DOING IT FOR THE PLOT

Stephanie Yeboah is a British-Ghanaian body image advocate, multi-award-winning content creator and freelance writer with nearly a quarter of a million followers on Instagram. She is the author of *Chaotic Energy* and *Fattily Ever After*, and is passionate about centring plus-sized bodies in TV and literature, especially within the categories of romance and romantic comedies. Stephanie currently lives in south London.

Instagram: @stephanieyeboah
www.stephanieyeboah.com

Also by Stephanie Yeboah

Chaotic Energy
Fattily Ever After

DOING IT FOR THE PLOT

Stephanie Yeboah

First published in Great Britain in 2026 by Trapeze,
an imprint of The Orion Publishing Group Ltd
Carmelite House, 50 Victoria Embankment
London EC4Y 0DZ

An Hachette UK Company

The authorised representative in the EEA is Hachette Ireland, 8 Castlecourt Centre, Dublin 15, D15 XTP3, Ireland (email: info@hbgi.ie)

1 3 5 7 9 10 8 6 4 2

A CIP catalogue record for this book is available from the British Library.

ISBN (Mass Market Paperback) 978 1 3987 2195 1
ISBN (Ebook) 978 1 3987 2193 7
ISBN (Audio) 978 1 3987 2194 4

Typeset by Born Group
Printed in Great Britain by Clays Ltd, Elcograf S.p.A.

MIX
Paper | Supporting responsible forestry
FSC® C104740
FSC www.fsc.org

www.orionbooks.co.uk

For my dear Sareeta

Chapter 1

'Oh . . . you're gonna order dessert as well? Aren't you full?'

I felt the hairs on the back of my neck prick up instantly as I slowly glanced over the dessert menu and laid eyes upon my date who was sitting across from me at the table. He had a confused look on his face as he glanced at me up and down, eyes full of judgement and – if I wasn't mistaken – slight disgust. This was my second date with Calvin and my sixth date this month overall; we'd matched on a dating app the week prior and as a part of my New Year's goals (framing them as 'resolutions' just sounded way too formal) to 'say yes' to almost everything and date as much as possible this year, because I wanted – nay, needed – to get laid; and if that meant having to sort through some questionable prospects just to make it happen, so be it.

I moved the menu out of the way, trying as much as possible to keep my cool while I looked him up and down. At some point I just knew it would boil down to my appearance; it always did.

'Why wouldn't I order a dessert? I've heard great things about their matcha cheesecake on TikTok and wanted to try it out. What's the problem?'

'It's just . . . the main was quite big, innit, and I'm absolutely stuffed, so I just – ya'know – thought you'd be full too.' Calvin flinched uncomfortably in his seat, his words slipping out before he could stop them. The discomfort on his face was unmistakable – but I knew he meant every word. I knew this scenario all too well.

He was the third man that I'd dated to inadvertently mention my weight/appetite this year, and we were only twenty days into January. Just so you know, he had swiped left on me first. He knew what I looked like: I'd uploaded nothing but full-length photos on my dating profile, alongside a disclaimer that read '*For clarity, I AM plus size so pls keep that in mind before you swipe left*' right at the top of the profile; something I didn't feel I needed to add, but a necessary evil nonetheless.

I had turned up to the date feeling and looking somewhat confident; I was wearing a short, brown minidress with white polka dots and a deep plunge neckline so the girls could breathe, complete with a pair of opaque tights and my black Maison Margiela Tabi ankle boots that I'd had to put in several hours overtime at work to be able to save up to afford, much to the chagrin of my mum, who preferred to call them my 'camel-toe shoes'. By all intents and purposes, I think I looked pretty damn good. Calvin was thirty-six years old and a secondary school teacher. His profile on the app was cute and funny, more or less: '*I'm here because I'm too lazy to find a soulmate, and my mum said that I'm getting old*'. And he was pretty handsome too; big, dark-brown doe eyes that were hidden behind a pair of thick, Malcolm X-esque glasses, with a chiselled jawline that would have put Prince to shame, may he rest in peace. Thick, pouty lips, and a mass of gorgeous dreadlocks that had been braided down into neat cornrows. All I had initially wanted to do was take him back to mine and let him have his way with me and, up until the last ten minutes, it looked as if the evening was due to end that way, but alas the universe had once again conspired to prevent me from getting my back blown out.

I glanced down at the menu, resisting the urge to snap back. Calvin's subtle jab about my alleged overeating made it painfully clear he had some issue with my weight. Honestly, if that was the case, he should have addressed it on our first date – though, to be fair, a date at the movies didn't leave much room for deep conversations. Instead, I'd gone through the effort of getting ready and booking an Uber to this ridiculously fancy restaurant, only to face the likelihood of being rejected yet again. Annoying didn't even begin to cover it.

'Me? Full?' I replied slowly, hoping to lighten the mood despite the brewing annoyance I was feeling internally. 'Oh, no, no, my friend, that was just my starter and main stomach. The dessert stomach is a whole different department!' I laughed, hoping it would in some way lighten the mood so that we would wrap this up and I could allow him to take me home and ravish me. At this stage in my dating life, I couldn't even be fussed about establishing a genuine connection. Now, don't get me wrong, in a perfect world that would have been ideal, but with the quality of men floating about these days, I was fully allowing my raging libido to take the lead in order to secure a quick shag and a dopamine boost. Sad times, really.

Dearest reader, not only did the mood not lighten, it dampened, significantly so.

Calvin placed his menu on the table and stared at me as I laughed. After what felt like the longest thirty seconds in the world, he cleared his throat and then, without missing a beat, proceeded to inform me of the benefits of healthy eating, and how I should perhaps look into intermittent fasting for faster weight-loss results? 'All I'm saying,' he continued on as I stared at him in disbelief, 'is that making small changes like cutting out desserts and including more protein in your diet can help with—' he looked at me with what looked like a hint of embarrassment in his eyes '—your issue.'

I forced an internal sigh. Was this really where I had arrived at with dating? How had it gotten so bad and how had I gotten it so wrong, so many times? All of a sudden, it seemed as if London had developed an influx of self-qualified nutritionists overnight.

I scoffed as I made eyes at the waiter to grab his attention so I could get the bill. My date with Joe Wicks was going nowhere, and all I wanted was to go home and cuddle up with Toby, my three-year-old Russian Blue cat.

'My "issue"? Heh . . . I see.' I scoffed, flashing a kilowatt smile and leaning back into my chair, surveying him. He really thought he was the prize here. The delusions of men shall never cease, it seemed. If only he had kept his mouth shut; I wasn't here for a lecture!

I picked up my half of the bill and proceeded to put on my coat while simultaneously trying to order an Uber home. So far, this dating-slash-trying to have a somewhat satisfactory sex life thing was turning out to be a huge flop. No amount of dick was worth this kind of humiliation.

'Not in a rude way or anything,' he said, trying to backtrack upon realising he'd fucked up. 'I'm just big on health and stuff, so I want to make sure that any future partner also takes health into account.'

I actually couldn't be arsed. As if one can judge someone's health based on their body type?

'Calvin,' I announced breathlessly as I struggled to put my coat on, 'I'm going to have to love you and leave you, I think. You knew what I looked like when you swiped on me, and when we met up at the cinema on the first date. You had no problem with my weight when you were grabbing on my thighs back then, funnily enough. Frankly, I just wanted to see if we could fuck but I can see there's no chance of that so—' I dramatically threw my scarf around my neck with a fierce flounce as I uttered my final line '—until next time, if there ever is one, I bid you adieu.'

'Ah, Cassie, calm down man, I wasn't trying to take the piss, I . . .' Calvin retorted before I held my hand out to shush him. I needed my dramatic exit and I was going to get it by any means necessary. 'Aht aht. Calvin, no more needs to be said. You're good. Take care, OK?'

And with that, I strutted out of the restaurant, head held high and hips swinging with a dramatic, sensual flair. It was an exit for the ages! It wasn't until I got outside that I realised something was missing.

I'd left my bag at the table.

I ran back in, hiding my face quickly enough just to see Calvin's stupid face break into a smirk. I grabbed my bag in a flurry and hot-footed it out of the restaurant again, post haste.

So much for a dramatic exit.

Twenty-five minutes later, I was back home, and switched on my favourite movie, *Pretty Woman*, to have it playing on the TV for some background noise as I wiped off my make-up and mentally unpacked yet another disastrous date. (Was it me? Am I the drama?) Just as I was spiralling into self-reflection, my phone buzzed. It was Mum, probably checking in to hear how the date went.

Back when she was single, we had this tradition: weekly catch-ups to debrief about our dating adventures. My parents had gotten a divorce when me and my younger brother Steven were teenagers. Frankly, it was the best decision my mum could have made (albeit the worst timing ever as they started their divorce proceedings slap bang in the middle of my GCSEs, but hey-ho) as we were tired of the daily arguments and disagreements in the house. Ever since the divorce was finalised, my dad had been on a steadfast mission to get my mum back despite her being outrageously happy in a relationship with her boyfriend Femi – much to her disgust and mine and my brother's occasional entertainment.

I put my phone on speaker as I slabbed on my Kate Somerville Goat Milk cleanser and gently massaged it into my skin as it disintegrated a night's wasted make-up. I tried to contain my anger as I recalled the events of the evening.

'Baby! How did the date go? Are you still on it, or should I call back later?' My mum's deep, melodic Ghanaian accent lightly decorated with a South London flair came through the speaker, brimming with excitement for the update. Like many Ghanaian mothers with their firstborn daughters, she'd been eager for me to settle down and start a family for the past ten years. Never mind the fact that I have a younger brother – already engaged and with a child on the way – at the end of the day, the weight of preserving our family legacy rested squarely on my shoulders. The future of her matriarchal lineage depended on my matrimony. Well, I hope they're prepared for a dose of disappointment!

'Ahh, Mum, please,' I started, using a facecloth to slowly take off the cleanser before I started to apply my trusty hyaluronic acid serum. 'I thought it was going well, but then he kept talking about how much I was eating and commenting on my weight and stuff so I just walked out, man. I couldn't be bothered with all that shit again. It keeps happening to me and I'm sick of it. Ugh.' It actually felt good to vent to my mum – we'd developed a really candid, casual relationship where I felt good being able to open up to her. As I began to unravel the events of that evening to her, I could begin to feel a prickle behind my eyes. I could feel the frustrations of the last few dates beginning to build up and, in that moment, I just wanted to cry. Why was dating this hard? Why couldn't I just find a nice, tall, intelligent, handsome man who had good conversation, worshipped the ground I walked on and wanted to have sex every once in a while? Was I asking the universe for too much at this point?

'So at the end,' I continued, stifling a sniffle, 'I just walked out but then I forgot my bag so I had to go back in to get it – it was so embarrassing. He was actually smirking at me when I headed back in so, yeah, I guess that's the end of that. Back on the apps I go, I suppose.'

'You actually went back in?' my mum replied, scoffing. 'Girl, you should have asked one of the waiters to grab the bag for you! But it's fine. You won't see him again, I guess. A shame, he sounded nice.'

'Is it me, Mum?' I said, now applying my Ole Henriksen retinol serum in a bid to keep the fine lines at bay. 'Do you think I need to do something about how I look? Because every guy that I've dated since the New Year keeps mentioning either my weight or my "appearance" as the reason why they don't wanna continue seeing me, and I can't lie . . . it's triggering me hard.' I wiped a tear as I applied the final product of my skincare routine – my Estée Lauder Advanced Night Repair night cream – in thick strokes before massaging it into my face.

'Cassie, baby, it's got nothing to do with your weight or whether you need to change yourself, darling. How many times have I told you this? You're fabulous in the body you're in, your mum doesn't make ugly children, and I've taught you to never base your worth on the validation of others – least of all, men!'

She made a gagging sound as she said this, which made me laugh, as I instantly knew she was thinking about my dad. Her rant continued.

'The men in the UK are very mad and have no one to tell them because of the patriarchy. Look at your dad, for instance; a very useless human being who also at one point tried to tell me what to wear and how to do my hair, talking about how he preferred it natural – d'you remember that? A very mad man. He met me when I had a wavy BLONDE weave and then all of a sudden he expected me to walk around looking like Angela Davis? At that point I knew that it was giving "Divorce" . . . Is that how you young people use that phrase?'

'Yes, Mum; very good,' I replied, smiling. She was up to date on her *Real Housewives* binge, it seemed.

'Speaking of Dad, he texted me again this morning, asking how we were – and of course by "we", he obviously meant you. When are you gonna tell him you're going steady with Femi? I can't keep being the buffer between you guys. You should just let him know and he'll probably stop bugging you once and for all?'

At this, my mum loudly kissed her teeth. 'Fuck him. I don't owe that man anything except for giving me you and Steven. Even when it came to making you two, he couldn't even last two min—'

'IIGHT MUM THANKS SO MUCH I'LL CALL YOU IN A COUPLE DAYS BYE.'

At that, I hung up the phone and applied some face oil to finish off my regimen.

As close as we were, some boundaries still needed to be had!

As much as I loved *Pretty Woman*, the thought of seeing a conventionally attractive woman getting the life of her dreams wasn't something I was particularly in the mood for any more, especially after tonight. I needed to ingest more relatable content.

'Hey, what's going on, guys? It's your girl Simi P and welcome back to yet another episode of The Jungle Diaries *where I go through some of your dating dilemmas and we talk about the absolute stress of trying to date in this here London! We've got a packed episode for you; I need*

to update you guys on this absolutely diabolical date I went on last weekend with this guy I matched with on Tinder; note to self and you guys – take out your Invisalign trays before leaning in for that kiss!'

I hopped into my pyjamas and brought Toby into bed with me as I listened to my favourite dating podcast. If I was going to go turbo mode on dating this year, I needed all the help and advice I could get. While listening to Simi P reading out this week's dilemma – a listener who wasn't sure if she should wear her lace front wig before sleeping with her new date who happens to be white – I opened up the message I'd received from Calvin twenty minutes prior and grimaced.

> **Hey Cassie. Um, I don't really know what that was about earlier; I was just trying to give you some advice and I don't think it was cool for you to take it so personally. Nice knowing you, I guess.**

Toby softly made biscuits against my forearm as I typed back; keeping it short and sweet.

> **One thing to learn on your next date, I think: don't preach on about the eating habits of the person you're on a date with; especially if they are bigger than you. It's rude, if you didn't know. Don't contact me again pls. xx**

Satisfied with my response, I sent the message and proceeded to block him. Mum was right: I *am fucking gorgeous.* I have a wonderful personality (if I do say so myself), I'm intelligent, I'm somewhat funny at times, I'm kind, generous, laid-back, yet for some reason, my curves always seem to get in the way of me achieving any kind of dating success. It's absolutely wild to me, dear reader, as I thought we were in the midst of a curve revolution. Body positivity and all that, huh? Weren't curves supposed to be in? It had been refreshing to see over the last few years a multitude of women who look like me being shown in magazines and online – all bodies are beautiful, after all – but somehow, this hasn't translated into the dating scene.

The truth is, I've never had a boyfriend. And it's something I carried a lot of shame about for years growing up, as it felt like a rite of passage at school to have crushes on boys and have them reciprocated and all that. The shame only intensified as I finished uni and started getting pressure from my parents about marrying up and settling down, despite only being twenty-one. I've always been somewhat confident in my skin, with the odd run-of-the-mill nervous breakdown here and there but, ultimately, I've never let my body hold me back from living my best life. Even in the dating scene I've always been someone to take up space and be unapologetic in my confidence but, for some reason, men see my body and suddenly decide they're no longer interested.

I'm at the point now where I really want to feel desired. I'm thirty-four, for crying out loud. I want to go out on normal dates, feel adored, be sexed up spectacularly on a regular basis and eventually settle down, but it's hard enough trying to get someone to swipe left on me, let alone marry me. But this year I told myself that I WILL have a successful dating life, by any means necessary. As a feminist, nothing gives me the ick more than seeing women revolve their lives around men. While I'm making a conscious effort to avoid doing the same, this year, I'm focused on having as much fun as possible – and if I happen to meet someone special along the way, that's just a bonus.

I could hear the low, hypnotic purr of Toby, who had fallen asleep in my arms as I lay back and allowed myself to be swept away by the drama of Simi P's hilarious listener letter:

'Babygirl, if it were me, I wouldn't wear a wig if I knew I was gonna sleep with him soon but you do you. As long as you don't use gorilla glue to secure the ting cus that shit'll ruin your scalp, still!'

I allowed the rest of the podcast to play out as I slowly fell asleep.

Date six? A complete disaster, but I wanted to cling onto the hope that something better would come for me soon; it had to.

Chapter 2

I woke up at 6 a.m. the next day and did my usual routine, which involved a fifteen-minute swipe-through session of the men who had matched with me on the app the night before, before going to brush my teeth and shower. I opened the app to look through today's applicants;

- Multiple men wearing hats in every single one of their photos – clearly bald and hatfishing
- Asian men with Black women fetishes (I always seem to score the highest in this category and I didn't know why)
- Men under five foot nine inches. (No discrimination here, but as someone who stands at five foot nine and wears heels, it would be nice to at least be eye-height with someone every now and again)
- Andrew Tate/red pill enthusiasts
- And one guy who was very clearly racist ['only into non-tanned, non-ethnic women, 👍']. Note to self: read profiles thoroughly before swiping

I sighed and swiped right through the twenty-eight men who had attempted to match with me, then switched over to the main app. I glanced through today's line-up of available men, questioning whether my standards were simply too high.

In my head I breezed through my list of what I wanted in my perfect man:

- A man
- Live/grew up in London
- Preferably South London
- At least six foot two
- No preference on weight or build
- Nice teeth and lips
- Nice eyes
- Well spoken
- Tattoos
- Educated [university level and beyond]
- University must be one of the top 20 best universities in the UK
- Earning at least £50k a year
- A stable, steady job that isn't so demanding that it takes time away from moi
- Should either have hair, or be completely bald with a full/long beard
- Dick size at least six inches and thick in girth; preferably circumcised
- Kind, generous, sensitive, fun blah blah blah
- Must have own car and live alone. No flatmates
- No red pill/Alpha male beliefs
- Must ABSOLUTELY NOT listen to any male podcasts
- Must not be a super active user of Facebook or Instagram
- Must not have more Instagram followers than me
- Must not be any kind of social media influencer
- Non-cigarette smoker [weed OK on occasion]
- Must not invest in or have anything to do with Crypto currency or 'stocks'
- Should be open to pets (especially cats)

I reckoned my list was pretty reasonable, to say the least. I was aware that I had slightly high standards, but it was only because I've always wanted the best for myself as someone who consistently brings a lot to the table. Having the man I deserve, is what I deserved; whether I was going to find him on these apps, however, was a different story altogether.

I got up and walked to the bathroom, phone in hand, swiping mindlessly while my mental checklist lingered in the back of my mind;

Right swipe on Rico the five foot eight Spanish PR Executive.

Right swipe on Matthew, bald architect, holding someone else's baby [allegedly].

Right swipe on Kevin the curly-haired bartender who liked to kayak and surf for fun.

As I brushed my teeth, I stopped at a profile that had caught my eye.

Michael, 35. Lives in Battersea. Full-time Personal Trainer. A Christian. Capricorn.

I scrolled through his photos; liking what I saw. He was six foot three with a full beard, and his hair twisted into cornrows. He dressed reasonably well, with a gorgeous smile, dimples and a muscular dad-bod build. He looked toned, but wasn't too muscular, which was what I liked. He had several photos of him at the gym working out with his clients, as well as a couple of photos of him at Notting Hill Carnival and a few of him celebrating Nigerian Independence Day. Normally, I try to stay away from Nigerian men and their chaos, but I wanted to make an exception for this Michael guy; he was pretty sexy. And a Christian, which would go down well with my parents. His profile simply read:

'Not looking for anything serious right now, but if my dog likes you then maybe we can give it a try!'

An animal lover too? Bingo. I swiped left on Michael as well as a couple of other potentials, and then stripped off to take a shower. This year was going to be the year that I found 'The One'. I just knew it.

After my shower, I quickly got dressed, grabbed a flapjack from the cupboard and made my way to clock into work. I worked as a Medical Secretary in the Trauma and Orthopaedics department at St Thomas' Hospital and had been working there for the last four years. My role wasn't primarily patient-facing, so I rarely felt the need to wear make-up – one of the few perks of the job that I really appreciated. It was a stable but monotonous job, and for the most part, the office was shared by just two of us – me and my manager-turned-best work buddy, Kofi, who served as the office coordinator for three of the six orthopaedic surgeons in our department. I managed the other three surgeons, though since they spent most of their time at their private practices, my daily workload was relatively light. I wasn't complaining though; it was a well-paid job and even though I didn't get to put my Law degree to good use, I had a good thing going at the hospital; it was peaceful, for the most part.

I sauntered through the main concourse, briefly stopping at the Pret a Manger by the elevators to grab myself a flat white and a pain au chocolate before making my way up to my office on the tenth floor. I bounded through the door, breakfast in hand, to see that Kofi was already at his desk.

'Here she is; Queen Cassie herself. I don't think I've ever seen you come in this early, you know? How come?'

I switched my computer on and scoffed while giving him a half-hug from behind. I may or may not have been known to show up between ten to twenty minutes late on occasion. I slumped into my chair as my old, dusty computer whirred and hummed until it reached the start-up screen. 'Not you trying to call me out for OCCASIONALLY being late. I had a bit of an early night to be honest so I guess I thought I'd try something rare and actually be ahead of time today.'

Kofi swivelled his chair around and fixed his gaze on me, his frameless square spectacles teetering precariously on the bridge of his nose, giving him the appearance of peering down at me in judgement. I'd previously told Kofi about my meetup with Calvin a week or so prior but hadn't updated him on yesterday's shenanigans. After I'd filled him in, Kofi exhaled deeply and turned back to his screen in silence.

'You good, Kof?' I said, blowing cool my flat white as I logged in to today's tasks.

'Yeah, I'm cool, Cass; it's just—' I heard him swivel his chair back around as I turned to do the same. Mrs Johnson's hip referral letter would have to wait another five minutes. 'I just – like – what makes you go for these types of guys? I just don't understand it. You're a great person with a lot to offer and I just don't understand what's not clicking. What are you like on dates? Are you confident? Because that's what men like the most, you know, it's more than just how a woman looks; it's how she carries herself.'

I looked at Kofi up and down silently, trying as hard as possible not to feel slightly offended. As if men's lack of interest in me was my fault? Absolutely not. 'Mm,' I started, sugar-coating my irritation with a smile. 'I'm actually fabulous on dates – I don't do the whole wallflower act or anything like that. If anything, I'm the entertainment. So no, men going out of their way to find me unattractive isn't a "confidence issue". That's a *them* problem, to be honest.' I was tired of people assuming that just because I was fat, I automatically had a problem with confidence. Can't a fat bitch just be happy and thriving?

'Oh, don't try it, man.' Kofi smiled coyly as he turned back around. 'I didn't mean it like that – I guess I'm just struggling to understand why someone wouldn't be bowled over at you

– it's nothing to do with how you look so I just wonder if it's something else,' he replied carefully. 'You're a good woman and you deserve someone special, you know?'

If I flinched, I didn't show it. I let out a weird and awkward laugh. Gratitude and embarrassment tangled in my stomach, each one trying to edge out the other. 'Aww, bless you. You always know what to say to cheer me up,' I replied, rubbing his shoulder and turning back around. 'Thank you so much. Hopefully said man will just fall into my lap at some point.'

Kofi touched my hand briefly as he turned towards me, his eyes barely hiding a mischievous glimmer. 'My absolute pleasure, and hey? Worst-case scenario, you can just hire an escort, innit? That's what all the strong, independent women are doing these days, haha.'

'Woooow, hilarious. Have you forgotten where we're from? We don't do those kinds of things, man. Can you imagine?!' I laughed and rolled my eyes at the audacity of his suggestion. I was all for sex positivity and all but the thought of being a woman and hiring the sexual services of a man . . . something about that screamed 'desperation' to me. I knew Kofi was joking, but was my demeanour really sending out signals of obvious desperation like that? Did Kofi think of me as somewhat pathetic?

'Yeah, yeah, I know, I'm just playing with you, Cass,' Kofi replied, a wide, toothy grin spreading across his face. 'I know you wouldn't do anything like that. You're gorgeous and you have a great personality – any man would be an idiot not to pursue things with you.'

As close as Kofi and I were, I could never quite pin down where he stood with me emotionally. Every so often, he'd drop these subtle little signals that made me think he might be into me – only to turn around a few weeks later with a brand-new situationship, or worse, slip back into his habit of playfully negging me, like he was doing right now. Sometimes he'd even recycle an old flame, and then – poof – back to being completely unreadable. He was a lovely guy, don't get me wrong, but he was more like a brother to me than anything else. He also had some traits that gave me the ick; his loud swallowing when he ate, always biting pen lids, and his weird laugh that sounded like a Labrador barking. Plus, I've never been one for, well . . . shitting where I ate.

I started answering emails as I took a bite out of my pastry, thinking of Kofi's last words. I deserved someone who would treat me like the diamond I was. He was right. I deserved the perfect date. To have someone not treat me as if I were a liability. I wanted to be wined and dined without the other person watching MY calories. I wanted to dance and flirt, to be coy, to have someone stare at me the whole night as if I were the most beautiful woman in the world, then take me back to their place and, quite frankly, fuck the absolute shit out of me. I wanted to feel confident and powerful and sexy for once, and it annoyed me that, at thirty-four years old, I'd yet to have an experience like that. I also thought about his 'escort' comment. Was that even a thing these days? To think I could – at any point – finagle my way into a relationship like this was a wild and probably ridiculous thought, but at this point, I might as well go online and hire someone to give me the night of my life; at least I'd know what I'd be getting, despite paying for it. If it was good enough for Richard Gere . . .

A couple of uneventful hours went by as I worked steadfastly at my desk with Kofi manning the outpatients' desk for the day. Today I had to focus on typing up and sending out dozens of patients' referral letters to private hospitals on behalf of my consultants, process fifty-two GP referral letters, and schedule the diaries of two of the consultants for the next three months, while manning the phones for enquiries. They were pretty simple tasks really, and I loved the monotony of it. I knew that my parents had instead wanted me to go down the legal route, go to law school and become some kind of highly esteemed corporate lawyer like my dad, but after three years of doing nothing but shaking ass and getting up to mischief with my friends at Hertfordshire Uni, let's just say I fell out of love with law, with my 2:2 degree being a testament to that.

I was halfway through translating Dr Foley's notes to a GP when I received a text message from my brother Steven. It simply read:

> **Cass! Are you able to grab me some lube from work? I'll swing by and get it tonight yh?**

I stared at my phone for a full minute, processing the message I'd just received. I knew my baby brother was blunt, but fucking hell. I scoffed as I typed back:

> **. . . ? What happened to 'Hello, how are you?' Mind you, this is the first time I've heard from you this week. Do I want to know what you need lube for? 😭**

A few moments later, Steven types back:

> **Lollll soz. Bianca's got me doing that taint massage thing so she doesn't tear when she's in labour and erm, yeah . . . I need lube, man. It's harder than it looks.**

My brother and his fiancée, Bianca, were expecting their first child – my nephew – next month. Ever since he learned he was going to be a dad, my brother had been putting in the effort to prepare as much as possible. I'd seen him diving into childbirth books, attending prenatal classes, and going all out on decorating the nursery. It was a remarkable transformation from the teenager who used to spend twenty-two hours a day holed up in his room, doing who knows what. Loved that he was making the effort, but there were *some* things I just didn't need to know, you know?

I replied back:

> **This sounds fascinating tbh, but I'm in Orthopaedics, we don't really have lube on hand here, I'm afraid! Can't you just get some KY Jelly from the pharmacist or Boots or something? xx**

I was met with an immediate response:

> **I don't want them to see me buying it though, it's embarrassing, man! As if I would ever need lube on a normal basis. Not meeee!**

I needed to wrap this up before I started getting mental images. I replied quickly:

> **All right, lol! You've officially made this interaction weird and so on that note, I'd suggest doing a quick next-day delivery on Amazon or something and I'll chat to you later – send Bianca my love xxxxx**

Because who needed visuals of their brother massaging his girlfriend's taint? Not me. The hours slowly whittled away as I continued to work in silence, thinking about my dating goals this year.

I quickly opened up one of the many dating apps on my phone again for any updates on matches. I'd been swindled into paying for the privilege of seeing who had liked my profile, and as I swept through today's selection of potential love interests and their messages, I groaned internally.

Uncles. All uncles. Again.

Tunde, 46, Camberwell: 'Hey babygirl. You're looking very succulent. I wud like 2 get to know u. Are you looking for marriage?'

Mr Tunde clearly had forgotten to Photoshop his wedding ring out of his pictures. Delete.

Nathaniel, 58, Horsham: 'My dear, you're very pretty. Write back.' Nathaniel conveniently dressed like a 1970's California pimp. No bueno. Delete.

Timothy, 32, Thamesmead: 'Hi am looking for a wife, do you have any children? How much do you earn?' Bold. Succinct. To the point. It also didn't help that Timothy was definitely at least fifty-one years of age and had used an obvious face-editing app to appear younger. Delete.

I sighed and exited the app. The Lord was clearly forsaking me for some reason.

I pondered briefly on the escort idea. Clearly it was a joke, but what could be the harm in having a browse online? If only just to see what the going rate was on male sex workers these days? I'd love to experience a 'Great First Date' for once in my life. I'd be doing it for research in order to share my findings with others who might be in the same predicament. It would just be a bit of harmless fun.

Right?

One more shitty date, perhaps. If I had more trash interactions, then I might allow myself to potentially consider the notion of even being open to that idea.

Parking that idea to the side, I'd taken a late lunch in order to make the day go faster; I crossed Westminster Bridge and took a right down Parliament Street to the nearest Pret a Manger. After buying my tuna and cheese panini, a packet of cheese and onion crisps (the only flavour that matters) and a Diet Coke, I took a seat in the corner and started googling escort services. 'Purely for research purposes, just in case,' I muttered to myself as I swiped lazily.

Little did I know that I would be bombarded with a litany of websites that catered to all kinks, fetishes and preferences;

there was a site called 'Feabie', which catered to people with Feederism and fat fetishes, a BDSM website that catered strictly to those over the age of sixty-five, and a foot fetish site where visitors were encouraged to upload photos of their feet in exchange for cold, hard cash.

I screenshot the feet one. That could potentially come in handy later on, finances depending.

As I sat in the corner, going through various websites and giggling to myself, I noticed a couple who were standing in line waiting to be served. The woman was stunning; she had a short, blunt bob and big brown, doe-ish eyes, and was dressed impeccably in an oversized suit and camel coat. Her partner on the other hand – who had his hand clasped around her as he hugged her from the back – was a little scruffier. Beard unkempt, hair all knotted, and wearing beat-up trainers with ill-fitting jeans and a jumper with holes all over it – whether that was intentional or not, I had no idea. After they had ordered (I'd noted that she paid for both of them) they came to sit down at a table across from me.

'So yeah, if you don't mind me crashing at your place for about three months, I'd really appreciate it, babes,' the man said, coyly. I briefly glanced up, almost admiring the audacity.

I was in the presence of a hobosexual, it seemed; I continued to eavesdrop under the pretence of looking through my phone. The woman's face was blank; unreadable. I could almost sense she'd been here before.

'Um, I mean, yeah, I don't mind, as long as you'll be able to help with the rent and stuff . . . if that's OK with you?' she replied finally. I mentally cheered for her for adding in the rent.

The man exhaled loudly, looking out of the window.

I glanced up again, looking past him slightly, pretending to look out of the window, hoping that shame and embarrassment would catch up to this man and that he would retract his earlier request.

I hoped.

'You know I'm in between jobs at the moment – why would you bring money up now? After everything I've done for you over the last six months, if I were you, I would have allowed you to stay with me for free! You clearly have the space – I thought you loved me?'

The manipulative prick. I was fully invested now; don't let him in, sis!

The woman looked up and quickly glanced at me before looking away, her face an illustration of anxiety and worry as the man continued chastising her for her reluctance.

'If you really loved me, you would at least consider it,' the hobosexual continued arrogantly. 'I told you how I'm trying to save up so I can invest in my Twitch streaming content. Why can't you be supportive? If I ever go viral and the cash starts coming in, we both benefit, don't we? I'm doing this for us!'

I almost threw up in my mouth. I'd heard enough. The bar for men was deep under the Mariana Trench's crust and it made me sick. If this was the best us women could hope for, then bring on the male escorts at this point.

I gave the woman a reassuring smile and nod as we briefly locked eyes again, internally praying that she didn't fall for this man's schemes and gaslighting. I was disgusted, and at that point, my mind had been made up.

I scrolled back onto Google's homepage and typed in 'Male escorts based in London', and clicked on the first non-sponsored website that popped up; it was called *OuiMeet*. The website was simplistic in its design, having looked like it was made in 2003, with a hyperlink button directing users towards its 'brand-new app' instead.

I felt some way about having this on my browser history,

so I downloaded the app instead and hastily made an account. Again, for research purposes; just in case.

I arrived at the profile section and hesitated. What if someone recognised me here? What were the chances that I would bump into someone I knew though? My Ghanaian family were way too conservative to be into these shenanigans, and if Kofi or any of my other friends showed up, I'd just mention that I had signed up as part of an investigative article I was writing for my made-up Substack site. Yeah, that sounded believable, right? Right.

Even though I knew I was signing up mostly as a joke, I still felt the need to remind myself not to take it seriously. Women using escort services to find male companionship was something I'd rarely heard of, and when I did, it was always the same stereotype: an elderly, wealthy heiress to a multimillion-pound fortune, recently widowed and seeking someone to share her final days with.

You never saw young, Black, somewhat hip women like me on these sites. Or so I thought. I guess I was about to find out. With one final push of self-persuasion, I decided to add my photo. I opted for my main photo to be a headshot; it was a selfie that I'd taken of myself at Bianca's baby shower. I was looking particularly hot that day with my long, auburn Senegalese twists wrapped into a high bun, a sharp winged liner and red lip convo for the make-up, and a V-neck silk blouse that I had picked up on sale at Marks & Spencer that hugged me in all the right places. Alongside that photo, I went for two full-length photos, wanting to be clear from the onset that I was plus sized. I didn't need for there to be any repeat situations of my previous dates. The first photo was me at the hospital Christmas party last year where I'd gone all out in a floor-length sequin fish-tail dress with a slit down one side, high enough for me to show off my legs (in a 'So Kate'

Louboutin shoe, might I add – courtesy of the 30 per cent sale at Bicester Village). The second photo was one taken of me by my mum and was of me sitting down on my sofa with Toby stretched along the entirety of my stomach and ribs. I had my head thrown back in fits of laughter, and it was always a photo that made me smile and brought back warm memories; it was wholesome. After adding the photos, I scrolled through the rest of the editing page until I approached the space where I had to write a little 'About Me' and what I was looking for. I wasn't planning on being on this app for long, so why not have a little fun? Again, clearly for research purposes of course. I wrote the following:

Hey! The name's CeeCee, and I'm an administrative professional based in South London looking for the perfect date. I'm looking for a gentleman who will wine and dine me, take me out dancing, and provide great conversation. My interests and hobbies include listening to podcasts, working out on occasion, playing video games (mostly The Sims), taking care of my gorgeous cat Toby and watching movies.

I read the profile back in disgust. I sounded like an eighty-year-old homebody with no life. Where was the fun in that? It low-key worried me that even on an app where I had the opportunity to be whoever I wanted to be, my first inclination was to talk about the real me, who sounded boring as fuck. I deleted the text and started again:

South London's finest; ready to be swept off my feet.

I'm a medical professional by day and a thrill-seeker by night. When I'm not busy helping to save lives or making rounds, you'll find me painting my imagination onto canvas, breaking a sweat in the gym, or feeling the rush of adrenaline on a go-kart track. I believe life is best lived boldly – and I'm ready for someone who shares that fire, if only for the evening. I'm here to meet someone who can reignite my faith in dating and romance. Show me that chivalry isn't dead and sweep me off my feet with your wit, charm, and love of life. If you can make my heart race faster than a go-kart and keep me smiling long after the night is over, then we might just have something special.

I took a mouthful of food as I assessed the paragraph; this sounded so much better. I actually sounded like a decent catch. Impressed with how my profile was shaping up, I saved the page and scrolled into the members' section to check out the talent. I set the 'looking for' options to 'Male, between 34-40 years old, 6ft or taller, London' and hit 'search'. The search results returned a meagre forty-three men, which surprised me; for some reason I assumed there would be a plethora of male escorts in the Big Smoke keen to make their fortunes by any means necessary, but maybe that spoke more to my stereotypes and assumptions of London men – heh.

Scanning my watch to make sure that I had enough time to browse before I had to make my way back to the office, I did a quick scroll of the talent on offer and was slightly disappointed; at least three of the men on this list were clearly lying about their age. There were two men who had bald patches – nothing against balding men, but a bald patch just wasn't an aesthetic I could embrace in my life at the moment. A couple of the other guys seemed sleazy from their profile photos alone – there is no reason why a thirty-eight-year-old man should be wearing a matching tight-fitting smedium denim suit with bedazzled pockets and a black satin shirt with the buttons open down to the navel. Also, the nerve of him to charge £300 for the night was abysmal, to say the very least. I laughed my way through the rest of the offerings; the app was looking pretty ghetto so far. As I gathered my things to leave and walk back to work, I came across one profile that piqued my interest.

His name was 'Jericho', he was based in Hackney and he was thirty-four, although to me, he looked significantly younger. He was six foot four, with small, almond-shaped dark eyes that almost disappeared under the weight of his luminescent megawatt smile. Faint wrinkles gently lined the sides of his eyes, and he had a short, neatly trimmed faded haircut, showing no potential bald patches or receding hairlines. A win! Jericho had medium-brown skin that glowed against his sharp, black well-fitted suit. In the photo he was sitting with some other men at what looked like a wedding or a birthday ball. He was gorgeous. What the hell was he doing here?

I scrolled through a couple of his other photos, which were a lot more delectable; mostly of him topless in a professional studio, shot in black and white, no doubt in order to make him appear more demure. He had abs and muscles for days, yet still had a softness to his torso that made him look quite huggable and playful. I snapped out of the quick daydream of me licking cream off his abs to peruse his profile; which was the most important thing:

> The name's Jericho and I'm a six-foot-four, clean-shaven, somewhat handsome lad from London with a passion for fast cars, intelligent conversations, good food, and beautiful women. I love the finer things in life, and being able to share my passions with the ladies who share my interests. One evening with me and I can guarantee that you won't be leaving disappointed. :) Oh, I'm also a huge cat person. 😃
> My menu is as follows:

> FaceTime/Video Call (20 minutes) – £40 // FaceTime/Video Call (1 hour) – £95 // My company during the day (up to four hours) – £200 // My company during the evening (up to four hours) – £350 // One-off special event (weddings,

school reunions etc) – £500 + expenses // Overnight stay – £600 // 'Group activities' – Please enquire // Vacation getaway for two nights – £1500 // Vacation getaway for more than two nights – Please enquire for tailored fee, plus expenses // Other kinks – Please enquire. All arrangements will be provided with up-to-date sexual health screening tests, as well as a CRB check confirmation for your security and safety.

Well, damn. Here I was, thinking I'd only need to set aside about £50 for the night. Turns out the cost of living has hit every industry hard. But, to be clear – AGAIN – this was purely for research purposes – I had no intention of actually going through with hiring an escort for the evening. I mean, I'm a Black woman in my thirties. That's just not something we do . . . right?

As I walked back to work, I decided to text my best friend, Sade, for advice. I needed someone to confirm that what I was doing was absolutely insane, and there was no one more level-headed than her. We'd met back at university while studying the same course and living in the same halls of residence. From the start, we became fast friends, with Sade often acting as the voice of reason to counterbalance my chaotic, impulsive decisions. The only annoying thing about our friendship was the fact that she currently lived on the outskirts of West London, meaning we always had to schedule our hangings-out way in advance instead of being more spontaneous.

Babes! A quick one; I joined this site called 'OuiMeet' a few mins ago (it's a sex worker app lololol) and I feel like I'm this close to renting an escort to go on a date with, 'cause all these dates I'm going on are fried and I just wanna feel nice for once. Questions? Thoughts? Concerns? PS The one I found also likes cats. Cats!! Toby could make a new friend! xx

I knew Sade would waste no time questioning my sanity and talking me out of it. What I was doing was, without a doubt, ridiculous. And let's not even get started on the social implications – if word ever got out that I'd rented an escort, I'd be done for. If my family ever found out? Game over. I'd have no choice but to pack up my things, move to a nunnery in the Vatican, and live out the rest of my days in shameful silence, reflecting on my poor life choices while a six-foot-four nun with a cowbell screamed 'SHAME!' at me every seven seconds.

OK, maybe I was exaggerating a little, but the absolute last thing you'd want is for your West African parents to find out you were paying for companionship – and, by implication, sex. Of course, all of this was irrelevant, because Sade was bound to knock some sense into me and remind me just how ridiculous this whole idea was anyway.

As I stepped into the elevator and pressed the button for my floor, my phone buzzed in my pocket. A message from Sade. Ah, good old Sade – my wise, level-headed friend. She'd set me straight, no doubt, and remind me that there were far better things ahead for me than stooping to this level of desperation . . . probably.

Call me xxxxxx

I looked at my watch. I had a few minutes before stepping back into the office. Would I have time for a full best-friend verbal flogging right now? I chanced it, and dialled her number. Sade picked up on the second ring.

'OK, talk to me,' Sade demanded, slightly breathless, as if she were sitting out in the cold. 'What's this about renting someone online?'

I talked her through everything I had done thus far – filling out my profile and attaching a photo, and finding a couple of profiles that had tickled my fancy. At the end, I waited for

Sade to speak; to tell me off for even contemplating such a ridiculous idea.

After about a minute, she spoke.

'I actually think it's a brilliant idea, babe,' she responded, somewhat enthusiastically.

Wait, huh?

I scratched my head in confusion. That wasn't how this was supposed to go at all. I replied impatiently. 'Erm, what? That's not the response I was expecting. Where's the cussing out? Where's the shouting? I thought you were gonna talk me out of it!' I was outside the main entrance of the hospital by now, stamping my feet side by side in a bid to create some warmth. I refused to go back in until Sade spoke some sense into me.

'Why would you think I would say that? I think it's super empowering, and in a way, it puts you in the driver's seat, doesn't it? And if all else fails, you could just see it as a completed side mission, you know? Like those quests you're always trying to complete in *Zelda*. Chalk it up to the game!'

I almost felt betrayed. I couldn't believe she was on board. She was supposed to be the sensible one.

'Yeah, but what if—' I started, and was immediately cut off.

'Bitch, life is too short for ifs and buts, let's be real. You only have one life, and you want to fill it with as many memorable and random moments as possible, you get me? You've been doing the dating thing for ages and people keep taking the piss. Take the bull by the horns and shag as many guys as you can on YOUR watch. Why? Because you deserve it. Now, we'll talk about this later – I popped outside to chat to you and I'm freezing my arse off. Love you!' and with that, the phone went dead.

I stared at my phone in disbelief. Oh, for fuck's sake.

Chapter 3

Once I was back at the office, I let Kofi head off for his lunch break, leaving me with a solid hour to sit in solitude and reflect on the questionable life choices that had brought me to this moment. A few minutes went by before I noticed that Sade was calling me, again.

'Can you talk?' she said breathlessly; it sounded as if she were running up a staircase.

'Yeah, for a few minutes, it's not that busy in the office today,' I replied, sucking on my pen cap nervously. Maybe she'd had a change of heart. Maybe this was where the real dragging was to begin.

'OK, so . . .' began Sade. 'Sorry I locked you off so quickly, I was outside when you called. So here's how I see it, yeah? I think it's safe to say that when it comes to dating in this here London, it fucking sucks, right? As women, we put so much effort into making ourselves look good, sound good, SMELL good, all to go on a date with a guy that turns up looking trash and talking shit, only for them to have the rabid ass audacity to expect us to go halves on a date!' I could sense she was projecting here, but allowed her to continue as no lies had been told thus far.

'So like . . . I don't see anything in paying for a service that allows us to have the experiences we deserve. I think it's empowering, and if men can do it, why can't we?' Sade had a point, I feared.

On one hand, I understood where she was coming from, especially the female empowerment angle, and being able to dictate how and when we as women experience pleasure and joy, but on the other hand, I couldn't get over the shame I felt in having to resort to paying to be made to feel good. Why would I have to pay for it, when other women around the world could get this treatment for free, with men who wanted to treat them to the best?

'I hear you,' I responded, a bit deflated. 'I guess I assumed you wouldn't be on board with the idea, and it just low-key annoys me that it feels as if I'm feeding into a stereotype.'

'What do you mean, hun?' Sade replied.

'Just that, when you tend to look at who typically pays for sex or company,' I began, wanting to choose my words carefully, 'it's never the super attractive, super slim or acceptably curvy women who are doing it, innit? It always seems to be be the undesirable dregs of society that end up having to pay for it.' I hear Sade laugh on the other end, even though I was being totally serious.

'Um, Cass – I'd hardly call you a "dreg of society", as you so put it – I'ma need you to have a lot more confidence in yourself; and while I hear what you're saying, in this case I just don't think it's the same. See it as you RECLAIMING your dating autonomy!'

'*Reclaiming my dating autonomy.*' That had a nice ring to it, actually. I guessed if I spun it that way, I could perhaps replace the initial shame I felt with a sense of righteousness about the whole thing. Was I really about to message a sex worker for a date? For Sade of all people to co-sign this random act, that definitely said something. Maybe I was doing the right thing, surely there could be no harm in it – what was the worst that could happen?

'You have a point, I guess. I'm a bit nervous of doing it, and if I DO do it, you can't tell a soul. Listen. Not a SOUL, Sade. We've gotta keep it between us, OK?' I muttered the last sentence through clenched teeth as a way to emphasise the seriousness of this whole situation.

'Oh, girl, please, I ain't telling anyone. As long as you keep me up to date with who you're seeing; name, car reg etc. Can't have you randomly turning up missing, can we? These London streets are tough, man. Oh, babe, this is so exciting! Honestly, even if you only do it once, just for banter, at least you can say you've done it, right? I wanna hear all about it, and also, send me a cute picture of you just in case you go missing and the news stations ask me for a portrait of you, 'K?'

I sighed. Do it for the plot; why not? Jericho seemed like the best of an awkward bunch in any case. 'Thanks, babe, I'll keep you informed IF I do it. Jeeze, man, I can't believe this is what it's come to, you know. And for you of all people to co-sign this randomness too.' Sade chuckled heartily, her high-pitched voice echoing through the phone and into the office. 'Sis? If I tell you the absolute scum I've been seeing on these dating apps? It's a jungle out here, man. I'm this close to probably hiring someone myself. Godspeed indeed.'

I got off the phone with Sade and after tying up a few emails and delivering some paperwork to a couple of the departments on the floors below me, I returned to my desk and took my phone out again; thankfully, Kofi was still on his lunch break so I wouldn't be peppered with questions.

I scrolled again to Jericho's *OuiMeet* profile; his 'last online' tab showed that he was online a mere twenty minutes ago and had replaced his main profile photo with a new one: a professionally shot studio photo of him wearing a tight white vest with a dog tag chain, teamed with some dark-blue baggy jeans and a pair of Timberland boots. A man of taste. I wondered what his demographic was. I looked through his menu again; how much was I prepared to spend? Would he even accept me as a 'client'? What if he had a certain type of person he went for? Were they even allowed to have types? I felt a twinge of guilt about my last thought [#TeamAutonomyAlways], but I couldn't help but wonder, just in case he didn't respond. I didn't think I would be able to live with the shame of being rejected by a sex worker whose job it is to spend intimate moments with someone for money.

I hovered over the 'delete profile' button. This was crazy.

I thought about everything Sade had said earlier. Outside of assault and/or murder, what was the worst that could happen? Well, for one, my parents finding out. I pressed the button, which signalled a 'Are You Sure You Want to Permanently Delete Your Profile?' prompt. Spontaneity had never been my strong suit – maybe it was time for me to start taking control of my life.

My finger found its way back towards Jericho's profile instead.

Fuck it. Let's do it for the plot, Cassie! 'You only live once' and all that. Before contacting, I had to figure out what I wanted. Should I opt for an hour-long FaceTime call with him – a sort of pre-date consultation – if you will? Or head in straight for the four-hour date? I pondered having a video call with him beforehand so he could get a full look at me and decide if he even wanted to take me out. What a concept. I exhaled as I heard Kofi's footsteps round the corner to our office – I had to be quick.

I tapped the 'FaceTime/Video Call (1 hour)' option on his profile, which instantly directed me to a payment page along with a calendar to book our session. By a stroke of luck, Jericho had an available slot that evening at 8 p.m. Without hesitation, I selected the time, entered my phone number, and quickly keyed in my card details, trying to outrun the wave of shame creeping back over me. Just as I hit confirm, the notification came through – right as Kofi walked through the door.

'Cassie, did you know they've opened a new South African bakery near the bridge?' Kofi burst in, his voice brimming with excitement and his right hand clutching two grease-stained white bags. 'I picked up this thing called Malva Pudding – it's like a fancy bread-and-butter pudding. Fucking STUNNING. I got you some to try.' He set one of the bags on my desk with a grin. Kofi was such a sweetheart, and under different circumstances, I couldn't help but wonder if we would have been a good match. But alas, it wasn't meant to be.

'Aww, thanks, mate, you shouldn't have!' I cooed as I placed my phone in my desk drawer and picked at the white bag – the dessert smelled heavenly. 'It's about time that Westminster dipped into some flavour; it can't just be Costa and Pret every day. I'll be sure to patronise them tomorrow on my break too.'

Kofi leaned slightly against my desk, his body angled towards my chair. 'Maybe we could go together sometime and grab takeaway, if you're up for it?' he suggested, expectantly.

'Um, sure, that'll be cool! Any excuse for a pastry, to be honest haha.' I laughed awkwardly, although his eagerness to hang with me did make me feel a small twinge of warmth inside. I would be lying if I said I didn't like the attention every now and again.

Kofi continued to linger against my desk for a while before my phone rang; saved by the bell. As I made to pick up the phone, I heard Kofi say under his breath, 'Great, tomorrow then, but don't get all excited haha.'

I rolled my eyes. 'Excited' indeed. So much had happened in the last ninety minutes. I decided to put my head down and just steamroll with work – I needed to zone out to curb the anxiety of tonight's phone date with the sex worker. Because that's a totally normal thing to do on a Tuesday night.

Hours had passed, and I was making my way through the dreary, rainy January weather to get to the bus stop. The wind howled like a wild beast, clawing at me as I wrestled with my umbrella, which had already flipped inside out twice and was now little more than a stubborn skeleton in my frozen hands. I cursed under my breath, blinking furiously against the stinging drizzle that sliced sideways through the air. This was the last thing I needed, especially as I had my phone call with this Jericho bloke in a couple of hours. I didn't want his first impression to be that of a heavily panting, windswept banshee with smeared make-up. I had half a mind to just order an Uber home, as the weather had clearly worsened since winding down at the office, but in the distance I eventually saw the faint glow of the 77 bus and decided to wait it out.

As I struggled to close my wretched mess of an umbrella, I made a mental checklist of all the things I needed to do once I got home, seeing as I would only have around an hour and fifteen minutes to get ready and make myself somewhat presentable. The nerves had started to set in and I could feel my hands shaking, whether from that or from the cold, at this point I couldn't tell. I got on the bus and sat at the very back, facing away from the rest of the passengers. I was three stops away from getting off when I received a text message from Mum.

> **Hello my dear. I hope you've had a good day! Can you and Steven come round this weekend? Maybe on Saturday? I have some news to share. xx**

Ominous. I texted back: **You're not dying, are you? If so, remember to update your will. As the first-born daughter (as per Ghanaian tradition), I inherit everything. Love you xx**

She immediately replied. **Nkwasiasem. You think you're so funny lol. No, nothing bad! Come around 1 p.m. I've texted Steven too xx**

I don't know why I had this feeling, but I had the sneaking suspicion that Femi had perhaps proposed to my mum. She was never normally this vague and suspicious, especially when it came to regular family news and announcements, which she'd normally always broadcast in our family group chat. Hmm.

No time to think about that now, though; I had to park it and clear my brain for this evening's events. I got off the bus and walked the short distance up Wandsworth Road to my flat. Through the living-room window, I spotted Toby's adorable, expectant face watching for me, his excitement unmistakable even from a distance. At least someone (or something?) was excited to see me these days.

I entered my flat, put away my bag, coat and umbrella and got to work. I had an hour to calm my nerves and make sure I looked somewhat decent. I'd already come up with somewhat of a checklist on my Notes app while on the bus:

- Feed and give Toby cuddles [5 mins]
- Take a quick shower [10 mins]
- Light candles [15 secs]
- Outfit??????
- Skincare routine [10 mins]
- Hair????
- Eat leftovers [15 mins]

I gave Toby his dinner and petted him for a few minutes to calm my nerves. I could tell he could sense my anxiety, as he snuggled into my arms extra tight, bathing me in a blanket of warmth. I'd probably bring him into the video call – it'd be something extra to talk about I supposed. Afterwards, I hopped into the shower and used my Sol de Janeiro Beija Flor body wash to give me a little confidence. Jericho wouldn't be sitting in front of me to smell it, of course, but doing these little rituals in the lead-up to the call would give me the confidence I needed to make it through. As I rinsed the lather off my skin, I suddenly realised that I hadn't checked the *OuiMeet* app since confirming the call. Had he checked out my profile? Had he rejected me? A moment of panic took me as I stepped out of the shower and hotfooted it to my phone to double check. I opened the app to see a message in my inbox. It was from Jericho and I felt my heart skip a beat. I opened it:

> **Hi Cassie, I hope you're well and thanks for booking in with me. I must say I found your profile really enchanting, and you're incredibly beautiful too. I look forward to speaking with your fine self later on. Have a great day. :)**

Oh, this guy was a professional, and you could tell he knew how to play the game. Charming. Polite. Succinct. We loved to see it. I 'liked' the text.

Noticing that I was standing dripping wet in the middle of my living room (curtains wide open btw), I took my phone and ran back to the bathroom where I carried out the rest of my post-shower skincare regimen. I placed my phone on the toilet, and covered myself in a Shea Butter body cream that my dad had brought back from one of his trips to Ghana, seeing as he owned a Shea Butter farm out there. I then slapped on a thin layer of coconut oil, making sure to pay extra attention to my decolletage area – in fact, I added a few drops of body shimmer for that extra razzle-dazzle. After making sure every inch of my body was moisturised, I headed to my bedroom and spritzed some body spray just to set the mood. I needed a scent to make me feel empowered and the light jasmine and oud fragrance had a subtle masculine note that made me feel quite sexy.

Now, the outfit. Cute or sensual – what vibe did I want to send Jericho? The unanswered message on my phone lingered in the back of my mind, but I still had forty minutes to spare. My ritual couldn't be disrupted, not now. I'd deal with it once I was fully dressed, the mood set, and everything perfectly in place. After trying out a few cosy, plush night robes and an old Christmas onesie, I settled on a simple black satin robe. I wanted to give off the impression that I hadn't put too much thought into the call, but still wanted to appear low-key sexy, with a vibe of nonchalance. I then wrapped my twenty-six-inch braids into a high bun to better show off my face, and then warmed up some jollof rice in the microwave while I started on my make-up.

Obviously not wanting to go all in, I decided to settle on a subtle, soft 'no make-up/make-up' look. A somewhat dewy look that didn't look too try-hard. I applied a Laura Mercier tinted moisturiser to my T-zone, making sure not to cake my face too much. I then applied one coat of mascara, added a dab of peach cream blush to the apples of my cheeks and my Huda Beauty peach translucent lip gloss to my lips. I gave myself a final once-over in the mirror; I scrubbed up well, considering how little time I'd had to prepare. I checked my phone for the time again: twenty minutes to go.

I walked back into my living room, drew the curtains and took the steaming jollof out of the microwave. Time to do a little multitasking here.

I took a spoonful of jollof while I rearranged the throw pillows on the sofa. My goal was to position myself in the middle, with a slight view of my candles on the side table in the background. I dug out my tripod and ring light from the ottoman near the dining table and positioned them in the centre of the living room, closest to the sofa. After five minutes of chopping and changing the positioning, I finally had the setup. I dimmed the main light and walked over to the kitchen to polish off the rest of the jollof rice, burning my tongue in the process. 'Ow! FUCK!' I screamed, spitting hot rice over the floor.

Of course, this would happen to me with only five minutes to spare. Toby sauntered over to the spilled rice, eagerly lapping up the spilled grains. *Fair enough*, I thought. With three minutes left, I poured myself a rum and Coke and settled onto the sofa, making sure to strike just the right balance between casual and composed.

I reapplied my lip gloss, which I'd placed next to me, and lifted Toby into my embrace; I needed something to do with my arms to stop me from looking anxious, and Toby provided the perfect foil for the distraction. With my phone on the tripod, I opened the app and waited.

Within moments, the phone started to ring, with the Face-Time screen lit up, showing my face on screen. This was it; all or nothing. I had no reason to be scared; after all, I was purely doing this for research purposes. It wasn't like I was actually going to ever meet the guy?

I adjusted my robe slightly and took one last look at my face, then accepted the call.

Chapter 4

Jericho's face lit up the screen, every bit as ruggedly handsome as his profile had promised. His chiselled features were bathed in a soft glow, accentuating the striking light brown of his eyes that practically sparkled with mischief. His wide grin revealed perfect teeth, while the corners of his eyes crinkled into delicate, dark-brown specks that added warmth to his megawatt smile. Despite his rugged demeanour, there was a slight boyish charm to him that made him seem far younger than his years. I couldn't help but make a mental note to ask him about his skincare routine later – whatever he was doing was clearly working wonders. I was slightly taken aback to see how incredibly FINE this man was. But, I could get through it. I'd look at it as an interview. Nothing more, nothing less.

'Hey Cassie! It's lovely to meet you,' Jericho said, his deep voice penetrating my ears like a low, velvety hum that wrapped around me, stirring something deep within me. For a moment, my heart betrayed me – thumping hard against my ribs, each beat a tiny jolt of anticipation I could feel all the way down my spine. A warm flush crept up my neck and in that moment I was thankful that my melanin meant he couldn't see me getting hot and bashful as hell. I knew I had to get it together and keep myself composed instead of acting like a giggly teenager. I had to be as cool and confident as I sounded in my *OuiMeet* profile.

I took a small breath and replied. 'Jericho, it's lovely to meet you too! I'll be honest, this is my first time doing anything like this so I apologise in advance if there are any awkward silences or anything.' I mentally kicked myself over saying this – I didn't need to apologise about anything, he was a professional!

Jericho chuckled sweetly and waved his hand at the screen nonchalantly. 'Don't worry about it, sweetheart – from the sound of your profile, I don't believe there's anything awkward about you. So, can I ask what brought you here? Tell me a bit about you.'

Oh. Diving straight in then. A part of me wanted to tell the truth, but another part of me wanted to lean into the facade of this super-confident persona I'd made on *OuiMeet*. I wanted to be someone else, if only for a few minutes. 'Haha, well!' I started, seductively tucking a stray loose braid behind my ear and looking up at the screen from below my eyelashes – Princess Diana-style. 'I don't know about yourself, but dating in London for me has been such a drag; a series of terrible experiences after another, and after a while racking up a plethora of shit dates, I just felt like I needed a bit of a change, you know? I wanted to be daring and try something new.'

Jericho listened intently, nodding in all the appropriate places and issuing a small smile when I'd mentioned that I'd wanted to try something different. He rubbed his chin enticingly and stared into the screen. 'Well, I can definitely try and help with that, Cassie,' he said in that low, seductive voice. There was something about the way he said my name at the end of his sentences that made the hairs on the back of my neck stand on edge; it was so . . . *sexy*.

'I'm hoping so too,' I replied, as coy as I could muster in a bid to match his seductive energy. Even through the video call, his eye contact was incredible; I could feel myself growing more shy as the minutes went on; minutes I had to keep an eye on as the call would only last thirty-eight more minutes.

'So, erm,' I continued, hoping to retain his attention, 'as you know my name's Cassie, I'm based in South West London and I work at a hospital. I absolutely love my job, and I live on my own with my little baby boy. His name's Toby!' I gently picked up Toby – who had been dozing lazily in my arms – and pointed him towards the camera before sitting him back down in my lap. Toby stirred briefly, gave me a dirty look, and hopped off my lap to use his litter tray in the kitchen. His aggressively flat ears were proof enough of his anger for waking him from his slumber. I knew he'd make me pay later.

'Awww! You have a cat!' Jericho suddenly exclaimed, a boyish twinkle in his eyes as his face cracked open into a huge smile. 'I love cats myself; there's an aloofness to them that I find charming. They just don't give any shits about anything and I respect that so much,' Jericho responded, his laughter warm and unguarded with a rich, deep timbre that vibrated through the air. Every move this man made was electrifying.

'I agree!' I replied, beaming. This was a good start. 'He's a cutie . . . I've had him since he was a baby and he's very high maintenance, but I don't mind – he practically considers me staff at this point. But anyway, more on why I'm here. Essentially, I want to have some fun with a kind, enigmatic, intelligent guy, you know? I want to have good conversation, and to be treated like the Queen I believe I am, if just for once in my life. I believe I deserve that for myself at the very least.' I smiled, cheekily.

At that, Jericho cocked his head to the side and stared at me intently, as if peering into my soul. What I thought would be a casual, light-hearted conversation slowly began to feel more like a deep therapy session. I hadn't intended to share so much – at least, not yet. But there was something about the way he looked at me that stirred . . . something inexplicable inside me.

There was a safeness and a kindness in his eyes that made me feel as if I could talk to him about anything, which when you looked at the bigger picture was horrifying. I could hear my mum's voice in the back of my head now: '*Cassie, after God, fear men!*'

'Cassie, two things,' Jericho responded, still staring intently at me. I straightened up as he spoke, as if suddenly having a serious conversation with a headteacher. 'One, I love how you mentioned that "you deserved" to be the recipient of these experiences. I've met a lot of women who come to these apps and have really bad confidence and self-esteem issues, which I get. But you're a breath of fresh air.' At this, he smiled, which instantly made me smile, the charmer.

'Two,' he continued, still maintaining eye contact, which I dared not break. 'I find it really hard to believe that you've had unsuccessful dates. I mean, I know dating in London fucking sucks at the moment, but you mean to tell me that not one of the dudes in this city has had the nerve to treat you well? That's fucking wild to me, man. You're beautiful, and you seem really cool.'

It took everything in me not to turn the camera off and kick my feet up in the air while squealing. Is this why people paid for escorts? Because if so, I'd take out a subscription. I could feel my cheeks slowly burn hot as I briefly looked away from him, before the realisation hit me like a ton of bricks. That was the whole point, wasn't it? I was paying him to be nice to me. I looked back at the camera and smiled softly. I'm sure there were rules to this whole thing, and I had to be careful not to get too ahead of myself.

'Why, Jericho, you're super kind, but I guess that's why you probably earn the big bucks on here, huh?' I scoffed playfully. 'I bet you say that to all the girls who swing by your page.'

Jericho performatively raised his hand to his chest in mock

hurt. 'Me? Absolutely not! I mean, sure, compliments are part and parcel of this whole experience at times, but I'll be honest, I don't tend to get a lot of phone calls, it's more so a case of, doing the do and going the go, so with you, I genuinely mean it.'

'Doing the do and going the go?' I replied, keeping an eye on the clock. I liked where this conversation was going and was wary that our time was drawing near. 'As in . . .'

'As in,' he finished my sentence, 'an evening or overnight experience that's purely physical, and I'd leave the next day. See? No time for compliments, so with you, I'm being genuine!'

'So about that,' I replied. Now I wanted to know more about him but, more so, I didn't want this conversation to end – I was having fun. 'Do you tend to get those types of requests often? The overnight ones? I'd love to know more about you and how you got into this.'

Jericho stared directly into the camera yet again and pursed his lips slightly, ending with a small, disarming smirk. I wondered if he had to do some kind of 'Art of Seduction' *OuiMeet* course before getting his account validated on the app, because he was brilliant at it, whatever his tricks were. I was hot and flustered by this point, but I was proud of myself for still being able to keep it together.

'Well,' he started, leaning closer to the camera, drawing me into an intimacy so compelling that I found myself leaning in too. 'No, Jericho isn't my real name; I try to leave personal details like that off these kinds of sites if I can help it. I already stress about my work being recognised, and if the worst were to happen, at least I could claim plausible deniability – just a case of mistaken identity or a catfish situation, haha.'

This admission caught me off-guard – I'd assumed that this was his full-time gig. 'Oh! So, you have a full-time job outside of this? That's dope – what do you do?' At this, the smile lines around Jericho's eyes faded slightly, and his sleepy smile had been replaced with a quizzical one. 'This call is supposed to be all about you, my love,' he started. The goosebumps sprouted up again at his term of endearment to me. 'I don't normally kiss and tell until I meet people in real life, I'm afraid, but also, try and see it like this: it only adds to the mystery. For the most part, I tend to keep my "online" life and my personal life separate when I can – that is, unless I strike up a bond with someone I suppose, d'you know what I mean?'

I nodded, though a little too aggressively, and felt a small tugging of one of the muscles in my neck. Girl, calm down!

'You mean, I'm gonna need to pay more money to see or speak to you again in order to get to know you more, huh? It's a good scheme, I have to say.'

Jericho laughed in response, clapping his hands enthusiastically, which for some reason, made my heart flutter. It made me feel good to know that I at least amused him. 'You caught me! Hey, if it ain't broke, and all that. But in all seriousness, these phone sessions are all about you; you tell me what you want to talk about, I'm here to fulfil your desires and fantasies. It's your world, I'm just a squirrel trying to get a nut – metaphorically,' he added hastily after noticing the sly grin I had been trying to hide.

'I understand all that,' I replied, aching to know more about him. 'But what if my fantasy was to know more about you and have an equal back-and-forth conversation, instead of just ranting on about me? I'm not that interesting of a person, to be honest.' That last part wasn't true – I am, in fact, a very interesting person, but the British trait of self-deprecation took over at the last minute for some reason.

Jericho paused, looking pensive. I was hoping I'd said enough to convince him. I took a nervous sip of my drink as I glanced again at the clock. Not much time left.

'I'll tell you what, Cassie. We've got ten minutes left, ask me whatever you want, and then if you want to have another chat at a later date, we can carry on where we left off. As you're new to this, I can probably go through how these arrangements typically work too.' He grinned wolfishly and leaned back, his straight, white teeth gleaming.

'OK, cool,' I said in mock defeat. I decided to get the main questions out of the way. 'I'd like for you to answer the following questions – in the same order – and if I'm satisfied, I'll think about maybe booking another phone call. Deal?'

'Gotcha,' Jericho replied, looking amused.

'OK. Answer the following please; one – what's your skincare routine? Because your face is flawless and I can't honestly believe you're thirty-four. Two – you're a gorgeous man, why are you here? Three, which is kinda related to two – do you have a girlfriend outside of this? Four – are you looking for said girlfriend? Five – who's the oldest person you've had sex with on here? And six, do you honestly find me attractive?' I exhaled and leaned back, allowing the lapel of my robe to gape slightly, showing a little cleavage. Jericho caught onto this and grinned his wolfish smile again. I was enjoying this little game of tennis we were currently playing.

'Oh, we really went in, didn't we? OK. One; it's just pure soap and water, I'm afraid. All of this—' Jericho points to himself cockily '—is genetic, baby. Second question, that's really an answer for a much longer conversation but, to cut a long story short, I'm using the money I earn here to save towards my future and to supplement my current income. Three, no. I'm single. I'm not really sure how it would work if I had a girlfriend while doing this job so I've stayed clear of that for now. Four. Wouldn't you like to know? Five. Again, wouldn't you like to know? And six. I think you're beautiful, Cassie. Given the nature of our interaction, I can see why you'd find it hard to believe, but you're a cutie.'

'Thanks for answering,' I replied, smiling awkwardly. I leaned back even further into the sofa, pondering his answers. We had four minutes left before he had to go and I wasn't really sure where to go from here, so I just asked the first thing that was on my mind:

'So, um, I saw on your menu thingy that you don't have a text option. Is that something you'd probably consider doing in future? You seem really nice and, I have to say, I like the cut of your jib. It would be cool to chat to you again sometime.'

Jericho smiled at this dozily, and scratched his perfectly square chin, as if pondering. After a moment's silence, he responded. 'You know, you're the first person to ask me that? I've never thought about the text thing because it seems silly to charge for a few messages back and forth each time – I wouldn't really know how to price it really. For now, I think I'm gonna stick to my current price list but if you ever want to talk again, you can always book another call, or—' at this, he took a dramatic pause and I held my breath '—or you can book a date night and we can talk some more – if you can afford me, that is.' At this, Jericho leaned back and burst into laughter.

'You're a bit of a cheeky shit, aren't you?' I baulked, also breaking into a chuckle at his insolence. 'I'll have you know I can definitely afford you . . . CHALLENGE-FUCKING-ACCEPTED, MATE.'

'Iight, cool. Well, until we speak again, Cassie. This is truly one of the strangest phone dates I've ever had.' He again stared at the camera intensely, drawing me in.

'Meaning?' I replied, a tinge of disappointment arising in my tone. Hopefully I hadn't offended him. 'Meaning,' he replied, 'this is the first time I've had a chat with a woman via the app who hasn't tried to accost me for phone sex or dirty talk. You seem like somewhat of a wholesome woman. I like that.'

I grinned, excited to have differentiated myself from the rest of the women he talked to. At that moment, I almost knew that I wanted to speak with him again.

'Well, I'm glad about that. I wouldn't count myself as wholly "wholesome", but that may be something you get to find out in time perhaps.'

His coy, wolfish smile returned as he looked into the camera hungrily. 'Game on. Goodnight.' He winked, as the phone cut dead.

I fell back onto my sofa, allowing the exhilaration to take over in that moment. I could feel my heart pounding a million miles a minute as I went over the last hour's events. Maybe it was just me overthinking, but I had felt an undeniable sexual tension in the air throughout that entire phone call – the kind I hadn't felt in who knows how long, even when out on a date. Usually, I'd fake a connection just to bring a guy home for some boring, passionless, mediocre sex. But this? This was different. This felt real, somehow. Maybe it was simply lust. Or maybe I was just a delusional single woman desperate for an ounce of passion in whatever form that came in. I was leaning more towards the latter. Whatever that was, I knew one thing for sure: I needed to fuck him at some point.

Chapter 5

'So how did it go? Did he look like his picture? Wait, send me a screenshot of his page, I wanna see!' I'd called Sade to give her the rundown of the night's events as I made my way to bed, rather proud that I'd gone through with the whole experience in the end. Sure, there was some awkwardness in the beginning, but as the night went on it felt more like chatting with a new social media friend on FaceTime than a co-ordinated, paid-for date with a male escort. Despite our brief conversation, Jericho had had a way of making me feel at ease and comfortable, and it was that feeling that I was desperate to experience again.

I lay on my bed, kicking my feet up in the air like a girl having her first crush. 'Sis! It was actually really nice, you know. He was such a gentleman, and he had this way about him, man . . .'

I took a screenshot of Jericho's *OuiMeet* page and sent it through to Sade. 'What do you mean "a way about him"? Finish your sentences, please!' Sade pressed, gagging for the tea as only a best friend would.

'Did you see the screenshot I just sent?' I replied, skilfully sidestepping her question. The truth was, I was still sorting through my feelings about the encounter – and, more importantly, whether speaking to him again was a good idea. I had started down a path, and I needed to be sure I didn't lose myself in it.

'Well, well, well. He's a hottie, isn't he? He's fucking sexy, I can see why he charges that much boy.' Sade swooned. 'What's he like? Did he give off "prostitute" vibes? Were you guys talking dirty and shit?'

'Rah, look at this one!' I replied, sounding mock-stunned. 'First of all, I think you're supposed to call them "sex workers" now. You're supposed to be the progressive one! Secondly, no, we didn't talk about sex, actually; we kept it nice and wholesome. Some might even say demure.'

'Ohh booo!' snapped Sade. 'I'm here trying to fish for dirty, sordid tales and you're here doing up Disney Princess with Prince Charming. This was your opportunity to get DOWN AND DIRTY Cass. DIR-TEE.' I laughed at her last sentence, thankful that I had a friend who encouraged all of my random exploits.

'Girl, we'll get to that in time, I suppose! I'm thinking about maybe booking another phone call with him, but actually I'm wondering if I should just take the plunge and go on a date with him? I'm struggling with it, to be honest.'

As empowering and fun as the last hour had been, there was still a huge part of me that was struggling with having to pay for a date. For me, it still felt like an admission of failure as a woman. There had to be some way I could twist the narrative so I didn't feel like such a loser.

'Well, babes,' summarised Sade in between what I could hear were sips of tea, 'if he was as nice as you say, I don't see any reason why you shouldn't chat to him again. If I were you I'd just go all out and book him for the evening. You only live once, and at our age, you gotta start creating random life experiences for the plot, and to do shit for the fun of it, because life only goes downhill from here, man.'

'Thank you for the life-coaching session, Oprah,' I replied, rolling my eyes. I knew she had a point; I supposed that one day when I was older, this would be a great story to tell the kids, that's if I ever went on to have any. They'd know all about Mummy's brief, torrid affair with the escort and how it led to nothing but probable heartbreak.

'Oh wait, he's just sent me a message!' I told Sade, noticing my phone's notifications going off.

'Wonderful!' Sade responded. 'I'm gonna go to bed, but catch me up on it later, yeah? I need to share some gossip with you at some point too, actually, so let's maybe make a night of it – we'll sort out the details tomorrow!'

'OK, sleep tight, my love, and thank you for everything – you're my favourite enabler!' I added. As we ended the call, I glanced back at the *OuiMeet* app, pausing slightly before opening. What if Jericho had sent a message asking me not to contact him again? What if he found the whole encounter weird? He did mention that our talk was one of the 'strangest phone dates he'd ever been on'. What if he actually meant it? Better to rip the plaster off, I supposed.

I opened the app and headed straight to my inbox. I clicked the tab to open it and read the message out loud to myself:

> Cassie. It was a pleasure to chat with you this evening and I want to thank you again for booking with me. You're a curious little sprite, aren't you? I'm intrigued. Hopefully we can talk again soon. Goodnight, beautiful. J x

I read through the message three more times, basking in the warmth and apparent sincerity of his words. Toby hopped up into the bed and began to make biscuits on my tummy, before curling into a ball to sleep. I held him close as I thought of something to write back; I didn't want him to think I was super eager to talk to him. I needed to play it cool and chill. Not *too* nonchalant; just the right amount of 'chalantness' to inspire intrigue, yet not push him away. After a moment, I typed back,

J, the pleasure was mine. Curiosity is a dangerous yet fascinating thing, you know – leads people down all sorts of interesting paths. Perhaps ours will cross again soon. Sleep well. x

Yeah, that's more like it. Mysterious, yet slightly ominous. I put my phone on charge, popped a melatonin pill and drifted into what I thought would be uninterrupted, dreamless sleep.

I woke up at five thirty the next morning, horny and irritated. As I fed Toby his wet food and slugged into the shower, I reminisced about last night's dream, which was essentially six hours of repetitive failed attempts to have sex with Jericho. I kept being woken up by the cold sweat that had gathered underneath my belly and between my inner thighs as a result of these dreams. In them, Jericho had me pressed against my kitchen counter, clearly struggling to lift me – but trying way too hard to play it cool. We fumbled from one unsuccessful position to the next until, finally, he sighed, pulled away, and admitted he couldn't perform – said he felt too awkward trying to navigate around my stomach. The dream ended with me bursting into tears, and that's exactly when I jolted awake.

Cut to me in the shower, warm water streaming down my body as I lifted my stomach, trying to catch a glimpse of my own genitals. Yeah, I had a FUPA – but I quite liked it, actually. It was plump and squidgy and it kept me warm. Plus, it was cute. The truth was, I'd been rejected more than once because of my weight, leaving behind a string of failed hook-ups and disappointing dates. At first, each one chipped away at my confidence, but eventually, I realised the problem wasn't me – it was them. It was always them. Still, there were days, especially when loneliness crept in, when that confidence wavered. What if I met up with Jericho and he did the same thing?

The more pressing question was, why was I becoming so

caught up in a random internet stranger I'd virtually met less than twelve hours ago? I tried to snap out of it as I lathered the rest of my body and got ready for another work day.

I slipped into my silk robe, tossing a couple of sausages into the air fryer while setting a pan to boil an egg, as per traditional Ghanaian customs. Since I'd woken up early, I had a rare hour to spare before leaving for work – plenty of time to enjoy a home-cooked breakfast, something I didn't get to do often these days. I sat on the sofa, Toby purring peacefully in my lap as I searched for the perfect playlist to start the day: I decided to go with a bit of Linkin Park's *Hybrid Theory* album to perk me up; a throwback to when I went through my brief period as a grunger back in secondary school.

Halfway through screaming out the lyrics to 'Crawling', my phone started to ring. To my surprise, it was my father, a man I typically only heard from when he needed a favour or if he wanted to complain about my mum. I wondered which one it would be today.

'Dad. You all right?' I answered casually as I went to check in on my sausages. 'I'm getting ready for work so I won't have a lot of time to chat, I'm afraid.' Silence on the other end of the phone as I waited for him to respond, followed soon by a soft sniffle. Was he – was my dad *crying?*

My dad's job as a big-time patent lawyer in the City meant that we rarely saw him around growing up and on the occasions when Steven and I did get to spend time with him, we only saw one side to him – pure stoicism. He was never one to show emotion outside of anger and frustration, so for him to be on the phone seemingly sniffling at stupid o'clock in the morning seemed somewhat concerning.

'Hello, my dear,' he finally replied, and it sounded like he was in his car. 'I'm actually outside your flat – I've got an early Zoom meeting at work with some international clients in

Jordan so I'm just making my way into the office – um, can I pop in for a second? It'll be like twenty minutes. I can drive you to work if you want?'

My guard instantly went up. My dad, offering me favours and wanting to spend time with me? Something was afoot. 'Um, sure, Dad, come up.' I peeked through the curtain to see his black Mercedes Benz GLB SUV parked outside my flat, opposite the park. After getting off the phone with him, I quickly texted the family group chat, lovingly named 'The Inheritance Squad', due to me and Steven accidentally finding our dad's will in his office a few years ago. The group consisted of Steven and me, alongside Mum when we told her that she was also named in the will too.

Cassandra: Um guys? Dad's downstairs. He wants to come up and talk to me about something. Has something happened?

Before I could check for a response, my intercom blared with its usual shrill tone. I hurried to the front door and glanced at the screen – there was my dad, as solemn and stoic as ever, dressed in a three-piece suit and a black peacoat.

I buzzed him in and dashed to my bedroom, swapping my slinky black robe for a thicker, borg-textured oversized one. Living on the fifteenth floor gave me a couple of minutes before he reached my flat – just enough time to brace myself.

I served up my boiled egg and slightly undercooked sausage breakfast before heading to the door to let him in. As I opened the door, I was greeted with a wall of the Tom Ford Ombre Leather cologne that I'd bought my dad for his birthday a couple of years ago. He stood there, solemn and somewhat morose, as if carrying the weight of the world on his shoulders. The moment he stepped into my flat, he made a beeline for the kitchen.

'They're not gonna ticket my car, are they, Cassandra? I parked in a resident spot. Actually, I won't be here long, just wanted a quick chat.'

His words came out scattered, his mind seemingly juggling seventy different thoughts at once. I made my way to my breakfast and took a couple of bites before responding, intermittently checking my phone for any updates in the group chat.

'Nah, you should be fine, it's still pretty early. Um, so . . . what's brought about all this? You're not dying, are you? If so, can you update your will so Steve gets the house in Ghana? I'm not ready to move there anytime soon, to be honest, haha.' My attempt at lightening the mood hung heavy in the air like a thick smog; normally he would laugh at my dry, awkward jokes but not this time.

'Oh, so my daughter thinks she's a comedian now, huh? Very funny,' he said quietly, his brow furrowing even further. 'Can you make me a quick cup of tea please?' Without hesitating, again as per Ghanaian 'Oldest Daughter' customs, I switched on the kettle and grabbed a mug as he sat down at the kitchen table, inhaling deeply upon impact. He stared slowly from me to the open plan kitchen/living space, before staring silently at me again. 'You've really made something of yourself, Cassandra. It wasn't the direction I wanted you to go in; if I had it my way, you'd be settled down with a nice man and a baby or two by now, but I'm proud of you regardless.' I let the sting of his last sentence wash over me as I poured the hot water into the mug, allowing the tea bag to steep.

As the eldest, it was always expected that I would follow in my father's footsteps and pursue a career in law. I ended up choosing a law course at uni, but by the middle of my second year, I realised my heart wasn't fully in it, much to my parents' dismay, anger and frustration. Still, I finished my degree, but instead of practising law, I wound up doing several admin roles before eventually finding my way into the NHS, where I worked my way up to where I was now. On a £45k-a-year salary I was doing all right for myself, but deep down, I always knew it was a huge disappointment for my dad. Mind you, I had a whole other sibling who did not receive the same career pressures as I did, the double standard of it all.

'Erm . . . OK, cheers, Dad, I appreciate it. What did you want to chat about?' I mumbled, handing him his tea and going back to bites of my breakfast. I had about forty minutes before I had to start getting myself ready for work and needed him to get to the point.

'Ahh man,' he replied, making a grand gesture of holding his head in his hands as if in pain. 'Have you heard from your mother lately?' Of course. Whatever this chat would be about, deep down I had the feeling that it would somehow revolve around Mum, the only woman he'd ever loved. I joined him at the kitchen table.

'Yeah, I spoke to her last night. I'm gonna be seeing her over the weekend too. Why, what happened?'

Dad brought his eyes – sad and wistful – up to meet mine. And then he dropped the bombshell.

'Did she tell you she was getting married to that guy?'

Ah. So that's probably why she wanted to gather me and Steven round at her place this weekend. What an interesting turn of events. But more so . . .

'Wait, how did you find out?' I asked, trying not to look shocked. I low-key found it hilarious that he kept referring to Femi as 'that guy', even though, a long time ago, he fully made it his business to be aware of his name, age, and job title. Dad turned to take another sip of his tea – no doubt using the delay to think of an excuse. My dad working at one of the top law firms in the UK meant he was used to acquiring the types of access to and information on people that your average person off the street wouldn't have. That wasn't to say that he acquired this information through nefarious means but . . . you never knew when it came to this man.

'Uncle Kwabena called me last night,' he said, referring to a mutual friend of both my parents who we affectionately called 'Uncle' growing up. 'Apparently he proposed a few days ago and your mum said yes and has started telling people. I can't believe it.'

This definitely wasn't how I wanted to learn about my mum's upcoming wedding, and I was pretty pissed off that he had deliberately ruined the surprise for me. Honestly, I was just frustrated that Steve and I kept getting caught in the middle of whatever one-sided grudge he had against Mum.

'Well, I didn't know that, and it's a shame I couldn't hear it from her directly,' I said, glancing at the time. After a few more bites, I took my plate to the sink. 'I'm happy for her, she deserves a happy ending—' I caught myself after seeing the pained look on my dad's face '—not that you didn't make her happy, of course, but . . . ehh . . . you know what I mean,' I continued as I leaned on the counter to look down at him. He genuinely looked heartbroken, but there was nothing I could do; he had to bear the consequences of being a bad husband and a bit of a shit dad, I supposed.

'It's OK,' he said, defeated as he took another sip of tea. 'I guess I just always thought that one day . . . after some time has passed . . . she would want to reconsider us getting back together at some point. We're both old and no one wants to be alone in their old age, especially with you and Steven all grown up and living your own lives now.'

As much as I wanted to tell him that he was the architect of his own undoing, I couldn't help but feel sorry for the guy at times; he had been pining over my mum since their divorce, unable to move on or get over her at all; it was sweet, in a sense.

'Well, Dad, I think even Stevie Wonder could see that THAT was never going to happen, no offence. You guys have been divorced for years and I would have thought that, in that time, you'd find someone else too! You're still young! You're still hip!' I popped the lapel on his very expensive tweed peacoat. 'At the very least, you're wealthy. I would have thought the women would be all over you.' At my last comment, he let out a guffaw, his chest heaving up and down frantically, almost as if he was going to have a coughing fit. 'You this girl, you're funny!' he chortled, taking a final long sip of his beverage. 'It's improper to talk about these things with you, but I have had my fair share of dates here and there . . . no one measures up to your mother though. She was the love of my life.'

I felt my heart melt there and then, knowing that if my mum had been around to hear that, she would have burst into fits of laughter before condescendingly consoling him while shading him at the same time. If there was one thing my mum loved, she loved hearing about how much my dad regretted letting her go.

'I hear ya, Dad, but maybe her getting married again can be the push you need to get yourself back out there and start dating again?' I sat at the kitchen table opposite him as he turned to face me, his sad eyes searching for a resolution in mine.

'Mum has moved on, and I know you love her and all that, but there needs to come a time where you accept that she's found happiness elsewhere, and use that as a motivational tool to search for what happiness means for you. It doesn't necessarily have to be another woman – you can take up a hobby or something; you've still got time to go through a midlife crisis and buy a motorbike.'

He laughed at this again, his glazed eyes twinkling momentarily. I preferred him in these vulnerable moments, as weird as they may have sounded. It was almost like receiving special access to a portal to a younger version of himself, a part of his personality that the family didn't know.

'You're wise beyond your years, Baba,' he replied, using the pet name he used to call me as a child. 'You probably have a point but – what do you think? Is she happy? Does she truly love him? Is he good to her?'

I exhaled. I give one rousing, emotive monologue about moving on and all of a sudden I'm Oprah. Well, Oprah had to leave for work in thirty minutes so I had to find a way to make this short.

'Dad . . . I think she's happy. I don't say this to make you feel bad at all, but she is the happiest I've ever seen her for a minute, I think. She's found something that works for her and I think it's important that you do the same; you're a handsome guy, you'll be able to find love again, if that's what you're looking for?'

My dad gave a slow exhale as he drained the rest of his mug. I excused myself temporarily to quickly get changed into my work gear and put my hair up in a top bun. I ran some mascara through my lashes and applied my peach translucent lip gloss from Hourglass Cosmetics, taking one final look at myself before heading back to the living room. I looked and felt tired, but was still living off the adrenaline of talking to Jericho last night.

As I headed back into the living room to rejoin my dad, I received a text from the family group chat again:

Steve: Nothing that I can think of, sis. Are you in trouble lmao? What did you do???
Mummy: What's happening? What has he told you?
Cassandra: He's pining over you (AGAIN) of course.
Mummy: . . . Jesus Christ of Nazareth. When will this man rest?

Cassandra: Loooool! When you decide to get back with him, I suppose.
Mummy: God forbid.

I wondered if my mum knew that Dad knew about her impending nuptials? I quickly sent a message to Steven separately.

Cassandra: It's about Mum. He found out that Femi proposed apparently???
Steven: Say whaaaa? IS IT? Rah boy. Maybe that's why she wanted us over the house this weekend?
Cassandra: Yh I think so. Don't tell Mum we know, though. It'll be nice for her to surprise us. But yeah, Dad isn't happy. He's been crashing out for the last 20 mins.
Steven: At some point he's gotta get over her, man.
Cassandra: Right? Smh. I'll ttyl xx

I put my phone away and went to join Dad in the living room as he made his way to leave. I felt a bit bad for how I had come at him regarding Mum, but it had to be said. The man had to move on and stop pining after her – he was only hurting himself in the process. I dropped my keys and hand cream into my bag as I slipped on my shoes.

'You all right, Dad? I hope what I said didn't come across as harsh or anything.'

'No, you're fine. You're right. We both have our lives to live, I suppose. Anyway, I said I would give you a ride to work, are you ready?' His eyes were still moist with tears. I couldn't handle this. In a rare display of affection, I went up to him and gave him a hug, which to my surprise, he actually returned, instead of the half-hearted, half-hug he would usually dish out. We embraced for what felt like thirty minutes, though it was only a few seconds. Yet in that brief moment, I could feel the entire weight of the world lift from his shoulders. I grabbed my bits and together we headed out and towards his car.

Poor guy. Mum had him absolutely whipped. I issued a soft prayer to myself that that kind of heartbreak would never find me.

As we headed off towards Vauxhall, Dad turned briefly towards me and asked, 'Cassie, are you seeing anyone at the moment? It would be nice to be a grandpa while I still have all my motor functions.'

I guffawed.

'Dad. You have a whole grandchild currently basting in its own juices in your future daughter-in-law's stomach right now, ready to drop in the next couple of months. What's with the pressure on me?'

Dad responded by sucking his teeth and tapping the steering wheel as we ventured down South Lambeth Road.

'It's not the same, Cassie. It's not the same. You were supposed to be first, you know?'

Yeah. I knew. My parents had never let me forget it.

There was silence for a few moments more, before he briefly turned to me again and let out a huge exhale, almost as if he were bracing himself.

'Thank you,' he started, his voice solemn. 'Thank you for your advice this morning.'

I smiled faintly, attempting to burn this moment into my brain, for it was rare for me to receive an acknowledgement of appreciation from him.

'You're welcome, Dad,' I replied. 'Careful, though – keep being this nice to me, and I might get used to it.'

Chapter 6

I arrived at work with thirty minutes to spare, and in that time, I decided to reflect on the last twenty-four hours with the whole Jericho situation. I quickly checked the *OuiMeet* app for signs of a response, but my message was still left unread. I wanted to gauge his response before booking another session, but the excitement from last night's shenanigans sat deep in my stomach – I needed more. I loved the thrill of it and was tempted to book without waiting for his reply. To hell with feeling embarrassed or ashamed about it; I had had too much fun to let this be a one-time occurrence. I checked Jericho's 'menu' again to see his rates:

> My company during the day (up to four hours) – £200 // My company during the evening (up to four hours) – £350.

I logged into my monthly savings accounting app to check how much I had accumulated so far. I'd set the account up five years ago to deposit automatic monthly savings of £400 in my bid to someday have enough to help with buying and doing up a house (most of the funds would be coming via help from my parents but I wanted to save a bit aside for renovations and such). There was currently £24,000 in there; I'd been strict on never touching it except for dire emergencies. I couldn't help but wonder: would withdrawing £200 to spend time with a strapping young man – improving my mental, emotional and (hopefully) sexual health – constitute a dire emergency? I transferred the £200 into my current account and went back onto *OuiMeet.* Fuck it; I deserved to have a good experience, and the money could always be replaced in time.

I thought it would be cute to schedule a nice weekend date during the day to do something wholesome at first. I wanted to establish a rapport with him that didn't feel quite so transactional and so I clicked on his 'daytime date' option on his profile. I checked his calendar for availability; Saturday was the only day he had available for a daytime date, the same day my mum wanted us to come over so she could spill her alleged engagement news. Damnit.

With fifteen minutes before I needed to officially 'clock in' to work, I quickly texted Mum, already anticipating her emotionally manipulative response:

Cassandra: Mum, what time do you need us over this weekend? I may have a clash . . .

She answered within a couple of minutes.

Mummy: Clash with who? And why?
Mummy: So you can't even take a day out of your busy schedule to spend time with the woman that brought you into this world? Who gave birth to you? Who gave you life???

Like clockwork. I quickly checked the available times Jericho had for Saturday; 10 a.m. and 2 p.m. Damnit. I replied:

Cassandra: Can you really say you 'gave birth' to me, though? I was a caesarean, wasn't I? So *technically* you didn't really give birth to me . . . I was forcefully removed from your body against my will. Ejected. Anyways, I was thinking I could swing by for a couple of hours in the morning?

Steven would most probably end up staying the whole day at Mum's with Bianca, which would take the heat off me. I crossed my fingers as I booted up my computer, hoping that she'd be OK with the early morning drop-in.

A few minutes later, the office door opened and instead of Kofi, a tall, bald-headed man came through the door and walked in my direction. He had on tortoise-shell horn-rimmed glasses (from Oliver Peoples, I assumed), a black Bottega Veneta intrecciato-woven briefcase, and a three-piece suit, most likely by Ozwald Boateng. Having worked around surgeons and consultants over the last few years, you quickly find out that they all tend to dress the same and reach for the same designer brands when outside of their surgical scrubs. This was a man I didn't recognise, however. He stopped at my desk, a beaming smile in tow.

'Hi there! You must be Cassandra. I just thought I'd pop in quickly to introduce myself.' He had a sunny, charming disposition, not dissimilar to a holiday representative. He held out his hand, which I took hesitantly, and gave me a firm handshake. I didn't think we were expecting any new consultants on our floor, and if so, HR hadn't alerted me to any staff changes, annoyingly.

'I'm Mr Paulson, but you can just call me Jeff. I'm one of the new orthopaedic consultants, I don't know if HR told you at all?' He stepped back slightly, allowing me room to go through the piles of letters and notices on my desk and, of course, there was nothing to tell me he was starting today.

'Hey! Nice to meet you – no, unfortunately HR haven't updated me at all but that's no problem,' I said, trying to sound as professional as possible to cover up the fact that I was completely frazzled. I absolutely hated being caught unaware, especially at work. If I had known that we were going to get a new consultant, I would have arrived at work at least an hour earlier to set up his new office and run through a few logistics with him. But, we move.

'Oh! Not to worry,' he chortled lightly. This Jeff guy seemed like a pleasant person; I was hoping he wouldn't be too much trouble. 'To be honest, I actually start tomorrow but I just wanted to move my bits into the new office beforehand – I like to be super organised ahead of time so thought I'd quickly introduce myself to you and just say I'm looking forward to us working together!'

He seemed nice enough, and maybe this was right on time too, as a couple of my consultants were currently on annual leave, meaning my workload over the last few weeks had decreased a little – it would be nice to have a bit more to do.

I flashed my widest megawatt smile and replied, 'I'm looking forward to working with you too, Jeff! Thanks for stopping by. I work with another colleague called Kofi who should be here by nine a.m., but when he gets here, I'll make sure to introduce you to him too! I'm normally in the office all day until half past five, so if there's anything you need or you have any questions, please don't hesitate to email or call me on my extension—' I picked up one of my business cards located on the desk '—here. My extension is three-five-five-three and you can call anytime. I'll also get on the phone to HR today so we can confirm your work email and some other bits that I can run through with you tomorrow morning?'

By the look on Jeff's face, I could tell he was impressed, which gave me a bit of a rush. I loved this job, and there was nothing I loved more than being in charge of a group of men, especially. There was something exhilarating about heading up some of the most brilliant medical minds, despite having no medical expertise myself. The unique power dynamic fed a superiority complex I had come to welcome and fully embrace. At this, Jeff beamed a wide smile and gave a short bow.

'Amazing! Thank you, Cassandra. I look forward to meeting Kofi too, and I'll be in the office until two p.m. or so moving in, so I'll shout if I need any help – have a wonderful day!'

I quickly sent an email asking for more information on Jeff through to HR after he left, which is when Kofi sauntered in, coffee in hand. 'Who's that?' he asked, cocking his head towards the door. He then kicked the door shut and placed his drink on the table. 'He's tall, innit?'

'That's our new consultant apparently. Jeff Paulson – he seems nice. I've just sent an email to HR for his new email and stuff. I guess they forgot to tell us he was starting this week.'

'Oh.' Kofi breathed, rubbing the back of his neck slowly. 'Yeah, my bad. I did get an email about someone starting this week but I kinda scrolled through it and forgot to forward it to you. Sorry!' He held his hands up guiltily. He knew how militant and organised I was when it came to work, and the last thing I hated was being caught off-guard – especially by one of our consultants. 'Can I treat you to lunch to make up for it?'

Damnit. I didn't really want to, but a free meal was a free meal. 'Ugh. I 'spose so,' I replied. 'I'll be ordering lobster for lunch, just so you know.' He laughed as he logged into his computer. It was nothing more than a work-friend lunch – that's all it was. I checked back on my phone to see a response from my mum:

> **You think you're so funny. You get your humour from your dad unfortunately. Anyway, I wanted to prepare a meal for us all, but if you have more important things to do, then . . .**

Ah, the good old emotional manipulation. The cornerstone of every mother–daughter relationship. I quickly replied;

> **It's just a timing issue, but I'll cook you a wonderful breakfast if that helps? The best breakfast you've ever had!**

'So, what time did you wanna head out for lunch?' Kofi said quietly over the humming of his computer. I could tell he was trying to sound casual, but the tension in his voice betrayed a quiet desperation, hanging awkwardly in the air. There was a part of me that wanted to lightly mention my interaction with Jericho to him just to throw him off my scent, but equally that would have been cruel, and I still wanted to keep that quiet for now.

'I don't think it's a good idea for both of us to be away from our desks during lunch, you know,' I replied cautiously, yet truthfully. 'I was planning to pick up a few things to get Mr Paulson ready for his official first day tomorrow but—' I turned around to see Kofi's face looking almost crestfallen. I felt the guilt run through me like a knife '—why don't you grab us something and we can just chill here maybe? Besides, it's way warmer here!' His face lit up again at that. Lunch came, and in the time that Kofi dashed out to grab us two boxes of beef lasagne, I decided to make my move and book Jericho's company for Saturday now that I'd sorted out early morning plans with my mum. I went to Jericho's *OuiMeet* page and saw that his 2 p.m. slot was still free, and booked it. After receiving the confirmation, I let out a slow grin; finally something to look forward to! I couldn't wait. I wanted to buy a new outfit and perhaps retwist my front braids so everything looked neat. I sent Sade a quick text.

> **Babe, I booked Jericho again for this weekend??? Gonna actually meet him for a few hours, I can't believe it. Need to find something to wear ASAP xx**

She immediately texted back:

> **Bitch, this is what we love to see! Happy for u, remember to text me where you're going and send me your location info so I know you're not being murdered, k? Also this**

just reminds me that I need to go on a date too man. Ugh. Hate this dry spell! I need to be hooked up expeditiously! xx

At that exact moment, Kofi walked through the door with our lunch, his face lit up with a wide grin – just as a mischievous, knowing smile spread across mine. Sade wanted to go on a date. What if the best way to keep Kofi from focusing on me was to shift the attention onto . . .

'Hey buddy!' I said a little too loudly, flashing my award-winning smile at Kofi as he kicked the door behind him. I helped him with the bag of food as he sat our two Diet Cokes on the table. 'Thanks so much for getting this, I've been craving lasagne for a good two weeks now, you star.'

'No worries at all, hun,' replied Kofi, beaming. 'I'm just glad we're able to do this!' Now that I thought about it, I couldn't believe I hadn't seen it sooner. Kofi and Sade. Sade and Kofi. They would be perfect for each other. Kofi was a bit of a golden Labrador – super romantic, excitable, super kind and generous – and Sade was a black cat: mysterious, sexy, nurturing and an undercover lover girl. Even thinking about it made me giddy and I knew I had to start sowing the seeds.

'So,' I started, turning towards him, fork in hand. I needed to tread carefully here. 'How have you been lately? What are the apps saying these days?' I blew onto a forkful of lasagne and was about to put it into my mouth when out of the corner of my eye I saw Kofi watching me, almost hungrily, his eyes fixated on my mouth. Shit.

I instinctively put the fork down and smiled at him – how could I have this conversation in a professional way when Kofi probably thought this was a work date?

'Hehe, why do you ask?' he teased. I didn't like where this was going. Time to nip this in the bud.

'Oh no reason! It's just . . .' I intentionally trailed off, enough to grab a few mouthfuls of pasta.

'Well, I have a friend, you see; my best friend, actually, and I've been trying to set her up for a while but the men in this City move mad, as you well know.' Kofi scoffed at this, eyes still searching for meaning in mine.

'Essentially, I haven't played matchmaker in a while and I genuinely think you and her would really get on! You're quite the opposite, but I think, in this instance, it could potentially work.'

Kofi reached over and grabbed his Diet Coke, studying me quietly as he opened it and took a swig, his eyes still grazing over mine. I couldn't read him; was he being coy or was he upset? Had he caught on to my game? I waited for his response as I swallowed a couple more mouthfuls of pasta, the air in the room suddenly feeling thick with anticipation. 'I see,' Kofi finally said, after what felt like hours. 'Um, well, haha, I'm errr . . . Yeah, I'm still trying to date and stuff, just seeing what comes along, but I also trust your judgement too, Cass. Um, what's she like, your friend?'

Phew. At that, I launched into my pitch. My plan was to set them up and have them hopefully like each other enough that it would get Kofi off my back if just for a little while.

'So her name's Sade, she's thirty-three and Nigerian. Works as a talent agent down Great Portland Street and she's very single and very beautiful, if I do say so myself. She's a little introverted but she's warm and funny and kind, and loves doing nerdy shit.' I raised an eyebrow at him while taking another bite of lasagne. Knowing Kofi's love for video games, I hoped my last sentence would grab his attention.

'Mmm OK, OK!' he nodded, his demeanour perking up. 'Is she anything like you personality-wise? And do you have a pic?'

'Why? What's wrong with me?!' I replied in mock disgust. I

grabbed my phone and brought up Sade's Instagram account for him to see.

'Haha, no, I wasn't insinuating that there was anything wrong with you, sis! What I was trying to say was that if she's anything like you, I'm sure I'd have a great time hanging out with her.'

The silence that followed hung in the air like a damp sponge. I took another mouthful of lasagne to keep my mouth full as I thought about how to answer. Eventually, I mumbled a quiet 'Aww thank you' and nudged closer to his seat to show him Sade's Instagram page. Kofi took my phone and started to scroll through her photos, every now and again mouthing his approval at a bikini or night-out photo.

'Damn,' he said, eventually, handing my phone back. 'She's gorgeous. She has a lot of hobbies too, by the looks of it. I like that. I'll give her a follow on IG and slide into her DMs haha.'

I tried as hard as possible to cover up the wide grin that had been forming across my mouth. This was great news for me; getting Kofi off my back for a while and potentially hooking my best friend up with a genuinely nice guy. Even if it didn't go anywhere long-term, at least he'd be busy for a short while.

'You won't regret it. You guys'll get on like a house on fire!'

Here was hoping.

A couple of hours later, I checked my phone to see if there had been a response from Jericho on my recent booking and to my excitement, saw the '**1 unread message**' tab on my profile page. I clicked on the tab and read his message:

> Why, if it isn't the brilliant-yet-mysterious Cassie with all the questions :) . Great to hear from you again! I see you've booked to have the pleasure of my company this Saturday

at 2 p.m.; someone was able to scrape up some coins then? ;)
J xx

This cheeky bastard had my heart doing somersaults. I scoffed loudly at the message, causing Kofi – who had his headset on – to briefly turn around to see if I was OK.

'Sorry, allergies,' I lied as I went back to my phone. I typed back:

Ha! You'd be surprised what I can 'scrape up' when the mood takes me. I must say you did leave quite an impression, so I thought an IRL meetup would be able to satiate my curiosity. Anyway, where are you taking me? Here's hoping our date will be more impressive than your weak chat-up lines. :)

I enjoyed the mildly flirty-yet-humorous tête-à-tête we'd gotten ourselves into, and was very much looking forward to our upcoming date. I wondered what he smelled like? Would he put effort into his outfit? How many dates like this had he gone on before? Would he end up regurgitating lines? More importantly, was there a specific way I needed to act? Rules I needed to follow? I'd been focusing so much on him that I'd completely forgotten to think about whether there was some kind of 'escort code' I needed to adhere to. *Note to self; get on some escort research once I get home.*

I put my phone in my drawer and went back to work, answering emails from GPs, collating various patient surgical notes for the consultants and booking pre-operative appointments. I willed the time to go quickly as I anticipated what Jericho's response to my message would be.

There was an hour left until the end of the day and I had just reached the office after spending the last hour in a consultant monthly meeting taking minutes. I opened the door to find

Mr Paulson in conversation with Kofi at his desk. I waved awkwardly at them both and went to my desk, praying for the last hour to melt away, when I felt a tap on my shoulder. I turned around to see Mr Paulson smiling down at me, his horn-rimmed glasses sliding ever so slowly down his nose. I guess you could call him 'attractive' – in a nerdy maths teacher 'Taika Waititi' kind of way.

'I've nearly finished moving in!' Jeff exclaimed proudly, pushing his glasses up to meet his nose. 'Cheers for also speaking to HR about my email, I'll likely be getting that tomorrow. I also wanted to ask—' he turned around and tapped Kofi on the shoulder '—if you guys perhaps wanted to do after-work drinks tomorrow with the rest of the team? It'll be great to get down to a local pub and get to know you all!'

In all the years I'd worked here, myself and Kofi had successfully been able to evade every single post-works-drinks night with the rest of the Trauma and Orthopaedic department. It wasn't that we purposefully wanted to be antisocial per se, but:

- I just never understood the fascination with the British and after-work drinking. Was it possible to ever relax around colleagues in a social environment where alcohol was being consumed?
- I never understood the fascination with pub culture in general. It always seemed rather exclusionary for some reason. On a . . . cultural level.
- Personally, after seven and a half hours of nonstop human interaction, the only company I wanted to keep was my own – preferably in silence, with snacks that didn't come in a communal bowl.

Me and Kofi briefly gave each other 'The Look'; the universally acknowledged unspoken gesture between Black people that signified confusion and increments of 'are you hearing what I'm hearing?'

Going for work drinks during the week sounded like a bad idea, but I would rather have gotten it over and done with now instead of it being on Friday night. I wanted to use Friday to mentally prepare for my date with Jericho . . . and spending time with the family, of course.

'Um, yeah sure! That would be nice – a lovely way to welcome you to the team.' I smiled, briefly looking over at Kofi who had an incredulous look on his face. 'I'll send an email round to the department now. There's a pub at the end of the road we can go to.'

'Brilliant! Love that idea, Cassandra, thanks!' Jeff exclaimed, clapping his hands together. As he left the room, Kofi turned again to look at me, his eyebrow cocked.

'Cass . . .' he started, before I cut him off.

'Oh . . . you're coming too. Don't try it! Strength in numbers and all that.'

At that, he grinned and turned back to his desk. Before getting back to work I decided to send a quick text to Sade to alert her to my matchmaking finesse with her and Kofi. So far I'd:

- Offloaded Kofi onto my best friend
- Secured a date with Jericho for this Saturday
- Had somewhat of a heart-to-heart with my dad
- Received a free ride to work

Small victories, but victories nonetheless. I smiled to myself as I completed the rest of my tasks for the day, as I looked forward to getting home, cuddling with Toby and picking up where I left off with Jericho in our messages. A buzz from my drawer alerted me to a text reply from Sade:

> **Clearly I need to take you on as my pimp or something because the speed with which you were able to supply cock on demand is truly a talent! Is he fine at least? I'll call you after work! #CockOnDemand**

My best friend was ridiculous.

Chapter 7

'So he's thirty-five and he lives in Clapham,' I said, emptying a packet of premium cat food into Toby's bowl. Toby had developed a taste for expensive meals ever since I fed him a packet of Applaws turkey wet food as a one-off treat a couple of years ago. Since then, he doesn't care to touch anything that isn't brand named. Toby snuggled against my leg for a few seconds until he could no longer resist the aroma of the white fish, salmon and prawn stewed in gravy. This boy ate like a king and, to be honest, I wouldn't have it any other way.

'Is he fit?' replied Sade.

'He's been working at the hospital for a while and he's such a lovely guy, Sade! He's into video games but not like . . . obsessively. He loves his music and he's a really sweet and outgoing guy.'

'Is he fit?' replied Sade.

'I think his last serious relationship was around eighteen months ago too, so still kinda fresh on the market. He's got a car and he's really really good at his job – you can tell he has a real dedication to it which is gre—'

'GIRL!' exclaimed Sade, the frustration in her voice clear as day. 'Is. He. Fit or nah??'

'Which is GREAT . . .' I continued, teasingly, 'if you're looking for a man with stability. Damn, you couldn't let me finish pontificating before going straight to the looks?'

'Babe? I'm gonna hold your hand when I say this. His personality sounds cool or whatever, but I'm trying to get put through the mattress and, in order for that to happen, I'm going to need to be sexually attracted to him so . . . let's see his photos please. Fast fast!'

At this, we both burst into fits of laughter as I screenshot Kofi 's Instagram account and messaged it to her. I was hoping that she'd be interested enough to at least try going on one date with him.

I waited with bated breath as I anticipated her response. I was met with a flurry of 'oooh's and 'mm OK's before she delivered her final judgement.

'He's cute, you know.' After what seemed like an eternity of waiting. 'He's tall too! He's got that whole "Mahershala Ali" thing happening, and his glasses are definitely giving "Zaddy" vibes. Yeah . . . I like what I'm seeing!'

Music to my ears. I grinned as I switched from my handset to earphones so I could get undressed and settle in for the evening. I needed to check and see if Jericho had responded to my cheeky response, as well as make some dinner and direct-message Kofi to let him know that he'd been given the all-clear to message Sade. I could see this being a match made in heaven, and I loved this for both of them.

'That's what I like to hear, sis! Honestly, he's a lovely guy. Am I OK to give him the go-ahead to message you?'

'Yeah, go on then. I'm not doing anything at the moment, so . . .'

'Wait,' I interjected, slightly concerned about her nonchalant disposition. 'Sade, take it seriously! He's a really nice guy so don't treat this one like a plaything because if you break his heart, I'm gonna have to hear it at work and I don't wanna be caught in the middle of any drama.'

The tinkling of her laugh echoed through my earphones as I undressed down to my underwear and made my way to the bathroom for a quick shower. 'Babe we haven't even spoken or texted yet; calm down! He seems like a really wholesome dude, I'll be gentle with him.'

'Mmmhmm,' I responded apprehensively. I knew my best friend like the back of my hand. Although a great girl, she could be a bit of a ghoster when she got bored; a habit I had been trying to get her to kick for the longest time now. I needed both of them to work together at least temporarily – selfishly – for my sake.

After getting off the phone with Sade, I stepped into the hot shower and allowed the scalding hot water to pour over me as I thought about some of the day's events: my dad's trauma dumping, and the revelation of Femi proposing to my mum. As mildly entertaining as Steven and I found the situation between my parents, I couldn't help but low-key feel sorry for my dad. Being single at his age must feel shitty – especially when experiencing unrequited love. I'd always had a fear of loneliness – especially the prospect of increasing loneliness as I aged and all I knew was that I didn't want to end up like my dad – alone, heartbroken and bitter.

After my shower, I warmed up some leftovers and settled onto the sofa with Toby, my phone and laptop in hand. I still needed to find something to wear for my first date with Jericho this weekend and had to place an order to make sure it arrived in time. Before that, however, I needed to check out Jericho's response on *OuiMeet*. I had no expectations for the upcoming date, which only added to the excitement. I didn't mind what we did that afternoon – as long as I enjoyed myself, that was all that mattered. I opened up the app to see a response from him:

Well, I'm glad to have left an impression! I'd be lying if I said you didn't leave a slight impression on me too. :) I hope that I'm able to satisfy your curiosity this weekend too; although I'm more than confident that I will, tbh. I don't have a high rating on this site for no reason – and that includes my so-called 'weak' chat-up lines! Where I'd be taking you depends on the following: What are your hobbies? What do you like to eat and drink? Are you more of an activities person or a chilled one? I can then take it from there. :) x

I swooned as I sank further into my sofa, with Toby wriggling out of my grasp, an indication that I was clutching onto him a little too tightly. This man knew exactly what to say; he was charming and cheeky without being corny or over the top, and he seemed attentive. Attributes escorts had to have in order to be successful, I supposed. I knew that I had to try as much as possible to keep from getting emotionally attached to this man as this was all purely transactional. I was just paying for a service; that's all this was. Still, it didn't stop me from being a little bit excited.

I messaged back:

The fact that you felt the need to drop in your rating is so bold of you. Hmph! I'll be the judge of that eventually. :) Also, we love an organised king so you automatically get a point and a half for that. In answer to your questions: 1) Hobbies include playing video games, eating good food and drinking great coffee, buying and reading books, live music and photography; 2) my answer to what I like to eat and drink is simply 'yes' (although I'm not the biggest fan of Indian food!), and 3) I can take or leave both – although I think I have to be in a certain mood to want to do activities on a date – I think that's more of a second and third date-type thing, don't you?

After sending the message, I hit up a few of my favourite clothing websites to see what they had in stock, opening up several tabs with my current top-three brands – Aligne, Marks & Spencer and Lucy & Yak – to see what they had. I went straight to their 'New In' filter tabs and clicked on my dress size – a size 24 – and watched as my clothing choices narrowed. Aligne stopped at a size 22, but the majority of their pieces were slightly oversized to where I could get away with wearing some of them.

I realised at that moment that I probably needed to wait to hear back from Jericho before deciding on what to wear, so, leaving the tabs open, I switched on the TV and put on an episode of *The Simpsons* as a distraction while I mindlessly scrolled through Instagram, waiting for Jericho to get back. For a moment I thought about asking him if there were any rules I should know before we met, but ditched the idea – figuring I'd just study up on my own and wow him with confidence and charm when the night rolled around.

I hopped onto Sade's profile to see that not only had Kofi already followed her, but she was following him back and they had been 'liking' each other's photos already. Damn, they moved quickly! I beamed with pride at my matchmaking skills and continued to scroll through for several moments until I heard the familiar *ping!* of the *OuiMeet* notification.

A prompt responder too? I mean, I knew it was probably all a part of his service, but I couldn't help but swoon at the level of communication I was receiving. Why couldn't the regular guys on dating apps be this rapid in their responses? Anyway, I didn't have to worry about them for now. I clicked on the message notification and read his response:

> I'm looking forward to you judging my hosting skills. Don't worry; I'll make sure you leave the date a happy woman!

Thanks for your answers too, I appreciate it. I'll get back to you soon with some plans in tow. I'm really looking forward to our date; I'm sensing something chill for this one, but I'll confirm once I've organised. :) Have a good evening x

My heart skipped a beat. Give me a handsome, suave, organised man any day of the week and I'm yours. As much as I was trying to see this whole interaction for what it was – a paid service he was used to carrying out with different women – I couldn't help but be taken in by the camaraderie of it all. He mentioned a 'chill' date, so I switched back to my laptop to browse the clothing pieces that were on offer. As the date would be taking place in the afternoon, I didn't want to go in with anything too sexy, but I didn't want a business/casual situation either. I needed something that cried 'confident-and-fun-yet-elegant'. I didn't want to show all the goods off there and then, but equally I didn't want him to think I was boring in any way. After a few moments of searching through pieces, I eventually landed on a baby-blue bow-tie knitted crop top from Aligne, which would show off just the right amount of cleavage and torso, alongside a pair of dark-red barrel leg jeans I found from Lucy & Yak. Teamed with a pair of slightly heeled black Chelsea boots, I thought that would make a cute first-date outfit that wasn't too dressy for a Saturday afternoon. The last thing I wanted was for Jericho to assume that I had tried too hard.

After ordering the outfit, I messaged Jericho a quick 'goodnight' back, and I settled into watching TV, though all I could think about was Saturday's date. Taking control of my dating history felt good, and I wasn't sure whether it was because things seemed to be going well at home and at work or not, but there was a calmness and a sense of control that swept over me that I hadn't felt in months. As I snuggled into the sofa, my phone started to ring. It was Sade.

'Hey sis!' I answered, leaning over to the remote so I could mute the TV.

'GIRL!' shouted Sade back in a way that could only indicate that she was about to spill some good news or gossip. I immediately pressed the 'video call' option, which she accepted; I was ready for some tea to be spilled. 'What's the gist?' Sade was lying on her bed in her onesie, sipping on a mug of something hot. She had a sense of coyness about her as she looked knowingly into the camera.

'I'm so mad at you right now, man,' she responded in mock anger as she kissed her teeth. 'I can't believe you've been hiding from me this whole time.'

I blinked twice in confusion. What was she on about?

'Huh? Come again?' I replied.

At that, Sade's face cracked into a wide smile, which then cracked into fits of giggles. She began to roll around on her bed while kicking her feet like a toddler who'd just been given her first Polly Pocket toy.

'I'm talking about your little friend Kofi at work, innit?' she replied giddily. Clearly there had been an update that I was unaware of. Excellent.

'Naturally, I followed him after you showed me his Instagram page . . . what? He's cute – I just wanted to have a gander!' she said after she noticed my raised eyebrow. 'I dunno why you're looking at me like that – you're the one that's trying to set us up. Anyway, he slid into my DMs and we've just been chatting and yeah . . . he's um . . . I like the cut of his jib.'

That was music to my ears. A part of me was a little surprised at how seamlessly this had all gone, but I didn't want to put too much thought into that, lest something go wrong at the last moment. Cuffing season was in full effect.

'Well, this is what I love to see! I'm only giving you this

look because I went on IG earlier and saw that you two had followed each other. You guys moved quickly, and to be honest I'm not surprised, you have to move quickly in this dating climate, to be honest.'

At that, we both laughed and I spent the next twenty minutes with Sade filling me in on their Instagram conversation. Apparently, Kofi had nothing but nice things to say about me (bless him), and they had begun to connect over their shared love of live music.

'I haven't spoken to someone for hours at a time like that for such a long time, you know,' Sade said, sighing. 'He's a cutie, and a bit of a nerd; I like that. We'll probably try and link up at some point soon – I'll text him and see what his calendar's looking like over the next few days.'

'Text? As in proper iPhone text messaging instead of the DMs? Already? Blimey; you guys aren't wasting time!'

Sade smiled; if she were capable of blushing, she would have been bright red by now.

'Time waits for no one, my friend! Also it's just a bit more convenient to text instead of going into the app so he sent me his number. Thank you again, sis, I'll let you know when we meet up but, in the meantime, lemme know what's going on with you! What's the update?'

I told Sade all about the drama with my dad coming over to mine this morning ('I've never seen simping like it, to be honest. Your dad is so whipped – it's cute!') as well as the arrival of Jeff, the new consultant at work. I then took a short pause for dramatic effect before I launched into the news with Jericho.

'Umm . . . so I'm gonna be seeing Jericho on Saturday for our first date, by the way,' I said, attempting to sound as nonchalant as possible. Sade, however, saw right through me.

'Not you trying to sound relaxed?!' she immediately

twigged. God, I couldn't hide anything from this woman. 'First of all, this is great news and I need you to send me your location when you're out so I can check throughout the day if you're still alive. Secondly, I know you're absolutely shitting yourself inside, it's OK to be excited! How are you feeling?'

'I'm all right, to be honest. Ordered an outfit tonight and I think because I know in my head it's all transactional, there isn't really a lot of pressure there. I'm expecting to just show up and be treated to the best date ever, to be honest. I don't have to go out of my way to impress him or anything so I feel all right!'

It was going to be a great day; I just knew it.

'I love this for you, it's what you deserve, sis! Not that you deserve to be paying for escorts—' she quickly added in, noting my scoff '—but like . . . taking control of your dating destiny is something I wanna see more and more women do. I'm gonna see what this Kofi guy is saying but if it doesn't work out, I'll be joining you on that *OuiMeet* site for sure!'

After we said our goodbyes, I made my way to my bedroom to lay out my outfit for tomorrow night. I didn't plan on changing completely after work – stepping into a sparkly number in the middle of the week just felt wrong – so instead I packed in a separate bag a green satin blouse I'd recently bought from Simply Be – that would go well with the black A-Line midi skirt I'd already be wearing – alongside a tube of red lipstick and some setting powder. I didn't want to seem too enthusiastic and give the team the wrong idea – if they thought I was really into it, they might start inviting me to even more after-work events and that's not a habit I wanted to create any time soon.

As my head hit the pillow, I received a message notification – this time from my mum – who had written the following:

Cassie. Your dad's been drop-calling me every hour for most of today. What's his problem? He really needs to back off before I pass this onto Femi. Am I a dickhead??

I squinted, rubbed my eyes and reread the message.

When did my mum turn into a 17-year-old college girl from South London? I typed back:

Who taught you the word dickhead?? Mum pls. I'll chat to you later. Goodnight!

Parents. Nobody warns you that after you grow up, the roles switch, with you being the one having to raise them.

I was in the middle of grabbing myself a cappuccino at the coffee machine at noon the next day when I bumped into Mr Jeff Paulson, our new consultant. Somehow he'd managed to look even more dapper than yesterday: he was in yet another three-piece suit but today's one was a dark-beige tweed situation, which had quite a slim fit against his physique. *Focus, Cassie.*

'Good morning, Cassandra!' Jeff practically shouted across the staffroom, drawing the attention of nearly everyone – much to my embarrassment, especially since I was a good ten feet or so away from him. I shifted onto my other foot clumsily as I gave a slight head nod and waved. There was something about the impeccably dressed Jeff Paulson that gave off 'Golden Retriever' vibes – a term I'd recently become acquainted with via TikTok – which described a man who had energetic, wholesome and affectionate energy. He seemed a little dorky, but it suited him. Jeff scooted through a row of plastic chairs, mug of coffee in hand as he made his way to me. I could already smell his Hugo Boss cologne as he edged nearer. On closer inspection, I noticed how incredibly tight-fitting his suit was against his torso and thighs, not that I was intentionally looking or anything. He must have noticed me staring, as he looked down at his torso, then back at me, confused.

'Oh, hey Je-I mean – Mr Paulson, how are you doing today?' I replied sheepishly, turning my attention again to my coffee, which had suddenly taken an age to brew.

'I'm doing well, thanks! Just wanted to let you know that I've received my email address from HR and they've sent me the other handbooks from the department, so I think I'm all moved in now. Did you receive my calendar request?'

A weird thing to ask, seeing as I sent him a thank-you email in response to it this morning.

'I did. I've added your calendar to my schedule. Now, whenever you want to pop anything in by way of meetings or anything like that, you can just ping me an email and I'll organise it on my side.' I grabbed my coffee and looked up at him, only to see him already staring at me.

'Amazing, thank you, Cassandra. I trust I'll be seeing you this evening? You and the rest of the team I mean, of course . . . ?' he quickly added in, looking flustered. It could have been the lighting of the staffroom, but he almost looked as if he was blushing.

Even though Jeff sorta, kinda, was attractive in his own way – his piercing, brown eyes, full, thick lips, and his neat, trimmed moustache – I told myself that I wasn't even going to entertain the thought of developing a crush on him. I had enough on my plate as it was with my little Jericho-shaped side project. Besides, there was something that seemed . . . off. I couldn't put my finger on it, it was more of a gut feeling.

'Yes, I'm looking forward to it, it should be a great night!' I lied, already wanting to go home.

'Yes, me too! Thank you for organising it. I guess I'll catch you later?' he replied as he took a sip of his drink, which appeared to scald his tongue as he cried out in agony, causing heads to turn towards us in the staffroom again. *Ick*. 'Shit! Oh – I'm so sorry, Cassandra – just burnt my tongue there haha! I'll, erm, I'll catch you later!' And with that, Jeff and his scalding coffee took off in a power walk towards his office. I picked up my cup of coffee and sauntered off towards the office, confused, yet annoyingly intrigued. I arrived back at the office to find Kofi in the corner with his back turned against me, shoulders moving jauntily up and down as he tried to stifle a giggle while looking at his phone. I took my seat, watching him silently, smiling.

'Ah, I'll talk to you later, yeah? Cassie's back in the office. Speak tonight,' Kofi announced, pocketing his phone and turning around to face me. He had the goofiest grin on his face, with his rectangular glasses perched halfway down his nose. Had I interrupted a moment?

'Hey, Cassie,' he continued, after clocking my knowing smile. 'What, so you couldn't even bring me a coffee too, yeah? I see how it is!' He laughed as he took his seat, sliding on his headset.

'OK, so I'm gonna go out on a limb and assume you were voice-noting Sade? We're on the voice notes already? I must say, if that's the case, I'm absolutely loving this progress!' I laughed, beaming. My plan was coming together smoothly. With Kofi now focused on someone else, I could finally shake that anxiety-ridden monkey off my back.

'Ha! Yeah, we've been voice-noting back and forth all day, to be honest,' said Kofi, grinning his ears off. I'd never seen him this animated over a woman before. Could this potentially be a match made in heaven? But also, he'd been able to get over me that quickly? Hmm. Slightly wounded ego aside, I was happy for him.

'She's a great girl; you didn't tell me how funny she was!' he continued.

'I did. Yesterday!' I replied, kissing my teeth in the process. 'You were too busy staring at her nyash to listen to anything I had to say though, innit?' I lightly patted my bum, by way of explanation.

'First of all, I wasn't staring at her nyash!' Kofi replied quickly, almost tripping over his words in the process. 'I was admiring her . . . . voluptuous beauty!'

'Voluptuous beauty, my ass. Or should I say, my nyash?' I scoffed. 'C'mon – let's try and finish out the rest of the day so we can get this damn work drinks thing over and done with.'

Chapter 8

I switched off my computer at 5.30 p.m. on the dot and let out a loud sigh. All I wanted to do was go home, order a massive pile of junk food and play with Toby until I fell asleep, but alas, I'd committed to doing the after-work drinks with Jeff Paulson and the rest of the team.

'I hear you sis,' replied Kofi, also giving out an exasperated sigh. 'Let's try not to stay for too long – maybe an hour tops or something.' We needed to treat this evening with military precision – I had heard too many stories of people getting in trouble with their company HR the day after the office drink-up or Christmas party to ever feel comfortable letting loose around the other office folk – especially our consultants.

'Agreed!' I replied, picking up the bag containing my green satin blouse. 'And let's not be too heavy on the drinks – let's aim for maybe two vodka and Cokes or a low-alcohol beer or something.'

'Why not just go alcohol free?' Kofi replied, putting on a very festive-inspired patterned jumper.

'Because I think we'll need a little sludge of something to get us through tonight to be honest,' I replied. 'I'll be back in a sec.' I took my bag, and as I made my way to the bathroom to change, I walked straight into who else but Mr Jeff Paulson who had just turned the corner. As my head cascaded into his chiselled, hard torso, I couldn't help but wonder about how many times he worked out a week; his body was rock solid.

'Ohh! Why, Mr Paulson, we simply must stop meeting like this!' I joked [or teased? I didn't know what the hell I was doing], feigning bashfulness and ending with a giggle.

Jeff took a step back and took his hand to his chest while making a small bow. 'I beg your utmost pardon, Miss – actually what is your surname, Cassandra? I'm embarrassed to admit I hadn't even checked!'

'It's "Mensah", as in the IQ organisation, but it's a Ghanaian name,' I replied, stifling a chuckle. Jeff was incredibly cheesy, but it worked for him.

'Oh, nice! I'm Jamaican but one of my great-grandmothers was Ghanaian,' he chortled happily, revelling in this shared connection. 'They say that Ghanaians and Jamaicans have a shared ancestry of sorts though, don't they?'

I stared into his eyes a moment longer than I should have before lowering my gaze briefly.

'That they do,' I eventually replied. 'Some of the same traditions and folk tales and stuff. But I'm going to go and quickly get changed for the drinks.' I narrowly squeezed past him as I made my way to the bathroom, flashing him a smile on the way. 'I'm looking forward to it! Remember we're meeting at the main reception in twenty minutes!'

'Noted, I'll see you – I'll see you all soon!' Jeff replied, beaming.

I threw myself into the nearest toilet cubicle and quickly changed into the green blouse. It was slightly creased from sitting in my bag all day, but I figured that as it would be dark, no one would really notice. I left the cubicle and went to stand in the mirror to size myself up. I looked OK, I supposed; the neckline of the green blouse went just deep enough to show whispers of cleavage, and my A-line skirt was still a respectable length. I blotted my lips and carefully applied a red lipstick; the key for tonight was to try and have a little bit of fun, but to not give the illusion that I got down wild and loose. The last thing anyone wants at work is to become the main character the day after the night before.

After spritzing on some perfume and checking myself over once again, I was ready. Considering I wasn't fully glammed up, I looked and felt cute enough. I grabbed my things and made my way to the elevators, where Kofi was already waiting – his vibrant, patterned jumper standing out like a beacon to everyone on our floor. He looked . . . conspicuous.

'This jumper is really something, I have to say, friend,' I said, gently nudging him in the ribs. Kofi turned away, then strutted towards me like he was on a catwalk, finishing with a flawless Naomi Campbell-inspired pose. 'Girl, don't hate because you're not into the latest fashions,' he uttered, playfully snapping his fingers in Z-formation. I just knew Sade would eat this up. We both loved a man who could give up generous amounts of banter. 'I bought this from the Crisis charity shop in Peckham Rye – you like?'

'I do! A bit loud, but if you like it, I love it,' I responded, and we both burst out laughing. 'OK, so remember the plan, yeah?' continued Kofi. 'We get to the pub, order our little drinks, make pleasant conversation with Mr Paulson and then do a staggered Irish exit after about an hour. Sounds good so far?' If it's one thing we Africans loved, it was an Irish goodbye.

'Wait,' I said, as we both got into the elevator. 'How many people are coming? It'll be hard to leave without saying bye if there are only, like, four of us!'

'Didn't you send out the invites, Ms Secretary?!' retorted Kofi, laughing. 'You didn't check to see how many people had RSVP'd? God, you had ONE job, dude.'

We both tried to stifle laughter as the other people in the elevator uncomfortably shifted from side to side, perhaps under the impression that Kofi was seriously berating me. As we left the elevator, we were greeted with the appearance of Jeff, as well as thirteen other members of the Trauma and Orthopaedic outpatients' team, including three other surgeons. Considering I'd invited twenty people overall on such short notice, this was a reasonably good turnout. Clearly I hadn't made that much of an effort in the outfit stakes, as I could see that a fair few of the team had gone out with the sequins and strappy sandals (it's January?!) for this event. Jeff had removed his blazer and waistcoat and was just in his crisp, white shirt and navy blue trousers, complete with an absolutely stunning camel fur peacoat that looked straight out of the MaxMara Autumn/ Winter collection.

'Do I scrub up well?' Jeff uttered, staring directly at me as if able to read my mind. He did look *good*, I had to admit. I could sense Kofi next to me turning his head slightly to the side towards me and, out of the corner of my eye, I noticed him giving me a very quick-yet-pointed side-eye before going over to join the rest of the group. I could suddenly feel a pool of sweat at the base of my spine, the weird energy between us still lingering. I met his gaze head-on, matching his energy.

'I suppose you do! I like the coat,' I said as nonchalantly as possible as I walked towards the rest of the group. I'd never wanted to be at home so much in my life. 'Shall we all get going then? The pub's just a short walk down the bottom of the road.'

As a group we set off to the pub, looking like a gang of primary school students off on a school trip. Ten minutes later, we arrived at The Lancaster pub, with Jeff and Kofi bringing up the rear having lagged for a few minutes while deep in conversation. As we entered the pub, Kofi gave me what looked like a sly grin as one of the last to pass through the pub doors.

'What have I done?' I whispered as we both walked up to the bar amid the cries of the rest of the team getting their orders in at the bar. Jeff was at the front, credit card in hand. 'First two rounds are on me, team!' he yelled, to rounds of applause. 'You? Why . . . you haven't done anything at all!' Kofi replied, smiling a little too sweetly for my liking. 'Unless you count undressing Jeff Paulson with your eyes as something, but hey . . . I don't know what counts as "things" any more.' I turned to look at him as we approached the bar. Damn. That definitely wasn't the vibe I was trying to give off . . . I definitely did not have a crush on this man – equally, I didn't see the harm in having a look every now and again – he WAS very handsome. And slightly goofy, which was endearing. And rich. And seemingly intelligent.

Focus, Cassie.

'Pfft. You're chatting shit. I have no idea what you're talking about and I'm just going to face my front moving forward!' I replied, lending him a side hug. Kofi laughed as Jeff came round to take our orders. His smile faltered a little bit upon seeing my arm around Kofi's.

'So, what'll it be, guys?' he said eventually, tossing his gold Amex card between his fingers, seemingly impatiently, while still looking at the space where Kofi's waist was. At that, I instinctively removed my arms away from his waist and gave Jeff a small smile.

'I'll take a double shot of rum and Coke, please, mate,' Kofi said loudly over the noise of the bar.

'I'll have the same please, if you don't mind.' I followed, smiling at him. I don't know why it felt as if I had to get on his good side so much, but it irked me. I was supposed to be off men at the moment. Well, most men.

'Coming right up!' Jeff replied, flashing his dazzling smile. I followed Kofi to the corner of the pub where the rest of the team had assembled: the three spine and major trauma surgeons Mr Jackson, Ms Liu and Ms Juma, and the majority of the outpatient team who were based on the ground floor of the hospital. The majority of them were bank staff who all looked to be under the age of twenty-five.

I sat in the corner booth next to one of the trauma receptionists who I believed was called Tanya. She had dolled up for the occasion especially, and was making eyes at Jeff across the room, which I found cute, considering he was probably old enough to be her dad (albeit a very young dad). Kofi was on his phone next to me, sending a flurry of text messages with a goofy smile on his face. No doubt he was texting Sade. After making small talk with Tanya ('Have you seen the new consultant? He's well fit, isn't he? How much do you think he makes?'), I then locked eyes with Jeff as he sauntered across to give us our drinks. I wondered whether he had a partner, not that it had anything to do with me, of course, but I wondered what he was like at home. Was he always this jolly and bumbling? Or were these just first-week-newbie-nerves?

I thanked him for the drink and took slow, steady sips. The plan was to make my drink last the duration of the hour, by which time me and Kofi would have made a clean getaway.

As the rest of the staff began to chat and laugh with each other, I could feel Jeff's eyes on both Kofi and me. At that point, he brought up a chair and sat opposite us, across the table.

'So! How long have you both worked at the hospital?' he uttered, his eyes already developing a glassy film. We'd only been at the pub for ten minutes. Kofi – distracted by his phone up until that point – put his device away and replied after taking a sip of his drink. 'I've been here about five years or so now, Cass started a bit after me, didn't you, Cass?' and gave me a gentle nudge in the ribs.

'Um, yeah!' I replied, shooting a subtle side-eye to Kofi. 'I've been a secretary here for a few years and I absolutely love it. But what about you? What made you decide to join our hospital?'

At that moment, I felt my phone vibrate in my pocket. A quick glance told me it was a *OuiMeet* notification, no doubt Jericho sending through details for our meeting on Saturday. I smiled slightly at this – I was interested in what Jeff had to say but I was also giddy with excitement at the thought of what to expect over the weekend with Jericho too.

'Oh, erm, I guess I just wanted somewhere a bit closer to home for the most part, and it just felt like a good time to leave my old Trust, really.' I acknowledged his answer with a smile, wanting nothing more than to go into the toilets so I could read Jericho's message in peace, but for the sake of trying to get to know Jeff, I questioned further.

'Oh nice! So um, where do you live, if you don't mind my asking?'

'I'm in Vauxhall actually; you heard of those high-rise buildings with the swimming pool linking the two together?'

I knew exactly where he meant, as that apartment building was a mere seven-minute walk from my flat. I remembered viewing one of the flats in that building out of pure curiosity, just to see what they looked like from the inside, and I remember the way I laughed when I was told that the two-bedroom flat I viewed (it was a 'price on request' at the time of viewing) was £4,800 a month.

'Oh, yes, I know it well!' I replied. 'Not far from me actually. The flats in those buildings are stunning; do you rent or own?' A bit of a personal one to ask maybe, but the rum had already begun to take effect, so fuck it.

'I own – but also cool that you're not too far. A fellow South Londoner is always a great thing. Also, if you're not too far, maybe I should offer some kind of carpooling service haha!' he offered, looking from Kofi to me. Neither of us laughed at first.

The silence stretched, heavy and expectant. Kofi shifted slightly, his expression unreadable. Realising the awkwardness, I forced out a small chuckle, the sound thin and unnatural, but at least it filled the space between us.

'Yeah, I suppose that could be cool at some point!' I eventually said, taking another sip of my drink to fill the silence. Mirroring my movements, Jeff also took a swig of his drink before eventually making his exit to the group next to us. 'I'm going to chat to these guys for a bit and get to know everyone, but I'll circle back to you guys soon! If you want another drink just let me know!'

'Thanks, Mr Paulson,' both Kofi and I said in unison.

'Please, for you two, it's Jeff,' he reminded us.

Jeff made his way towards the other corner, leaving me and Kofi to stare at each other before bursting into laughter.

'That was awkward, wasn't it? Not him inviting himself to drive you to work!' said Kofi between laughs. 'I think he has a thing for you, Cass. I've seen him giving you the eye.'

'I very much doubt that, to be honest,' I replied, shaking my head. But did I truly doubt it? There was . . . something there, a tension humming beneath the surface. I decided that I wanted to just let it lie, untouched, unread.

'I have no idea what you're talking about, mate . . . and ANYWAY, when are you and Sade gonna hang?' I answered quickly, wanting to change the subject. At that, Kofi grinned sheepishly and took out his phone.

'We just set a date for this week actually; we're doing a running club on Sunday.'

Kofi and Sade? Running club? He must have been referring to another Sade, because the Sade that I knew didn't run.

'Umm. Which Sade are you talking about? You mean you're

gonna be listening to Sade, the eighties music band, while you're out for a run, right?' I corrected him, looking baffled. Kofi laughed in response, but it wasn't a joke; Sade was one of the most unfit people I knew. If she could, she would Uber Eats a delivery driver to her fridge and back.

'Ahh whatever, man! She said she's a frequent runner so I thought doing a running club would be a cute first date – and then afterwards I was thinking that we'd go to a cafe for brunch, and then who knows?'

I stared at him, shocked yet incredibly entertained at this turn of events. I could not wait to bring this up with Sade later. Wanting to impress a guy on the first date, I could kind of understand – but flat out lying about something that I knew she hated? This could only end in tragedy.

'And so . . . Sade told you that she ran? OK. Well, God bless, and I cannot wait to hear how it goes on Monday. I'll absolutely be here for the update!' I said eventually, giggling.

'Oh, doesn't she run?' Kofi replied, quizzically.

Meanwhile I was fighting for my life not to crack a smirk. 'Hey . . . the important thing is that you guys are going to get to know each other and hopefully have a wonderful time, innit? Happy for you! I'm glad that you're with someone who actually likes you back; you absolutely deserve it. Iight, I'm gonna go and take a slash quickly.'

Kofi turned to look at me, confused.

'What do you mean "with someone who *actually* likes me back"? I don't get it,' he said, taking a sip of his drink.

Shit. The alcohol was making its way through me faster than I thought. Why couldn't I shut the fuck up? Actually. ACTUALLY. Why did I use that word?

'I'll be right back – one sec!' I shouted as I bolted it to the bathroom, phone in hand as I sent a text to Sade while deciding on how I was going to respond to Kofi when I got back:

RUNNING CLUB? Lmao. Girl.

Within a few seconds, Sade had replied with a meme gif of a man looking guilty and 'shhh'ing the camera. I was now more excited for Sade's and Kofi's date than my own with Jericho. Speaking of which, I still needed to read his message.

After using the bathroom, I snuck into a little alcove by the bar and went into my *OuiMeet* app. There in bold font was an unread message from Jericho. I felt my stomach knot up with anticipation as I opened the tab to read the following message:

Dearest Cassie,

I'm looking forward to seeing you this Saturday afternoon, and I hope your week is going well so far! I wanted to let you know I've created a short itinerary of sorts of what I think we could do. Look it over and see if you like what you see. Let me know if you have any reservations. If it's too much, I'm happy to revise. J xx 😃

2 p.m. – We'll meet at the Watchhouse coffee shop on Hanover Street in Mayfair for a coffee

3 p.m. – I'll take you to the new ***Squid Game*** Escape Room in Piccadilly

4 p.m. – We can then grab a bite to eat at Fortnum & Mason, before perusing the Waterstones next door where we can get to know each other even more. After that, I can drop you home, or near home if you don't want me knowing where you live directly.

I reread the message several times, with a huge smile spreading across my face. This man had taken the time to really take into account my hobbies and likes/dislikes, and had come up with my idea of a perfect date. How the hell did he know that

I was a big fan of the *Squid Game* show and, more importantly, how was he able to get tickets?? I had put myself down on the waiting list for the escape-room experience months ago, due to the activity always selling out. I figured I could skip the bookshop browsing for now – I'd rather spend more time talking with him than getting lost in the shelves.

Aside from that, though, this date felt perfect. I appreciated the level of organisation this had taken on his side, right down to him offering me the option to be dropped off near my house for security reasons – what men were offering those kinds of considerations?

I smiled to myself as I sent my response:

Jericho,

My my, this is very impressive and organised, even by your industry standards (although with this being my first time engaging in your industry, I have no idea what the standards are like tbh – I assume not as rigid as yours?). Thank you so much for sending this through! One small amendment – I'd love to be able to maximise our time getting to know each other, so would you mind us leaving out the bookshop browse for now? Outside of that, everything looks perfect, and I'm looking forward to seeing you soon! Cassie x

I rejoined the rest of the crew, periodically checking my phone to see if Jericho had responded. I had already checked out by this point and wanted to leave sooner than the one hour minimum that Kofi and I had agreed on, but in the interests of trying to be supportive, I decided to stay. I only had thirty minutes left to go; I could do this. I could see Kofi beckoning me over to sit with him and then I remembered how I'd left. Damnit. I hadn't had time to come up with a good lie, which at this point – given how tipsy I was – probably wouldn't have been the best.

'Hey babes!' I called out, sliding into the seat beside him with a little too much enthusiasm. 'What's up?'

'Yeah, so—' Kofi set his glass down and turned to me, his eyes narrowing in mock suspicion '—what did you mean earlier about me seeing someone who *actually* likes me back?'

My brain scrambled like eggs in a hot pan. Lie? Deflect? Fake faint? Nope. None of those would work. Honesty it was – well, my own tipsy brand of it.

'What I meant was, we're all deserving of being liked, right?' I said, forcing my voice into some semblance of calm. 'Like, take me – I'm absolute trash in the dating scene, I can never seem to get it right. But you? Setting you up with Sade was perfect, because now you two found each other and—' I gulped so hard I nearly swallowed my dignity. 'Well, no, what I *meant* was I'm glad I set up two people I care about. That's all.'

'Mmhm.' He leaned back, lips twitching like he was enjoying this way too much. 'But see, you said "someone who *actually* likes me". And since I haven't really updated you about my dating life outside of Sade . . .'

He trailed off, eyes suddenly widening as the penny dropped.

'Oh my God.' He pointed at me, half laughing, half offended. 'You set me up with Sade to keep me busy, didn't you? Like a kid with a colouring book or something.'

I winced, covering my face with my hands. '. . . In my defence, it's a very high-quality colouring book.'

Kofi continued to shake his head disapprovingly at me. 'For the sake of your friendship with Sade, I'm not gonna tell her that we had this chat, but honestly, Cassie, it was never that deep. I may have flirted with you here and there but I honestly didn't ever think it would go beyond that. If I've ever made you uncomfortable though, I do apologise.'

Now I felt even worse. My banter with Kofi was always very

light-hearted and I feared I might have now caused somewhat of an awkwardness between us.

'Don't apologise! I'm the one who should apologise,' I blurted, throwing my hands up dramatically and nearly knocking his glass over. 'Maybe I was just . . . arrogant, thinking you were – actually, no, nope, we're not opening that door. You and Sade are a thing now. And we want that, right? We *like* that.'

Kofi let out a reluctant laugh, shaking his head. 'Yeah. We like that a lot.' But his eyes still held a flicker of unease, like he was humouring me but filing the whole incident under 'things Cassie says that keep me awake at night'.

'Good! Excellent!' I declared, a little too loudly, as if we'd just signed a peace treaty. 'So let's leave it at that. I apologise for saying what I did. You're an amazing man, you deserve all the great things, blah blah blah—'

'Blah blah blah?' he repeated, incredulous.

'Fine! Marvellous, magnificent, king among men,' I said, throwing my hands up so dramatically I almost pushed my glass off the table.

Kofi burst into laughter then, the kind that bubbled out despite himself, though I could still see the trace of tension in his shoulders.

I leaned in and wrapped him in a hug, whispering, 'Truce?'

He hugged me back, but with a measured squeeze. 'Truce. But Cassie . . .' he pulled back just enough to look me in the eye, half grinning, half serious '. . . let's not mention this again, yeah?'

I nodded sheepishly, grinning anyway. We both laughed, but the warning was clear.

Another twenty minutes went by. At that point, Kofi was interacting with a few other members of staff, leaving me to nurse my drink alone. As I looked around the pub, trying to ascertain why people found this sort of social gathering fun, I caught the eye of Jeff yet again, whose gaze lingered on mine a fraction too long before he sauntered over to sit next to me.

'How are you enjoying the evening, Cassandra?' Jeff asked, with slightly slurred speech. Clearly by then, he'd had a few; I just hoped that this wouldn't become another embarrassing encounter.

'Yeah, it's . . . um . . . it's really nice!' I said, smiling sweetly. He didn't need to know that I would rather be anywhere but there at that moment. 'I'm not really someone that does pub drinks and things so it's a new experience for me, I suppose.'

Jeff took another swig of his drink, seemingly nodding his head in agreement. In my peripheral vision, I could see Kofi's head turned slightly towards us, as if eavesdropping on our conversation.

'I feel you,' replied Jeff, his eyes scanning mine thoroughly, as if looking for me to expand on my answer. As my eyes looked into his, I realised that he had the longest eyelashes I'd ever seen on a man, and that his lower set of lashes had flecks of grey among them. 'So . . . tell me more about yourself,' he finally said, his voice lower, smoother, as his gaze dragged over me from head to toe. The playful, easy-going energy he carried just days ago seemed to dissolve, replaced by something heavier – charged. It almost felt like we were in a very sexually tense movie scene where I played a nervous interviewee and he was the CEO of a company, where the interviewer's interest shifts from professional to something far more primal. The way he leaned in, the way his eyes lingered – there was no mistaking it. His interaction definitely felt suggestive.

'Um . . .' I began, scrambling to find the most boring and uninspiring facts I could find; the sudden physical closeness between us felt awkward and inappropriate and I wanted any reason to escape it. 'Well, I'm born and raised in South London and I live with my cat Toby. Um . . . I'm Ghanaian, as you know—' Jeff's eyes lit up as I said this '—and I have a law degree. I'm quite boring, to be fair; there isn't really that much to tell.' Of course this was a lie, friends. As confident and as awesome as I liked to think I was, I knew better than to reveal too much to this man. He was already unsettling me more than I cared to admit. I took another sip of my drink to fill the space – I was nearly done with it now – an indicator that I could leave soon. Why did each minute in Jeff's presence feel like an hour?

'Oh, I very much doubt that to be the case, Cassie – I'm sure you're a lot more fun than you care to let on,' Jeff replied eventually, studying me. There was something nefarious in the way that he said it. What did he mean by that? Was he coming on to me, or was it the alcohol teamed with the building tension between us getting to my head? I smiled a strained smile at him, fighting for my life to not give an inappropriate reply.

'Well—' I started, trying to measure my words carefully. I didn't want to egg him on by entertaining it. 'That may or may not be so, who knows? I find that the older I get, the less I like talking about myself, in all honesty. My boyfriend hates that – he thinks I should be a lot more outgoing, haha.'

Boyfriend? Like I've had one of those before, lol.

The word was out of my mouth before I could stop it and, in that moment, I saw Kofi out of the corner of my eye snap his head towards me, with an unreadable expression on his face due to the cloud build-up on his glasses. Jeff took off his own glasses to clean his lenses, probably realising how he had sounded in the moment. I couldn't tell 100 per cent from his expression, but he looked embarrassed. I don't know why I mentioned having a boyfriend, but if it could get Jeff off my back, then hey ho.

'Ah. Well that's fair enough, I suppose. I'm sure you're a

remarkable person nonetheless!' Jeff cried, putting his glasses back on and giving me a wide, yet unreadable grin. I couldn't tell if he genuinely meant it or if he was forcing a smile, but at this point I didn't care.

'I'm going to grab another drink at the bar – would you like another?' he asked. I saw this, however, as my opportunity to start phasing out my exit.

'I'm actually OK, thanks. I'm going to get going soon – early start tomorrow and all that,' I muttered, making an effort to gather my bag and coat. After Jeff had gone back to the bar, Kofi slid over next to me, downing the last of his drink, and stared at me – incredulous.

'So . . . a boyfriend, huh?' he scoffed, smiling slyly.

'No, silly! I just said that to get him off my back. That thing you said earlier about noticing him giving me the eye – you weren't completely wrong. It was making me feel . . . some way.'

Kofi exhaled and looked from me to Jeff, then back again. 'He works quickly, boy! He's only been here five minutes. So, if he starts making you feel uncomfortable at any point, just escalate it to me, OK? I'll deal with it.'

Sweet, protective Kofi. A surge of gratitude fell over me as he said that, and I gave him another side hug for good measure. 'Thank you, friend,' I replied, and started to put my coat on.

'Now?' I asked, looking around to see if we had the all-clear. The rest of the staff were three or four drinks deep and had reached the tipsy stage of the evening, with people shouting, laughing and slurring their words. Jeff had been dragged into a game of darts by a pair of strangers on the other side of the pub, which gave us a way to leave undetected.

'Now,' replied Kofi. We slyly packed up our things, shuffled towards the doors and slipped out into the frosty night. Pub drinks after work? Yeah; not for me.

Chapter 9

It was now Saturday and, like a child on Christmas Eve, I was awake at 2 a.m., excited about the busy day ahead. The last two days had fortunately flown by; the day after the pub drinks was full of semi-hungover admin staff so it was a quiet day. Jeff was starting on a part-time rota, so he wasn't scheduled to be in on that day anyway, which was great for me as I didn't fancy bumping into him after our awkward interaction at the pub. I still didn't quite know what to make of it; I couldn't 100 per cent tell if he was flirting with me or not, but the weekend wasn't the time to worry about that just now.

My clothes had been delivered yesterday and, after trying them on for size, I laid them out on my sofa, excited for what was to come. A few hours before, I had received a message from Jericho:

> No problem about the book store; I'm sure we can find something else to do! I'm looking forward to seeing you tomorrow – sleep well. :) J xx

I was so used to men cancelling on me at this point, however, that I knew I wouldn't believe he would still be coming until I saw him in the flesh. I was paying good money for him, so a part of me believed that he would hold his end of the bargain, but I couldn't help but wonder – what happens if an escort doesn't show up? Would the client get a refund? The thought of reaching out to the app to report being ghosted on a date gave me the ick. I just hoped it wouldn't come to that.

As Toby purred in bed next to me, I scrolled through Jericho's profile again, looking at his profile photos and imagining what he would be like in real life. Did he smell good? Did people stare at him everywhere he went? Would they stare at us? I was used to being the target of judgemental stares from strangers who had already decided that the men I dated didn't align with my appearance, due to me always being bigger than said man. I wondered if that would happen to me and Jericho – this man was an absolute knockout to all intents and purposes and was by no means small in stature, but I knew it wouldn't stop people from staring.

First, I had to go to my mum's house and hear about her engagement. My phone alarm eventually buzzed for 8 a.m. and after brushing my teeth and changing Toby's food bowl, I headed straight for the coffee machine for some much-needed caffeine, considering the fractured sleep I'd had.

I then took a long shower using some fragranced toiletries and, afterwards, put on the outfit I'd bought, looked in the mirror, and whistled. 'You scrub up quite well, bitch – I know that's right!' I said to myself while doing a 360 turn. The jeans fitted immaculately, shaping my bum to perfection. The blue tie-string top showed just enough cleavage, and the colours of the pieces complimented each other perfectly. I carefully wrapped my hair in a high bun to accentuate my cheekbones and did my make-up – I didn't want to do too much – a slick of pink blush here, a dab of mascara there and a generous offering of my rose rude Fenty lip gloss and I was set to go.

I grabbed a small bouquet of flowers for my mum on the way to her house – I had to practise my surprised face – Steven and I could not under any circumstances let on that we knew about the proposal. Despite our feelings about her and Dad, she deserved this second chance with Femi. He was a nice guy, very quiet and he kept to himself for the most part, but we could see how much he loved and adored Mum – practically worshipped the ground she stood on – and if she liked it, we loved it.

'Oh, well, look who it is! Are these flowers for me? You shouldn't have, but also, you should have. Thank you, dear.' My mum grabbed the bouquet from me as she ushered me into the house. I could see Femi in the kitchen making breakfast as I placed my bag in the living room.

'Cassie, my dear, good to see you! I'm making breakfast, would you like some?' Femi yelled from the kitchen, with a huge grin on his face. Mum had disappeared upstairs, so I went into the kitchen and half-hugged him while he was at the stove. Femi had no children, and so I think he saw Steve and I like his own. He wiped his hands on the tea towel draped across his shoulder and opened his arms for a full embrace. His hug was warm and he smelled of Old Spice, which immediately made me feel hungry.

'What's for breakfast? And when is Steven coming?' I asked as I made my way to the dining table. Before I could sit arse to chair, I heard my mum's voice thundering down the staircase as she strode into the kitchen. 'Sitting down for what, please? Didn't you say you were going to treat us for showing up early? Or was this bouquet the treat?' she said, peering over at the bouquet of hydrangeas that so happened to match her violet-coloured moomoo dress.

'I mean, Femi's already got breakfast covered but I can help?' I replied, trying to avoid staring at the blindingly sparkly ring that had caught my eye just at that moment. It was obvious she'd gone upstairs to put it on. Femi must have spent an absolute grip on it, for it was a unit of a rock. In response,

Mum very conspicuously raised her left hand to her forehead, feigning tiredness as she sighed loudly, making sure her left fingers were in full view. 'Oh, don't worry about it, my dear. What have you been up to anyway?'

Now was my cue. I looked from her to her hand and made sure my mouth formed the perfect 'O'. I stood up, looking from her to Femi and back, and started to dance up and down on the spot. An actress! Viola Davis who??

'I KNOW that ain't what I think it is, Mum?' I screamed, reaching to give her an embrace as well as pull her hand in for a further look. It was a gorgeous emerald-cut diamond set in a single gold band. Classic, elegant, and absolutely stunning. She waved her hands to her face, wearing the biggest smile I'd ever seen. She looked so radiant, happier than I'd ever seen her with Dad, anyway. I turned to Femi, who was standing by the stove – spatula in hand – beaming at us both.

'Come here, mate!' I said as I pulled him into an embrace. 'I'm so happy for the both of you! It's time you made an honest woman out of her at last, because at one point I thought she was headed for the streets.' I was met with a light slap around the back of my head as Femi burst into fits of laughter.

'It was about time, I agree!' replied Femi, as he went back to attending the sausages. 'I love your mum so much, and already knew this was the woman I wanted to spend the remainder of my life with. A kind, upstanding, strong, intelligent woman. And one heck of a mother, too – look at how you and Steven turned out!'

I gestured with a short bow as I continued to coo at the ring. Femi and Mum were the cutest couple; I could only hope to find the kind of love they did one day. 'OK, so . . . engagement story, how did it happen?'

Femi grabbed Mum by the waist as they stared into each other's eyes lovingly. They were so heartbreakingly cute. 'Well,' began Mum, 'we'd gone to one of our favourite restaurants in St Paul's and we'd just finished dessert. So Femi goes to the bathroom, comes back and suddenly all the lights in the restaurant start dimming! So I was like, "Oh, someone hasn't paid their light bill".'

'She had no idea!' joined in Femi, beaming. 'I didn't actually go to the bathroom by the way, I was just setting up last-minute arrangements with the staff.'

'Oh you!' my mum squealed. 'Lemme get back to the story – anyway – so he comes back and the lights have gone down and I'm like, what the heck. Then when he comes back to the table, he pretends to start coughing, I guess, and then he gets down on one knee next to me and that's when the ring pops out!'

'Your mum had no idea, she just stared at me for, like, forty-five seconds, you know. My knee was killing me being on the floor for that damn long!' Femi joined in.

'Pfft! A small price to pay for eternal happiness, I reckon,' Mum scoffed, playfully tapping Femi on the arm. Ugh. Love is sweet.

After chatting a bit more with them both and finding out that Steven and Bianca were most probably due to arrive that afternoon, I sat at the kitchen table facing the window, playing with my phone.

After a moment, Femi came to join me.

'I don't know if your mum said, but we've set the date for the wedding quite soon. Thirtieth of May, in fact. At our age, we don't have time to waste, to be honest.'

I raised my eyebrows in shock. Four months to plan a wedding. An African wedding? In fact, scratch that . . . a WEST African wedding? That was going to be one hell of a feat.

'Whew! That's cutting it a little fine, but I hear you on the time thing. I'm so happy for the both of you, you deserve each other so much!' I responded, briefly glancing at the clock on the wall. Don't get me wrong, I was having a great time, but my date with Jericho would be happening in a mere three hours and I could already feel the subtle onslaught of moths attacking my insides. The nerves had already begun.

'Don't worry, sweetheart,' Femi replied, rubbing his head. 'It's going to be a small wedding, nothing too fancy. Obviously we'd love it if you could bring a plus one? A nice partner maybe? I'm not going to pry into your dating life or anything, but I know your mum wonders sometimes . . .' His voice trailed off, leaving an awkward silence hanging between us. Here we go: the annual 'HAS CASSANDRA FOUND A BOYFRIEND YET?' crusade Femi and my mum loved to do. Which had always been wild to me, considering I had a whole younger sibling with a baby on the way, but it's me that they wanted to concern themselves with. It just made no sense whatsoever. Besides, they knew how I felt about that subject. Being forever single has always been somewhat of a wound for me, and being forced to be reminded of the fact was beginning to take its toll.

I responded with the generic response. 'I'm working on it, guys, don't worry! The dating scene in London is rubbish, but I'm trying.'

'Mm well, try harder then,' I overheard my mum call out from the corridor. 'I won't rest until everyone in this family is married off and happy. Well, nearly everyone. As for your father, he can choke.'

I spluttered as Femi looked towards Mum sternly across the hallway. He and Dad weren't on the best of terms, but they were at least always cordial to each other, which was more than I could say for Mum. 'Regina? Be nice now,' he said in a stern, yet tender manner. I'm sure it must have grown bothersome for him always getting in between Mum and Dad, but hey ho. I had bigger things to worry about. My date with Jericho was happening soon and I needed to psych myself up for what was to come. After spending the next couple of hours pottering around the house, picking at breakfast and annoying my mum as much as possible, it was finally time to set off.

I gave myself a final once-over in the bathroom mirror, making sure my face hadn't broken out into any oily patches. I sprayed myself with a floral perfume and went downstairs to bid goodbye to Femi and Mum.

'So where are you going that is so important that you couldn't spend the day with us then? You're also going to miss your brother too!' moaned Mum, sucking her teeth.

'I'll catch up with Steve later, Mum,' I replied, putting my jacket on. 'And actually, I'm trying to do what you want me to; I'm going on a date, innit?' I turned around to see her beaming at me, eyes wide open with what looked like pride?

'That's my girl! Doing what needs to be done. Finally! We'll have your uterus up and working overtime in no time!'

'On that note, it's time for me to leave,' I said, shaking my head. The woman had no filter, clearly, but it was also something I absolutely loved her for. 'I'll call you later and fill you in on how it goes – Femi – congratulations to you both once again! I can't wait to get into all the wedding planning and obviously I'm going to be maid of honour so we'll need to run through a full itinerary at some point.'

As I made my way to hug them both goodbye, I heard my mum whisper to me, 'Actually, Femi's sister is going to be my maid of honour this time; she's not that well and the wedding is one of the last things I think she wants to be a part of before the worst happens.'

'Oh no!' I gasped out loud. I'd only met Uwa – Femi's sister – a small handful of times, but she was always very pleasant. 'I'm so sorry to hear that – of course, that's fine. Is she OK? How long does she have left?'

'What? Oh no, nothing like that. She has gout. But you never know with these things, innit?'

I rolled my eyes and took my attention to my phone. Time to cram, apparently. But what exactly does one google here? 'Client/escort etiquette'? 'First-date manners for sex work 101'? In a moment of desperation, I tried 'how to treat sex workers on a first date', only to be bombarded with Reddit threads on how to respectfully meet female escorts. Not exactly my situation, but hey—at least the internet wasn't a total cesspit. Small wins. I tried again: 'etiquette when dating a male sex worker'. A *Medium* article written by a male sex worker came up. I clicked into it and read what they had to say:

Before the meeting:

- **Confirm the time and be punctual. Being late and/or ghosting is just as rude here as in any other professional service.** (He didn't have to worry about that – with the amount I was spending, I was for sure going to turn up.)
- **Hygiene is key! Shower, brush your teeth and clean up.** (Again, obvious but I chucked a mint into my mouth just to be extra sure.)
- **During the encounter, respect his boundaries. Just because you've booked his time, it doesn't mean you can do anything. Stick to the agreement.** (Wait, what was our agreement?)
- **Treat him like a person; if something isn't a part of the agreement, don't push for extras.** (Were we supposed to have an agreement beforehand? Was a contract needed? Maybe I should have asked for his non-negotiables before agreeing to the meetup.)
- **Don't ask him anything personal unless he gives you the go-ahead.** (That was pretty self-explanatory.)

I skimmed a few more blogs, all repeating the same commandments of etiquette. Suddenly, a jolt of panic iced my veins – what if I reeked? What if he took one look at me and thought, *no thanks*? Or worse, what if I blurted out something tragically stupid? I did a final mirror check on my phone, confirmed my make-up was still serving, and pulled out my perfume for a liberal spritzing before saying goodbye to Mum and Femi.

'Have fun, dear!' Mum called after me. Then, with the timing of a stand-up comic: 'Although, what perfume did you just drown yourself in? It smells like cat piss!'

Fantastic. Exactly the confidence boost I needed. Nothing like stepping out the door smelling like Eau de Public Toilet.

On the Tube into town, I opened up the *OuiMeet* app to reread the itinerary that Jericho had laid out, but not before seeing his latest message to me that he'd sent that morning:

> Good morning, Cassie, I'm looking forward to seeing you this afternoon. Take care!

He was too sweet. After writing back saying I was looking forward to seeing him too, I hopped off at Bond Street and marched straight into the first fragrance shop I could find, which of course turned out to be a Middle Eastern oud boutique – aka, the Holy Grail of perfumes. Crystal bottles glimmered under spotlights like holy relics, while I slunk in looking like I'd just lost a fight with a Yankee Candle.

Channelling fake confidence, I prowled the aisles with my best '*hmm yes, I'm very discerning*' face, while inside I was screaming: *please God, just cover the pee smell.* I paused at a £250 bottle of tobacco oud, lifted the tester dramatically, and thought, *well, if Jericho doesn't like this, maybe his grandad will.*

'Hello there! Do you need any assistance?' A sales assistant materialised out of thin air, dazzling me with veneers so white I nearly ducked for cover.

'No, thank you,' I croaked, then, in a voice two octaves lower than usual, added, 'I'm just browsing . . . for my brother.'

Smooth.

The moment she pivoted away, I lunged at the tester like Gollum with the One Ring and unleashed a panicked spray storm all over myself. One spritz turned into three, three into seven – I basically hotboxed myself in a tobacco oud cloud. My eyes watered, my throat closed, and I coughed like a Victorian orphan, waving away perfume fog before the assistant noticed.

By the time I staggered out, I smelled like Santa's grotto had been set on fire inside a Lush shop – but hey, at least it was an upgrade from Eau de Cat Litter. Barely.

I sprinted towards the WatchHouse coffee shop located on Hanover Street. It was one of those super classy, Scandi-inspired coffee shops filled with patrons on their laptops, sipping their iced matcha lattes. The coffee shop was situated just behind the station off the public pathway, so there was a degree of privacy there which was perfect. Jericho had clearly done his homework.

I checked my watch; in true Cassandra fashion, I had arrived fifteen minutes early, so I found a booth seat in the corner of the shop. I took a couple of deep breaths; I wasn't sure whether I was nervous or excited – maybe both? I tried to steady my heartbeat as a myriad different thoughts flew around my head. What if he changed his mind after meeting me? What if he didn't find me attractive? What if he was a weirdo? Was I crazy for doing this in the first place? Well, it was too late to look back now. Just then, I received a notification ping on my phone – from Jericho. He'd cancelled, hadn't he? I knew it.

I sighed as I opened the app, gearing myself for whatever excuse he'd written:

Just walking down Oxford Street; I'm about seven minutes away or so.

Oh. That'll teach me.

I responded back telling him I'd grabbed us a seat, took out my make-up bag and touched my face up one last time, dabbing at my T-Zone to clear up my oil patches, and put on a fresh layer of lip gloss. I was in control, not him. What I was doing was empowering, not degrading. I could almost see it as self-care. Some people pay £500 for a month's worth of Pilates classes; I pay for the pleasure of being in good company. Self-care was self-care.

I took another couple of deep breaths. It was all going to be fine. I smelled somewhat OK, at least. And even if the date turned out to be awful, I could say that I'd tried it. As I went to put my phone in my pocket, I looked up briefly and that's when I saw him; all six foot four of him. He was wearing a crisp, white T-shirt with a pair of navy-blue slacks and its accompanying utility blazer. On his feet were a pair of white Nike Air Force Ones (rarely worn). He had a gold wristwatch on his left wrist, and had a smattering of gold chains around his neck. As I glanced up towards his face, it took everything in me not to let out a choke. Jesus Christ.

Jericho was *beautiful*.

His chocolate-brown skin almost seemed to radiate in the sun's rays, with his small, piercing eyes squinting narrowly as he approached the shop. His hair was freshly trimmed, and from my field of vision I could see that he had a small tattoo inscription on his neck. There was nothing – and I mean NOTHING – that drove me wilder than a man with a neck tattoo. I crossed my legs and tried to stifle a huge grin – this gorgeous man was here to see me, and it was what I deserved.

As Jericho opened the door of the coffee shop, every female

eye in the vicinity turned towards him. It was as if an Adonis had entered the building. He glanced at his phone briefly, then looked up and did a sweep of the room before eventually locking eyes with mine. His mouth immediately burst into one of the most beautiful smiles I'd ever seen. His teeth were absolutely perfect. I stood up awkwardly and returned the smile, suddenly feeling embarrassed although I wasn't sure why I felt that way – I was just as cute as him, if not cuter??

Jericho weaved in between the tables, staring at me the whole time, eyes unflinching. I suddenly felt incredibly exposed; almost as if he were sizing me up. He looked like a predator about to attack his prey. His stare was intense; almost intimidating, but equally, incredibly hot.

'Cassandra. Here you are,' he said, his sexy, almost-baritone voice permeating my eardrums. I studied his face again; he was thirty-four years old, but he had a charming, youthful look about him. I wondered if he'd had Botox or any other tweakments; he looked good.

'As I live and breathe, Jericho; the icon herself. It's lovely to meet you!' I managed to utter eventually, opening my arms to give him a hug. He welcomed my embrace and as we briefly hugged, I noted the intensity of his cologne; it was fresh, yet woody, and smelled amazing. After a short moment I sat down as he remained standing.

'Can I order you a drink? What would you like?' he said. A true gentleman. We loved to see it.

I had surveyed the menu beforehand so knew exactly what I wanted. 'Aww, thanks!' I responded, smiling sweetly under his intense gaze. I couldn't allow him to intimidate me in any way – I was in control here. 'Could I please have a medium skinny cappuccino with a shot of vanilla, and an almond croissant?'

'Absolutely. I'll be over shortly, sweetheart.'

Sweetheart.

And I was SAT. Was this whole thing transactional? Sure, but it didn't stop my heart from skipping a beat on impact. I took a seat, emitting a low whistle under my breath as I checked him out from behind. So far, so good. I took out my phone, put it on silent and snapped a sneaky photo of him while he was at the counter and sent it to Sade with the following message:

> **Babe. Look at this specimen pls. A true FINE BABE omg?! We've just started the date, I'm so excited! Also for safety's sake, we're currently at the WatchHouse coffee shop behind Bond St station. Love you! xx**

Within two minutes, Sade had responded. I briefly glanced at my phone while Jericho walked back with a tray full of our drinks and food. Sade had responded:

> **Fucking hell, mate. Maybe I need to join OuiMeet too, man. A very FINE BABE indeed, damn! I'm expecting a FULL debrief this evening, keep me updated and remember, you got this, it's all about you and you're in control! xxxxxx**

I turned my phone over and tried my best to concentrate on this beautiful man who had come to see me. Jericho sat down and passed my almond croissant and cappuccino to me, again while staring at me intensely. What was his game? I decided to match his energy and stare back.

'Thank you so much, Jericho – if that is your real name?' I finally said, matching his stare.

'Ha! Uhhuh . . . You're welcome, Cassandra, and thanks for booking me; I'm keen to ensure you have a great time today.' He took a sip of his beverage, and I caught him stealing a glimpse of my cleavage in my tie-up blouse. I knew it was a good decision to buy it.

'OK, OK . . . let's cut the BS now – do you talk like an AI

bot all the time? You can call me Cassie, by the way, and feel free to be a bit less formal because you're really giving me double-o-seven vibes at the moment. Also, is there anything I need to sign? Like a contract or a disclaimer or anything like that?'

At this, Jericho's eyes widened as he burst into a grin, then into a bellowing laugh showing his pearly white teeth – the infectiousness of it all automatically made me want to laugh too. 'You're hilarious, Cassie,' he said as he laughed, his shoulders shrugging. His idiolect had relaxed somewhat at this point – it became less of the Received Pronunciation that I had heard on the phone and was now a little bit more East London. He continued, 'And straight to the point too. You're the first person to mention my demeanour in that way, you know. To be honest it's a bit of a persona I created for clients – a lot of them seem to like the whole dapper, suave, Regé-Jean situation, you know?'

'Uhhuh. And let me guess . . . most of your clientele are . . .' I tapered off, hoping he would get where I was going with this. He did.

'Yeah . . . they are. You're probably the third Black woman I've seen since being on the app, to be honest,' he replied. I wasn't surprised by that at all; the prospect of women paying for company and sex in Afro-Caribbean communities was still something that was considered taboo.

'Anyway,' he continued, 'there's no official disclaimer you need to sign; you kinda already signed up to the terms and conditions when you joined the app. But also, I've gotta say, I'm surprised you even felt the need to do this – you're absolutely stunning. I hope I'm not being too forward but you have a gorgeous figure.'

I froze mid-sip at the unexpected compliment, my cheeks burning with a deep blush. After years of being conditioned to believe my desirability was tied to my weight, hearing that bit of validation felt unexpectedly refreshing. And though it shouldn't have mattered, for some reason, the words hit even harder coming from Jericho – an undeniably attractive man.

'You're good at this, aren't you? I bet you say that to all your clients, but I'll take the compliment anyway,' I replied, bashfully taking a bite into my croissant. I wanted to know more about him – starting with his name. I also needed to be careful, thinking back to the tips I'd read on the various sites before about etiquette. *Don't be too personal*. Surely just asking about his name was fine enough? 'Speaking of which – if I could ask – what's the story behind the name Jericho? And what *is* your real name?'

Jericho took another sip of his drink – his piercing eyes still boring into mine. He looked hesitant. After a moment, he spoke. 'Heh – I'm not gonna share my name on this occasion right now, but "Jericho" kinda started off as a stupid joke that eventually stuck. You know the whole thing in the Bible with the walls of Jericho being blasted down and stuff? I equated that with me, erm, blasting down women's *walls* and er, yeah. Obviously now I know it's stupid but the name stuck – and so here we are, I suppose.'

I looked at him, dumbfounded.

'Wow. Blasphemous and factually incorrect, what a combo,' I replied, stifling a giggle. 'Shouldn't you have called yourself Joshua instead? He's the one who blew his trumpet that caused the walls to fall down in the first place; it would make more sense that way.'

Jericho narrowed his eyes before picking up his phone and appearing to search through for something.

'Shaking my damn head. You didn't know this beforehand? Tut tut! Someone clearly wasn't paying attention in Sunday School it seems,' I playfully teased, catching his eye as he looked up from his phone. He broke into his trademark smile again, rolling his eyes. He glanced at the screen again, a hint of disappointment crossing his eyes, and put the phone down.

'OK, well . . . you got me there. I just googled it. I always fell asleep in Sunday school, OK? What can I say?? Anyway, enough about me, this is your time. Tell me about you.'

'With all due respect, I booked this date to find out more about you, not me,' I replied, smiling innocently. 'You intrigued me, *Jericho.* And I kinda like the cut of your jib. You may not tell me your real name now, but you will at some point. And besides, on the phone you did say that there were a couple of questions that you'd prefer to answer in person so . . . here we are!'

His smirk was infectious. I'd got him there.

'You're quite the curious creature, Cassie,' he admitted, nodding his head. 'You're right; I did mention that – OK, in that case, feel free to ask away, but also just to let you know we'll be making our way towards the *Squid Game* escape room in about forty minutes or so.'

'Thanks, Dad,' I said, rolling my eyes in mock annoyance. 'Tryna breeze through the date already, huh? I'm peeping your game, bro.'

'Heh. Not at all! Look, I'm open to anything within reason – ask away.'

I made a display opening my phone's app to take a look at his profile on *OuiMeet* as he looked on, amused. There was an interesting power play situation that was currently happening here, and I enjoyed it.

'OK! So the last time we spoke, I asked the following questions; what's the oldest person you've slept with, and if you were looking for a girlfriend, have you ever slept with anyone famous, are there any rules or boundaries I should know when it comes to this kind of thing – oh and a bonus one – what's your job outside of all this?' I'd slipped in two new questions, hoping he wouldn't notice.

Jericho cupped his head in his hands as he leaned on the table, pensive. He had this deliberate way of taking his time when he spoke, making sure the pacing was just slow enough for me to want to hang onto his every word.

'OK so—' he began, his smile breaking into a smug smirk. 'I think the oldest woman I've been with was around sixty-three or so. Maybe sixty-four? Am I looking for a girlfriend? As of now, I don't think there would be anyone who would feel comfortable with my current lifestyle, so as much as I sometimes crave intimacy, connection and companionship, I don't think it's something that may be feasible right now. Slept with anyone famous? Maybe, but that was a long time ago. When it comes to boundaries and etiquette in these kinds of circumstances, I'm pretty flexible for the most part; I guess I don't reveal too much about my personal life, no wandering hands unless it's consensual on both sides, and uh, try not to fall in love with me, haha.'

I baulked at him.

'. . . And as for your final question, I work at a building design firm right now.'

I mulled over his answers as he took a bite of his pastry. *Sixty-four?* He'd also slept with a famous person? Also, fair do's on the personal stuff; I supposed this line of work was the kind of thing people wanted to keep separate from their personal lives. I had follow-up questions; I wanted to know the gist, but didn't want to scare him off.

'I feel you on your second answer. I mean, given the way you look and the amount of women you must meet on a weekly basis, whoever you end up with would probably need to have nerves of steel and the confidence of Beyoncé.'

Jericho laughed at this, his eyes twinkling in the diffused afternoon sunlight. I simply couldn't get over how pretty and young he looked. I stared at him – transfixed.

'I mean, it would probably be like that at first, but it would depend on how much money I've been able to store by the time that special lady comes into my life,' he replied. 'If I've been able to pack away a significant amount, then maybe I won't need to continue with these shenanigans any more. But we'll see!'

I imagined myself as being the woman who had to share him with a harem of different women each week – it couldn't be me; I was way too possessive.

'That's fair enough,' I replied, finishing the dregs of my coffee. 'How much are you looking to save overall? AND ALSO, what was sleeping with a sixty-four-year-old like? Don't try and gloss over that part – you thought I forgot. AND ALSO . . . who's the famous person you slept with?'

'Oh, Cassie.' Jericho's voice had an authority to it that drove me crazy. He knew exactly what he was doing. 'You're annoying, you know; nothing super personal, remember! I low-key like your confidence, though.'

'Why, thank you. I'm a curious little pixie, like you said – now make with the answers, Jerry.'

At my impromptu nickname, he cocked his brow.

'Erm, WELL, I'd like to be able to buy a house soon – a really nice house, like . . . a "four-bedroom townhouse in Zone 2 London" nice – so let's just say that I've been making some really good progress in that department. I'd probably say that I'd only need to keep doing this for another couple of months or so before I have a healthy deposit. As for sleeping with older women, it's not really that much different from sleeping with women our age, I suppose – there's a sexual confidence that comes with maturity that I definitely find to be a turn-on, but sexual confidence can be found in women of all ages really. There's nothing sexier than a woman who knows what she wants and is willing to teach along the way, too. And as for the famous person, don't you worry your pretty head about that.'

'Mmm, I see. Well, thanks for answering my questions; I'll try not to nag you any more,' I said, somewhat satisfied with his answers. There was something really refreshing about the brutal honesty of it; I wanted to know more but equally, I didn't want to fly too close to the sun. His 'don't you worry your pretty head about that' carried enough finality to warn me off.

'You're not nagging me, actually,' he replied, finishing up the dregs of his drink. 'You amuse me more than anything; I like your questions and I like your vibe so far. And your perfume is so . . . interesting. Strong and vibrant, like you.'

Oh, for God's sake. I'd hoped the oud would tame the vinegary nightmare of my first fragrance, but thanks to scent blindness, I had zero idea what I actually smelled like. Had he been silently waving for fresh air this whole time?

'Oh! Erm . . . yeah, I may have gone a little overboard this morning,' I blurted, crossing and uncrossing my legs like a nervous metronome. 'I love perfumes . . . sometimes I get a bit . . . enthusiastic. Hopefully it's not too strong?'

Jericho gave me a slow, calculating wink. 'No, no . . . not at all. I mean, it's strong . . . in a heroic "call the fire brigade" kind of way. But I can handle it.'

'Heroic?' I squeaked. 'Like Superman or more like Godzilla?'

'Hmm,' he said, leaning in slightly, clearly enjoying this. 'A bit of both. Definitely unforgettable.'

I gulped. 'Unforgettable . . . that's comforting. Or terrifying. I can never tell with men.'

'Oh, trust me,' he said, grinning, 'I'm more "memorably charming" than "tragedy in a bottle". But don't worry, if anyone else faints from the scent, I'll heroically save them from their oud-infested prison.'

I blinked, half amused, half impressed. 'Well, if I survive my own perfume apocalypse, maybe I'll get a medal too.'

'Deal,' he said, winking again. 'Medal ceremony immediately after dinner.'

So this is what falling in love felt like, huh?

In true hopeless-romantic fashion, I let out a soft sigh and smiled at absolutely nothing. He was perfect. We spent the next few moments asking each other random questions before setting off on our next venture. So far, I'd found out the following about him:

- Jericho was left-handed
- He lived in East London **(ugh)**
- His family were St Lucian
- He had a degree in Architecture **(a smart one!)**
- He owned a car **(an Audi, very fancy)**
- Due to his work schedule, most of his escorting activities were now either online or over the phone – he limited in-person meetups to weekend occasions once or twice a month.

We also discovered we had a lot in common – same taste in TV shows, same music, a shared obsession with Japanese food, and, best of all, a soft spot for video games.

'Wait, you're a *Zelda* fan too? No way,' Jericho scoffed, half impressed, half amused. The more he spoke, the more I felt like I was peeking past that mysterious, charming exterior of his and catching glimpses of the big, excitable kid underneath – and honestly, it was ridiculously endearing.

'Listen!' I said, already matching his enthusiasm. 'Don't even get me started on *Tears of the Kingdom*. I've been stuck on that Phantom Ganon boss for six months. Six. Months. I'm at the point where I might actually throw my Nintendo Switch out the window.'

Jericho burst into this deep, hearty laugh that made my

chest warm and my face break into an unintentional grin. For someone who seemed so composed, the laugh was disarmingly boyish, and I couldn't help but adore it.

'Phantom Ganon?' he chuckled, shaking his head. 'That's nothing. Quickfire way to beat him: bait him into the corner, shield parry, then just hammer away. Honestly, if we hang out again, I'll beat it for you in, like, ten minutes.'

He said it so casually, but the thought of him actually sitting beside me, controller in hand, solving the one problem I hadn't been able to crack for half a year . . . well, that sounded suspiciously like bliss.

It was silly, but I could feel myself warming to him more and more. Not just because he might be my ticket out of Phantom Ganon hell, but because it felt like we were tuned to the same frequency. And somewhere between the laughter, the nerdy game talk, and the easy flow of conversation, I realised – I might just be developing a little crush.

As we made our way to leave the coffee shop, Jericho stretched his hands out towards mine.

'Your hand, madam, if you're OK with that?' he asked devilishly, to my surprise. I'd never been on a date where a guy had done this before – at least not in public. It felt like he wanted the whole world to know I was his for the day – that he was proud to have me on his arm. For a moment, the tears nearly made it to the surface, but reality hit me hard, yanking me back to the truth: I was paying for his time. For all I knew, this was just part of the performance. 'Why yes, kind sir; you have my consent,' I replied.

My smile temporarily faltered, yet I took his hand all the same as we left the coffee shop, hand in hand.

We arrived at the *Squid Game* escape room ten minutes ahead of schedule, where we were paired up with another couple for the hour. After filling out all the forms, we started playing the game, and I was impressed to find that Jericho was actually excellent when it came to the logical and physical puzzles, as we breezed through those rooms with ease. I spent most of the hour just watching him with awe; he seemed to be in his element as he furiously solved Sudoku puzzles and tore the rooms apart looking for clues to get to the next rooms. He was like a big kid, and the more I watched, the sadder I became that this meeting might be our only interaction – unless I paid for us to have another date.

As we rushed into the next room, I decided in my head to think of a plan; Jericho had friends, right? I could just be another friend of his, and maybe then I wouldn't have to keep paying to be in his company. I might do one more session with him and then float the idea and see what he thought.

As we arrived at the last escape room with at least fifteen minutes to spare, Jericho looked at me, gesturing me to come towards him.

'We've nearly beaten it! I can't believe how fast time's flown, man.' His eyes practically had sparks shooting out of them as he darted from corner to corner, diving under tables, kicking over cushions, and waving his hands like he was conducting an invisible orchestra, all in pursuit of the brass butterfly ornament. Meanwhile, me and the other couple stood frozen, doing absolutely jackshit – well, except me dramatically leaning on the table, pretending to be part of the scenery.

'To be fair,' I said, 'you've basically carried all of us. My contribution was minimal at best. Aside from looking flawless, of course. Honestly, my radiant aura probably powered your stamina and sheer will to victory. You can thank me later.'

He lunged for the butterfly, tripped over a chair, and somersaulted into the corner. The ornament went flying – straight past him, clanging against the wall and disappearing out of sight.

'Wait . . . are you saying I lost because you distracted the butterfly with your beauty?' he wheezed, tangled in cushions.

'Exactly,' I said, holding my hands dramatically over my heart. 'I am the secret final boss of this game. Bow before my power!'

Somewhere in the chaos, a cushion hit the other couple in the face.

I shrugged, grinning. 'Collateral damage. Worth it.'

At that, Jericho finally paused his wild butterfly hunt, brushing off a pile of discarded cushions. He walked over, gave me a half-hug that was just enough to make my heart stutter, and grinned.

'You're absolutely right, Cassie,' he said, eyes twinkling. 'Now . . . if you could help me find this butterfly so we can finally win, we'll get a celebratory meal. Sound fair?'

I blinked at him, part mortified, part amused, and muttered, 'Fair . . . but only if I get to take full credit for your heroics.'

After a couple of minutes of searching, I saw the brass butterfly ornament out of the corner of my eye – it was perched behind a photo frame on the floating shelf.

'Got it!' I yelled as the other couple (who were absolutely useless by the way) whooped and clapped. I dropped the butterfly ornament into the task bin provided, and the game was over.

As we walked out onto Piccadilly and made our way to our final pit stop for a light dinner – Fortnum & Mason – I made a mental recap of the day so far: everything was going well, me and Jericho were getting on and we seemed to have established a playful banter that kept me on my toes. Yes, I had to acknowledge that it was perhaps a part of the performance on his end – but I was having fun and I could feel a little crush rising from the depths of my loins. I knew that I had to find a way to taper it somehow, though – the last thing I needed was to get hurt.

Fortnum & Mason gleamed like a cathedral of edible decadence, and Jericho was clearly on a mission to make it a full-contact sport. He darted between displays of glittering tea tins and stacks of fancy biscuits, nearly toppling a tower of shortbread in the process.

'Earl Grey?' he asked, lifting a tin with exaggerated reverence, only for it to wobble dangerously on the edge of the shelf.

'Careful!' I cried, lunging to steady it, and somehow ended up knocking over a jar of honey. It rolled across the floor like a sticky bowling ball, almost knocking into a toddler standing by the teddy-bear biscuit tins.

Jericho didn't skip a beat. He dabbed a bit of jam from a sample tin by the till on my finger. 'Taste test,' he said, grinning like a cat who had just found the cream. I licked it off and immediately left a streak across the sleeve of my jacket.

'Perfect,' he said. 'Now we match. Team sticky-fingered chaos.'

On our way down to the stairs to the lower ground floor, heading towards the bar, I became acutely aware of a gaggle of teenage girls behind us, muttering and laughing together. Every few steps, I'd glance back at them and smile, and they'd smile back before leaning into each other to whisper. I couldn't help but wonder – were they whispering about me? About Jericho?

It wasn't until we were on the fifth or sixth step down that it happened. The lead giggler from the pack of girls suddenly broke formation, strutting straight up to Jericho with the kind of boldness only teenagers have.

'Hey! Sorry to bother you, but aren't you the guy who used to date Ca—'

'Hey!' Jericho cut her off, a little too loudly, his voice cracking with forced cheer. His boyish grin stayed plastered in place, but I caught the flicker of panic in his eyes as he looked from me to the group of girls in quick succession.

'Um, yeah that's me; but I'm kinda busy right now. Really sorry, can't talk.'

The girl blinked at him, then shrugged with a grin. 'Oh, nah, that's cool. You're so much fitter in real life, man. Nice to meet you!'

And just like that, she rejoined her squad, all of them squealing and skipping off like they'd just won a bet. Behind us, I could clearly hear, 'See! I told you, I TOLD you it was him!'

I raised an eyebrow at Jericho, trying (and failing) to suppress my smirk. Teenage superfans ambushing us outside a wine bar was not on my bingo card for the day. And yet, underneath my amusement, I couldn't ignore the little itch left behind: *Ca – who?* 'He was fitter in real life'? What did that mean? He'd shut it down fast, maybe too fast. I told myself not to pry; after all, it was none of my business at the end of the day, and he'd clearly laid out his boundaries surrounding his personal life, but the curiosity was already nibbling away at me. I tried not to think about it too much, however, and tried to just stay in the moment even though he seemed a little flustered after the interaction. I told myself that there would be plenty of time for detective work later.

Jericho was obviously slightly shaken by this interaction, on the other hand. He picked up his pace as we continued on our way, seeming a little skittish. 'Sorry about that, by the way,' he said eventually, rubbing the back of his neck while we walked.

I hadn't planned on bringing it up but seeing as the mountain had come to Mohammed . . .

'Don't worry about it! What were they on about? Did you date someone well known or something? Are you some kind of local CELEBRITY?'

Jericho laughed; however, he seemed slightly on edge.

'Ha! No not at all. I'm a no one. I guess they knew someone I used to date; it's not a big deal.'

I was intrigued. To be honest, with the way he looked, I wouldn't have been surprised if he had told me right there and then that he had previously been a contestant on *Love Island* or something similar, gorgeous as he was.

'Ohhh.' I grinned. 'Did you used to date an influencer or something?' I wouldn't have put it past him.

He slowed his pace slightly as he replied. 'Something like that; d'you mind if we don't talk about it? And could you maybe not mention it to anyone else?'

Whatever it was about that interaction had him spooked. Why would he assume I would gossip about it? Unless his ex was mega famous, why would I even want to know? I didn't need anyone to compare myself to, thank you very much.

'Uh sure, I mean I wasn't planning to go on a gossip spree or anything, but you have my word,' I eventually said.

The man didn't like to bring up his exes. Fair enough, to be honest. I'd just met the guy.

We continued on our way to the wine bar and took our seats, with Jericho very kindly pulling my chair out for me. I pretended to swoon a little – just a fraction, nothing dramatic – and opened the menu. My eyes immediately widened.

Oh, wow . . . this is . . . ambitious, I thought, mentally calculating whether my bank account could survive a single salad. Deciding to play it safe, I hovered over the Caesar salad option, ready to declare fiscal responsibility my top priority.

'Get whatever you want,' Jericho said with a grin, leaning back while his eyes bored into mine hazily.

I raised an eyebrow. 'Even . . . Wagyu beef?' I asked, half joking, half testing the limits of his generosity.

'Even Wagyu,' he said, shrugging like it was no big deal, which made me laugh – I wasn't used to men covering the bill like this, and he had already been so generous as it was. I felt my face flush with gratitude.

As we waited for our food, we recapped the day: the chaos of the game, the perfume disaster, the near-catastrophic honey spill upstairs. Jericho laughed at my commentary, adding his own exaggerated replays of my 'secret final boss' antics. I found myself laughing harder than I had in ages, the sound warm and easy, and realised my little crush had been quietly growing all afternoon.

I hesitated for a second, then asked, voice almost sheepish, 'So . . . d'you think this date is going well then?'

Jericho tilted his head, flashed that mischievous grin, and said simply, 'Yeah.'

Cue internal swoon.

By the time our mains arrived, the conversation had settled into a warm, easy rhythm. I ended up going for prawn and mushroom ravioli with a side of sweet potato fries, while Jericho had gone for a steak the size of his head. But as we ate and chatted, I realised how much I was enjoying *just being with him*. He was funny, unpredictable, and somehow managed to make even mundane observations feel like a private comedy show. I caught myself smiling at him more than I probably should have, and felt a flutter of something dangerous and exciting.

When our desserts arrived – a glorious, wobbling mountain of chocolate profiteroles – things hit peak ridiculousness. Jericho tried to be suave, lifting a fork with the utmost care, only for chocolate to escape and streak down the side of his shirt. I snorted so hard that a rogue puff of whipped cream went flying towards his face. He ducked, chocolate splattering a little on the edge of the table.

'See?' I said between giggles, smearing a bit of chocolate on my finger like a tiny flag of victory. 'Romance is messy.'

'Exactly,' he said, leaning across the table with a grin, swiping a dollop off my plate and shoving it into his mouth like it was a covert mission. In his reach, he accidentally nudged one of the profiteroles, sending it wobbling towards my shoulder. I caught it with a squeal, holding it triumphantly above my head like a golden trophy.

'Truce?' he asked, holding up his chocolate-covered hands.

'Truce,' I agreed, though we both ended up flinging tiny smears of chocolate at each other anyway, laughing so hard we drew curious glances from other diners. The way he laughed, teased, and somehow made the chaos feel intimate and light, made my heart flutter. By the time we finally settled back, sticky fingers and all, I realised that I might just be falling for him anyway. Just a little bit, perhaps.

'You know, you're a lot more laid-back than your profile implies,' Jericho said as we made our way to leave. True to form, he helped me slip into my jacket, and I used that small window of closeness to lean in just a little, letting my arms brush against him as I threaded them through the sleeves. For a brief moment, I was enveloped in his cologne again, and for some weird reason, I felt safe.

'Is that so?' I replied, feigning shock, though I'd known it for hours. There had been a part of me that wanted to maintain the top-tier, snooty elegance my *OuiMeet* profile promised – a brooding, mysterious, slightly unattainable persona designed to make him chase me. But all of that had crumbled the second he made me laugh at the coffee shop earlier. With him, I didn't need to perform or pretend; I could just be me. And somehow, that ease between us made my chest tighten in a way I wasn't prepared for.

'You know,' I added, letting a teasing smile curl at my lips, 'you're dangerously good at making me forget how to be intimidating.'

He leaned slightly closer, and I felt a little thrill of daring. 'Oh? Maybe I should keep doing that, then,' he said softly, his voice low enough to make my heartbeat spike. In my head, I ran through my preferences again, matching Jericho against them:

- A man **(tick)**
- Live/grew up in London **(tick)**
- Preferably South London **(unfortunately not, but God bless the London Overground)**
- At least six foot two **(six foot four! We have a winner)**
- No preference on weight or build **(built like a stallion – tick)**
- Nice teeth and lips **(tick)**
- Nice eyes **(beautiful ones, tick)**
- Well spoken **(we love an eloquent babe – tick)**
- Tattoos **(on the neck! THE NECK!! Swoon. Tick)**
- Educated [university level and beyond] **(tick!)**
- University must be one of the top 20 best universities in the UK **(tick!!)**
- Earning at least £50k a year **(haven't asked, but would assume so based on what he said about his savings)**
- A stable, steady job that isn't so demanding that it takes time away from moi **(mmm. I'd need to revisit this; on one hand . . .)**
- Should either have hair, or be completely bald with a full/long beard **(sexy low fade – tick)**
- Dick size at least six inches and thick in girth; preferably circumcised **(Let's pray I get to find out)**
- Kind, generous, sensitive, fun blah blah blah **(seems to be so far – tick)**
- Must have own car and live alone. No flatmates **(another win – double tick!)**
- No red pill/Alpha male beliefs **(so far so good – tick)**
- Must ABSOLUTELY NOT listen to any male podcasts **(I absolutely fucking hope not)**
- Must not be a super active user of Facebook or Instagram **(remains to be seen)**

- Must not have more Instagram followers than me **(wouldn't be surprised if he did – he's gorge)**
- Must not be any kind of social media influencer **(tick, I think)**
- Non-cigarette smoker [weed's OK on occasion] **(tick)**
- Must not invest in or have anything to do with Crypto currency or 'stocks' **(tick – we thank God)**
- Should be open to pets (especially cats) **(triple quadruple tick)**

I caught his gaze, the mischievous glint in his eyes daring me to match it, and for a brief, perfect moment, the space between us felt electric; charged with laughter, teasing, and the delicious knowledge that we were playing a game neither of us seemingly wanted to end.

Chapter 10

'So . . . how did it go? What did you guys do? Was he sexier in person? Are you gonna see him again? I'm requesting all the tea, post-haste!'

It was the evening, and I was at home on the sofa with Toby purring on my freshly showered and moisturised thighs as I recounted the events of the day to Sade on the phone. Since finishing the date with Jericho, I'd been in a bit of a weird trance. On one hand, it was certainly the best date I'd ever been on; he was kind, funny, paid for everything, witty, smart, compassionate and fun – all the things I wanted in a guy on a date for the most part. I'd felt seen and prioritised throughout. He listened to my lame jokes. We flirted and bantered continuously throughout the day. He repeatedly told me how attractive he thought I was. All these things were great and all, but again, I couldn't help but note the annoying feeling that I knew to be true; it was all performative.

A few minutes after I had arrived home earlier, I received a notification from the *OuiMeet* app, informing me that my payment had been released to Jericho, as well as a message from him a few minutes afterwards:

> Cassandra. I had a wonderful time with you today; you were truly a delight, and I really hope you had a nice time too!

Thank you once again for requesting my services, and I hope we're able to talk again soon. J x

Hmm.

I read the message over and over again, confused. There was something about it that just seemed so rehearsed. So impersonal. So stoic and formal; almost as if it was an automatic message that the app sent out on his behalf, with only my name being added. I'd be lying if I said it didn't put a bit of a dampener on my mood at that point. We'd had such a great day, I don't know what I was expecting with regards to his response, but it certainly wasn't . . . that.

I stroked Toby's belly slowly as he made biscuits with his paws into my thighs and purred softly while I responded to Sade, pensive.

'The date was cute, man; it was really cute,' I replied, sighing softly – the uncomfortable knot in my stomach bubbling slowly. 'Jericho was a real gentleman throughout.' At that, I heard Sade mutter a smooth 'We love to see it!' under her breath. I could hear her sigh of relief after hearing that it went well.

'Yeah. We went for coffee, and then he took me to an escape room, which was pretty cool, and then after that we went for something to eat and had a great chat, and yeah he is, like, EXTREMELY sexy in real life. He was holding my hand and everything in public, like he was proud of me or something. And Sade, man . . . we have SO much in common. He loves horror movies and video games too. He loves CATS. I felt really . . . I don't know . . . relaxed around him. Like I didn't have to pretend to be someone I wasn't. He's really comfortable to be around.'

'Well, duh, babe,' Sade retorted, and I could almost hear her scoff in the background. 'You're a gorgeous, intelligent, well-rounded babe. Why wouldn't any man be proud to have you on his arm? I'm so glad it went well, and that you're still alive to tell the tale! He sounds amazing.'

'I dunno man, I really loved it – it really was my idea of the perfect date but—' and I stopped here, not sure if I wanted to confess how I really felt to Sade, considering how much she had rooted for me to go on the date in the first place.

'But what? Spill!' she snapped impatiently, already gearing up to put on her problem-solver hat.

'Ugh! Like . . . there was something so performative about it all. And I know from a logical point of view, I shouldn't have expected any more because, ultimately, I was paying for a service; I expected to be treated like that, but I couldn't help but want for him to actually . . . I don't know . . . *like* me in that way, you know? Like, I wish it were real.'

Sade stayed silent for a while before responding.

'Hmm. It sounds to me like someone has a bit of a crush on old Jericho, you know?' she said playfully.

'Ahh shut up, man, I totally don't!'

'Oh, you totally do! And that's fine! I think it's good that you've been able to establish the performance aspect of it though and can separate the two – it keeps you from going full delusional. I think if you feel like you'd wanna spend more time with him and get to know him offline, maybe it's something you could have a conversation with him about? Or . . . meet up with him and suggest it there?'

I mulled over her words while also trying to piece together who Jericho truly was – beyond the app and outside of his 'escort' persona. Was he really as charming and as chivalrous as he made out to me today? I wasn't sure, but I had enjoyed his company, and I knew that I wanted to feel the way he made me feel today, again.

'You're right, I guess. I don't know, I'll send him a message on the app and just see where his head's at. I'd have to play it smartly though. He told me today about his boundaries with this kinda thing, and personal questions are off limits.'

'That's fair, babe,' replied Sade reassuringly. 'If you're thinking of seeing him again, you'd need to take it slow. Build trust and all that. And then once that's there, go in for the kill.'

I giggled. As much as I wanted to see him again, I wanted it all to feel organic. The last thing I'd want to do was feel as if I was strategically setting him up.

'Thank you for your advice, baby,' I said as I rose slowly to plant myself on my bed. Tomorrow was another long week at work and I'd almost forgotten that I had to face Jeff tomorrow, which I anticipated would be somewhat awkward, considering the way Kofi and I snuck out of the pub last week. I hadn't really spoken or bumped into him since as he was starting off at the office part-time, with tomorrow being the first time I'd be seeing him. Speaking of . . .

'Oh! Before I forget – what's going on with you and Kofi, by the way? Last time I spoke to him, he was practically giddy and kicking his feet in the air. Did you do your so-called "running club" then? I still cannot believe you peddled that lie, you know.'

'Girl, whatever! We're actually meeting up after work tomorrow now. I had to really talk him out of that running club stuff because I actually don't know what came over me when I mentioned it. I wanna be cute as fuck when I first meet him, not breathless and sweaty! I'm gonna meet him at the hospital and we're going to a bar around Clapham after, so I'll see you tomorrow.'

Sade's update instantly lifted my mood; this was what I loved to hear! Two of my favourite people potentially getting together was my Roman Empire, and I was determined for them to be a thing even if it killed me at this point.

'HA! I warned him about doing the running club. I did try and suggest he do something else! What was your excuse?'

'I told him I had a pre-existing injury – I think I said I tore my ACL or something and that it had been flaring up this week, I don't know,' Sade replied, sighing.

'Sade? Where is your ACL?' I asked, shaking my head.

'I don't know, like . . . the ankle?' she responded with full confidence.

'OK. I see,' I replied, trying not to burst out laughing. 'Anyway . . .' I continued, 'Going for drinks? In his neighbourhood? Where he lives? We love that.'

I could already see where this could potentially go, but it wasn't my business.

Sade seemed to sense my pessimism too. 'Girl, don't even try it. Nothing like that is going to happen – when have you ever known me to be a "sleep with a guy on the first date" kinda gal?'

'Umm, let's see,' I began, counting on my fingers. 'Four months ago with that guy with the wide jaws from Hinge. Last July with that Nathan guy. Last May with the guy on Bumble – need I contin—?'

'Would you look at the time?' Sade cut in, fake yawning. 'It's time for me to get some beauty sleep, I think. Let me know how you're feeling with your Jerry guy tomorrow and I'll see you at the office!' and with that, Sade put the phone down. Heh. Got her ass. Not that I've ever had anything against people who sleep together on the first date, mind you. I've had my fair share of one-night stands in the past.

I hopped under the covers and opened up Jericho's message again, thinking about how to respond. There was no doubt that I wanted to see him again, but I needed to see whether that was what he wanted too before I made my next move. I thought back to that weird interaction with the group of girls and how taken aback he'd been. Who was the person he'd dated before and why did random people know about it? Was he well known? Had that interaction maybe put him off meeting again? I typed back, deciding to not mention that incident:

> I had a wonderful time too, Jerry, thank you so much for today; it was almost the perfect date but I reckon you could do better, don't you think? ;) How about we go for round two if you're up for it? I have a Nintendo game that needs solving. Cassie x

A mere five minutes later, Jericho had responded:

> 'Almost', you say? Hmm. Challenge accepted. You know what to do. :) And yes, I'd like to see you again; I had fun with you too!

Much better! Without hesitation, I swiped to his menu, this time looking for the 'evening company' option, which was £350. I transferred the funds from my savings account to my current account and looked through his calendar; his earliest availability was tomorrow night at 7 p.m.

I finalised the booking, switched my phone to airplane mode, and tried to fall asleep before I could dwell on what I had just done. £350 – was this what gambling felt like?

The next day, I was up bright and early, rummaging my cupboards for what to wear that evening for my second date with Jericho. I'd received a message from him early that morning:

> Oh, someone is keeeeen. Thank you once again, Cassie, I'm looking forward to seeing you. Would you like to go somewhere near where you are for ease? Jerry x

He'd signed off as 'Jerry', and I took that as a sign that he was warming to me. After texting him back the location of my neighbourhood (as my plan was to hurry home at 5.30 p.m.

and get ready in time for 7 p.m. – the privileges of living fifteen minutes away from work!) and getting dressed for work, I quickly tried to pair together an outfit for the evening, to keep me from rushing when I got home.

As it was to be an evening date, I really wanted to make an impression, so I decided to go for my killer dress: my burgundy, long-sleeved bodycon ribbed midi dress with a slightly plunged open back. It wasn't just any dress – it was *the* dress. It sculpted my figure in ways I never thought possible, especially in the back, and let's just say, it had a well-earned reputation. I called it my 'fuck 'em' dress, and nine times out of ten, it lived up to its name.

I laid the dress and a pair of black high-heeled boots to the side for later, and hurried out the door to grab the bus for work. My plan for this evening was to hopefully try to entice him to the point where he would want to potentially start seeing me more casually, outside of *OuiMeet* – a girl could only dream.

I arrived at work a few minutes before 9 a.m., awkwardly bumping into Jeff in the elevator going up to our floor. My mind was so preoccupied with my upcoming meetup with Jericho that I had zero interest in making awkward small talk with Jeff right now. He was wearing a navy-blue suit complete with a salmon shirt and blue tie; it was kinda giving 'Tory MP' but I let it slide. I gave him a brief smile and uttered a quiet 'Good morning' before reaching for my phone in a bid to feign productivity, but he didn't take the hint.

'Hey! So did you enjoy the drinks last week? You left a bit early, I noticed.'

Damnit. Why did everything involving this man always feel so *awkward?* I looked up from my phone, trying to come up with an excuse on the spot.

'Oh, no, I had a fab time! I had to leave early to feed my cat actually – silly reason, I know – but he only eats wet food and well, you know . . . ?' I tailed off, hoping he would get the hint.

'Ah, I hear you. Not to worry!' he replied, as we finally reached our floor. 'It was really great getting to know the other members of the team. I didn't realise how young everyone was – it feels like everyone's in their twenties here!'

'Ahh yeah, haha, we're a young bunch in this department, I suppose,' I muttered quietly as we walked in tandem to the department. 'I hope you had a great time, though! We should probably hold events like that in the department more often, to be honest.'

I knew I was just saying it to make small talk, but I had no business suggesting it as an idea. It's not that I didn't have an OK time; it's just that pub nights weren't really my cup of tea.

'Yeah, it would be good for workplace morale, I think – it'll be nice to get to know everyone better. Anyway, had a good weekend?' Jeff responded; we were almost near the office now. I used this as a chance to casually remind him of my marital status – just in case it had slipped his mind. It was a harmless little lie, one he never needed to know wasn't true.

'Um, yeah, it was great actually! I was in the West End for most of it with my boyfriend, just hanging out and stuff.' Smooth, Cassie. Real smooth.

'Oh, lovely . . .' Jeff said in an almost whisper. Cue an awkward silence yet again as we finally made it to the office. I opened the door to see Kofi already at his desk, headphones on. We smiled at each other as I entered. 'OK, well—' continued Jeff, who seemed to be addressing me but looking at Kofi instead '—when you're all settled in, can you please send me the new patient appointment doc for today, as well as their past medical records, if possible? Oh, and I have a meeting at midday with one of the spinal surgeons – if you could book meeting room two, that would be amazing.'

'On it; no problem!' I responded as I took my seat. In true 'Cassie' fashion, I'd already typed up the new patient list and had placed it on his desk along with the patient records on Friday before leaving for the day.

Kofi removed his headphones and swivelled over, his eyes meeting mine. His eyes were swollen and bloodshot, and exhaustion was written all over his face.

'Well, that wasn't awkward at all was it?' he said, smirking.

'Ugh, don't even get me started, man. I'm going to try and not make it too awkward, though – he's OK, really. Anyway, what's going on with you? You got four cases of Samsonite luggage underneath each eye. You all right?'

Kofi laughed and patted his eyes lightly, stifling a huge yawn.

'Yeah, I'm good. Didn't go to sleep until three a.m. though. I was, erm, I was on the phone.' Kofi attempted to swivel his chair back before I was able to stop him and swivel him back to face me. He looked up at me through his finger-smeared glasses, then quickly looked away bashfully. I knew exactly what he'd been up to.

'Speaking with Sade, huh? Oh boy, you guys have it bad, don't you?!' I teased. Their interactions with each other brought me so much joy.

'Oh, shut up man!' Kofi retorted, trying desperately to hide a smile. 'You don't know what you're on about, it's not like that at all.' He returned to his desk and I returned to mine; silence followed us for the next couple of minutes until I couldn't resist:

'I bet you were in bed grinning your teeth and kicking your feet in the air like a schoolgirl the whole night, huh?'

'Maybe,' came Kofi's response. He told me that he was planning to take Sade to one of the local bars near his house that evening, which led to me giving him the rundown over how I expected him to behave.

'Now, as I said earlier,' I began as I typed up a GP referral, 'this isn't a dating app situation where you can just ghost her or treat her weird and dip. You're accountable to me if this goes tits up, you hear me?'

'I hear you,' replied Kofi; I could almost hear the smile in his voice.

'And if you guys are going to make whoopie tonight—'

'Wait – make what? What the heck does that mean?' replied Kofi, laughing.

'Make whoopie! Having sex! Wait, don't the kids say that any more? Ugh – we're really losing recipes this generation, aren't we? ANYWAY, if you guys must feel the need to do-the-do, just remember to use protection, and be aware that, as my best friend, Sade will at some point give me a play-by-play of the events that go down, so keep that in mind when you're romancing, innit?'

Kofi stood up and stared at me, incredulous.

'You guys are actually sick, you know that?' he said eventually, kissing his teeth. 'Women! Anyway, I'm going to grab a coffee, want one?'

'I could murder a flat white if you're offering!' I said in response.

The rest of the day went by without much interruption, with only Jeff and a couple of the other doctors swinging by the office a few times with things for us to do. That afternoon, Kofi had to attend an outpatient clinic with one of the spinal surgeons, leaving me in the office alone to ponder tonight's date with Jericho. I opened up the *OuiMeet* app (I restricted myself to checking the app just once or twice a day – I didn't want to get too obsessed with him) to see his response to my earlier message:

Oh, you're pretty central, aren't you? Lucky you! OK in terms of options we can do the following: Flor de Samba if you're into Brazilian food, Vagabond Bar in Battersea Power Station if you like your wines, The Alchemist Bar if you want to be a bit experimental with your drinks, Cinnamon Kitchen in the Power Station for Indian food, or . . . a Wetherspoons. :)

Jericho was like my own little *Time Out* city guide when it came to this whole dating thing and I absolutely loved it, although he really thought he ate with the little Wetherspoons mention at the end. I enjoyed his humour, and the more I reread his messages, the more I could feel myself growing feelings for him. Damnit. He was doing all the right things, and I was eating it up.

I settled on drinks, hoping it might get him to open up to me a little more. Was that manipulative? Only time would tell. I replied back, smiling:

I love how organised you are; you must be an Earth sign, am I right? Thank you for sending through this list; I'm not the biggest fan of Indian food, so I quite like the idea of The Alchemist, to be honest. What do you think? It would be cool to try out some quirky cocktails with you. Also, Wetherspoons? You're a comedian. By the way, I'm totally bringing my Nintendo with me – you think I'm kidding? I need this shit solved immediately. 😃

Satisfied with my response and excited about the evening, I worked through the rest of my workload with methodical precision, making sure my consultants had follow-up appointments with their inpatients, scheduling meetings for various doctors and tackling a few difficult orthopaedic patients on the phone. I left Kofi in the office for lunch as I headed to the cafeteria to grab a bite to eat. I'd taken my headphones with me, so as not to be disturbed; I really wanted to get into the zone for tonight, which meant turning on a nineties R&B playlist and letting Boyz II Men take me away.

Out of the corner of my eye, I noticed Jeff standing in line to pay for his food. Instinctively, I tried to avoid eye contact, but it was too late – he'd already seen me and started to wave erratically. God, he was cheesy. Forcing a quick smile, I waved back and tapped my earphones, signalling that I was on a call. Thankfully, he got the hint, nodded, and headed to the far end of the cafeteria to join a group of other consultants. Phew. I was fresh out of small talk that day. I returned to the solace of my food and my music; Mya slid seamlessly into Destiny's Child, their harmonies dripping with promises of honeyed love and devotion. I poked at my meal, wondering what being in a relationship was actually like. According to the R&B babes, it sounded like the sweetest thing on earth; silky, effortless and beautiful. I'd suddenly realised in that moment that since speaking to Jericho, I hadn't opened up any of my dating apps once, which was quite the achievement. With Destiny's Child still in my ears belting out the lyrics to 'Dangerously in Love', I opened up Hinge and took a brief look at the offerings on parade for the women of London today:

Fraser, 34, Brixton. Freelance Creative. 'Message me if you're a gym nut like me. Under thirties with athletic bodies only.'

Emmanuel, 39, Stoke Newington. Creative. 'Don't just message me saying 'hi'. Be a woman of substance. Don't message if u have masculine energy.'

Robert, 36, Stockwell. Finance (Crypto). 'Looking for my Lori Harvey, Chloe Bailey or Zendaya!!! Holla at man if you look like any of them innit xx.'

Malachi, 33, Shepherd's Bush. Entrepreneur. 'Here for casual dates only. Say hi.'

Jesus Jerome Christ.

I took a deep exhale as I closed the app. I could see why so many peers of mine were beginning to date internationally at this point. I'd been reading more and more think pieces lately from women who were in long-distance relationships, waxing lyrical about the benefits of dating someone from a completely different culture. I'd be lying if I said I hadn't thought about taking an impromptu trip to New York for a week or two, just to check out the local talent. Desperate times called for desperate measures.

I ate the rest of my meal in silence, while casually swiping through different guys' profiles on the main three dating apps I was on. I'd decided that I couldn't just rest all my laurels on Jericho – I still had to actively put myself out there, lest I randomly one day come across my Prince Charming. As I swiped, I saw a notification ping from the family group chat; it was from my mum and she sounded mad:

My dear children??? Your dad is pissing me off. I need for one of you to speak to him before I KNOCK HIS HEAD!!

I decided to take the bait and ask what had happened; nothing wrong with squeezing in a little last-minute family drama before heading back to the office.

Lol Mum, what's happened now?

The fact that Mum was texting me in the middle of her workday was a clear sign that she was furious. She had a prestigious job – Senior Client Service Officer at Coutts Bank, no less – and would never normally call or text during work hours unless it was something incredibly urgent or wild. What had Dad done now? I had assumed that my little chat with him last week would have settled things down, but fucking alas!

As I made myself a coffee to go, I received a flurry of notifications in the group chat:

> **Steve: Oh ffs. What's he done now? I'm at work at the moment so if I don't respond immediately, that's why.**
> **Mummy: He's been sending me angry text messages all evening and morning. Asking me to leave Femi . . . asking if we can catch up and have a conversation . . . he's saying he's a changed man and all of these things. I'm so tired of this. Why can't he just leave me alone?**

I read the messages and shook my head, annoyed – not just at my dad's petulance towards my mum, but at her insistence that we, as her children, be fully aware of all the chaos. As African kids, we weren't usually meant to be tangled up in grown folks' business like this. But as I got older, I realised I was increasingly stepping into a role that felt more like parenting my own parents. Didn't they have friends or other relatives to confide in? I couldn't shake the feeling that I knew too much about their private lives – about things that were never meant to be my burden.

I sighed as I made my way back towards the office to relieve Kofi as he took his lunch. Kofi had come into work looking casket sharp – he seemed to have had his hair and beard trimmed up cleanly, and had come to work wearing a seemingly fresh pair of dark-brown slacks – complete with what looked like a dark-grey Thom Browne sweater with its signature four white stripes down the left arm. He had drenched himself in some kind of amber- or clove-scented fragrance that took up the whole office, and for the first time ever, it looked as if his hands and lips were moisturised. I was impressed.

As Kofi made his way to go to lunch, I couldn't help but make a playful dig:

'Thom Browne, you know. I didn't know we were doing *that* in this economy? We love to see it!'

Kofi laughed and straightened his sweater, ending with a silly pose, showing off his biceps.

'It's not my fault that *some* of us can afford designer, babes. Well . . . sixty per cent off on The Outnet actually. You either have it or you don't, and as you know, I've got a hot date tonight, so . . .' he replied, sassy as ever as he left the office.

After sending out a few emails and attending a couple of scheduled meetings with two of my consultants, I briefly opened the message group to catch up on the latest family drama.

> **Steven: Mum, just block him, man. There isn't much we can do at this point.**
>
> **Mummy: Can you not talk to him??**
>
> **Steven: No disrespect, Mum, but it's not for me to do. Bianca is due really soon so I've got my hands full with that and doing final bits for the spare bedroom, innit. Sorry.**
>
> **Mummy: Wow. OK. I rarely ask you for help and the one time I beg you, you say this? I see.**
>
> **Steven: . . . ?**
>
> **Mummy: @Cassandra ??**

Oh Lord.

As I geared up to type a diplomatic response, I received a separate, private message from Steven:

> **Cassie, wtf, man? Is she serious? Why is she crashing out on me like that? I really can't be bothered with them two, I can't lie.**

I groaned. Steven had a lot on his plate as it was without having to play mediator to our parents' issues too. I felt for him, but as the oldest sibling, I knew that ultimately it would be down to me to somehow try and fix things between Mum and Dad. Either that, or find a way to let them both know that they were old enough to sort their issues out themselves and to leave the kids out of their post-marital woes. I didn't fancy choosing the second option at present.

I replied back, trying to play peacemaker:

> **I hear you, bro. I think she's just a bit stressed with her and Femi having to plan the wedding in a few months and stuff. She shouldn't have said what she said to you; it's quite unfair and a bit manipulative tbh. You and Bianca have your own things to be worrying about at the moment!!**

I switched back to the main chat and wrote my response:

> **Cassandra: Hey Mum. I'm at work at the moment so I'm not that free to talk, but I agree with Steve. Just block him. I'm not sure why you haven't already. Also, Steve is right; he's having a baby next month. I didn't think it was fair for you to say what you said above to him, but I'll call you later, OK?**

A swift text back read:

> **Mummy: Wow. I see. All right.**

I knew I would feel the brunt of her wrath later on at some point, but it needed to be said, one way or the other.

At 5.25 p.m., Kofi and I began to wind our computers down; we both had busy evenings ahead of us and needed to get into the zone.

'Got a busy evening tonight?' asked Kofi as he propped his headphones into the charger.

'Um actually, yeah!' I replied hesitantly, suddenly realising that I hadn't really filled Kofi in on the whole 'fake boyfriend' charade at the pub last week. 'I've got a second date with this guy I met on Hinge, not a big deal really.'

'Oh nice, I'm happy for you!' he replied, smiling. Phew. 'Hopefully this guy is a good one.'

'We can only hope,' I replied, switching off my computer monitor. 'Anyway, how are you feeling about your date tonight with Sade? What time is she getting here?'

'She should be here in about fifteen minutes or so; I'm gonna meet her at the ground-floor reception. Wanna come with?' he replied, putting on his jacket.

At that moment, my phone buzzed with several notifications at once. The first was a text from Sade saying: **Hopefully see you in a bit! En route to you and Kofi xxx** and the second was a notification from the *OuiMeet* app from Jericho, which read: **Alchemist it is. If you send me your address, I'll pick you up. I'll see your fine self later. :).**

Pick me up?! I wanted to practically swoon at the proposition. He was really going all out with this, and it made my heart (and ovaries) swell up even more. I sent him my building address as I planned to meet him outside instead of having him come directly to my door. I was an excited babe, but I was also a safe babe.

'Sade just texted me to say she's on route, by the way. Let's make our way downstairs!' I said, also grabbing my coat. I had everything crossed that Kofi and Sade's date would go well, and I also couldn't wait to hear any tea she might have afterwards too. Kofi and I made our way down in the elevator and through the hallway to the main hospital reception point. I had to be honest, when he put the effort in, Kofi actually scrubbed up real nice. We waited at the reception together while he doused himself yet again with his perfume.

'Are you nervous about tonight?' I asked, checking my phone for the time. I'd decided to wait until they were both here before jetting back home to change for the date.

'A little bit. We've spoken on FaceTime and stuff so we both know what to expect, but it's just different in real life, isn't it?' Kofi replied, and I could hear his voice slightly shaking with nerves, bless him.

'You guys are gonna be fine, don't worry about it! Sade's a great girl, man. You're gonna get on great,' I reassured him. At that moment, I had a short daydream of the four of us: me, Jericho, Sade and Kofi, enjoying a double date together. It irked me how consumed I'd become with Jericho after such a short amount of time, but his company was almost too perfect to pass up on. I enjoyed the way he made me feel; it ignited feelings in me I hadn't had in so long while being in the dating scene. It was like a drug, and I needed more.

A few moments later, I saw Sade walk through the hospital doors. She looked absolutely sensational, with her long hair flowing in big, bouncy waves past her shoulders. She was wearing a pale-pink bardot cut jumper that showed off her perfectly toned shoulders, and had teamed it with a pair of black skinny jeans and a pair of hi-top Converse trainers. She looked sensational.

'There she is!' I exclaimed, moving towards her to give her a hug. 'The Queen herself. You look incredible, babes!'

'Thaaaaanks, lovely!' Sade exclaimed, bashfully tucking her curls behind her ear and looking towards the floor. I'd never seen her appear so shy before – especially when it came to dates. They both must have caught more feelings for each other than they were letting on.

'Let me take you to your suitor for the evening,' I announced, as I linked arms with her and strolled towards Kofi. Kofi 's face had changed completely. His demeanour – a moment ago a picture of calm – had broken out into a wide grin, and he was looking at Sade up and down, taking her in. They both stared at each other a moment, before going in for an embrace. It was quite romantic, actually.

'You look beautiful,' said Kofi breathlessly, with the biggest, stupidest grin I'd ever seen on his face.

'And you know it! You scrub up well too, I guess, hehe,' replied Sade cheekily. After a moment of watching them both size each other up and get into a bit of small talk, I checked the time and realised I definitely needed to get going if I wanted to make the date on time.

'Now. I have to run as I've got my own thing going on—' I mentioned after a brief moment of allowing them to take each other in. 'But Kofi, do you remember what I told you in the office earlier?'

Kofi broke his gaze from Sade to me, rolling his eyes. 'Yes, madam. I heard everything and it was all noted.'

'Iight,' I continued, looking to Sade. 'And Sade, babes, do you remember what I told you as well?' Sade turned from Kofi to me, giving me a mock salute. 'YES, MUMMY.'

'All right, guys,' I replied, slowly backing my way towards the exit. 'I hope you both have a wonderful time! Don't do anything I wouldn't do, and if you do, please for the love of God use protection because I'm not ready to be an aunty just yet!'

After saying my goodbyes, I raced towards the bus stop across the street from the hospital, just as my bus was arriving. I had timed it perfectly. Seventeen minutes later, I was home, and after feeding Toby, taking a quick shower and meticulously doing my make-up, I was ready. The 'fuck 'em' dress fitted a bit more snug than I would have liked, but it still got the job done. I'd paired the dress with my red lipstick – the signature Ruby Woo by MAC – alongside a winged liner and some burgundy blush. I looked like a fucking siren and I loved it.

I checked the *OuiMeet* app for any update on Jericho's side (note to self: try and ask for his number tonight), which there was:

Hey beautiful. I'll be seeing you soon at 7 p.m. My car will be the silver Audi outside your building. :)

I smiled to myself at the mention of 'car'. That's how low the bar was for me within the dating sphere at the moment, my friends; the fact that he owned his own vehicle excited me somewhat, even though he'd already mentioned it in one of our previous conversations.

I quickly typed back Looking forward to seeing you soon! and went into the bathroom for one final checkover. As tonight's date was more formal, I wanted to make sure that everything was perfect. Teeth? Brushed and flossed. Breath? Doused with mouthwash. Make-up? Flawless, however I gave my face one final blast of setting spray just to lock everything in. After that, I lightly spritzed on one of my top perfumes that I only ever used for dates: the Hugo Boss Elixir for Her. It was the fragrance I'd gotten complimented on the most over the last few months, so here was hoping it would work in seducing Jericho tonight.

With ten minutes to go, I perched on the edge of my sofa like a nervous job applicant, obsessively going over possible subjects to cover during the date like a weirdo. I normally didn't put so much effort into trying to come across as 'likeable' when it came to dates – my natural effervescent personality was normally enough to carry me through most scenarios – but there was something about Jericho that – despite the setup and circumstances of our date – slightly intimidated me. It was almost the same feeling I got from Jeff at work but where my intimidation with Jeff was laced with a lingering feeling of the ick, with Jericho it was laced with a feeling of – lust – maybe? Desire? Whatever it was, I just knew I wanted to see more of him.

A part of me wondered whether this desire to get it right with Jericho maybe stemmed from the pressure I was getting from my parents to date and settle down soon. As much as I would usually shrug it off, I couldn't help but have that niggling feeling in the back of my head; the urge to please them, to live up to the image of the perfect daughter they'd always envisioned. It was a weight I could have done without, yet one I felt duty-bound to carry.

I screened my cul-de-sac discreetly through my living-room window, channelling my inner nosy neighbour as I searched for any sign of his silver car. Jericho struck me as the type to obsess over his car – meticulous, polished, and undeniably well kept.

I saw it a few moments later.

What looked like a really fancy silver Audi TT crept slowly up the cul-de-sac, its blue headlights illuminating the empty crisp packets littered outside my flat. The car eventually stopped right outside my building, and as the engine dimmed, I heard my phone ping loudly with the good old *OuiMeet* notification sound that I had come to know so well.

I quickly grabbed my coat from my coat stand and spritzed another generous helping of my Hugo Boss fragrance for good luck before grabbing my bag and heading for the door, phone and Nintendo Switch in hand. As I made my way down the stairs, I stopped to glance at the message:

Miss Cassandra, your carriage awaits. :) J x

I reached the bottom of the stairs, took one last breath and opened the door to meet him. By the time I'd gotten downstairs, I found him outside, leaning against the front passenger door of his car, smirking at me wildly. He looked incredible. He was wearing a pair of dark indigo slim (but NOT skinny) fit jeans with some beige Adidas Samba trainers. On the top, he had on a beige sweater, covered by a black, waist-length peacoat. One thing about Jericho? The boy knew how to dress.

'We meet once again, Jerry; you look good, by the way,' I said, trying to look at him up and down as seductively as possible as he opened the car door for me. He chuckled as he stepped aside for me to enter the car, before slamming it shut and heading to the driver's side. His car smelled of oud; it was a heavy, yet rich scent, and I instantly sank into the plush, heated seat, still trying to fathom how this was my life right now. Jericho got into the car and before starting the engine, turned to stare at me as he smiled that wolfish grin. I melted.

'Wow. Cassie, you look sensational. Drop-dead gorgeous.' His gaze swept over me before locking on my eyes, that damn smirk of his aimed straight at my soul. 'And you smell incredible too – just the right amount of perfume this time.'

I raised an eyebrow, pretending not to melt under the compliment. 'Careful, Jericho, you keep talking like that and I might actually believe you.'

He opened his mouth to say more, but then his eyes flicked down to what I was holding. 'Wait . . . is that—?'

I wiggled the console in my hand, grinning like a cat with cream. 'Yes, sir. Yes, it is. You didn't seriously think I was going to let you get away with that little promise, did you?'

Jericho laughed, low and incredulous, as I flicked the Switch on and slid it across to him.

'You said you could take Phantom Ganon down in ten minutes flat,' I reminded him sweetly. 'So I figured . . . why not now? That way, we can have the rest of the evening free to talk about other things.'

'Other things, huh?' His smirk deepened, eyes glinting as his fingers curled around the console. 'This is either the flirtiest boss battle setup I've ever seen . . . or you're just ruthlessly efficient.'

'Why not both?' I shot back, leaning in, enjoying the way he looked at me like I'd just played the winning move.

Jericho leaned back against the driver's seat, Switch in hand, suddenly all business. The smirk was still there, but now it was paired with a laser-sharp focus that made me laugh out loud.

'Wow,' I teased, watching him navigate the opening moves. 'I've never seen anyone look this intense outside of an Olympic event. Should I be quiet so you can concentrate?'

'Shhh,' he said dramatically, narrowing his eyes at the screen. 'Greatness is happening.'

And, honestly? He wasn't lying. Six minutes later, Phantom Ganon was down, my months of hair-pulling frustration evaporating under the sound of the victory jingle.

I blinked at him, equal parts impressed and slightly annoyed. 'OK . . . wow. I don't know whether to thank you or be offended that it really was that easy for you.'

Jericho flashed me a grin, basking in the glory of his digital triumph. 'What can I say? Some heroes wear green tunics. Others drive silver Audis and clear boss fights in record time.'

I rolled my eyes, but I couldn't hide my smile. 'You're kind of insufferable. D'you know that?'

'Charming, though,' he shot back, waggling his eyebrows. 'And, listen – if this becomes a regular thing, we could always play more games together. I've got plenty of tricks up my sleeve. Think of it as . . . bonus entertainment if you keep me around.'

I pretended to mull it over, though my grin gave me away. 'Hmm. So what you're saying is, you'd chuck in the gaming lessons for free, as well as some good company?'

'Exactly.' He handed the console back to me with a flourish. 'A package deal.'

Ugh. I wanted him. But I forced myself to play it cool, to keep it cute and composed, at least for now. Sliding my now-conquered Nintendo Switch into my handbag, I shifted in my seat with deliberate ease. My legs crossed slowly, a subtle performance, the sheen of my oiled thigh catching the moonlight like liquid gold. You could cut the tension in the car with a knife.

I didn't look at him directly, but I didn't need to. Out of the corner of my eye, I caught Jericho's gaze dipping, lingering on the curve of my legs. His sly, hungry glance told me everything I needed to know.

Got him.

He started the engine and slowly reversed out of the cul-de-sac – using one hand to steer nonetheless (a HUGE sexual green flag for me; I shall not explain!) – as we made our way down Wandsworth Road towards Battersea Power Station and The Alchemist bar.

Less than ten minutes later, we arrived and slipped into a quiet booth at the bar. The Alchemist had a low, intimate hum tonight – mostly couples on dates, with a few scattered groups of friends. Jericho slid in beside me, effortlessly helping me with my coat as I took my time easing it off my shoulders. The body oil I'd so strategically applied to my décolletage shimmered brilliantly under the soft lights – exactly as planned.

'You have the most beautiful skin; almost looks good enough to eat, if you don't mind me saying,' Jericho said, licking his lips. Again, my womb quickened. This guy was GOOD.

'Well, if you don't mind me saying – I've been told I taste good in the past so you're probably correct in that assumption, Jerry,' I responded cheekily. Because why not? I'm paying for the entertainment. Jericho's grin turned into a wide smile as he winked at me and turned towards the menu.

'So. Couldn't wait to see me again, huh? Did I make that much of an impression? Am I that irresistible?' He laughed at his own joke as I playfully prodded him with the menu.

'I'm really annoyed that you're correct in your assumption,' I replied, trying to be careful with my response. Ultimately, I didn't want to come off as too desperate to the point where he would feel no way in taking my money for dates – I wanted *him* to *want* me.

'But I suppose you piqued my interest yesterday. I like you, and ideally, I'd really like to get to know you better if that's . . . if that's something you do?' I peered at him, as I tried to judge his reaction. His face was expressionless as he continued to smile somewhat politely at me.

'Shall we order some drinks in and get this party started?' he said eventually, avoiding my question. Too soon, Cassie. Too soon.

After a short wait, our drinks arrived, and we spent the next thirty minutes chatting about our favourite things and catching up on recent happenings. I found out that his favourite movie was *Scarface*, that his favourite food was a jacket potato with tuna and cheese, and that in his spare time, he liked to draw. All wholesome. All cute.

By now, we were about three drinks in, and I could feel myself starting to relax. Jericho's eyes had taken on a hazy look as he lounged back in the booth, gazing at me sleepily. As I sipped on my spicy margarita, I decided to take my chance and amp up the questioning.

'So. What would you say is your ideal woman? Both from a physical and personality point of view? Hopefully that's not too personal to ask?' I asked, slightly slurring my speech. I figured it would be a good thing to find out before I continued on my offensive with him. Jericho scratched his head briefly, before finally answering.

'Haha, not personal at all. Hmm. Well, from a personality aspect I suppose I love a strong woman,' he replied, staring directly at me with those piercing eyes yet again. 'I love a woman who knows what she wants, is compassionate, kind, creative, intelligent and funny. I guess it's one of the things that attracted me to this job, you know? Being able to meet women who know what they want and are determined to get it at all costs. Ignoring the gender roles that society puts on them regarding sexuality and desire, and taking the bull by the horns. It's fucking sexy to me, really.'

I straightened up in my seat as he spoke – transfixed. I felt like I ticked all the boxes under the traits he'd mentioned thus far; so far so good. But what about the physical?

'With regards to how a woman looks?' he continued, taking a sip of his drink. 'Honestly, I wouldn't say I have a specific type, but I do tend to prefer curves, I guess? I grew up surrounded by confident, curvy women in my family who celebrated their bodies and were unapologetic in their confidence, so growing up, that was always my norm. I guess that appreciation naturally carried over into my dating preferences.'

It took me a second to notice that I had stopped breathing. I subtly got it together, while taking in the information. Before I could allow the sense of relief to wash over me however, I had to ask the crucial question.

'When you say "curves", do you mean "Instagram model hourglass curves", or—' pointing to myself '—my kind of curves?'

At that, Jericho looked at me up and down, slightly biting his lip in the process. The hairs on the back of my neck stood up as his eyes travelled from my face, down my cleavage and towards my hips. I subtly moved closer to him, allowing him to get a better view.

'You're definitely more my type, Cassandra,' he said finally, his eyes travelling to meet mine again. He inched closer towards me as he maintained eye contact, as if daring me to look away. 'As I said yesterday and tonight, you're very . . . alluring. And before you say anything, I'm not just saying that because of the nature of our date; I genuinely mean it.'

Far be it for me to swoon under the weight of external validation from a man, but Jericho had captivated me from the very start, and I was completely under his spell. No man had ever treated me like this; I wasn't used to this level of attention and focus before. It was like a drug, and I was hooked.

A moment lingered as we both stared at each other longingly, the weight of his words hanging in the air with a degree of sexual tension neither of us saw coming. At that moment, I wanted nothing more than for him to kiss me, and I stared at his lips, hoping he would take the hint. Instead, his eyes came up to meet mine and the longing vanished from his eyes as he smiled meekly and sat back.

The moment had gone. What had just happened?

'So, what if I wanted to get to know you more?' I said, slightly frustrated and going for the jugular. 'I know this is only our second date, but say I wanted to keep dating you, would I – would I have to keep paying for it? Even if you liked me too?'

Jericho then switched to take a sip of water, straightening up suddenly. I'd pressed him too much. *Fuck.*

'This isn't the first time this has happened with someone I've dated from *OuiMeet*, Cassandra. I go on a couple of dates with someone, and then over time, they develop feelings and want to see me for real. If that were to happen between me and you, I suppose a separate conversation would have to be had but, for now, this is my job so I need to keep those certain boundaries in place. Do you understand where I'm coming from?'

I faltered. 'So . . . what you're saying is, in order to keep seeing you, I have to keep paying for you. Even if we at some point ended up as friends and I wanted to hang out with you outside of all of this, with no expectations – you'd still make me pay?'

Jericho sighed and took my hand in his, stroking the back of my hand lightly. I flinched at the warmth and softness of his touch.

'Essentially, yes. That's how this arrangement works. At least for now,' he said, apologetically.

I sighed and backed away, returning to my drink. Suddenly, I was ready to go home. But after a couple of awkward minutes, another thought struck me; something I had wanted to delve deeper into on our first date, but wasn't sure it was appropriate at the time. I had nothing to lose by asking him now, plus I wanted to change the tone of our conversation.

'So, I know you said that you got into this whole game 'cause you're trying to save for a house,' I started, smiling meekly. 'But is there more to that? Not trying to get in your business or anything, but I find the whole industry fascinating; I wonder what drives people into the lifestyle I guess, and whether it satisfies them. I mean, I'm as sexually liberal as the next person, but doing it as a job – I dunno – it seems like it must get physically exhausting after a while?'

Jericho shifted in his seat before facing me again, studying me with exaggerated suspicion. 'You're not some kind of investigative journalist doing a piece on escorts, are you? I've never had anyone so intrigued about my work before – it's new.' He broke into a grin, making it clear he was teasing.

'Sir, I promise you, I am but a homely medical secretary who earns a modest living in order to care for my feline son,' I said innocently, making the Scout's honour hand salute. 'It's not often I encounter these kinds of situations, plus I'm *really* nosy and—'

Jericho raised an eyebrow and giggled at that part, which I responded to by giving him the middle finger.

'—Oh, whatever. You don't have to answer of course, but I am intrigued!'

'Well,' Jericho began, taking another sip of his drink. 'When I started, I was a little nervous, I won't lie. Getting paid to have sex was not on my bucket list by any means, but when the opportunity arose, I thought I'd only do it a couple of times, just to say I'd done it. A little life side quest, you could say. But then I saw how lucrative it could be and . . . well, the rest is history.'

I cocked my head to the side as he spoke, wanting to know more.

'So, it's just about the money then? Nothing else?'

'For the most part, yeah,' Jericho replied, fully facing me now. His eyes were locked onto mine, and he was barely blinking. My ovaries squelched at the intense eye contact; it was hot.

'Even though I make a decent amount at the design firm,' he continued, 'it's not "zone two London mortgage"-decent, so it's been one of those instances where I've had to learn how to compartmentalise when I'm on dates and . . . overnight stays and stuff, and think about my end goal.'

'And how do you compartmentalise?' I nudged. 'Does it ever take its toll on you? Are you . . . are you compartmentalising now?' I asked the last question before I could decide whether I really wanted the answer. Jericho flashed that wolfish grin at me again, never taking his gaze from me.

'Well, it's easier to compartmentalise when the women that often book me are either significantly older, or just not my type appearance-or personality-wise; it makes it a lot easier to not develop feelings or crushes that way. You're probably the first woman I've gone on a date with in this capacity who is my type; both physically and chemistry-wise, so yeah, I guess you could say that I'm having a bit of a shitty time trying to compartmentalise that right now.'

I smiled, a wave of bashfulness falling over me. I was his type, but I had to be cautiously optimistic here. I couldn't allow myself to get too excited. I couldn't deny that it did feel nice to be the exception to his rule though.

'Oh, Jerry,' I said playfully, matching his intense gaze. 'I'm not the kind of girl you'd ever want to compartmentalise or forget, I'll have you know. I'm quite frankly wonderful. Nothing but five-star Amazon reviews, me.'

He laughed, his eyes twinkling in the low light. 'Oh, don't worry, Cassie. You're not someone I think I'll be forgetting in a hurry. I'm enjoying this.'

After a few more moments of coy flirtation and banter, I eventually picked the bill, and we made our way to leave.

'Shit, I just clocked, I'm not gonna be able to drive,' Jericho mumbled twenty minutes later. We were both slightly tipsy, and were walking through the Power Station to get to the car park when he realised. 'I'm going to book us an Uber that'll drop you off at your place first, and then I'll just pick the car up tomorrow after work.'

'I'm sorry,' I said, as we made our way to a small side road near the car park so he could book the Uber. 'This was my fault. I shouldn't have suggested a bar when I knew you'd be driving. My bad.'

'Nah, it's cool!' he replied, sliding towards me. The biting frosty air seeped through my coat, chilling me to the bone. He wrapped an arm around me, and I melted into him. 'This was really fun. I enjoy spending time with you.'

'Yeah . . . for a fee . . .' I muttered under my breath, low enough to not be heard. We spent the next seven minutes in silence as we waited for the Uber to arrive. I burrowed further into his chest as the bitterly cold winds tore through me, with him holding me closer to him in a bid to share some of his body heat. He really knew how to do all the right things when it came to performing the role of the 'perfect' boyfriend; how many dates like this had he gone on per week? I also wondered how many women he slept with per month. A dozen? Thirty? Why did I even care? It wasn't like I was catching feelings or anything like that. I needed to remember that I was in charge here, and that this whole experience was transactional. On my terms.

We both hopped into the Uber as it pulled up to us moments later, with Jericho slightly leaning into me, his head lolling about lazily as he tried to sober up.

'Well, this has certainly been fun. Informative, even,' I said eventually, staring out of the window as we turned onto Vauxhall Bridge. Jericho took my hand and kissed it lightly. Ugh. Such a gentleman. He was making this really fucking hard; I couldn't help but swoon slightly.

'What do you mean by informative?' he asked, his normally piercing stare suddenly becoming doe-like in comparison. He sat up straight, body turned towards me. I had his full attention now.

'Oh, just . . . you know. You letting me know about your boundaries and stuff – which I completely understand, by the way – you're absolutely entitled to boundaries and I get the whole "not shitting where you eat" thing, so yeah . . .'

Jericho edged closer to me; so much so that I could feel his breath on the back of my neck. He then ran one finger down the length of my arm, ever so lightly that I immediately broke into goosebumps. I looked back at him briefly, then turned away again. I refused to be seduced by his gaze yet again.

Ever so gently, he whispered, 'I appreciate that you understand, Cassandra. For what it's worth, if this were under any other circumstances, I wouldn't hesitate to take you out on a few more dates . . . and then some.'

At this, I turned back around, meeting his gaze, because at this point, why were we playing games? '. . . And then some. So then, let's arrange things so they can fall under "other circumstances" then, no?' Nothing wrong with trying my luck here. Jericho laughed and fell back into his seat, his mouth formed into a half-grin. I lay back into the seat with him, wary that I would be getting dropped off home in mere minutes. I didn't want this strange, fun, peculiar night to end.

'Mmm,' he murmured at last, his tongue grazing his lips as the arm closest to me slipped lower, his hand resting against the small of my back. The touch was deceptively casual, but I knew better – this had to be page one of the *How to Enchant Your Female Clients* sex worker manual. My body betrayed me instantly, heat coiling low in my stomach, every nerve ending sparking like he'd flipped a switch only he knew existed. I clenched in response, frustrated at how easily he could unravel me. It was infuriating, really – because while he might have had the upper hand, I couldn't decide if I wanted to wrestle it back . . . or just let him keep it.

'Mmm? Is that the only answer I'm getting from you then?' I teased, my voice softer now, threaded with a dare. Slowly and deliberately, I let my hand drift onto his upper thigh. Because why the hell not? Problematic as it might sound, he was still on my dime – and if he thought he was the only one allowed to play this game, he had another thing coming. If we were going tit-for-tat on touches, then I wanted a fighting chance at leaving a mark he wouldn't forget.

The effect was instant. His eyes flickered, heat sparking in them as they locked onto mine, then slid deliberately down to my mouth. That stare alone was enough to short-circuit my pulse; it was hungry, and so intense I almost forgot to breathe. For a heartbeat, the Uber melted away – the traffic, and the lights of Wandsworth Road. There was only him, and this unbearable closeness of what might happen if either of us gave in.

I knew he wanted to kiss me; it was written all over him. But something – duty, restraint, or maybe that professional boundary – held him back, and the tension between us stretched tighter and tighter, maddening, really. Just as I leaned the tiniest fraction closer, the car jolted hard to the left, snapping the spell as we rolled into my cul-de-sac.

As the car came to a stop, I decided to ask one last question before departing:

'Can I at least know your real name?'

Mind you, we were still staring intensely at each other at this point, both of us tipsy – on some *50 Shades of Grey*-type shit. My whole body was practically humming, every fibre aching to drag him upstairs and let him do unspeakably delicious things to me. But I forced myself to keep it cute, to hang onto a shred of composure, even if my self-control was hanging by the flimsiest of threads.

The silence between us stretched, thick with sexual tension, until finally Jericho leaned in, his breath brushing hot against my ear, and whispered—

'It's Theo.'

I leaned in and kissed him, soft at first, testing the waters. He didn't flinch, didn't hesitate – if anything, he leaned in harder, like he'd been waiting for me to finally make the move. And oh my God, the second our mouths touched, it was like a light switch flipped – *bam* – fireworks. His lips were warm, moist, and, honestly, a little unfair in how good they felt. Then he deepened it, and suddenly my knees – even though I was sitting down, decided they no longer believed in supporting my body weight. Rude.

I let out a tiny gasp (in my head it was sexy, but in reality, it probably sounded like a baby sneeze), and of course he just stole it, swallowed it whole, his tongue sliding against mine in this ridiculously slow, teasing way that had my spine tingling almost erratically. Meanwhile, my body was full-on betraying me – heart racing, legs wobbling, practically vibrating like a faulty washing machine. At one point I accidentally shifted too quickly and nearly knocked my forehead against his, but managed to style it out as a '*passionate head tilt*' (very professional of me, thank you).

Inside my brain? Pure chaos: *keep it casual, don't moan, don't drool, don't let your leg cramp in this position, Bloody hell, is this what they mean by sexual tension?* Outwardly though? Cool, calm, collected. OK, maybe not that cool. Definitely not calm. And collected? Eh. But hey, the kiss was good enough to make me forget all of that . . . at least until oxygen became an issue.

Just when I thought I might actually combust from the sheer intensity of it, a polite little '*ahem*' floated up from the front seat – the Uber driver's gentle reminder that, in fact, he had *not* signed up to chauffeur a live-action soap opera. We both broke apart, laughing under our breath like guilty teenagers caught behind the bike shed.

As I glanced down, I noticed our little encounter had clearly gotten to him – he was hard. A rush of smug delight ran through me, a secret thrill that made me feel powerful, like I'd just unlocked some forbidden achievement.

'Well—' I began, brushing a stray smudge of lipstick off his mouth as I gathered my things '—this is my stop. I've had a wonderful evening with you, *Theo*. Message me on the app to let me know you got home safe, yeah?'

Jericho – or Theo, as he would officially be known from now on – let out a low, almost pained chuckle, his eyes flicking up to mine with something that felt like . . . longing. He tried to hide the evidence of his reaction, fumbling awkwardly, but failed spectacularly.

'That'll cost you,' he said, eyes still glazing hungrily over mine. I made a show of getting out of the car – making sure to get out slowly so he could see the shape of my butt in all its glory in slow motion. I turned around and it had done the job; he couldn't take his eyes off me.

'Uhhuh. We'll see about that. Oh, and thanks again for completing the game – I owe you,' I said finally, with a smirk. And with that, I sauntered back into my building, hips swaying side to side, with a newfound confidence in my step. I turned around again to see he was still watching me leave from his side of the car.

He was going to be mine at some point. He just didn't know it yet.

Chapter 11

'The lunch has been bought. The tea is brewed, and I am ready to hear all about your night last night, my friend,' I said as I crossed my legs and took a sip of coffee, waiting for Kofi to spill all. The last twenty-four hours had been wild; I'd woken up this morning feeling brand new, with a new pep in my step. I'd even managed to get through an awkward chat with Jeff in the hallway with ease before he headed off to perform surgery.

I'd taken an extra-long shower that morning, remembering the evening's events. Although I didn't quite get the answer I wanted from *Theo* regarding dating outside of the app, progress in some form had been made. I'd woken up thinking about the kiss we'd shared the night before.

It was so tender, yet primal. Aggressive, yet passionate at the same time. There was something so inexplicable powerful about how that interaction took place, and I yearned to feel that way again. Theo had texted on the app that same evening to let me know that he'd gotten back safely. As I went to bed, I felt a quiet sense of triumph and confidence. To me, it had been the perfect date.

On the way to work, I'd received a very short and to-the-point text update from Sade:

Girl . . . THROUGH THE MATTRESS. xxx

Normally I would have been all up and in her business trying to get details, but seeing as the other party was someone I knew, it was way more than I needed to know at this point. Still, I'd be lying if I said I wasn't the least bit intrigued by what had happened.

It was lunchtime, and I was keen for all the gossip. I knew Kofi wouldn't tell me everything, which was why I was planning to call Sade that evening for the full rundown.

Kofi had come into work that morning tired as ever, yet in a relatively jolly mood, which I took to be somewhat of a good sign. He swung his chair around to face me, with his lunch – a jacket potato with a mountain of cheese and tuna – in hand.

'My dear, I'm waiting. I wanna know how it went! Where did you go? What did you talk about? And keep in mind that I will be calling Sade to hear her version of events at some point too. I'm VERY invested in this.'

Kofi took a bite of his jacket potato before starting.

'Um, well. We had a good night, you know? It was great, actually.' He gave a knowing smile.

'You're gonna have to give me more than that, mate,' I whined. 'I want details. D'you think you'll see each other again, or? Given that I set you guys up, I deserve the deets, at least!'

'OK, OK! Yeah, it was a great date actually! We went to this bar near my place and the first ten minutes were actually spent talking about your annoying ass.' At this, Kofi laughed at my unintentional scowl.

'Bonding over your favourite person, OK, noted,' I said, gesticulating for him to continue. 'And?'

'Sade's an amazing person, Cassie. We just talked all night about stuff and things, you know? Video games, music, TV, past relationships, that kinda thing.'

'And then . . . ?' I replied, hoping that he was picking up what I was trying to put down.

'And then what?' he replied.

'How did the date end? Did you shake hands and go? Did you guys kiss? Are you gonna see each other again? You're actually very terrible at recaps, you know.'

Kofi laughed as he sipped on Diet Coke. 'Have you spoken to her this morning or something?'

'Not quite,' I responded, grinning wickedly. 'She gave somewhat of an update but I wanted to hear it from you.'

After a few mouthfuls of his food, I think Kofi realised I wasn't going to let it go.

'OK damn! Fine. We had a few drinks and got to know each other. I think she's really funny and cute and engaging and we had a really good time. We had a lot of the same interests which was dope, and then yeah . . . we left the bar and went to mine for a nightcap and stuff. End of story.'

I squinted at Kofi knowingly, looking at him up and down. We both knew what had gone on to happen.

'A nightcap and stuff, huh? Mmhm. Well, I won't question you any further, that's your business and all that. I just hope it went well!'

Silence once more as we both got back to work. Out of the blue, Kofi said, 'You are both gonna talk about what we did at my house anyway, aren't you?'

'Yep,' I replied.

My plan tonight included getting home and having Sade over for an hour or so for a catch-up, then later, try to catch up with Theo to see how he was doing. 'Operation: Make-Theo-Somehow-Fall-For-Me' was officially under way, and after the night we had yesterday – especially in the car – I knew that I wanted to see him again. There was, however, still the unresolved family issue. In my haste to meet up with Theo last night, I'd completely forgotten to call my mum to make sure she was OK, and to find out what my dad had been doing. A part of me wanted to call him first to ask, but I also could no longer be bothered with their ongoing drama.

Despite me telling her to talk to the man himself, I decided to bite the bullet and do it myself, knowing she'd never contact him. After dinner and a shower, I called my dad, who picked up on the third ring.

'Cassandra, my dear, how are you doing? Nice to hear from you.' Yeah, yeah, whatever.

'Hey, Dad. Erm, so . . . what's going on with you and Mum again? She messaged me incredibly upset because you guys had had a row or something? What's going on? I—'

'Let me stop you right there, Cassandra,' he interrupted, clearing his throat loudly. 'This is between me and your mum, and I don't appreciate her ranting to you about our problems. This is grown folks' business, so you don't need to worry about it.'

This? Coming from the same man who showed up at fuck o'clock in the morning on my doorstep, ranting about his feelings for Mum? Do me a fucking favour. My parents always had no problem with trauma dumping on me and Steve (but mostly me), until it came to me wanting to get more information in order to give more informed advice, then suddenly it turned into 'grown folks' business'. Hmph.

'OK, understandable, but I need you to remember that you came to me asking for advice the other week. And now she's upset because you keep telling her to leave Femi despite knowing that she doesn't have any interest in you any more – with all due respect.'

This whole debacle was frankly embarrassing. Did my dad not know the meaning of shame? The whole thing would almost be romantic if it wasn't so deranged and delusional. I braced myself for his retort but, instead, was met with silence on the other end for a few moments. After about forty-five seconds, he responded.

'Fair enough. I – I'd had a bit to drink, that was all. I shouldn't have called your mother. You'll talk to her for me – yes?'

That. Wasn't. My. Job.

'Fine. At some point, I guess,' I responded, giving in. 'But you have to promise me that you're going to give her some space – this is supposed to be a really happy moment for her and it seems like – well – it seems like you're intentionally trying to ruin it.'

At that moment, I received a text from Sade saying she was about five minutes away. I needed to get off the phone and find some picky bits for when she arrived – this was far too much drama for one evening.

'I'm not trying to ruin anything, don't say that!' he needlessly shouted down the phone – as if I were the problem here. As well as anger, I could also hear the fear in his voice. He really did love her. Either way, that wasn't my issue, as this was something he was going to have to find a resolution to himself.

'I didn't say it's your fault, but yeah, I'll speak to Mum at some point. I've got to go now as I have a friend coming over, but I'll check in with you soon, yeah?'

He mumbled a begrudging 'Goodbye' as I hopped off the phone and got out a couple of packets of crisps, some trail mix, a couple of cans of lemonade and, more importantly, chocolate. I heard the low rumble of a car pulling up outside the building and moments later, the doorbell rang.

Sade had arrived in what could only be described as 'sleepover chic'. She was wearing a pair of red tartan pyjamas teamed with a bright-orange platform Crocs, complete with a red silk bonnet over her hair and a brown fur coat. It was fantastic.

'Don't even start, my friend,' Sade said, walking past me and into the living room. My face must have said it all already. 'To be honest, it's no biggie – I drove here and I couldn't be bothered to dress up, man.' I didn't care how she chose to show up; all that mattered was that she was now living closer to me.

She dove into the snacks as I opened my can of lemonade – the look of nothing but pure judgement written all over my face. I sat down opposite her in silence, looking at her up and down and she munched on a packet of crisps.

'Ahem. Some of us are waiting, you know,' I said finally.

Sade stopped mid-bite, confused. 'Waiting for?'

'The GIST!' I shouted eventually, seeing that she still didn't understand. Toby – who had been asleep nearby, stirred at the extra noise, and trotted off into my bedroom. He wasn't here for the gossip exchange, it seemed.

'Ohhhhhh THAT! Yeah, I was getting to it! I just needed to lubricate my throat . . . with your food and drink first, though.' She winked. I gagged.

'I want to hear every sordid detail,' I continued, making myself comfortable in my armchair, 'but I don't wanna hear anything that may make me look at him in a negative light moving forward, so before you start – was he a gentleman and did you have a good time?'

Sade got comfortable, as she settled into the sofa opposite me – with a sly grin that could only imply that she had been dicked down thoroughly within the last twenty-four hours.

'He was an absolute gentleman, to be fair. We had such a great time – he's so easy to talk to! And he's such a big nerd too, I fucking loved it, man.'

I smiled as I knocked back more of my drink – that was what I'd wanted to hear. So far so good.

'OK, I love this! Also, Kofi kinda covered what you guys got up to on your date so you don't need to run through that with me – I want you to elaborate on – wait – let me check my notes—' At that point, I made the grand gesture of pulling out my phone to locate the text she'd sent earlier. 'Being put

"THROUGH THE MATTRESS" it says here. I want to know what that was all about, please!'

At this, Sade shifted in her seat uncomfortably, her glasses perched on the edge of her wrinkled nose as she smirked wickedly.

'Girl. Sis. Babes,' she started, eyes already animated as she leaned forward, ready to tell all. 'OK so, first of all, his flat is SUPER cute. Like, you could tell that he's into his plants and interiors and stuff. We did a mini-tour of the place and then had a couple more drinks and stuff.'

My phone suddenly vibrated with a notification, but I was too locked in to Sade's story to notice. I leaned in closer as she continued.

'So yeah! We vibed for a while, he was telling me about his fam—' I had to stop her there.

'My friend. I didn't ask you over here to "David Attenborough" his life story. Tell me about the SHAGGING.'

We then both erupted into cackles of laughter, and out of the corner of my eye, I noticed my phone going off again. I quickly turned it over to notice that it was coming from the *OuiMeet* app. My heart fluttered almost instantly. I wondered what Jericho – or should I say Theo now – wanted? Still, I pushed my phone to the side, keen for Sade to continue, but she immediately clocked my grin.

'Wait. Is that your fancy man? You know you're gonna need to let me know how your date went after I tell you about mine, right? Because this whole thing is low-key giving *Pretty Woman* but in reverse. I'm fully invested!'

'Yeah, yeah, I will, but at the moment I'm waiting with bated breath, so . . .'

'OK! So we're on his sofa and at first we're just making out and stuff, and then he pulls me in closer. At this point, I can't lie, man . . . I was READY to go. So I lean in and start stroking my hands on his chest and he seems to be liking it. And as we're kissing, he basically *pulls* me on top of him. So now I'm straddling him on his sofa and erm . . . yeah, man.'

I was fully locked in at this point, even though imagining Kofi doing the nasty with my best friend was something I really didn't want to picture all that much, I knew I simply had to adhere to the Girl Code, which dictated full sexual exploit rundowns with your best friend after the deed had been done.

'So—' Sade continued, fully getting into the storytelling aspect now; she'd even put her snacks down and everything '—we just start dry humping on the sofa at first, you know, nothing too deep. And then! He picks me up and takes me to his bedroom. Fam, I felt like I was in a romcom or something, it was so sexy. So then yeah . . . we start undressing each other and, Cassie, babe, when I tell you that this man was PACKING? I was shocked.'

The last thing I wanted was to imagine Kofi naked; that man was like another brother to me and the very thought of it made me wince, but I had to persevere for Sade's sake, at least (and for my own nosy self).

'Cassie. Sis. He had Trojan condoms. The XL kind too. He said they were the only ones that would fit him and I believed it. His dick was at least nine inches.'

NINE! I knew I would never look at Kofi the same way again. I leaned back into the sofa, eyes wide open in shock.

'So then, he pushes me back onto the bed and then he just goes to town, just absolutely nailing me through the mattress. Honestly, Cassie, I've never felt anything like it. The thrusting? Militant! Precise! Deep! I could fucking feel it in my lungs, I tell ya. And he kept going for at least twenty minutes, which was a record for me anyway. And erm, yeah. Let's just say we received an angry knock on his wall from his neighbours. I couldn't contain it, man. That man unleashed something in me last night that I hadn't felt in such a long time. That dick is a menace to society. Anyway, I say all this to say, I'll be seeing him again, don't you worry about that.'

I sat back into the armrest and stared at Sade silently for a few moments while she continued to dip into the snacks nonchalantly. It was my fault; I was the one that pressed for more information, but fucking hell. I didn't know Kofi had it like that. I feared that I would never be able to look at him the same way again. Equally, however, I was also happy for both of them; my work, as far as they were concerned, was done.

'Bloody hell, man. All this time I've been working next to a man who's a fucking stallion. I know that's right, sis! Don't worry, though, I won't let him know that you told me all that extra info – the last thing I need is for things to be awkward at work, you get me?'

We chatted over the next twenty minutes whilst gouging serious kilograms of chocolate. I updated her about my mum's upcoming nuptials and Dad crashing out, and she told me about her recent work dramas and updated me on her family gossip. Now that Sade had rented a new flat way closer to me, we had vowed to do in-person home calls at least once every couple of weeks or so in a bid to kinda rebuild that sense of friendship community that our mum's generation used to have, where they would randomly go to each other's houses and stay there all day just because, and our friendship has grown so much stronger because of it. None of this 'having to book to hang out three months in advance' nonsense that a lot of our generation have unfortunately become used to; we try and make it work when we can.

'OK, enough about me 'cos I've gotta go soon. Fill me in on this Jericho guy then. How did your second date go?' Sade asked as she finished off her drink. I filled her in on the details of our date – really going to town when I brought up the car situation – and spoke of my plans to see him again. She looked at me, beaming.

'And here was me thinking this was just going to be a one-time thing! It sounds like you're low-key catching feelings for him a little bit, don't you think?'

I pondered on this. I didn't think it was 'catching feelings' per se. For me, I was just having fun with someone I was incredibly sexually attracted to. At least, that's what I'd been trying to tell myself. Did I want to be paying so damn much for it? Not necessarily, no.

'I enjoy him,' I said coolly. 'I think so far, we've had a great time together and he's been the perfect gentleman every time. I do want to see him again, and as much as I'm enjoying the whole control element of me paying for it, my bank account isn't. I'm tearing into my savings and the thought of having to keep this up does make me feel a little anxious, I can't lie.'

Sade and I sat in silence as we both pondered the tricky situation. I wanted to keep seeing Theo casually, but I didn't want to fall for him – that in and of itself would create a whole stack of problems that I wouldn't be able to face – such as trying to explain to my family and other friends how me and Theo met. That's if we were to ever get together in the first place.

Luckily though, I didn't think it would ever come down to that so I wasn't necessarily worried about that part. I mean, in another reality, it would be nice . . .

'Well, to play devil's advocate, I would see it as investing in your happiness and in things that bring you joy,' Sade said eventually. 'Instead of spending three hundred pounds on a pair of sunglasses or a new bag, you're spending it on your emotional and – dare I say at some point – sexual wellbeing. The way I see it is, why have money if we can't spend it on the things that make us feel good? We spend our lives saving up in order to have security when we get older, which I get, but while we're doing that, a lot of us forget to have fun and actually cultivate experiences that bring joy!

'One day, Cassie, you're gonna look back at this moment in your life while with your grandkids and you're going to be able to tell them that back in the day, you were a bit of a hussy playing it fast and loose, getting your back blown out and all sorts. Isn't that what we all want, at the end of the day?'

I never understood why Sade refused to go into politics. She could sell sand to the Sahara Desert. And she was absolutely right. Life was for living, not for waiting around. I deserved to have as much fun and feelings of spontaneity as I could before getting older and having to be more responsible.

'When it comes to you and your advocacy for the devil, you really give Greta Thunberg a run for her money you know,' I replied, newly emboldened and empowered by my best friend's speech.

Sade went home a few moments later, leaving me to deal with the situation in my *OuiMeet* app. I'd purposely refrained from opening Theo's message there and then as I wanted a little treat for myself to open before going to bed. I entered my bedroom, seeing Toby soundly snoozing on my side of the bed. I hunched up beside him on the opposite side, donned my bonnet and opened the app. There were two messages waiting for me:

> Cassandra, I hope you had a wonderful time the other night. I sure did. I'd be lying if I said you didn't make an impression on me, especially in the car. You're an amazing kisser, by the way. Speaking of cars, I was able to pick up my car eventually. I hope you're having a wonderful evening. T x

The next message seemed to have come through a couple of minutes after the first one:

I haven't had someone make me feel like that for a while, actually. You're a cold piece of work, Miss Cassie. :)

The fact that he felt the need to send a follow-up message was important here. It meant that I'd left something of an impression on him. I smiled to myself as I read the messages back. What was my next move? In my head, the natural progression would be for us to sleep together at some point, right? As someone in the sex worker business, surely he wouldn't be surprised if I were to book that in? My quest to continue seeing him, but to not pay for it, was under way, but I didn't want to press that issue on him again.

When he'd mentioned that other clients had tried to do the same thing to him, it did make me feel a little bad. After all, I've always been keen to support independent Black businesses; it wouldn't feel fair if I cheated him out of his wages by seeing him outside of the *OuiMeet* app. But on the other hand, if he started developing feelings for me, who was I to say no?

I typed back:

Evening, Theo. :) I'm glad you were able to get your car back in one piece! Praytell, how exactly did I make you feel?

It felt like a game of cat and mouse, and at the moment I wasn't sure if I was the cat or the mouse. I spent the next twenty-five minutes reading and scrolling through TikTok, laughing at memes before I got another notification from *OuiMeet* – Theo had responded:

Evening, Cassandra. :) If you'd like to know how you made me feel, you know what you need to do. :) My menu is on my profile. Sleep well. :) x

Shit.

And to think I assumed that I was slowly reeling him in. I

went onto his profile to remind myself of his 'menu'. I knew I absolutely wanted to see him again, but for what? What could I possibly do to get him to forgo the app so we could see each other more regularly? I knew that he was into me; I knew that much. But I just needed something to tip me over the edge, and my personality could only get me so far. What if I—?

I scrolled back onto his menu to check out my options again.

Overnight stay – £600.

Six hundred pounds. I needed to find a way to justify the cost to myself. On one hand, I could see it as an investment. Like Sade had said earlier (I could really use her right about now), we only had one life to live, and if there was any time to live a bit spontaneously, it would be now. I could make the money back eventually, after all.

My heart raced as my finger paused over the 'book' button. I'd need to root through my drawers to find the cutest lingerie at my disposal. I knew that if I chose that option, I'd have to put it on him, hard; really unleash my inner sexual prowess and utilise all the skills at my disposal to make him become enamoured with me.

I quickly scrolled from the *OuiMeet* app to my banking app, transferred £600 from my savings account to my current account and hopped back into *OuiMeet* again, hovering over the 'book' button. I was making the right decision; I was sure of it. It was an investment in my happiness after all. I was in charge. I was taking control of my joy, and what was that, if not empowering.

I clicked the 'book' button, which took me to his calendar and a list of times. The only availability he had for the next few weeks were on Fridays and over the weekend, no doubt due to his day job taking up time, I assumed. He had availability this upcoming Friday and weekend as it stood. Was it too soon? I thought back to our encounter in the car and how the passion and heat exchanged between us was undeniable. I needed more of that. I deserved it, and if this is what it took, then so be it. I made the appointment for Friday night, put in my bank details, and made the booking. After getting the confirmation email, I lay back in bed, nervous, but ultimately content and satisfied in my decision. As long as I kept telling myself that what I was doing was empowering, I had no reason to feel shame.

Damn. Maybe I was the mouse after all.

Chapter 12

The next day, as suspected, a new message notification from *OuiMeet* greeted me as I got ready for work. For some reason, I had a tiny bit of anxiety about reading it. What if Theo had rejected the booking? What if, instead, he wanted to take things slower, and have us go on a couple more wholesome dates before approaching that step? I waited till I was on the bus before I opened the message, slightly holding my breath as I did so. This time, the message came with an attachment.

> Cassandra, I feel very honoured that you like the pleasure of my company, obviously I wasn't the only one that felt something the other night. :) I'll be honest in saying that when I received the email and your username came up on the booking, I got a little excited. Thank you for booking the overnight stay with me; I can't wait to spend more time with you, you gorgeous human. Attached are my recent sexual health results for your peace of mind.

I exhaled a sigh of relief as I read the message back a few times. It was happening; it was actually happening. I had paid for sex, and in just a few days, it would finally happen. I'd expected to feel shame, but instead, all I felt was empowerment and pure bad-bitch energy. Sex work wasn't just a man's domain any more – women could claim that power too. We had the right to take control of our own sex lives, free from stigma and shame. I also noted that he'd attached his recent STI results; I didn't even want to begin to think about how many people he had slept with – or how often he was sleeping with clients in order for him to have an up-to-date test result. If I dwelled on it too much, I feared I might talk myself out of it. That was a worry for another day, as far as I was concerned.

I messaged back, smiling as my stomach began to bubble with excitement. I was actually going through with it! I decided to tease him a little:

> Hi Theo. I'm looking forward to it too! Although I'm a little confused as to why you sent over your STI results? My plan was for us to stay up all night playing Monopoly and Cards Against Humanity. Maybe even do each other's hair at some point. Unless you had something else in mind? Please advise x

A stop before getting off at my bus stop, Theo returned the message:

> You're funny x

Heh. Funny indeed.

Kofi hadn't been able to look me straight in the eye for two consecutive days. Apparently, Sade had let slip to him about our girl chat, and now, things had become slightly awkward in the office. After the third day, I'd had enough.

'Kofi, I know you've been avoiding me,' I said eventually, after getting off a call with a patient. 'I'm assuming it's because of my chat with Sade—'

'Aht aht!' Kofi said, turning around to face me, even though his eyes were darting in every direction except mine. 'I really don't wanna know what you guys were talking about, let's just . . . let's just gloss over it and pretend this conversation didn't happen. It's embarrassing, man.'

'But it did happen, Kof! And while I won't divulge what we spoke about, I'll tell you this! I'm proud of you. You just keep making her happy, you hear me? If she's happy, I'm happy. Mmkay?'

Silence as his eyes finally landed on mine. I could see he wanted to laugh – the corners of his eyes were turned up slightly, and he was struggling to hold in a smirk.

'OK. Fair enough, man. Also, who's this guy you're seeing then?'

Sade and her mouth. I loved that girl, but she could be a bit of a jabberjaw at times. I really needed to sit down with her at some point and tell her to rein it in sometimes. I really hoped she hadn't told Kofi how me and Theo had come to know each other.

'Err . . . how much did Sade tell you about that?' I replied warily as I swivelled the chair back to my desk. All of a sudden, I felt incredibly awkward talking about Theo outside of my best friend.

'Oh, not much,' he responded. 'Just that you had started seeing someone and that he was treating you well so far. I'm happy for you, Cassie – you genuinely deserve it.'

I turned around and patted him on the shoulder. That was really sweet of him to say. 'Thanks, buddy. Yeah, he's a nice guy. Erm, we just met on a dating app, same as all the others, and it's going well so far.'

He smiled. 'Good, I'm glad to hear it.'

The rest of the day went by in a bit of a blur, with me predominantly thinking about what to wear for that Friday. During lunch, I downloaded a few of those sex podcasts in a bid to hopefully learn about any new tricks or tips that could come in handy. The whole point of this arrangement was for him to satisfy me, but I couldn't help but want to do my part too. I wanted to leave him wanting more, and if it meant learning how to get my leg around my head for a few minutes, then so be it!

'Oh, by the way, Jeff is doing a training course thingy at St George's Hospital for the next two weeks so I cleared his calendar while you were at lunch and assigned his new patients to Miss Shimoda for next week.'

'Oh?' I replied confused. He hadn't sent me an email about it. I'd wondered why I hadn't seen him around recently. Had he been avoiding me? 'I didn't get any emails or anything from him, that's annoying that he wouldn't let me know.'

'Oh, interesting. He sent the email to about six of us the other day.' I checked my emails; nothing. Not that I was overly concerned or anything. Ever since our awkward encounter in the staffroom, and at the pub, I'd been trying to keep a bit of a wide berth, so him being absent for the next couple of weeks suited me just fine.

I'd planned to meet my mum for a quick drink and a chat in Whitehall – which was just up the road from me – after work as I wanted to check in with her to see if she was feeling a bit better after the whole Dad debacle. After saying my goodbyes to Kofi and packing up, I decided to stretch my legs and walk across the bridge to meet her, instead of taking the bus.

Fifteen minutes later, I had arrived at a tiny wine bar on the corner of Whitehall, and saw that my mum was already there. She looked so beautiful and corporate in her salmon-pink waistcoat co-ord set and black kitten heels. She was sitting in a corner booth, shouting into her phone, which was on loudspeaker, not giving a damn about the other patrons in the bar. Would she be an African mum if she wasn't shouting loudly into some kind of device? She looked up, beaming as I approached, and gave me a hug.

'Baby! It's good to see you. I ordered you a rum and Coke,'

Mum said, as she put her phone away and turned to face me, eyes sharp and piercing. My mum was one of the most beautiful people I knew and, growing up, I was always slightly in awe of her. The way she was able to light up a room with her confidence, her effervescent personality and her beauty amazed me. She was a size 18 and had been that size her whole life, and she never let what others thought of her body hold her back from feeling confident and secure in her skin. She brought me up to be the same way, which is where I think I got the savage confidence in myself from. She swirled her glass of red wine as she surveyed me quietly.

'How are you doing? How's work? How is the dating going?' The barrage of questions caught me slightly off-guard at first. I wasn't used to my parents asking about my life outside of 'when are you going to get married?' and 'when are you going to start thinking about having children?', but she did ask about my dating life so we'll probably get to the breeding part of my life eventually.

'Everything's good, Mum! Work is great, I'm great. Err, I'm not really seeing anyone . . . not really. But we'll see.' I took a cautious sip of my rum and Coke. My mum didn't need to know about my recent hobby just yet.

'But enough about me,' I said hastily, trying to change the subject. 'How are you feeling? Have you spoken with Dad? I chatted to him earlier and told him to back off a little bit. He doesn't really seem to be getting the picture, annoyingly.'

At the mention of Dad, my mum straightened up and almost hissed. If their beef wasn't so ridiculous and draining, I'd almost low-key encourage them to get back together. The whole 'divorced-parents-who-have-a-love–hate-relationship' trope was really working for them here.

'Please. That man was the biggest mistake of my life. The only good things I got out of it were you and Steven,' she added hastily. 'Outside of blocking his number, I don't really know what else to do. I've even spoken to his mum about it and she agrees that he needs to move on! I think it's something about Femi that threatens him.'

'I mean, that's obvious enough, Mum. Femi is consistent and generous and caring. And, more importantly, he loves you loudly and unapologetically. Everyone can see just how much he dotes on you – he treats you like the queen you are and I think Dad can see that too.'

Mum gazed thoughtfully at her glass, lost in contemplation. I'd never seen her happier than recently with Femi by her side, but my dad – ever the stubborn thorn – refused to leave it.

'You know he called your auntie Gifty and talked to her for three hours about me? Telling her all this nonsense about how I'm going to regret marrying Femi. How Femi is a conman out to take my money, and all this rubbish about how he still loves me? He makes me sick; especially with how he treated you and Steven – but especially you – growing up. You didn't deserve that. My children didn't deserve that level of neglect at all.'

She stared into the distance – talking more to herself at this point than to me – and I could see her eyes begin to well with tears. I took her hand in mine, and for a fleeting moment, we shared something unspoken as memories of my childhood washed over me. For the most part, it had always been just me, Steve and Mum at home – Dad was rarely around, always blaming work for his absence. Years later, we would learn that 'work' was just a convenient excuse for something else – other women. Being at home was always a tense affair when he was there due to his heated temper tantrums and all the emotional abuse. We didn't have the best time of it growing up, but Steve and I somehow managed to turn out fine for the most part. Steve more so than me, but here we are.

'You did your best, Mum,' I said reassuringly, now blindingly aware that we were two women sitting in a bar trying not to cry. 'The only person that should be sitting with themselves to really internalise what they've done and how they've acted is him. At least we know he's not invited to your wedding, hey?'

'Oh! Speaking of which, we've already done all the invites now so yours should be coming soon. I've given you a plus one, but don't feel forced to bring anyone if you know . . . if you don't want to.'

'And be harassed by all the aunties and uncles on the day about why I'm single? Absolutely not, Mum; I don't need all that stress. Thank you, I'll work on bringing a date.'

Mum took another sip of her drink, thankfully in better spirits. 'If you need help with finding someone, I was speaking with your second cousin Mabel the other day and she was telling me about this guy at her accounting firm who—'

'Mum, please, it's fine. I can find my own date,' I said, exasperated.

'No, but he's a really attractive man, Cassie!' she persisted, now becoming more animated. 'His name is Carl and he's from one of those islands – Martinique, I think? He makes six figures and—'

I held up my hand to cut her off, trying to hold back a laugh. If only she knew what I'd been getting up to of late. 'Honestly, Mum? It's fine. I'll find someone to bring along, don't worry.'

Damnit. My first thought was to possibly consider taking Theo along to the wedding with me as my plus one, but I absolutely could not allow that to happen, given his profession. I could potentially have him lie by omission, but what if there was a slim chance that someone recognised him from somewhere? That wasn't a risk I was willing to take, frankly. I didn't want to be the only one at the wedding without a plus one, so I had some strategising to do. Thankfully, the wedding was in three months so I at least had a little time.

After our catch-up, I walked my mum to the station and stood with her as she waited for her train.

'At some point, Cassandra, you have to learn how to drive so you can take me to and from work, you know. I'm an old woman; I shouldn't be taking public transport like this from Croydon and back every day.'

I rolled my eyes and grinned at the guilt-tripping of it all. First I was a marriage counsellor, then a conflict resolution officer. Now a chauffeur. How many things must I be expected to do at once? I replied, 'First of all, you have a fully grown son who is self-employed who has a car and is flexible with his hours, have you asked him? Secondly, you're only fifty-six AND you do Pilates twice a week. You're fitter than me. Third of all, maybe you and Femi could move further into London so you wouldn't have to travel as far? You know you guys can afford to at this point.'

Mum tutted as she shifted from foot to foot. 'I'm too old to be moving, my dear. Also, I don't think I'll get my money's worth if we move further in. Let us stay where we are.'

'Great,' was the only reply I could muster at that point. Parents. God love 'em.

I got home to find Toby scratching at his post and meowing loudly at me, no doubt furious that I'd come home late and missed his allocated dinner slot.

'I'm sorry, baby! Mummy had to go and see Grandma for a bit.' I cooed at him as I cleaned out the old food from his bowl and replaced it with his favourite chicken and salmon gravy packet. I cleaned out his litter tray, took out the bins and put on a load of washing before sticking some leftovers in the microwave. I stood by the counter scrolling aimlessly through Instagram as I waited for my food to warm up. As I scrolled through my notifications, I saw a flurry of engagement directed towards my page, which all seemed to be coming from the same account:

TheoCam_1996 is now following you

TheoCam_1996 liked your photo

TheoCam_1996 liked your photo

TheoCam_1996 liked your reel

TheoCam_1996 liked your photo

TheoCam_1996 liked your story

TheoCam_1996 commented: You are so incredibly beautiful, wow.

TheoCam_1996 commented: This is such a beautiful shot of the lake; you have an eye for photography!

TheoCam_1996 commented: 😍 There she is.

TheoCam_1996 liked your photo

With my curiosity piqued, I clicked onto the person's profile and scrolled through the first two photos. When I realised who it was, I did a double take. Surely it wasn't?

It was Theo. But this username had '1996' after the name. But Theo wasn't twenty-eight years old. He was thirty-four years old. Maybe it was an error? I ignored the ping of the microwave as I sat on my sofa, digesting the fact that Theo had just followed me on Instagram.

I scrolled through his photos, a mixture of fear, disbelief, bashfulness and curiosity all fighting for dominance inside my brain at the same time. It was Theo all right, but a more relaxed, candid version of him; photos of him out with friends, his paintings (he painted too, as well as drew, it seemed), him on holiday, and the odd portrait or two of him. I scrolled through his entire profile, taking in every photo, every moment. Images of him in Saint Lucia with his grandmother, images of him as a child in a pair of funky overalls . . . images that provided a raw, unfiltered side to him, without all the performance or pretence. Also, only 642 followers. A low-key babe. We loved to see it.

I followed his profile back, giddy about his comments and engagement on my photos. But also, what did this now mean? Did he typically follow his clients on Instagram? Curious, I skimmed through his 'follow' list. To my surprise, it was mostly other guys and branded accounts. The few women he did follow didn't exactly scream 'clientele' to me. Then again, at first glance, would anyone assume I was the kind of person who sought the services of a sex worker? Probably not, to be fair. Did this mean that he was beginning to like me? There was far too much to think about right now, alongside his username, which was still a niggle in the back of my head. Why would he use 1996? Unless it was a typo? But he *did* look a lot younger than he said he was. I decided that I would ask him about that when I saw him on Friday. In the meantime, I decided to send him a message on Instagram. At this point, the less time spent on the *OuiMeet* app, hopefully the less I'd need to spend in order to communicate with him.

After 'liking' a few of his photos, I opened up the direct message window and wrote,

> Well well well. Look what the cat dragged in. I hope you know that as this is a public platform, I'm not required to pay for this additional form of communication. Is following your clients part of your service or did our kiss leave more of an impression than I thought?

As I went to retrieve my now-lukewarm leftovers, I came back to the sofa to find that Theo had already responded:

I plead the fifth on all counts, Cassandra. Your profile actually came up on my explore page for some reason; must be an algorithm thing, I believe. Small world, huh? I thought I'd have a gander at your page and throw you a few likes here and there. It's a complimentary service I provide every now and again. xx

I shook my head. He's hard-headed, this one. We spent the next thirty minutes or so messaging our quick whips back and forth as I ate my dinner. His dry, sarcastic humour mirrored mine perfectly, making our conversations effortless. In an ideal world, he'd be the perfect date for my mum's wedding. I kept that thought on the back burner – just in case I could make it happen.

I sent a final message before getting ready for bed:

Well, *Theo*: it's been fun. Thanks for all of your cute comments by the way; it's nice to know you appreciate something beautiful when you see it. *tosses braids* I'd be lying if I said I wasn't excited for Friday; I'm going to try and be the perfect host. What time were you thinking of coming over?

I took a quick shower, thinking of Theo as I did so. I was actually going through with spending the night with him and that's when the small bubbling of nerves began to appear in the pit of my stomach. Sade would be so proud of me right now; I was actually about to go all the way with this incredibly sexy man and it was what I deserved. For the first time in my dating life, I felt empowered.

After my shower, I hopped back into bed and checked my Instagram for the last time before knocking out. Theo had replied one final time:

Well, according to the booking, I'm to arrive at yours for 7 p.m., right? I'll pull up to where I came before, oh and let me know if your place has free parking or if I'll need a permit. And don't toss your braids too much now – I know how heavy they can be. Save all of that for Friday. 😃

I smiled to myself and put my phone on charge. Friday was going to be fun.

The next day however, I couldn't get out of bed.

I'd woken up with the most excruciating stomach pain I'd ever encountered, as well as the overwhelming need to throw up. My alarm buzzed at 6.30 a.m., and as it continued to drill itself into my eardrums, I threw the phone across the room. As I tried to get myself out of bed, I suddenly felt the room spinning, and had to lie back down. Toby was in the corridor, crying for his food and my phone's alarm was still going off in the corner of my room. It was pure chaos this morning and I didn't understand what was happening.

I crawled off my bed, getting on my hands and knees as I slowly made my way towards my phone. After turning off the alarm, I crawled towards the bathroom, my eyes squinting in a bid to keep the room from eternally spinning. I finally reached the bathroom and that was almost like a signal for my stomach to expel whatever demons it had lying inside it – via both my upper and lower orifices.

I slowly clambered my way to the toilet bowl, and by this point I was sweating from every pore, horrified at this sudden and mysterious illness. As the remnants of last night's meal began to pour into the bowl, I tried to recall the events of yesterday; everything was pretty normal at work and I didn't believe I had come across anyone who had presented as ill? Everything seemed fine when I came home.

I'd spoken to Theo for a while, and had some leftovers . . .

Now that I'd come to think about it, the leftovers – which consisted of a piece of chicken breast, vegetables and some fried rice I'd cooked about three days ago – did have a little bit of a smell to them, but I'd ignored it. Did the food taste a little funny at the time of eating it? Sure, but I had put that down to me constantly reheating it in the microwave. I'd never had food poisoning before, so after flushing the toilet and crawling back on all fours to my bedroom (Toby would have to wait a few more moments for breakfast, I feared), I picked up my phone and texted Kofi:

> **Morning, Kofi, I'm so sorry to do this last minute, but I don't think I'll be able to come in today! I had some dodgy leftovers and I've woken up in absolute agony; I don't want to risk being ill and distracted at work. I'll log into work from home in the afternoon though so if you need anything, please just pop through an email xx**

After sending the text, I groaned and attempted to open my eyes fully. The room was still spinning and my guts were still on fire. With all the strength I could muster, I stood up and slowly shuffled to the kitchen to give Toby his food. Finding some paracetamol in the drawer, I knocked a couple of the pills back, filled my Stanley cup with water and went to lie down on the sofa in my living room. I needed this virus gone within the next twelve hours, PRONTO. Wasn't my body aware that it needed to prepare itself for Friday? I suddenly had a fleeting thought of me accidentally defecating on Theo's penis mid-stroke.

Absolutely fucking not. Desperate times called for desperate actions. And *Desperate Housewives*. The show had long been my 'sick day' guilty pleasure to watch whenever I was feeling under the weather, so gathering the little strength I had, I lined up a few episodes of the show for background noise, gathered my laptop and charging cable to the living room and opened up Deliveroo on my phone. I needed to force myself to be well before tomorrow night, by any means necessary. Using the grocery tab, I ordered myself a bottle of Pepto-Bismol and some Gaviscon tablets, three 1litre bottles of water, some peppermint tea, a packet of ginger biscuits and Jacob's crackers, a packet of mints and a loaf of sourdough bread.

Of course this happens to me – right before the most anticipated night of my life. Cancelling was simply out of the question too, I'd let too much excitement build over the last few days for me to back out now. After twenty minutes, my delivery arrived and I crawled my way to the intercom to let the delivery driver in. I was in absolute agony, still waiting for the paracetamol to kick in. The driver knocked on my door and I somehow gathered the strength to get on my feet to open it. The driver gave me a concerned look as he passed me the grocery bag – I was doubled over, with my hands on my knees, squinting up at him. I'm sure he thought I was in labour or something.

'You all right, love?' he muttered behind his balaclava. The concern in his voice was touching.

'Oh yeah, I'm OK, thanks!' I said back, trying to sound as chirpy and as upbeat as possible. It didn't work, however, and it came out as somewhat of a distressed groan. I took the bag from him and hastily closed the door, one hand cradling my aching belly and the other arm cradling the groceries. After making myself a cup of peppermint tea, I hotfooted it to the bathroom once again to relieve my poor bowels.

The rest of the morning was spent splayed out on the sofa with my laptop, periodically checking and responding to my work emails. Kofi texted me back:

Yeesh! Sorry to hear that, sis! Take all the time you need and I hope you feel better soon. It's mad quiet today anyway so I've got you covered xx

Sade following suit with a text a few minutes later:

My babes! I'm hearing you're unwell, what's up? Is there anything I can do??? Xxx

Word of my stomach upset had travelled fast it seemed. These two were moving like an old married couple already. I texted Sade back.

Rah. Kofi already told you, huh? You guys are getting very comfortable, innit? Love that for you both, and, no, I'm OK, thanks; I've got water and some dry food so I should be OK! Xxx

As much as I was ecstatic that Kofi and Sade were getting on like a house on fire, I couldn't help but feel light twinges of envy on my part. Kofi and Sade getting together just seemed too easy. But that was the amazing thing about Sade when it came to her dating life and relationships; she always seemed to come across the good guys. Her dating stories – whilst sometimes chaotic – always ended well. She was always able to find the good guys when dating in London. Meanwhile, I was out here paying for the privilege of being treated like a halfway decent human – totally of my own free will, obviously. Sade, in the meantime, could land a date or get laid without even trying. I swear, the woman made it look like a hobby. Love her always, but it was definitely something that bubbled to the forefront of my mind on occasion.

Halfway into season three of *Desperate Housewives*, I'd taken a nap and had awakened to find a flurry of messages from my brother. It wasn't like him to randomly text in the middle of the afternoon, so I knew it was something urgent.

> **Cass! Bianca's in labour we think. Are you at work? We're coming to St Tommy's.**
>
> **Please call or text when you're free. I'm panicking man. Mum and Dad aren't answering.**
>
> **We're at the hospital, sis. They are saying something about her birthing plug still being intact but she's in a lot of pain. Call when you're free.**

Oh shit; was I about to be an auntie? Bianca wasn't due for another couple of weeks, but I was in too much pain to even think about leaving the flat today. Equally, this would be a once-in-a-lifetime opportunity and I had to be there for my little brother. I suddenly felt a lurch in my stomach as the room spun, and threw up in the bucket I had sitting nearby. This was incredibly frustrating. It had been four hours and I'd given my body loads of water, medication and even a little nap. What more did it need??

After pulling myself together, I called my brother on FaceTime, silently praying that Bianca hadn't given birth yet. He answered on the first ring – God, I was grateful. I could hear the excitement in his voice, feel the weight of what this moment meant for him. He's wanted to be a father for as long as I can remember, and now, he was on the cusp of everything he'd dreamed of.

'Cass! Ahh, fucking hell, man, thanks for calling back – are you at work? We're in the hospital now – did you get my texts?' He was a bramble of nerves as he tripped over his sentences, frantic. I needed him to calm down.

'Bro? I need you to take a couple of deep breaths for me,

OK? Just follow me. Breathe in . . . and breathe out. Just like that. Do that for me a couple of times.'

Steven followed my guidance as he took a couple of deep breaths; his expression was slightly frantic, but overall he looked excited, making me feel a lot more at ease. 'Sorry, sis. I just didn't know what to do, Mum and Dad aren't picking up or anything. Are you – why are you wearing a bonnet at work?'

'Because I'm at home! You really think I'd wear a bonnet to work? I'm really sick at the moment so I'm not in today – is Bianca in labour? How is she??'

Steven panned his phone camera to a smiling-yet-still-heavily-pregnant Bianca, who was sitting on one of those exercise balls, rubbing her stomach and bouncing up and down.

'Hey Cassie! Girl, I'm still pregnant haha. The doctors said I have Braxton Hicks, which is what I said when we were at home, but your bro didn't wanna hear it!' Bianca looked radiant; her skin was glowing unlike anything I'd ever seen and she was wearing a beautiful white oversized maxi dress that showed off her perfectly round bump. She was going to be such a beautiful mother.

At that, Steven jumped in. 'Nah, I was just trying to be careful, innit? She woke me up this morning talking about contractions, and then—'

Bianca cut him off. 'Yeah, and *then* I told you the contractions and pain stopped after an hour! I said we didn't have to come all the way here – that it was probably just Braxton Hicks.'

Steven turned the camera back to himself with a look of exasperation. 'OK, but what do you expect me to do when you're yelling in pain, and then suddenly start going on about "Braxton this" and "Braxton that"? In my head, I'm thinking: what's Toni Braxton got to do with her going into labour?!'

At that, Bianca and I burst into fits of laughter. Men could be so clueless at these things.

'Bro? I actually CANNOT with you right now. What did the doctor say? Are they gonna observe her or what?' Steven panned the phone camera back to Bianca again, who answered.

'Yeah, basically. They said we can go home. I'm definitely not in labour and they had me bouncing on this ball to see if it would trigger any further contractions just to be on the safe side. I've been on this for an hour but nothing, so we're gonna get going in a second.'

Phew. Good to know they weren't in labour yet. That brief moment of chaos weirdly gave me a second wind – a little shot of adrenaline when I needed it most. After getting off the call with Steve, I took another dose of Pepto-Bismol and decided to walk around the flat a little to see if I could walk upright without my stomach doubling over in pain again. After a few laps around the living room and a quick cuddle with Toby – who was confused and almost resentful of my presence in the house due to him being so used to having the flat to himself during the day – I took another dose of Paracetamol and headed back to the sofa with the packet of Jacob's crackers. If I could keep a couple of the crackers down without throwing up, then it would be a sign that I was on the mend. I slightly chewed on the edges of a cracker as I scrolled through my Instagram feeds – it had been so long since I'd had a sick day that I almost didn't know what to do with myself outside of sleeping or watching TV. I needed to be productive in some way, shape or form, and rotting on the sofa all day just wasn't going to cut it for me.

I scrolled through my notifications to find a fresh onslaught of engagement from none other than Theo himself, with his last 'likes' being sent just over forty-five minutes ago. I'd wanted to believe that this was just an extra service he'd added on to the 'overnight stay' option perhaps; something to make his clients feel extra special. I logged into the *OuiMeet* app just to see if I'd missed any fine print or extra services, but I hadn't. All of his Instagram engagement was organic.

I couldn't quite work out what his game was, in all honesty. On one hand, he'd initiated a boundary with his clients regarding developing a relationship outside of the app but, on the other hand, he was getting pally with me for free on social media. I was definitely receiving mixed messages from him, and it was something I would potentially bring up on our date tomorrow evening – that and the '1996' at the end of his username. I was more inclined to believe at this point that he was twenty-nine years old instead of thirty-four. I also couldn't help thinking that him being younger than me was a slight *turn-on* for me. From my brief experiences being around him, he presented himself as quite a dominant man, but maybe that could all change tomorrow – especially with what happened in the back of the Uber the other day.

I opened my inbox to see a new message from him:

Hello beautiful lady. I hope you're having a wonderful day so far. :)

I was conflicted. On one hand, this was lovely, but on the other hand, I couldn't help but wonder how many other women he'd sent texts like this to. Was he 'dating' other women this week as we spoke? As much as I wanted to lean in to the prospect of developing some kind of whirlwind love affair, I couldn't allow myself to develop feelings for him, knowing that he was probably fucking other women at the same time. I'd decided that our relationship had to be purely transactional, for the sake of my mental health at this point.

I decided to play along and send a message back:

Hello to you too, somewhat-handsome gentleman. I've had better mornings, but I'm otherwise OK. Looking forward to tomorrow. I hope you're well too, and I hope you don't charge these interactions to my card btw. ;)

The 'read' notification text appeared instantly. Almost as if Theo had been waiting on tenterhooks for me to respond. I could almost bet that he wouldn't have been so forthcoming with his texts if he could see me now; shitting and puking up a storm. I decided to withhold my current health status in case he decided to postpone. I read his reply:

I'm sorry to hear you aren't having the best morning and I hope this improves throughout the day. Hopefully we can have some good fun tomorrow that'll counterbalance today. Haha, no, these messages are free of charge, just wanted to check in and see how you're doing. :)

He was adorable. I closed the app, downed almost half a litre of water and tried to get in a bit of a nap to expedite the healing process. I'd never had food poisoning before, but from what I'd read online, it seemed to be one of those twenty-four bugs that could pass even sooner provided you got adequate rest and hydration.

Over the course of the next few hours, I slipped in and out of sleep, feeling slightly more energised every time I'd wake up, which was a great sign. I watched a bit more TV and after being able to muster a bit more strength, did a bit more work on my laptop, which mostly consisted of me forwarding any 'big' emails to Kofi and apologising profusely while he kept emailing me back, telling me to rest.

Around 2 p.m., I received an email from Jeff, who I hadn't seen or spoken to in a little while. Thinking it was a meeting or appointment that needed rearranging, I opened the email, to be met with the following:

Subject: Wishing You a Speedy Recovery

Dear Cassandra,

I hope this message finds you well. Kofi informed me today that you're currently on sick leave due to food poisoning, and I just wanted to check in to see how you're feeling and whether there's anything we can do to support you.

Please don't worry about today's itinerary – Kofi has everything well under control.

Wishing you a swift and smooth recovery.

Best regards,

Jeff

I couldn't quite tell if Jeff's message came from his 'Type A' personality – always diligent and attentive – or if it was a genuine act of kindness. Maybe it was both. Still, I couldn't shake the uneasy feeling it left me with. Did he send thoughtful emails like that to everyone who called in sick . . . or was there something different about the way he treated me? Especially considering *that* night during the staff drinks.

Sighing, I sent a quick email back, trying to sound as professional as possible:

Dear Jeff,

Thank you so much for your kind message – I really appreciate you checking in. I'm on the mend and hoping to feel back to normal soon.

It's reassuring to know that everything is under control with today's itinerary. Please extend my thanks to Kofi as well for stepping in.

Looking forward to getting back to work once I'm fully recovered.

Warm regards,

Cassandra

I hit 'send' and stared at my screen, confused. Was I just looking too deeply into it? Jeff was a nice guy – maybe I was the one who'd been acting strangely around him. Perhaps I'd been reading too much into the lingering glances and the quiet tension in the elevator, mistaking them for something they weren't. In any instance, I decided to cross that bridge when I got to it.

After deciding that was enough laptop screen time for the day, I ran a bubble bath, hoping that could, in turn, help heal my body. I even threw in some magnesium flakes for good measure. I sank into the tub, letting the steaming, fragrant water envelop me, soothing and relaxing my aching muscles. I closed my eyes and lay completely still for a few moments. It had been quite a while since I'd been able to take time for myself and practice a bit of wellness, so I wanted to drag it out for as long as I could. With my phone on the side of the bath, I lined up the most recent episode of *The Jungle Diaries* to see what drama Simi P had cooking up this week, knowing that for the first time, I wouldn't be able to relate:

'What's up, guys? It's your girl, Simi P, back again this week with The Jungle Diaries *podcast, where we talk about the harsh realities of trying to survive what I like to call "The Dating Jungle", because it really is a jungle out here, guys! This week I wanna talk about dating scammers, trappers and drug dealers. I'm seeing so many babes on Instagram living their best lives online with the blurred-out faces of their men who are so obviously criminals, but what I wanna know is, is the glam and glitz of that lifestyle worth the stress of potentially going to prison? In this day and age, why are so many of us lowering our standards for these temporary lifestyle changes? Just so you can stunt on the gram? I'm gonna talk more about that, and then we'll get into our listener letters later!'*

I agreed with Simi in that it felt as if so many women my age were constantly lowering their standards for financial and aesthetic reasons. With the economy in shambles and the cost of living climbing like it's trying to win an Olympic medal, I couldn't really blame those women. The dating scene was a mess, and good men? Practically an endangered species. Honestly, I had to respect the hustle – some of us decided to stop waiting around for Prince Charming and go out and snatch what we wanted, even if it meant tossing the rulebook out the window and setting it on fire.

Chapter 13

'Sorry, love, what was that? Diarrhoea? How long have you had the diarrhoea for?'

I squirmed in utter embarrassment over the pharmacist's repeated loud use of the word 'diarrhoea' for everyone in the hospital pharmacy queue to hear. It seemed as if my sickness had broken overnight and I'd woken up that morning feeling ten times better than the previous day. Aside from a slight headache and a slightly runny stomach, I felt back to normal.

'Sorry, could you lower your voice please?' I said in hushed tones, as if I were an undercover police officer trying to score some heroin off the street. 'I've had it for about fifteen hours or so, and it's slowly going, but I just need something to help with the symptoms for a couple of hours.'

The pharmacist – who clearly paid no attention to my pleas of discretion – continued. 'OK. Well, we've got Imodium – that really helps with a running stomach – but it depends on which one you want. We've got Imodium classic, Imodium Dual Action or Imodium Instant Melts if you're looking for something on the go.'

'I'd go for the Dual Action if I were you, love.' I turned around to see an old woman behind me, smiling up at me warmly. This morning truly couldn't get any worse. 'The Dual

Action treats wind and cramps too; may as well get two for the price of one, I say!'

'Thanks so much,' I muttered darkly, wishing the ground would swallow me up. After purchasing the medicine, I hot-footed it to the staff elevator entrance corridor and made my way up to my floor, missing my daily cappuccino ritual. Today was not a day to be playing around with dairy, of all things. I had my date with Theo tonight, and I absolutely had to make sure that everything went according to plan, right down to my plumbing downstairs. If it meant having to plug my bumhole with cotton wool for the night to prevent any accidental leakages, then so be it.

I'd arrived at work a full thirty minutes ahead of schedule, giving me time to log in to the computer and swiftly knock back a couple of the Imodium double-strength pills. I prayed they would start working immediately; everything would be counting on how the next few hours would go. Luckily, my work inbox was looking a little thin on the ground, meaning there wasn't that much for me to catch up on outside of arranging the new patient appointments and scheduling the pre-operative assessments, which would probably take no longer than a couple of hours.

Just as I was starting to get into the swing of things, a gentle knock at the door pulled me from my focus. I turned to find Jeff standing in the doorway, a faint smirk playing on his lips. He wore a grey houndstooth tweed suit – something that seemed far more fitting for a day at Cheltenham races or a wedding than a shift at the hospital, but he looked great nonetheless.

'Hey, Cassandra!' he said brightly, entering the room and sitting in Kofi's seat to face me. 'Good to see you back in the office – how are you feeling?'

I'd never had anyone at work, bar Kofi, be so invested in my health and wellbeing before. I would almost be touched if I didn't find the situation slightly weird. But again, maybe *I* was being the weird one and making our whole interactions weird thus far. At that moment I decided to just give Jeff the benefit of the doubt and talk to him like a normal human being.

'Thanks so much, Mr Paulson, I feel a lot better. I think it was one of those twenty-four-hour bug things where I'd eaten some bad food. But I'm all good now – I'm just lining up your post-op appointments as we speak actually, so if there are any more patients you want to add on, you can email them to me throughout the day.'

Jeff continuously stared at my lips as I spoke, which threw me off. But, I had to tell myself that I was probably reading too much into it. Maybe that's just how he looked at people. He was a surgeon, for God's sake – surgeons had the reputation of being precise and meticulous. Maybe that was just his thing.

As I finished speaking, he wiped his glasses on his blazer and blinked rapidly. Now I don't know why this slightly turned me on, but it did. He was so suave with his movements and body language and, in that split second, I found myself imagining him as my plus one for Mum's wedding. He would make a great plus one, to be fair: he was tall, refined, handsome, and most importantly, he was a surgeon. I could already see him fitting in with my family.

His reply snapped me out of my very brief daydream as he put his glasses back on and looked up at me once again. 'I'm glad to hear you're feeling better, but if you do feel ill at any point in the day please do feel free to leave early – food poisoning can sometimes leave people feeling very weak for a while and you'll need all the rest and hydration to make a full recovery, OK? Hopefully your partner is taking good care of you, at least.'

Although grateful for his concern, I was probably going to

take him up on that offer in order to have a couple more hours to prepare for Theo tonight. I'd decided to order us a takeaway instead of stressing myself out by trying to cook something over the top and impressive. That way, I could spend the time I would have used cooking to clean up the flat a little, take an 'everything' shower, and beautify myself even more.

'My partner – yes. Yes, he's . . . been very supportive, thanks!' I said, trying to not let the panic reach my eyes. I'd completely forgotten I'd told him a fake story about having a boyfriend. 'Thank you so much, Mr Paulson, I—' Jeff held up his hand to silence me and said:

'It's Jeff, please.'

'Jeff, please . . .' I repeated, smiling up at him. 'Sorry, yes, I'm . . . I appreciate you checking up on me, thank you so much. I'm sorry we haven't crossed paths lately by the way, I know you've been away for a bit so when you're available at some point within the next week, it would be great to pencil in a quick catch-up meeting between us, if that's OK with you?'

It was nearly impossible to have a conversation with Jeff, his gaze fixed on my lips with an intensity that felt almost hungry. For a moment, I couldn't shake the feeling that I was the star of his favourite TV show, with him watching me as though I were performing for him. This whole exchange was filled with an unmistakable air of tension that I think we both felt. Before Jeff had time to respond, Kofi walked in at that very moment, rucksack swinging to and fro. He stopped dead in his tracks upon seeing Jeff in his seat, looking from Jeff to myself, his face full of concern.

'Morning, Mr Paulson, hey Cassie – um, is everything OK? How are you feeling?' he asked finally, as he patiently waited by the photocopier for his seat back. This was so awkward. Jeff – finally realising that he'd been sitting in Kofi's seat, awkwardly got up and began to slowly back out of the room, slightly tripping over a stack of files as he did so. It took everything in me not to laugh.

'Yeah, Kof, I'm good! I was just asking Mr Paul – Jeff – if we could arrange some time over the next week for a quick catch-up over his schedule, is all!' I came across way too excitable, which Kofi might've taken as me being awkward and uncomfortable – and, to be fair, I was.

'Right . . . right,' came from Jeff eventually, bordering the door frame now. He puffed himself up to his full height like a rooster about to challenge Kofi to a duel – minus the feathers, unfortunately. It was a weird sight and again, I had to cough to conceal my laughter.

'Yes, Cassandra, we should get a date in the diary to go over some things. Check and see when I'm next free and you can book it for then – thank you so much.' With that, he turned on his heel and left the office.

Kofi stared at me, baffled, before taking his seat. 'What the hell just happened there, bruv? That was so awkward, man. Did he say something to you again?'

I shook my head as I went back to scheduling appointments. 'Nah, he just wanted to see if I was feeling better and then I mentioned us having a quick meeting over his patients – and that's when you came in.'

'I see. He's a bit of a weird one, that one. Anyway, how are you feeling, love? If you need to dip out early at any point, let me know, OK?' Kofi was being extra nice today; he seemed to be in a good mood. I wondered why.

'Thanks so much. I'm feeling much better and I've taken some meds this morning but I'll let you know if I take a turn. Anyway, how have you been? Got any weekend plans?'

Kofi spun around like he'd been *dying* for me to ask what he'd been up to. A grin lit up his face, stretching wide until it turned into a full-on, all-teeth smile. I could already tell what he was about to say, and honestly, I was delighted for them both.

'I'm seeing Sade this weekend; she's actually staying over at mine tomorrow so we're just gonna chill and stuff. It should be good,' he said, now switching his demeanour to sound a little suave.

'Oh, you guys are into each other DEEP, huh? To be honest, I can tell she really likes you because she's been a little quiet on me lately. She's normally like that when she's into someone heavy; tunnel vision and all that. I'm loving this for you both!'

Kofi smiled again, his mouth spreading to the far corners of his face. You could tell that he was absolutely besotted with Sade, and to know that I had played a part in their impending love story/future marriage filled me with so much joy.

'I can't lie, Cassie, I feel like she may be the one. She's just . . . she just has such a beautiful soul, you know? We talk and text literally every day and she's just this radiant light that fills me with – well – I don't know what it is, but I've never met anyone quite like her . . . she's amazing, so thank you.'

Hearing Kofi talk like that about my best friend nearly reduced me to tears. Sade deserved all the amazing things coming her way and I was glad that they were getting on well. Now if only I could get someone to talk about me the way Kofi talked about Sade, I'd be set.

'You're welcome; you guys deserve each other, you're brilliant people,' I said, turning back to work. I'd decided to play up my upset stomach throughout the day and leave at 3.30 p.m., giving me plenty of time to get ready for tonight.

At lunch I decided to send Theo a text through the *OuiMeet* app instead of through Instagram this time. As endearing as our informal chats were, due to his boundaries I wanted to try and keep things as professional as possible. The last thing I wanted was to fall for him completely, only for him to keep me at bay. Being rejected by a sex worker was not something I ever wanted inscribed on my epitaph.

Hey Theo, hope you're well. I'm looking forward to tonight. :)

Just something plain and simple. Nothing too flirty for now. I'd be saving that for that evening.

'Ooh . . . d'you know what? I think I may take off a bit early, if that's OK, Kofi? My stomach's been cramping up all afternoon. I've been taking painkillers and trying to ignore it, but it doesn't seem to be going away – I'm so sorry.' I exaggerated the dramatic arch of my 'aching' back, really laying it on thick. It had finally hit 3.30 p.m. and I'd already wrapped up everything I needed to do – including setting up a quick meeting with Jeff next week. Honestly, the anticipation for tonight was getting unbearable; I was buzzing to just buckle down and start getting ready. Besides, thanks to staying on top of my meds, I was actually feeling *way* better. Not that Kofi needed to know that just yet.

'Aww sis. To be honest, you shouldn't have even come in! I didn't wanna say it earlier but you don't look one hundred per cent,' Kofi replied, looking concerned. Oh great. I quickly scanned my face in the nearby mirror – I didn't look that bad, did I? I made a show of doubling over in my seat, adding a bit of a wince of pain for dramatic effect. Kofi leaned over to see if I was OK, to which I replied I was. After switching off my monitor, I bade him farewell and to have a great weekend, before slowly 'hobbling' out of the office, semi-crouched over. All I needed to do was to keep up the ruse until I hit the elevator, and then—

'Oh, hey!' I heard a man's voice to the left of me, booming down the corridor. It was Jeff again, mug of coffee in hand as he walked in my direction. I wondered if he showed any of the other members of staff this much attention? I was still trying to figure out whether I should have been bothered or flattered by his interest in me, but now wasn't the time to figure that all out. I just wanted to leave as soon as possible.

'Oh! Hey . . . hey, Jeff, how are you? Is there something you need? I was just about to head home early for the afternoon – the stomach bug is still bugging unfortunately.' I chuckled meekly as I rubbed my belly, pretending to wince at its touch.

Jeff genuinely looked concerned as he followed my hands to where I'd perched them on my tummy.

'Oh, that's awful, I'm sorry to hear that! Wait here a second, will you? Let me just put the mug in the staffroom quickly—' he lightly jogged over to the staffroom at the opposite end of the corridor, leaving me standing near the elevator, confused. After a moment, he trotted back, seemingly out of breath.

'I think it's good you get yourself some rest. I was gonna say, um—' Jeff pressed the 'down' button for the elevator as we both waited awkwardly together. 'I'm actually heading out for a meeting at a spine clinic in Fulham. I remember you saying that you lived in Vauxhall or Nine Elms or something? It's on my way to the clinic, I'd be more than happy to drop you home. It'll save you having to wait for the bus or walk too far.'

Right on cue, the elevator arrived – and out poured a small army of no less than twelve or so people. The chaos bought me a few precious seconds to think. Was Jeff overstepping by offering me a ride home? Would *I* be crossing a line by saying yes? Or was this just peak Nice Guy™ behaviour? Did he have an agenda? And more importantly – did I really want him knowing where I lived before I even knew his coffee order? I had about ten seconds to decide, because the elevator had emptied and was now staring us down like, 'Well? You in or what?'

We both stepped into the elevator and as it closed, I replied:

'Um, yeah . . . sure! As long as it isn't out of the way or anything. That's very kind of you, Jeff, thank you.'

'The pleasure's all mine,' he replied chirpily. Maybe he was just being a nice colleague after all. We walked in silence to the staff car park and to his car: a dark-green Range Rover. Nothing fancy, then. Jeff opened my door before going round to his, and after giving him my postcode, we set off home, with me mostly sitting in silence as Jeff talked about his upcoming meeting at the spine clinic. So far, so innocent.

'I've been working with that clinic for the last three years,' he told me, 'and I find it so frustrating how they always seem to deliver biopsies and frozen sections late. It's absolutely unacceptable, so I think this meeting with the clinic manager and the owner should hopefully change things, but to be honest if it doesn't, I may have a chat with you during our meeting next week about potentially doing research to find a list of new spine clinics with their own labs in London, if that's OK?'

'Yep, that's totally fine. I'll remember to make a note of it, thanks,' I said, distracted by the utter cleanliness and organisation of his dashboard. He had a bobble-head Jesus figurine centred on the cream-coloured dash, with a compartment above the gear stick that included a spare iPhone charger, a packet of chewing gum, hand sanitiser, lip balm (Tatcha lip balm, nonetheless!) and a small tube of Rituals hand lotion. In the air-conditioning tab he also had a Rituals car perfume stick. A woman's touch, perhaps? Although I didn't want to assume. I couldn't see any evidence of children in the car – no loose crayons, empty juice cartons or games consoles to be found. I wondered if he did have a family and, if so, what they were like.

No, Cassandra. That wasn't the aim here. The aim was to get home and get yourself slut-ready for the handsome man due at your place this evening. I had all week to think about Jeff's private life.

A few minutes later we arrived at my flat. As Jeff parked outside and switched the ignition off, he turned to face me, his eyes boring into mine. *Weird*. I suddenly felt anxious; what was going on?

'I really do hope you feel better, Cassandra; you're a highly valued member of the team,' he said, his eyes lowering to my lips as he spoke, which put me even more on edge. You could have cut the tension in the car with a knife, and all I wanted was to run up into my flat.

'Ahh well, thanks so much – Jeff. That means a lot. I'm sure I'll be fine once I've had some rest,' I replied, forcing a small smile. My hand headed towards the door handle – then froze. A weight settled on my shoulder. I turned around, startled to find Jeff leaning towards me; his face suddenly far too close and his hand now softly squeezing my shoulder. My stomach dropped and ice shot through my spine. What the hell?

'Umm, sorry but what do you think you're doing?' I replied, horrified and mentally making a note to report to HR as soon as possible. This was NOT OK.

'Oh, I'm, I'm sorry I . . . maybe I mistook the signs. I thought—' Jeff jerked back as if burned. His words tumbled over themselves as he scrambled back in his seat, the colour draining from his face.

He looked genuinely mortified; as he should. I couldn't believe this had happened.

'Signs? Signs where?' I stuttered, trying to control my emotions. I didn't really know how to react; all I wanted was to be at home. I continued, 'I'm sorry if you got the wrong impression, Mr Paulson, but I was under the impression that our relationship was purely professional. I would like to keep it that way,' I said, gathering all the maturity and professionalism I had in my arsenal as I turned towards the door and slowly let myself out.

'No, yes of course. That was inappropriate of me, Cassandra. I'm sorry, I . . . yeah. I hope you feel better soon,' he said, his voice shaking. I'd barely slammed the car door shut before he tore off, tyres screeching as he fled the scene.

I ran into my flat, feeling more annoyed than anything. I didn't believe that I'd given off any vibes of liking him and, if so, why would he even think to act on it on company time? Work was going to be incredibly awkward; I pondered whether to seriously approach it with HR. He hadn't hurt or abused me in any way, and I suppose it was just crossed wires as he said, but still . . .

I felt awkward, and weird. Weird because in the back of my head I wondered if I weren't so emotionally invested in Theo, would I have stayed in Jeff's car? And if so, would I have wanted anything to happen? Also, was I unknowingly giving off signs that I'd wanted anything to happen between us? I didn't think so? Sure, he was nice to look at, but that was as far as it went. What an odd thing for him to do.

Hmm. Questions that needed answers.

I didn't have the time to contemplate what had just happened. I needed to compartmentalise the interaction for now – just for tonight, while I dealt with my upcoming date; I would cross that Jeff-sized bridge tomorrow.

After making sure Toby was watered, played with, cuddled and fed, I sent Sade a quick text, briefly letting her know about tonight's date for security reasons. Theo was a lovely guy, but so was Ted Bundy, and as a single woman living alone, you could never be too careful.

> **Hey sis! I hope you're having a great day. FYI; Jericho/Theo coming round to mine tonight for the first time. Letting you know for security reasons. If I end up missing, make sure the news use that pic of me when I had the red curly hair at your birthday party last year, that's a cute one xxx**

Tonight definitely called for an 'everything' shower – the kind that felt like a full reset. Although Jeff didn't actually kiss me, I still felt as if I needed to wash away his aura – his essence, so to speak – and feel brand new. For me, that meant co-washing my braids, doing a full-body shave – paying particular attention to my nether regions – indulging in a deep scrub, a thorough wash, layering on an in-shower body oil, and topping it all off with a face mask. By the time I stepped out, I was glistening and slippery, feeling like a dolphin. I then reached for my shea butter moisturiser and lathered my body in it, before going over everything with a cocoa butter body oil to seal in the moisture.

I still had three-and-a-bit-hours before Theo's arrival, so I decided to use the time to pick out what I was going to wear. If all things went well tonight, I'd already decided on a burgundy mini chemise that I'd picked up from Ann Summers a few years ago. It still had a good amount of mileage left, and made my boobs look amazing. I'd wear that with my dressing robe on top to lounge in afterwards.

For my main outfit, I needed something that didn't come off as too 'try-hard', yet I didn't want it to be super casual and basic either.

After rooting around for twenty minutes, I finally decided on wearing an Elomi push-up bra underneath a plain white fitted cropped tee. I paired the tee with a patterned silk maxi skirt from Whistles – also known as my 'good luck' skirt. Somehow, every time I wore it, something good seemed to happen. I was wearing it the day I got a pay rise at work. The second time, I had two unexpectedly great dates . . . with two different guys. And the third? During a hospital strike, I ended up with an unexpected three days off. Coincidence? Maybe. But I wasn't taking any chances.

I gave everything a good iron and laid the outfit out on the bed like a proud stylist prepping for a red carpet moment. I also decided to take another swig of Gaviscon, just to be safe. My stomach had mostly chilled out, but I wasn't about to let indigestion crash the party. Not tonight.

I went out into the living room and gave it a last-minute clean, and popped a bottle of Whispering Angel I'd been given a few months ago into the fridge to chill. Fast forward the next couple of hours and the dishes were washed, a plethora of scented candles had been lit, my bedding had been changed and Toby's cat hair had been meticulously scraped off the sofa. I'd changed into my outfit and, by my own standards, I looked *fucking* hot – if I did say so myself. I had that effortless, cool-girl energy going on, with just the right touch of sex appeal thanks to the push-up bra and the way the fitted tee hugged my curves, cinching in at the waist and giving my hips that extra hourglass drama. I loved to see it, and I hoped that Theo would too. It was twenty-or-so minutes until I was due to expect him, so after a healthy spritz of my evening fragrance (Cairo by Penhaligons, if you were wondering), I sat down on the sofa and tried to relax myself. I hadn't had sex in nearly six months; I was practically a virgin again. If the worst came to the worst, Theo could always take the lead anyway. I checked my phone for any last-minute updates; Sade had eventually texted back:

> **OOOWEEEE I know that's right! Wishing you the best of luck tonight, sis – we will debrief in the morning and, yes, I agree the red hair pic is v nice. Will keep in mind if you get murdered or anything xx**

Theo had also sent me a message; this time on Instagram:

> **Looking forward to seeing your gorgeous self soon, lady. I'm on my way. Anything I can pick up along the way? :)**

I smiled as I read his message; he was too sweet. I texted back:

Looking forward to seeing you too! And the only thing you'll need to bring tonight is your A-game. Can't wait for all the board games we'll play tonight xx

I gave myself one final glance-over in the mirror and a final spritz of perfume before surveying the living room to make sure everything was in order. As I exhaled, a bubbling of nerves began to fill my stomach. Or was that just my upset stomach playing up? At this point, I couldn't tell and was hoping that it was indeed just nerves, but decided to swig a quick dose of some Pepto-Bismol I had in my kitchen cupboard, just to be on the safe side. At the end of the day, Theo was here for me, not the other way round – HE should be the nervous one. I glanced at myself one final time in the mirror, mouthing affirmations in a bid to hype myself up.

'You've got this, Cass.'

'You're in control. Always in control.'

'You're a beautiful, confident, hot piece of ass. He's lucky to be spending time with you.'

I needed to stay in control. I wanted Theo to see me as some untouchable sex goddess about to lead him straight into Wonderland. Part of me even toyed with the idea of slipping fully into character – seductress extraordinaire, dripping with confidence, all velvet and mystery. Really, it was just smoke and mirrors, a performance to distract from the inconvenient truth: inside I was absolutely shitting a brick. Thankfully, only metaphorically.

As I stared at myself in the mirror, it hit me – I'd completely forgotten to use my trusty fanny wipes. Not exactly dermatologist-approved for daily use, sure, but they're absolute lifesavers on those spontaneous shag nights. You know, when there's a chance someone might go spelunking in the southern hemisphere and you want things to feel a bit more 'spring meadow' and a bit less 'forgotten laundry hamper'. I raced to the bathroom and took care of business using the wipes – splashing it with a bit of water beforehand to get rid of the harsh fragrance of the wipes; there was smelling neutral and then smelling like a 'tropical paradise', whatever that was supposed to mean.

No sooner had I cleaned up than I heard my intercom ring – Theo was early – ten minutes early, to be exact. *Just treat it like a normal sleepover with a friend*, I mentally told myself on the way to the intercom. Except I would probably be smashing my 'friend' to smithereens by the end of the night. Go figure.

I looked at the video screen attached to the intercom. Theo was standing there, looking directly into the camera wearing a slight smug smile on his face. His arms appeared to be full with a few things. Toys, perhaps? Tools? No, no, I couldn't let my mind go there – not just yet.

'Hello?' I answered, picking up the receiver and attempting to sound as husky and as sexy as possible. 'Who is this?'

Theo smiled more broadly into the camera this time, his dark eyes twinkling through the grainy video footage. 'It's the best thing that's ever happened to you – and I brought snacks,' he replied, laughing.

I buzzed him up and did a final once-over of the living room. I'd brought an extra blanket out and had arranged it nonchalantly on the sofa like I'd seen on all those hygge interior Instagram accounts. The flat smelled warm, sweet and earthy due to the candles, and I'd put on Clairo's lo-fi *Charm* album to set the mood. I was ready.

A moment later and there's a knock at the door. I opened it to find Theo, all six-foot-and-a-bit inches of him, taking up the entire frame of my doorway, both in height and width. 'Hey there,' he said in his deep voice that made my insides quiver. He knew exactly what he was doing. In his hands were a bouquet of hydrangeas – which were actually my favourite flowers – alongside a Marks & Spencer Food carrier bag.

'Please, come in,' I replied, trying to stop my voice from quivering as I posed awkwardly on the door frame. I wanted to jump his bones there and then but the night was young; we had all night, after all.

'Thanks. You look gorgeous, if you don't mind me saying. These are for you—' he presented me with the bouquet '—and these are just a few things I picked up to snack on just in case.'

I set the flowers on the counter, my fingers lingering on the stems as I stared at them, unexpectedly moved. I couldn't remember the last time a man had given me flowers – let alone ones that felt like they *meant* something. The gesture tugged at something in me, something I thought I'd tucked away. But even as my heart fluttered, a voice in the back of my mind whispered a quiet reminder: this was probably just part of the service. A carefully crafted charm. Nothing personal . . : or at least, it wasn't supposed to be.

'Thank you, Theo, that's really kind of you to say, and I love how you've gone all out with Marks and Sparks too! You're determined to show off tonight, huh?'

Theo took off the backpack he was wearing, staring at me the whole time he did this, as if toying with his food before devouring it. 'In more ways than one, if I play my cards right,' he answered. After laying out the spread of snacks he'd bought on the coffee table – croissants, chocolate chip cookies, mango bites, Percy Pigs and a couple of fruit juices – I decided to show him around the place. I made sure to give it my best Beyoncé saunter as I strutted around the flat, twisting my hips to and fro to accentuate my curves. *Remember, you're in control, always.*

'OK, so obviously this is the living room,' I started, entering tour guide mode, again trying to keep my voice steady, rocking my hips as I walked alongside him. His gaze – his intimidating, sexy, steady gaze – threw me off-guard every time. 'This is where I spend most of my time when I'm not out being a social butterfly and stuff.'

'Mmmhmm. I like what you've done with the place – nice decor.' He playfully stroked his chin as if admiring a Banksy painting.

'And if you follow me and look down to your right, you'll see the bathroom. For all your peeing and shitting needs,' I added, as he broke out in a chuckle.

'On your left, you'll see a storage cupboard. It contains suitcases, ironing boards, irons, a washing machine and other home admin and cleaning supplies, and just far ahead . . .' I trailed off as we reached my bedroom at the far end of the corridor. I took a deep breath as Theo began to rub his hands together in mock anticipation. 'We have my bedroom. This is where absolutely no magic happens, I fear.' I slowly opened the door and guided him inside where Toby – who had been sleeping soundly on my bed – woke up, stretched and hopped off the bed to rub himself against Theo's leg.

'Ah. And this is the man of the house, Toby! Apologies for him, he's just sussing you out, you know . . . making sure you're kosher and all that.' Theo bent over, picked Toby up and whisked him into the air, making cooing noises as he did so. 'Ahh! I love cats so much, I grew up with a couple! He is a very distinguished gentleman, isn't he?' He set Toby back down and gently stroked him behind the ears. Much to my delight, Toby purred and gently butted his head against Theo's leg, essentially giving his seal of approval.

'He likes you! That's a first,' I said, as Theo watched Toby hop onto the end of my bed and curl back to sleep. 'Let's go back to the living room, shall we? I'm a little thirsty.'

'Of course. You have a cute place, by the way – I dig it. It's . . . it's earthy,' replied Theo, still looking at the artwork on my walls as I led him down the corridor and back into the living room. After pouring us both a glass of Whispering Angel, I joined him on the sofa and clinked our glasses before taking a sip. Upon that first sip, I felt my entire body relax, and could tell that Theo's did too. He leaned back into the sofa, exhaling as he did so.

'Um, did you hurt yourself earlier, by the way? You were walking a little funny. Are you in pain?' Theo said, taking a sip of his glass, his eyes full of concern.

Panic hit me like a rogue brick. *Oh no. My sultry 'I'm-a-sexy-goddess' strut? More like 'I just rolled out of bed with arthritis.'*

'What? Oh, no!' I stammered, waving my hands almost erratically. I could feel myself beginning to panic already out of sheer embarrassment. 'I was . . . haha . . . no, I was . . . it's just how I walk when I'm at home.' I mumbled the last bit like a guilty confession and downed a long gulp of wine to wash away the embarrassment. Mortified didn't even begin to cover it. He probably thought I was a total nutcase.

Theo waved a hand, a small grin tugging at his lips. 'Heh – I see. I didn't mind the walk at all – it was . . . kind of charming.' I felt the tension drain out of me in a slow, satisfying whoosh. A sigh escaped me before I even realised I'd been holding my breath. *OK, Cassie,* I mentally told myself, *relax. Be normal. Maybe you don't need to be some walking, talking sex goddess 24/7. Just . . . exist. Smile. Don't trip over your own feet. Sip your wine like a semi-competent human.*

For the first time in what felt like hours, I let myself genuinely smile, letting the nerves loosen just enough to remember that Theo was, thankfully, more human than I'd feared. Maybe I could just be myself.

'So. How has your week been? What have you been up to, outside of talking to me?' Theo asked, thankfully changing the subject, taking another sip. I'd noticed that he'd put his phone on 'Do Not Disturb' and laid it face-down on the table. I loved that for me; I'd be getting all of his attention tonight.

'Work's been cool, thanks. Just your run-of-the-mill operation; booking appointments, having meetings with doctors, that kind of thing,' I replied, wanting to change the subject swiftly as the image of me alone with Jeff in his car popped up in my head. Definitely didn't need to be thinking about him right now.

'Nice! I'm glad to hear you're not totally run off your feet,' he said with a smile. 'So . . . did you have anything in mind for how you wanted tonight to go?'

As he said this, he moved closer to me on the sofa, his cologne wrapping around me in warm notes of amber, sandalwood and oud. The top two buttons of his shirt were undone, offering a teasing glimpse of his sculpted chest. I nearly drooled; I felt completely under his spell and wanted nothing more than to lean in for a kiss, but – the night was young.

'Well, I figured we could talk a bit more, I'd then order us something to eat and then . . . we could play games,' I said coyly, taking a sip from my wine glass while staring at him seductively.

'Games, huh? I see. I'm always up for that,' he replied. After we'd downed our drinks, we quickly discussed dinner options and settled on me ordering in some Japanese food – the last thing I needed was anything that would have been too aggressive on my stomach.

As we waited for the food to arrive, we spent the time getting into some wholesome chatter to pass the time. I talked a little about Sade and how I'd set her up with Kofi at work. I shared a bit about my family too – my mum's upcoming wedding, and how my brother was preparing to become a dad. There was something comforting about it, being able to open up like that. I didn't usually share much outside of my close circle, and honestly, aside from Sade, there weren't many people I talked to on that kind of level. But with Theo, it felt natural.

Safe, even. As I spoke, he listened intently, cocking his head to the side, his gaze unflinching. Every now and again he'd slowly look me up and down and give a little smile, as if surveying me. If it had been anyone else I would have called them out for objectifying me, but with Theo? It was hot. I moved closer to him, mirroring his gaze.

'Enough about me, I actually had a question for you – something I've been curious about ever since you started following me on Instagram.' I straightened up, suddenly remembering the question I'd wanted to ask.

'Oh? Shoot for it,' he said.

'Um, so your username has 1996 at the end of it. Is that your birth year?'

If Theo was in any way taken aback, he didn't show it. He continued staring at me, his smile fixed and unchanging. I noticed his jaws clench slightly as he continued to sit there in silence, completely still. He then started blinking rapidly, before finally facing away and exhaling.

So he *had* lied about his age.

'So . . . are you really twenty-eight or not?' I said eventually, breaking the awkward silence. I hadn't really made up my mind about whether I should have been annoyed about it or not. Sure, he wasn't a child, but a six-year age gap wasn't exactly tiny. I didn't want to feel like I was grooming the guy.

Theo shifted in his seat slightly as he exhaled. His gaze broke away from mine as he sat his wine glass down and again turned towards me. This was all a little bit dramatic, to be honest. It didn't need to be that much of a big deal.

'I'm sorry, Cassie. I'm twenty-eight, yeah. I'm sorry for lying to you. I put thirty-four on my *OuiMeet* profile to try and show up more on the results page for prospective clients I suppose. You'd be surprised, us young ones aren't really all that popular on the app. The clients sometimes consider us "inexperienced" for some reason.' He scoffed at that last part, and to be honest, his reasoning made sense; it was a strategic business decision, more or less. No wonder he looked so bloody young.

'I'm not necessarily upset per se, I can definitely understand the reasoning, I guess. It's just a bit weird now because you're essentially a *child*. Also, were you ever going to tell me?'

Theo let out a low, melodic laugh that echoed through the living room, rich and contagious. I couldn't help but laugh along with him.

'Cassandra, up until you discovered my age, have I given you any reason to feel awkward or weird around me? Have I been giving off "childlike" vibes to you? And yes, I had planned to tell you at some point.'

I shifted in my seat, maintaining my eye contact with him. 'I suppose you haven't given me a reason to feel weird around you, no. Still though, I'd consider it something important to disclose, you know.'

'I hear you,' Theo said quietly, his head flopping down as if he were a cute dog who had just been punished. 'Again, I'm really sorry for not saying anything. I guess some women find it empowering too, you know – the whole "younger guy" thing. Sometimes I play up to it if that's what a client wants but, for the most part, I think I'm quite mature for my age. I handle myself like a grown man, and that's all that matters.'

Whew. The authority in his voice when he said that made me shiver with pure lust. 'OK, so since you're bringing up other women while on the clock with me—' I teased, edging even closer to him '—let's talk about that some more. When did you start using *OuiMeet* and would you say – I mean – how many "clients" would you say you see per week or per month? Do you have any favourites?'

I could see Theo getting slightly uncomfortable upon being practically bombarded with yet more nosy questions, but I didn't really see any other time to bring it up; I was still so fascinated by his world and genuinely wanted to know what a typical week or month looked like for him when it came to his clientele – not that I was jealous or anything . . . I didn't think I was, at least.

At that exact moment, my intercom rang, signalling the arrival of our food. Saved by the bell, for now.

After dishing out the food, we both returned to the sofa. I'd decided to play it safe with a few Californian tuna rolls and tempura, while Theo had gone all out with his feast of sashimi and yaki udon noodles. After a few moments of silence as we enjoyed our food, it was time to get back to the matter at hand.

'OK, OK, now back to my questions – you can't avoid them forever I fear! If you feel like I'm overstepping, let me know, but you intrigue me, Theo.'

After a long, satisfied slurp of his noodles, Theo set his plate down on the coffee table and turned to me with that wolfish grin I'd grown to like more than I cared to admit. I was probably being a pain in the arse, but whatever – I was the one footing the bill for him to be here, after all, so why not?

'Are you sure my answers won't make you feel weird? I've had other clients ask me this same thing a few times in the past and, any time I discuss it, things either end awkwardly or I end up losing a client. I wouldn't want to hurt your feelings in any way.' He genuinely looked apologetic when he said it, forcing me to scoff. Did he think I would be jealous? I mean, I was still trying to grapple with how I felt about this whole thing myself, but for him to assume that was the case was bold.

'Pah! Me? Jealous?! A bold assumption to make, my friend,' I said, laughing, as I playfully tapped him on the arm. 'I understand that what we currently have is purely transactional, so you don't have to worry about me.'

Theo cocked one eyebrow at me, disbelieving. 'If I remember correctly, you were the one talking about us potentially developing a friendship or relationship outside of *OuiMeet,* or am I misremembering?' His smile was beginning to annoy me, because he was right.

'Maybe . . . maybe I did.' I said with a teasing smile, slipping another piece of sushi between my lips. Theo's gaze followed the movement, lingering on my mouth before flicking up to meet my eyes. I felt the pull of him, electric and impossible to ignore.

I watched him watching me, tension curling tight between us until our eyes finally locked – no words, just tension. The air thickened, humming with the unspoken. The chemistry wasn't just there; it was crackling, undeniable. I could feel the slow burn of desire pooling low, aching and alive. I just needed to wait a little longer.

The tension suddenly broke as I realised I'd stopped breathing temporarily. At this moment, I wanted nothing more than to jump on top of him, but patience was key.

'Hehe, OK, fair enough. Well, in answer to your first question, I've been doing this for about three years or so now.'

'Mmmm, I see, I see. Look at you now; living your best life and all that,' I replied. Theo's smile faded slightly at that. Had I hit a nerve? I decided not to intervene from that point and just let him speak.

Theo then shifted his weight, his shoulders dipping as though he was trying to make himself smaller; a nervous tell that didn't match his normally confident demeanour. He then immediately straightened up upon detecting my staring, his jaw tense and the expression in his eyes more pointed, as if remembering a sad story. Did I detect a flicker of shame?

'I guess you could say that. It's a bit of an isolating experience at times, having to live a double life almost. It's not as if I can go around telling my friends and family that I'm a gigolo on the side, you know? I know I told you before that

I tend to dissociate when doing dates and stuff, and when it comes to the physical stuff it's fine but I'd be lying if I said it wouldn't be nice to sometimes have someone to talk to about the industry.' He sighed.

I said nothing and, instead, kept a neutral face. I didn't want to interrupt the flow as he spoke. I wanted to see how much he would be willing to tell me. I was fascinated by it all, but I also appreciated him being vulnerable with me at that moment; I liked this side of him.

'Awww. Don't you have any gigolo mates you can vent to about stuff?' I asked, shifting towards him.

'Gigolo mates,' Theo repeated, trying to refrain from smiling, but failing drastically. 'No, Cassie, I don't have any gigolo mates. There aren't any conventions or monthly meetups, unfortunately – it's very much an individual freelance gig – but I love how invested you are in my wellbeing.'

I gazed at him, thankful that he wasn't upset by my line of questioning.

'I'm nothing if not caring, my friend. And besides, if you ever need to vent, you can talk to me about it. I know it probably sounds awkward but, you know . . . I'm always down to listen.'

Theo smiled warmly, took my hand, and kissed it as a sign of thanks. My pelvic floor clenched.

'I appreciate you, Cass. Also to answer your other question before I forget: when it comes to clients, I'd probably say it's like three to four different women a month at the moment – depending on the month. It used to be quite a bit more but I decided to calm down a year or so ago. It's almost like a retainer basis with those women, I suppose, and before you ask, yes, they are all older, haha.'

'How much older?' I asked.

'Two of them are in their fifties, one is forty-six and the other is forty-three,' Theo replied, matter-of-factly.

'And so . . . with me included, that makes five in total?' I responded.

'Yes.'

'And . . . do you use protection with all of them?' I asked.

'I don't have sex with all of them. Two of them just tend to hire me to escort them to their work events and be their dates.'

'And does that make good money?' I continued.

'Yeah, it's decent enough, I suppose.'

'And the other two?'

'Are you sure this isn't making you uncomfortable?' Theo asked warily.

'Nope. Continue. I'm intrigued!' I replied.

Theo looked at me warily, bless him. It was cute of him to want to protect my feelings.

'The other two, yes, on occasion . . . if that's what they've booked, then that's what will happen.'

'I see.'

We both sat in silence for a while as I processed the information. Of course I always knew that sex was a big part of the job description but I couldn't help feeling a little . . . weird about it. Not so much from an emotional point of view, more so feeling like I was just another client he needed to tick off the list. Yet, that was the whole point of this transactional relationship, I suppose.

'Are you OK?' Theo murmured, his voice barely above a whisper. His fingers lingered as they traced the curve of my cheek, sending a shiver through me. I turned towards him, trying to force a genuine smile. I had to get it together.

'I'm great! Thanks for sharing, by the way. I find it all so fascinating . . . that world.'

'As long as you're sure, love,' he responded. We continued eating our meal as we chatted throughout the evening. The more we talked, the more I found myself drawn to him – irresistibly, and somewhat a little annoyingly. There was something magnetic about him, an intoxicating charm laced with just enough mystery to leave me wanting more, needing to unravel every layer of him. He had the dry wit of Richard Ayoade and the suave aloofness of Jon Hamm, which appeased my interests. The night carried on, with us getting into playing a few card games (I won them all), cuddling with Toby, who'd ventured out of my room temporarily to use his litter tray, and laying into the dessert (I'd gone all out with a Viennetta ice cream cake and an M&S apple pie).

I switched the TV onto a streaming network for a bit of background noise, flicking through different movies and asking if there was anything he was in the mood for.

'There's that new gangster movie starring Al Pacino I could put on? When isn't there a gangster movie featuring Al Pacino at this point? Or we could try a cheesy Morris Chestnut romcom if you're in the mood for *love*. Oh, hang on . . . I remember getting a notification about that new superhero movie starring one of the famous Chrises, that Steven guy, and Catherine Thom—'

'No. Anything but that,' Theo interjected suddenly, sitting up, his voice stern.

I looked at him in confusion; his face had become solemn as his eyes squinted rapidly. He turned to look at me slowly, his face gradually relaxing.

'Sorry, erm, I'm just not the biggest fan of superhero movies is all,' he replied, trying to ease the sudden tension. I decided not to press the matter, just in case I'd said something that had triggered him. This night needed to go perfectly.

'Alrighty . . . cartoons it is!'

At 11.30 p.m., we were both on the sofa watching *The Simpsons* idly, me on the floor trying to keep myself from crashing due to the amount of sugar I'd eaten, and Theo gently slumped over on the sofa, his eyes glazing over at the TV. Annoyingly, I could feel my eyes growing heavy, which was not ideal. The night was still young, and I needed to get my money's worth.

'Hey, so um, I'm gonna go to my room and get changed quickly,' I said, standing up suddenly. It was the best segue I could think of at that time, as awkward as I was. Theo looked up at me, and then at his backpack, which was in the corner of the living room. 'Hmm. Yeah, I should probably do the same too. Can't be in my outside clothes all night.'

As he stood up and walked over to his bag, I pointed him in the direction of the bathroom for him to get changed. Before closing the door, he turned to me. 'Should I make my way to the bedroom afterwards or would you prefer to hang out on the sofa some more?'

That was the push I needed. I suppose he knew where this was going, which would hopefully make it less awkward on my side. I'd never done anything like this before, so I wasn't sure whether to summon him to the bedroom or just tear his clothes off on the sofa.

'Make your way to the bedroom, please,' I replied, with all the sass and confidence I could muster. *I was in control.* As he smiled and closed the door, I hotfooted it to my bedroom and disrobed immediately, stuffing my clothes lazily into my wardrobe and bringing out the Ann Summers chemise. I quickly put it on, making sure the outfit hugged every square inch of my body. The chemise was a little tight, but it was tight in all the right areas, which only helped my case.

I spritzed some of my bedside-table room spray lightly onto the bed, and went to half lie on my side of it, facing the door, my back straight so my boobs poked out prominently, and legs crossed over another so the thigh meat was on full display. Moments later, Theo walked into the bedroom, wearing a fitted white vest that showed off every muscle in his torso, and a pair of butter-yellow Calvin Klein boxers. He looked incredible. Before I could get a word out, Theo quietly shut the bedroom door and turned to look at me – as in *really* look at me. His eyes swept over me slowly, and then he bit his lip like we were in some kind of steamy movie scene. Part of me wanted to laugh at how dramatic it felt . . . but the other part? The other part was too busy remembering what it was like to be wanted – and wow, had it been a while.

'Damn, Cassandra – you look so beautiful. I hope this isn't too forward, but I love how you look . . . you're so gorgeous.' Theo walked towards the bed, his eyes not moving away from my body. I felt giddy inside, like a child on the morning of Christmas. This was it; this was going to be my mattress moment. I uncrossed my legs and slid underneath the covers, making space for him to lie next to me as he slowly lay down on the bed and went underneath the covers too. Finally, we were facing each other, and all of a sudden I felt awkward.

'Um. So what do I do now?' I blurted out randomly. I'd let my intrusive thoughts win once again. What kind of stupid question was that? *I'm supposed to be in control; CONTROL YOURSELF!*

Theo laughed as he moved closer to me.

'You're so cute. You haven't done this in a while, huh?'

'NO. That's the whole point! My pussy's probably ground itself to dust by now!' I said, trying to stifle laughter. So much for trying to come across as confident and in control of the situation.

'Haha, well, we can lie here and talk or cuddle, or we can go to sleep – it's your night. We can do whatever you want to do.'

'Mm, well, what do you want to do?' I replied cheekily, noting the glint in his eye.

'Well, I want to do what I've been dreaming about doing

since our time in the back of the car,' he replied; that familiar wolfish grin crept back onto his face, bold and irresistible as ever. Theo closed the distance between us in one smooth motion, his eyes locked on mine like he couldn't wait another second. Then his lips were on mine – kissing me with a hunger that sent heat rushing through my entire body. It was passionate and purposeful, like he'd been holding back for far too long. His fingers tangled with mine as he eased himself over me, his body pressing against mine in a way that felt both grounding and electric at the same time. When I bit his lower lip, he let out a low, breathless moan that made my skin tingle and my pulse race. The sound alone had me aching for more.

I felt him hardening against me – a silent invitation I didn't hesitate to accept. With a teasing smile, I gently pushed him onto his back and swung my leg over to straddle him, giving him a full, unfiltered view of me. *That's it, Cassie. Take the reins.*

He just lay there breathless, eyes locked on mine, completely at my mercy – and whew! Did that make me feel powerful. Slowly, I peeled off my chemise, letting it slip down my shoulders, taking my time as I watched his gaze darken with desire. My body, in all its soft, plus-size glory – the full curve of my breasts, the love handles, the stretchmarks etched across my skin – was laid bare before him. And at that moment, none of it mattered. I had never felt more desired . . . I felt sexy.

'I want you badly, Cass,' Theo whispered breathlessly as his hands made their way towards my breasts, cupping them gently, yet firmly. 'You're so fucking beautiful.'

'Oh, I know,' I murmured, leaning in until my face hovered just above his, our breath mingling. Our lips met again, hot and eager, as his hands slid down to my hips and then to my bum, gripping me with a delicious intent. His mouth left mine and found its way to my neck, kissing slowly, deliberately, before trailing down to my breasts. He took his time, circling my nipples with his tongue, sucking gently until I was squirming beneath him, every nerve in my body lit up.

Then, with a low growl, he flipped me effortlessly onto my back, reclaiming his place above me. His mouth returned to my chest, worshipping every inch as his hand wandered lower – slow and teasing, until he found the centre of me, which was already soaked. He stroked me softly at first, then deeper, more purposeful, and I couldn't hold back the moan that escaped me, aching, desperate for more. I wanted him inside me at that moment – but not just yet.

At first, I thought I was hallucinating; maybe I'd just imagined it. But then came the unmistakable sound: a soft, persistent scratching opposite the bed, paired with a dramatic meow chorus. Yep, Toby was outside my bedroom door, meowing for his life. He wasn't used to me locking him out of my bedroom and I guess he'd decided to protest. I tried to ignore him, but apparently Theo got the memo too.

'Oh, someone's annoyed I'm in here then?' he said, chuckling softly as he leaned in to kiss me. Turning my attention back to Theo, I parted my legs wider as he bent over the bed to retrieve a condom from his jeans, which were lying by the bed. I briefly looked down to catch a cheeky glimpse of what he was working with downstairs and was very happy with what I saw. One of the many reasons why he was so popular on the site, I suppose.

I tried to drown out the noise of Toby's cries and focused on the activity at hand; Theo had rolled the condom on with expert precision and leaned into me yet again.

'Are you ready?' he breathed softly as he stared at me intensely, before slowly kissing my neck.

'Yes,' I mouthed quietly. This was it. Everything had built up to this moment.

'Meow!' came a long whine from behind the bedroom door yet again.

'SHUT UP TOBY!' I shouted; I'd had enough. Why was he trying to ruin Mama's groove? At that moment, Theo and I erupted into fits of laughter; this wasn't ideal, but whatever.

'OK, OK, I'm serious now, I'm ready. Dive in,' I said, shutting my eyes.

'Dive in? Who says that?' Theo said in between laughs.

'Hey, hey! Don't get distracted now, you were doing so well a few minutes ago – you're on the clock if you don't remember. Get to fucking!'

'I . . . Jeeze, you're hilarious,' he said, struggling to control his laughter at this point. He then made a mock salute as he spread my legs a bit wider. 'Aye aye, ma'am. Right away, ma'am.'

He eased into me slowly, tenderly, until there was no space left between us, like a dam breaking, releasing a wave of feeling from somewhere deep within me. He started out slow, like he was teasing me on purpose. Each deep, lazy thrust had me squirming, half whining, half laughing.

'Having fun?' he asked, smirking down at me like he already knew the answer.

'You're the worst,' I muttered, breathless, and then he shifted gears, hips snapping harder, faster, knocking the air right out of me. Was this what it felt like to be put through the mattress? God.

'Oh my *god* – OK, OK, you're not the worst,' I gasped, clinging to him like my life depended on it. 'You're . . . alarmingly good, actually.'

You're talking too much. Shut up and enjoy it, knobhead.

Every time he moved, it was this mix of pleasure and something deeper, and suddenly it was like we were speaking a language only we understood. I held onto him, not wanting the moment to end, just wanting more – of him, of us together, of everything. He grinned, and kept going, his rhythm picking up, his manhood hitting that perfect spot that made my back arch and my brain go fuzzy. I tried to say something witty, something smart, which looking back, probably wasn't the best time, but all that came out was a string of broken moans.

'You were saying?' he teased, sweat beading on his forehead as he drove into me with purpose now – no games, just the kind of pace that said we were both chasing that same electrifying end.

I could feel it building, my thighs tightening around him, nails digging into his back.

'Don't stop,' I breathed, 'seriously, if you stop now, I will fucking haunt you.'

'I'd let you too,' he said with a grunt.

And we both came – me first, coming hard with a cry that might've woken my next-door neighbour, and him right after, with a deep groan and one last, perfect thrust.

He collapsed beside me, breathless, sweaty, grinning like an idiot.

'So,' he said, 'was that . . . medium haunting, or full poltergeist?'

I burst out laughing, still half delirious. 'You're such an idiot.'

So much for me taking control. He'd completely wrecked me, in the best way.

Theo turned towards me, breathing rapidly as he coaxed a stray hair from my face. He looked almost angelic in a way. Outside of the sexual pleasure, I'd never had anyone make me feel that way before; so desired, so seen. Like I was beautiful in a way I hadn't known I could be. I wanted to feel this way all the time.

He grinned at me as he pulled me close to him. No words were exchanged as I buried my head into his chest, absorbing his scent, the taste of his sweat and feeling comfort with his body being intertwined in mine. I felt at peace as I lay there, with him gently caressing my shoulder blades as I slowly fell asleep in his arms.

Best use of £600 ever.

Chapter 14

The dull aching of my pelvis was what woke me up first. The sweat was the second thing. I stirred, waking from my slumber to look at the time on my phone. It was 6.30 a.m. I turned over to find Theo still next to me, snoring soundly. I quietly slipped out of bed, softly rubbing my lower belly before putting on an oversized T-shirt. I hadn't been worked over like that in a while and now my kitty didn't know what to do with herself. I went into the kitchen and downed a couple of painkillers before going back to the bedroom, grabbing my phone and heading to the living room.

I was met there by Toby, who greeted me with a hiss as I went to go and pet him.

'Baby, I'm sorry!' I pleaded, filling up his bowl with dry food. 'Mama needed some time to herself last night. She needed her back broken, thoroughly – I hope you can understand.'

After brushing my teeth, I crept back to the bedroom – Theo was out like a light, looking beautiful against the soft glow of my bedside lamp. Last night was everything I could have hoped for and more. I even appreciated the awkward giggles and small talk throughout – it had made me feel closer to him – connected somehow. But equally, I knew what this was – he was just doing what I'd paid for him to do, but a small part of me feared that I'd want more.

I texted Sade a couple of hours later.

> **Sade. Girl. You know that whole 'THROUGH THE MATTRESS' thing? I'm joining the club. Last night was a movie; I'll fill you in later. xxx**

I needed to fully debrief the events of last night, as well as hear some reassuring advice on what I should do moving forward.

If I slipped back into bed with him and tried to initiate sex again, would he charge me for it separately? What about oral stuff? Before I had time to overthink any more, I turned around to see Theo standing in the hallway in nothing but his boxers, looking down at me, smirking.

'Coffee?' I said, making my way to the kitchen.

'Please,' he replied, joining me as I headed towards the coffee machine. Then, in one smooth motion, he stepped behind me, wrapped me in his arms, and spun me around. Before I could even process what was happening, he somehow lifted me up and set me down on the counter like it was nothing.

Were we in a damn movie? What was even happening right now?

He stepped in close, eyes locked on mine, and kissed me deeply, hungrily – while the coffee maker gurgled behind us like background music to the chaos of whatever this magical, steamy moment was turning into. The pain I'd felt in my pelvis suddenly disappeared into the abyss as his hands slowly crept up my thighs, grabbing onto my bum.

'Wait, stop – do I need to pay separately for this?' I murmured, not wanting him to stop, but also thinking about my ever decreasing savings account. Theo broke from kissing my neck and smiled.

'This is on the house.' His fingers gently made their way towards my clit as I exhaled sharply.

'Your coffee,' I breathed, not giving a solid fuck about the coffee in question.

'It can wait,' he replied. He crouched down as he made his way towards my thighs, inching his way slowly towards my labia. What the heck was happening?

Fifteen minutes and a broken coffee mug later (me having an orgasmic spasm on the countertop clearly not helping things) and I was absolutely exhausted again, drinking my now cooled coffee on my sofa in my dressing robe; all orgasmed out and loving life. After getting dressed, Theo waded into the living room, wearing a very self-satisfied smile.

'I trust you've had a good few hours then?' he said, grinning slyly as he swung on his backpack.

'I've had the best time; thank you. The service was absolutely out of this world and I'll definitely make sure to leave positive feedback on your profile thingy.' I sniggered as I stood up to see him out. As we walked to the door, I could feel the heat, still hot, still lingering between us. The last few hours had surpassed my expectations completely; Theo had been the perfect gentleman throughout, treating me with the care and attention I deserved, and as for the sex? Mind blowing. I hadn't been taken care of like that for a long time; it had been long overdue, and I felt incredible. Empowered, even.

'I loved spending time with you, Cassie,' said Theo as he turned to face me at the door. 'Getting to know you more over the last few hours has certainly been special. And before you say anything—' he added, no doubt catching the very slight grimace on my face at his remark '—I genuinely mean it. This has nothing to do with you booking me or anything like that. You're just – you exude this really calm, yet confident energy that I vibe with. Yeah . . . I had a really great time with you, so thank you.'

'I should be the one thanking you, I had a wonderful time

and err . . . yeah! Not really sure what happens now, but I guess I'll hopefully catch you soon? Thank you for your service – I mean . . . thanks for everything.'

Could I *be* any more awkward? Honestly, I had no idea how these things were supposed to go. One-night stands, I could handle – those had a script. But this? This felt different. A little more . . . formal? Like there should've been a sign-off or something. I tried to remedy it by leaning in for a hug, which he returned. When we broke away, he gave me a kiss on the forehead.

I exhaled. This guy.

'I hope I get to see you again, Cassie,' he said, as he turned on his heel and left.

'We shall see about that – give a girl a discount next time though!' I shouted behind him as he finally departed.

I spent most of that Saturday in bed, replaying the last twenty-four hours over and over in my mind. With the exception of that awkward encounter with Jeff earlier, it had been everything I'd hoped for, and then some. And while part of me couldn't help but quietly resent the fact that I had to pay to access that kind of experience, another part – the confident, empowered, unapologetic part whose back and pelvis were currently sore from the workout – absolutely loved it. The next few hours were spent in an almost catatonic, post-coitus bliss.

I'd caught up with Sade earlier and spilled all the tea ('I know that's right, sis! I hope you destroyed each other – in the best possible way, of course.') and managed to dodge a few calls from my dad who instead, kept sending me a flurry of texts (**'Have you spoken to your mum? Do you know when the wedding is? Can you ask her to call me please? Sorry to bother you xxx**) which I then relayed to Steven:

Cassie: Bro, does Dad keep calling you too?

Steve: Yeah man. I'm ignoring it at the moment. He hasn't even checked in on how me and Bianca are doing you know? We think she's due any day now.

Cassie: Oh bless you! Let me know as soon as she's in labour and I'll come down. I'm sorry Dad's being a bit of a dickhead at the moment – but yeah, I don't plan on telling him the date or venue of Mum's wedding.

Steve: DON'T do that. I bet you anything he'll crash the wedding. He seems the type. It's giving 'Stalker Ex' vibes at the moment.

Cassie: I can see him on a season of *Worst Ex Ever* on Netflix tbh. You don't think he'd ever do anything to Mum, do you . . . ? Like . . . something serious?

Steve: Don't think like that man. Dad is a 50-something-year-old short-sighted lawyer. He wouldn't hurt Mum. He's harmless.

Cassie: D'you know who else was a lawyer . . . . ?

Steve: Who?

Cassie: Ted Bundy.

Steve: SMH.

Cassie: Also! Serial killers can also suffer from short-sightedness and astigmatism! Jeffrey Dahmer had the thickest spectacles of all time.

Steve: Bye, sis. And stop listening to those true crime podcasts, yeah? xxx

In any case, I started googling old people's homes in the area just in case we needed to refer my dad. Who knew what he could be capable of?

In the late afternoon I saw a DM from Theo. That didn't take long.

Hey Cassie, I hope you've had a restful day today. I just wanted to check in to see how you were doing? xx

The fact that I was on his mind was quite sweet, I couldn't lie. I grinned to myself as I typed back:

What is this? Like an aftercare package now? I love how you go above and beyond for your clients; that's the kind of service I'm talking about haha! But to answer your question, I've had a wonderful day, thanks; spent it at home, trying to catch up on some rest from the last 24 hours. My body's really been through it, as you well know . . . 😃

The message was read immediately, which I found interesting. This was coming from the same person who had spoken about 'establishing boundaries' with clientele, by the way.

Ha! I'm glad to hear you're getting some rest in, and NO this isn't part of any package *tuts* – I've just been thinking about you all day, that's all. I really had a good time with you . . . !

Hmm. Was the sex that good? I mean, it was incredible, but surely not good enough for him to be breaking his boundaries like this? I decided to prod further.

Thinking about me, huh? Doesn't that go against your so-called 'boundaries'? Was my gorilla-grip moose knuckle that sensational? Damn. Maybe I should join *OuiMeet* and have my own clientele.

An almost immediate response:

HA. Go ahead and join *OuiMeet* then. Just remember to list your 'moose knuckle' as a separate account. It deserves its own rate. xx

We traded playful banter for about an hour, and as time

passed, Theo grew noticeably more talkative. He started opening up, chatting about work, sharing a few of his *OuiMeet* Hoe Adventures, and even letting me in on a bit about his family. I learned he was an only child, and that his parents had moved back to Saint Lucia four years ago, leaving him alone in London.

The fact that he was beginning to open up to me about his life felt like real progress. As long as I was careful not to overstep any boundaries or press him with anything *too* personal, I hoped things would continue moving in the right direction. I eventually bade him adieu and went to bed – exhausted yet quite content. I'd started the weekend off right, and dozed off, thinking about possible things I could get into tomorrow. There was a farmer's market on Battersea High Street that I'd always wanted to visit. Perhaps I'd swing by tomorrow morning – maybe with Theo, if he was free? It would be wholesome, and cute. I grabbed my phone from the bedside table and sent him a DM on Instagram:

> **Hey! I know this is really random and by all means please feel free to decline, but I'm thinking of going to a farmer's market tomorrow morning or early afternoon in my area and I was wondering if you wanted to tag along? It's on Battersea High Street!**

Two minutes later, a response:

> **This one can't get enough of me, can she?? Haha, I may have some time tomorrow, I know the market you're talking about. That's the place that does the viral sourdough ploughman's sandwiches right? I saw it on TikTok. I can be at yours for say, 10 a.m.?**

YES. I was in. This was shaping up to be, by far, an excellent weekend. I quickly typed back:

Ha, well, what can I say? A girl enjoys your company. And yes, that's the same place! We absolutely have to get a sandwich while there; I'll see you at 10 a.m. 😃

I loved this for me – this whole 'grab the bull by the horns' energy was really paying off, and honestly, I was thriving. In my head, the script was already written: a picture-perfect, cutesy, wholesome morning with Theo, after which I'd somehow (very smoothly, of course) persuade him to come back to mine. There, we'd spend the entire afternoon making sweet, passionate love before seamlessly transitioning into more quality time, like some sort of erotic romcom montage. It was all going to unfold exactly like that. Obviously.

Except, that didn't bloody happen, did it?

I was jolted awake at 2.44 a.m. by the crackly 8-bit Sonic the Hedgehog ringtone I'd assigned to my brother. I groggily rolled over to get the phone, having missed the call again, only to see a string of text messages he'd sent over the last thirty minutes, alongside texts from both my mum and dad. Bianca must be in labour! I called him back and my theory was confirmed immediately.

'Cass! She's in labour. She's in labour! For real this time; we're in the labour ward at St Tommy's.'

'OhmiGodohmyGod OK. OK . . . has she had the baby yet? How far away is she?' I cried, clambering out of bed and putting on the first item of clothing I could find. Steven was equally as excited and nervous as I was.

'The doctors are saying she's eight centimetres dilated or something like that; she's in a lot of pain though – Cass, I'm scared, man. What if something goes wrong?'

Bless him. Steven had been waiting his whole life for this moment and I already knew that he would make a better dad than the one we currently had, which reminded me . . .

'Bruv, I'm on my way. By the way, are Mum and Dad there? Together?' There would be enough drama this morning without them being in the same room as each other.

'Erm, Mum just got here, she's in the waiting room. Dad . . . I think he's on his way but I'm not sure. You're gonna have to run interference with those two 'cause I'm not gonna have the patience today, to be honest.'

'Leave it to me, bro. I'm getting an Uber to you guys now. See you soon. Love you,' I replied, putting on an old Reebok sweatshirt and grabbing my keys.

Twenty minutes later, I was at St Thomas' hospital racing my way to the labour suite, where I was greeted by Bianca's parents who were frantically pacing up and down the waiting room, alongside Mum, who was sitting closest to the door, her hands tightly cupped under her head as she rocked back and forth, seemingly in prayer.

'Hey Mum,' I said breathlessly as I sat next to her, trying to catch my breath. I'd had to run up the last two flights of stairs due to elevator doors suddenly failing on me at the last minute. I hadn't done that much cardio in a while, and my lungs were not coping well with the sudden increase in heart rate.

'Cassandra? Do you know you're wearing two different trainers?' she replied, kissing her teeth for good measure. I looked down to find that I was wearing one bright-red Adidas Samba trainer and one burgundy Nike running shoe. Because of course that would happen to me.

'Eh. I'm trying out a new fashion thing; get with the programme, innit? Anyway, where's Steve? Is Bianca OK? You haven't bumped into Dad yet, have you?' For some reason I felt more anxious about my parents running into each other than the impending birth of my future nephew. They hadn't seen each other in a while and after all the harassment my dad had been putting Mum through of late, I didn't anticipate their reunion to be a good one.

Mum sighed, wringing her hands in an ever-so-dramatic fashion. She looked exhausted – bless her – as she tried to stifle another yawn.

'Steve's in the birthing suite with Bianca – we've been told to wait out here, which is ridiculous. This is my first grandchild, I should be in there with them!'

As she said the last sentence an octave higher than the rest, a few heads in the waiting room turned towards us.

'Mum, I think it's because they don't wanna stress Bianca out, to be honest. Having too many people in the suite can be a bit of sensory overload, I reckon.'

But Mum wasn't trying to hear it.

'"Sensory overload" my backfoot. What is with your generation making up random words? Back in my day – even when you were born – we had both sides of the family in the room encouraging and cheering me on. She needs support!'

At that, she stood up and started pacing up and down, getting herself more and more agitated. I couldn't tell if it was the general situation that was getting to her, or perhaps knowing that she'd probably be bumping into my dad at some point soon – sans Femi by her side.

'Mum, calm down. The doctors are in there and I'm sure she's being well taken care of—' and it was at that moment, that the loudest, highest, most piercing scream I'd ever heard erupted through the halls. That was definitely Bianca, bless her. Steven had a huge head, so my thoughts were with her and her poor pelvis.

Twenty minutes later, Steven popped out of the delivery suite for a short break dressed in blue scrubs, complete with a hairnet on, excited, but shaken.

'Rah, boy. Labour's a bit intense, innit? Bianca's such a

trooper, Cassie, I love her so much.' Tears filled his eyes as he said this, causing me to start silently weeping too.

'How's she doing?'

'She's fine, we're just taking a quick break right now. She's fully dilated now so hopefully the baby will come soon – just wanted to update you guys quickly. Is Dad here yet?'

Mum took a break from speaking with Bianca's parents on the other side of the waiting area to give Steven a quick hug. 'It doesn't matter if your dad is here or not – listen; I'm so proud of you, do you know that? You're going to be a brilliant father, as long as you don't name your son after the dad you have now. His so-called "legacy" must end with you.' Steven and I both guffawed in unison and I struggled to contain my laughter before the sounds of Bianca's moans took him back into the birthing suite.

And – almost as if by fate – the doors to the waiting room creaked open, revealing Dad as he stepped in slowly, offering a subtle nod to everyone present. He paused when he reached Mum, his eyes locking onto hers with a quiet, longing gaze. She returned his gaze with a steely, cold glare. It was at that point that I realised that I was going to need a coffee; this was indeed going to be a long morning.

'Daniel,' said Mum curtly, using his Christian name instead of his Ghanaian one. That's how I knew she was pissed off. Dad responded, but used her Ghanaian name instead, as if using it would make her feel any less pissed off with him.

'Adwoa? How are you doing? It's good to see you.'

My mum responded with a short grunt and faced forward. I was in the centre, looking from one person to the other as if watching a tennis match, wondering if I needed to intervene. The last thing I wanted was to leave them alone together.

'Hey, Dad. Nice of you to join us eventually. Steve's just with Bianca but we can't go in there at the moment. Um, I'm gonna go and find some coffee somewhere, you wanna come with me?'

Dad broke his stare from Mum long enough to offer a casual glance at me. Despite it being early, he looked good. I could smell the faint aroma of his Hugo Boss fragrance – a signature scent that I knew was Mum's favourite. He had recently shaved his beard, judging from the fresh stubble across his jawline and chin, and he was wearing a brand-new pair of trainers. A part of me wondered whether he had come here to show support for Steve or to try and win my mum back, yet again. My inclination was to go with the latter.

'I'm fine, my dear – I'll stay here but can you get me a coff—'

'No, no,' interrupted Mum suddenly, standing up and glaring at Dad venomously. 'Cassie, I'll come with you to find a drink.'

As Mum crossed the room to join me, Dad attempted to take her hand, but with the instincts of a cat, she sideswept his gesture in an instant.

'Not here, Daniel. Your son is having a baby right now. Don't come and embarrass yourself.'

Dad stared at her, affronted. 'Adwoa, don't be like this. Please . . . if we could just find somewhere to talk—'

'Alrighty!' I said, clapping my hands like a primary school teacher. 'Mum? Let's go and find those drinks, yeah?' and with that, I took her arm in mine as I almost dragged her to the corridor outside.

'What the heck is his problem, Cassie?' my mum said, trying to lower her voice but failing miserably. We'd arrived at a nearby coffee machine and I was doing the duty of making the three of us (including Dad, for his sins) a drink. 'Do you see why I cannot stand that man? Why is he making this experience about him? Femi wanted to come with me but I told him to go back to sleep. I should have asked him to come. This is such nonsense! I'm already stressed as it is.'

I let her vent for the next few minutes as I collected the coffees, and together, we started making our way back to the waiting room. When we got back, Dad was sitting in the far corner, looking quite sorry for himself. A part of me felt a little bad, but I had to remember who I was dealing with here. I went to give him his coffee, as well as give him an empathetic shoulder pat.

'Have you seen Steven yet? How d'you feel about being a first-time grandad?' I asked, trying to make conversation while keeping an eye out for Mum. She was pacing up and down the room, occasionally glancing at Dad menacingly.

'Yeah, I'm happy – I'm really happy. Steven is going to be great,' he replied, staring at Mum the entire time. Honestly, Channel 5 couldn't produce a daytime drama this captivating.

The next hour or so passed in strained silence – Mum and I sat at one end of the waiting room, pretending to be engrossed in our phones, while Dad positioned himself at the other, chatting away with Bianca's parents, who were no doubt silently wondering what kind of dysfunctional circus their daughter had stumbled into.

I was beginning to fight sleep as I went in between lightly dozing off and playing games on my phone. In the distance, I could hear what I thought were the strained, agonising moans of Bianca as she pushed the newest member of our family into the world.

'Adwoa, can we please go somewhere to talk? Please?' my dad said, catching me completely off-guard. It was 4.30 a.m., and we were all running on fumes. Steven popped into the waiting room every twenty minutes or so with updates – the labour was progressing, just at a snail's pace.

'Daniel, now is not the time. Please, just be here for your son,' Mum said, her voice heavy with exhaustion and irritation. Then, without missing a beat, she turned to me. 'Oh, by the way, I'm having my wedding gown fitting next weekend if you're free. I'd love for you to come. Thanks.' She shot Dad a pointed look, and his face fell. Oof. Ruthless; but the game was the game.

At one point, Dad stood up suddenly and left the waiting room, with a speed that caused us all to lift our heads in confusion. Through the glass doors, I could see him pacing up and down, his hands occasionally rubbing his eyes as he bowed his head. Despite everything that had happened over the last few hours, seeing him like that tugged at something soft inside me. He looked smaller somehow – deflated – and for a moment I just watched him, torn between the habit of keeping my distance and the instinct to take care of him.

Eventually, that instinct won. I pushed myself up from the chair and slipped out through the doors into the corridor. Up close, the sadness on his face was unmistakable. A couple of tears had escaped down his cheek, hastily wiped away, but not fast enough for me to miss. He didn't notice me at first – he just kept pacing, fighting whatever storm was happening inside of him.

'Dad?' I said softly, stepping towards him.

He looked up, startled, before trying to hold himself together. 'Cassie. What's wrong? Is the baby here?' He looked past me and into the waiting room, panicked.

'No, no, not yet. I just wanted to come out and check on you; are you OK?'

The man had several pieces of luggage under each eye, which was red and bloodshot. He looked at me silently, and sighed.

'I'm OK, my dear,' he started. 'I think it's a mixture of nerves for the baby, tiredness and everything else. I . . . I really made a fool of myself in there, didn't I?'

'Um . . . yeah . . . yeah, you kinda did,' I admitted, deciding there was no point dancing around it. Today was supposed to be all about Steven and Bianca, and the tiny new human joining our family. 'But it's OK, we just need to focus on getting through the next few hours until the baby is born. Now isn't the time to dig up things between you and Mum.'

My dad stared at me, squinting, as if looking at me through new eyes. 'You would have been great if you'd decided to take up family law, you know; our little mediator, always trying to fix things.'

I smiled thinly. That was exactly the problem.

'Maybe, but it's not my job to be the family mediator though, is it? You and Mum are the parents. You're the ones who should be there to help and support me and Steve – not the other way round. I want to be parented too, sometimes – and not just when it's time for you to tell me off.'

Dad's face shifted almost instantly, showing a mixture of surprise and what looked like embarrassment. He glanced away briefly, his jaw tightening as he folded and unfolded his arms. For me, though, the moment felt strangely freeing. It was as if this knot I had been carrying – tight and silent for years – had finally come loose. Saying it out loud, naming the thing that had been eating at me, left me feeling a little lighter.

Dad swallowed, his voice a touch rough when he finally spoke. 'I . . . I hear you,' he said quietly. 'I could have . . . done more. I've leaned on you more than I should have. More than a parent should.' He rubbed the back of his neck, still avoiding my eyes but inching a little closer.

'I don't want us to—'

At that moment, Steven came bursting through the waiting room – a huge grin plastered on his face, followed by the sharp, beautiful cry of a newborn, indicating that my nephew was finally here.

'Dad! Cass! He's here! He's beautiful!' Steven cried, before disappearing into the delivery suite again. A wave of relief and quiet joy washed over us. As much as I wanted for this conversation with my dad to continue, there was a new priority in town.

I quickly caught my dad's eye. 'Can we talk about this later?' I said breathily, making my way back to the waiting room with him trailing behind me, panting with excitement.

'Yes, of course; I'm a grandad! I can't believe it!'

After Bianca had been cleaned up and made comfortable, we were finally invited into her room – just a few at a time – to meet their new bundle of joy.

'We're calling him Aaron!' Steven beamed, his face glowing with pure joy and pride. My little nephew lay nestled in Bianca's arms – an oddly fascinating mix of tiny limbs, soft skin, and the rawness of just having entered the world.

I spent most of those first hours in my brother's arms, sobbing erratically as our families all stared down at this tiny new bundle of life that had just appeared. I was officially an auntie now – Auntie to little Aaron – which meant I suddenly had responsibilities that stretched beyond myself. I would have a hand, however small, in shaping the person he would become, and that was a role I needed to take seriously.

For so long, I'd been consumed with trying to be the perfect daughter, the model child who lived up to my parents' expectations of what I should be (if we exclude the whole 'not becoming a lawyer' bit, that is . . .). But holding Aaron, I realised I simply didn't have the emotional energy to carry both loads – to keep being what my parents wanted, *and* to give him the example he deserved. Something had to shift, and maybe that brief conversation with my dad in the hospital corridor was just the beginning. My nephew needed me to show up as the best role model for him, not as some ideal version of myself sculpted to satisfy my parents.

I got back home at around 8.30 a.m., exhausted, yet laced with a warmth and joy I hadn't felt since yesterday morning. After feeding Toby his breakfast, I flopped back into bed, fully prepared to have a quick fifteen-minute nap before taking a shower. But just as I was settling in, a DM from Theo lit up my screen. I bolted upright like I'd been hit with a taser. We were supposed to meet at 10 a.m. today. Shit. I hadn't slept a wink and I looked like absolute shit.

> Morning, beautiful. Looking forward to seeing you soon! I'm going to head down in the next twenty minutes or so. Also, could I get your number? I figure it would be easier to text than through the app. No worries if not. X

I read the message, a flicker of panic running through me. Every fibre of my body was begging for rest, and the Rimowa-sized suitcases under my eyes were doing me no favours. But Theo had asked for my number. *My number.* Was he breaking his own carefully drawn rules and boundaries now? Oh, baby. He wanted me. This was it. The tide was turning. Tiredness be damned—I wasn't about to stop the flow of destiny now.

I messaged him back, first sending him my phone number, followed by:

> Of course you can have my number: there you go. I'm excited to see you! Also, apologies in advance if I look a little rough, it's been a long night! x

I ran into the bathroom, brushed my teeth and had the quickest shower I'd ever had. Afterwards, I threw on one of my luxury sheet facemasks while I moisturised my body and hastily put on an old-yet-comfortable and well-fitted Lucy & Yak sunflower-patterned jumpsuit, complete with a pair of Adidas Sambas. It wasn't glamorous, but it had to do for now.

As I tore off the mask and prepared to make a mad dash

on my make-up, I heard my phone ring; it was Steve. Halfway through putting my concealer on, I grabbed the phone.

''Sup Daddy?' I said hastily. There was an awkward silence as I processed what I'd just said. 'I mean, not in that way – don't make it weird or anything, I—'

Steven cut me off halfway through. 'I'm gonna forget you said that, weirdo. Anyway, I was calling to ask a favour, if that's OK? I forgot to bring a few things for Bianca and Aaron, and the doctors want Bianca to stay at the hospital for another day because of something to do with her blood pressure. They wanna monitor it.'

'Oh shit, I hope everything's under control?' I replied, using my beauty sponge to blend out the concealer under my eyes. I had an hour before Theo was due to arrive.

'Yeah, they're both fine. Mum doesn't wanna leave my side and Dad's fucked off back home, so I was wondering, pretty please, if you could just pick up a couple of baby vests, and a few cheap nighties and underwear for Bianca? I would ask if you could go to our flat but it's too out of the way, and you're closer to the hospital. We need it for this morning if possible as we're fresh out.'

Shit. So much for my date with Theo – looked like auntie duty decided to show up ahead of schedule.

'Ahh, yeah, no worries, bro. Text me the full list of things you need and I'll swing by this morning,' I replied, accidentally stabbing myself in the eye with the mascara wand.

'Love you, appreciate you!' called my brother from the other end of the phone.

I put the phone down, slightly annoyed at having to change my plans so last minute. Theo was probably on his way and a pit of guilt made its way to my stomach over the thought of having to cancel so suddenly. I also looked . . . dishevelled. And not in the sexy, tousled, French-girl way. No – this was more 'sleep-deprived pigeon who lost a bar fight'. My eyeliner had gone rogue, tilting at an angle like it was desperately trying to escape my face. The concealer under my eyes had crept into every fine line, basically sending out a public service announcement that I had crow's feet. My braids were shoved into what could generously be called a bun – more realistically, a haystack in witness protection. My edges? They'd staged a walkout and were now somewhere around my ears.

I opened my messages and texted him:

> **Hey Theo. I'm so so sorry to do this, but I can't make today any more. I've got a bit of a family emergency at the hospital and need to get some bits for my bro; can we reschedule?**

As I screenshot the list of items Steven had texted to me, I continued getting ready, dismayed over not being able to chill with Theo today, but feeling excited about being able to see my nephew again. Minutes later, I receive a text back from Theo:

> **I completely understand, I hope your brother is OK? I've actually just started making my way and it'll probably take me about forty minutes or so to get to South; do you need any help or anything? I can be your chauffeur perhaps if you need to pick some things up . . . let me know. Send message. Siri? Send message. Oh shit, SEND! Mate, get out of the lane, you're blocking–**

I reread the text and cackled at his attempt at using the voice-to-text function on his phone. There was something so sexy about him offering to help me in my time of need. I smiled to myself as I texted back:

> **Thank you so much and apologies for the change of plan! I'm making my way into town, but if you meet me at**

> **St Thomas' Hospital, that would be great. Let me know when you get there; looking forward to seeing you! Also we're gonna have to get you a few lessons on how to send a voice text, Gramps. x**

Thirty minutes later and I was in my local TK Maxx breezing through the baby and beauty aisles like a contestant on Supermarket Sweep. I picked up a couple of newborn vests and Babygros, some cute yellow cotton mittens, water wet wipes, a pack of five panties and two nighties for Bianca, and a little toiletry travel set. As I ordered an Uber to take me to the hospital, I got another text from Theo:

> **Listen, it's my first time doing one of these speak-text things, OK? Cut me some slack. Trying to be a responsible driver and all that, or would you rather I text with my hands and I end up DEAD? Haha, I'll let you know once I get to the hospital. Send text. No . . . delete the 'send text' bit and just SEND THE TEXT.**

I made my way up to the delivery suite after arriving at the hospital – shopping in tow – as I decided to pick up some pastries and a few bottles of water and juice for Steven and Bianca at the hospital shop. Bianca and little Aaron were fast asleep, and Steven was sitting in the chair, looking like a man who hadn't slept for a week. He looked up and smiled at me dozily as I placed the shopping bags on the side cabinet and crept over to the hospital crib to gaze at Aaron, who was sleeping peacefully, gently sucking on his thumb. He was absolutely perfect, and incredibly hairy for a newborn. My heart swelled as he began to do a little stretch.

'He's amazing, isn't he?' Steven cooed, peering behind me to look at his son. 'He and Bianca have been amazing, man. I still can't believe it; I'm a whole dad. A dad!'

I gave him a hug, feeling teary-eyed. I knew he would make the best dad and was just so happy for him at this moment.

'Thanks so much for the stuff too; I really appreciate it, man. Sorry if you had other plans by the way; I'm just so exhausted.' Steven rubbed his eyes as if on cue.

'Boy, please. I'm your sis. This is what I'm HERE for,' I replied, wiping my own tears. 'I got everything on your list and some food too, just in case you don't have the energy to go downstairs. Is there anything else you need?'

Steven had a dig through the bag before picking up an almond croissant and a bottle of water.

'This is perfect. Thank you so much, sis. I'm actually gonna see if I can have a little nap after this, seeing as they are both still asleep.' He nodded over to Bianca, who was snoring loudly.

'After pushing out a nine-pound baby, shit, I'd be snoring too,' I said, laughing. Me and Steven said our goodbyes as I left him to rest and headed downstairs to the main reception to wait for Theo and try and salvage what was left of the day.

Twenty minutes later, I receive a call from Theo.

'Hello, hello, I just parked up outside the hospital; which wing are you in?'

'Oh, let me come out to you; those parking fees are an absolute piss-take,' I said, gathering my handbag and making my way to the exit.

'Your wish is my command; see you in a minute, love,' Theo replied. I quickly nipped to the toilet to powder my face, making sure I still looked cute, took a deep breath, and strutted my way out of the exit to see him.

Theo was by his car, as suave as ever, this time wearing a casual rugby shirt and a pair of light-wash baggy jeans. Everything about him was so effortlessly cool, in comparison to myself, who currently looked like a hyper nursery teacher who had been attacked by her students.

'Hey, so—' I started, trying to address the elephant in the room '—please ignore the aesthetic today. It's been a *morning*, and I'm fully aware I look like I've been dragged through a bush.'

Theo just smiled, tilted my chin up with one hand, and pressed a soft kiss onto my forehead.

'I have no idea what you're talking about. You're gorgeous,' he said, his teeth practically sparkling in the sunlight like a Colgate ad.

Still, somehow, Theo looked at me like I was a vision. Which just proved my theory: men really don't notice eyeliner smudges – or maybe he was just into feral woodland creatures.

As we got into his car, I turned to face him. 'OK, so basically, my brother had his son early this morning and I needed to swing by TK Maxx to pick up some last-minute bits for him. Sorry about the chaos of it all!'

Theo started the car and turned to look at me in mock sadness. 'First of all, congratulations, Auntie! I hope everyone is doing well; that's major! And secondly, I see that this was all just a ploy – a *ruse* if you will – to get me to be your free chauffeur for the day, huh? I see how it is.'

I playfully punched him. 'First of all, don't flatter yourself. If I was really trying to scam a free chauffeur, I'd have picked someone with a Mercedes, at least. Secondly, I'll have you know, I am a *delightful* passenger – I come with witty commentary, questionable singing, and an endless supply of mints. You're welcome.'

He smirked, shaking his head. 'Uh huh, sounds like a hostage situation in the making.'

'Exactly.' I grinned. 'And you're the lucky victim. Buckle up, babe – today you're officially my UberXL with benefits.'

Theo made a right turn out of the car park, back towards Vauxhall.

'So, where to next, m'lady?' he asked.

I didn't mind what we did, as long as we did it together. But a random thought did occur to me.

'What about seeing a random shitty film at the PeckhamPlex on Peckham Rye? I used to go there all the time as a kid. A fiver for a cinema ticket! You can't beat those prices these days; and it comes with an extra serving of sticky carpets and overzealous Jamaican security guards. We'll have all the fun. Or we can just walk around the area and complain at the gentrification of it all.'

Theo laughed, typing the venue into his satnav as he did so. 'If we survive the carpets and the security guards, I'm buying you popcorn. It's the least you deserve. We'll go in that direction anyway and see what we feel like.'

'You're on!' I said, giggling like a little schoolgirl. For the first time in my life, I was going on a normal date, with a normal guy, with a shared chemistry, who was incredibly gorgeous, who liked me back, and it felt exhilarating. It felt as if all my Christmases had come at once.

Chapter 15

Three weeks had passed since the Jeff incident, and I had barely seen him at the office due to him 'coincidentally' booking more consultations at his private practice. For the most part, we had been able to keep out of each other's way, with the exception of the odd email here and there, which were always to the point, and professional. As my manager, I suppose I had a duty to report what had happened to Kofi, but decided not to tell him after thinking about it for a while; I didn't want to escalate it any further; the less people that knew about it, the better. I just wanted to forget it ever happened.

It had also been three weeks since my cute '*Theo: free chauffeur and Peckham Rodeo*' adventure. After meeting up with his cousin for a drink, we decided to ditch the PeckhamPlex idea and he'd decided to take me to his flat in East London. This was in fact A Big Deal. He was letting me into his world, little by little, and it was something I didn't want to take for granted.

His flat was small, yet beautifully decorated. It followed a very earthy aesthetic, with loads of wood panelling, soft beige decor, candles and African artwork – he had a good eye for interiors, I'd give that to him.

His bedroom was simple, but classically decorated and incredibly tidy. He had a poster of Pam Grier as Foxy Brown near his window (an iconic movie tbh), and several houseplants that trailed underneath the window, with photos of him as a child, as well as photos of his parents and grandparents decorating the window sill. I picked up a photo of his mother – a gorgeous woman with a huge Afro, caramel complexion and the biggest, kindest eyes I'd ever seen. His father was handsome and quite dapper – I could see where he got his looks and his dress sense from.

'What do you think of my humble abode?' Theo asked shyly, coming up behind me to wrap me in a hug. 'It's not much, but it's comfortable for now.'

I turned in his arms, giving him a mischievous smile. 'I love it. It's cosy – like a man cave, but without the smelly socks vibe. And your stack of vinyls? Very impressive.' I raised a brow. 'Honestly, it almost feels too good, like you're secretly trying to charm me.'

He smirked, tightening his hold just a little. 'And is it working?'

'Maybe,' I teased, biting back a grin. 'I'll let you know after I see the bathroom.'

His bathroom was small and clean; and not a '10-in-1' body wash to be seen in sight, thank God.

I decided to indulge my curiosity and peeked inside his bathroom drawers, expecting the usual; face creams, body lotions, maybe a few hair products. And sure enough, everything was premium; fancy, fancy, fancy.

I moved on to the second drawer and froze. There, neatly stacked, were at least fifty condoms. Next to them: boxes of Tampax in every size, a bottle of lubricant, edible body oil, and a packet of wet wipes. And tucked in the corner, almost innocently, was a diamond bracelet with the initials 'C.T.'

I quietly shut the drawer, my stomach twisting in a way I couldn't fully unpack. I mean . . . OK, considering Theo's line of work, at least the man was prepared and responsible. Condoms? Check. Safety first and all that. I reminded myself not to take it personally. He slept with women for money; this wasn't new information, and jealousy had no seat at the table here.

But the bracelet; that one prickled. Who was C.T., and why had he kept it? I considered confronting him in a light-hearted way, something teasing but not heavy – just enough to satisfy my curiosity without making a scene. Was this 'C.T.' the same 'C.T.' those girls had asked him about on our first date? My fingers itched to ask, but I had to be smart about it, knowing some answers were better revealed on Theo's terms.

A couple of minutes later, Theo came to find me in the bathroom. I leaned against the doorframe, casual but with a teasing glint in my eye. 'Hey! So . . . random question,' I said, tilting my head, bracelet swinging around my index finger. 'Who's C.T.?'

He paused mid-step, raising an eyebrow. 'C.T.?'

'Yeah,' I replied, tilting my head with mock curiosity. 'I noticed a little diamond bracelet tucked away in your drawer. You've got me curious! Is it a secret admirer, a keepsake . . . or should I start interrogating you?'

Theo froze for a millisecond, and then laughed low and warm, the kind of laugh that made my chest do that little fluttery thing. It was disarming. 'Oh. Err, I can't remember – maybe something a previous client accidentally left here, I think. Don't worry about it.'

Hmm.

I smirked, hiding the little flutter his laugh caused in my chest, even though I was suspicious of his secrecy. 'Mmm . . . OK, Mr Secret-Keeper. I'll let it slide . . . for now. But don't think you're getting away with hiding all your treasures from me.'

He chuckled, leaning closer with a playful grin, before taking the bracelet from my hand and practically throwing it back into the drawer, then slamming it shut with such force that it made me slightly jump.

'Noted. I'll make sure you get full VIP access eventually – you are one of my top clients, after all.'

He then took me into an embrace where we kissed passionately, his hands slowly reaching down my back, and landing on the top of my butt. He knew which buttons to push to make me think about nothing else but him, and it worked. He then walked me to his bedroom, where we spent the day wrapped up in each other. Making love, sharing food, and drifting through his vinyl collection in the living room like it was our own little world.

The last two weekends had followed the same rhythm, split between our homes, and honestly? It was fun. No labels, no pressure, and – most importantly – no monetary transactions.

Last week, Theo had even invited me to a work event as his plus one – a move I considered a major step in our . . . whatever-this-was. Even though the evening was informal, the invitation itself made my heart skip: he was starting to see me as more than a transaction, more than just a temporary distraction.

I arrived at the sleek Liverpool Street building feeling every inch the showstopper. I'd finally broken out my red, sequined Eloquii bodycon dress – the one I'd been saving for the 'perfect' moment – and paired it with low-heeled black strappy sandals from Simply Be. I felt like an absolute vision.

And, unsurprisingly, Theo thought so too. I could feel his eyes on me the moment I stepped inside, an intensity in his gaze that made my pulse quicken. He didn't take his eyes off me all evening, and I couldn't deny it: I loved every second of being the centre of his attention. It was interesting to have the roles reversed in that instance, where *I* was the one escorting *him*; he needed *me*. And despite a few misunderstandings during the evening (everyone seemed to think I was his girlfriend, which I didn't deny!), we had an amazing time.

Of course, that didn't stop the chaos. Within minutes, I'd made the first fatal social error: approaching a cluster of his colleagues with a smile far too wide and a cocktail in hand. 'You're Theo's girlfriend?' someone asked, wide-eyed. I hesitated for a millisecond too long before shrugging and replying, 'I suppose I am tonight!' Theo turned about fifty shades of red – rare, for his complexion – and just sighed, shaking his head at me.

By the end of the night, I had somehow:

- Been declared his 'girlfriend' by literally everyone at the party
- Knocked over at least three trays of food
- Spilled a drink on the CEO's jacket (sorry, Mr CEO)
- Almost started a minor civil war between the wine and canapé stations

Through it all, Theo remained by my side, half mortified, half amused, shaking his head as if he'd been cursed to witness my brand of charm in full effect. And despite the chaos, or maybe because of it, we had the most fun I'd had in ages.

After the eighth time we slept together, I joked that he could start putting everything on my tab. He just smiled and said everything from that first Sunday up until now was on the house. Shit, I wasn't going to complain; no siree! The monetary transactional arrangement had now turned into a somewhat casual arrangement, and I was just fine with that.

The days were slowly stretching out again, and with the extra light came little pockets of time where Theo and I would meet after work – usually for a drink, followed by a cheeky fumble back at mine before he headed home.

With every encounter, I felt my confidence building, especially in bed. Something was shifting. I was beginning to explore a more dominant side of myself, a version I'd never even thought to tap into before. And honestly? I liked her. Theo did too, which made things even hotter. I'd even popped into Ann Summers and treated myself to a couple of sexy lingerie pieces, plus a few toys, you know, for solo missions and joint operations. I was turning into a whole new woman: sexually enlightened, freshly stocked, and feeling myself in more ways than one.

Who knew all it would take was paying someone once to unlock my inner sex goddess? Honestly, money well spent.

In that time, Sade and Kofi had quietly become exclusive, much to my absolute joy. They had been seeing each other nearly every day, as well as spending time at each other's homes constantly. They had even planned their first couples trip to Turkey in a few months' time.

'Sis, I know it probably sounds like we're moving a bit fast, but it just feels right, you know? And when you know, you know!' Sade said one day across a bowl of shared Ceviche at our local Peruvian restaurant in Stockwell.

'I know,' I replied, tucking into a bite. 'I trust your judgement, and I think I know him well enough at this point to know he's a great guy. You guys are adorable, I must say. You both deserve each other!'

After a few more minutes of casual catching up, Sade hit me with the one question I'd been silently dreading for weeks.

'So! When are we finally doing that double date with you and Theo then?'

As much as I loved spending time with all of them equally, Kofi was the only one who was still unaware of the circumstances of how Theo and I had come into contact, and a huge part of me wanted to keep it that way. I decided that honesty would be the best policy in this case.

'To be real with you, Sade, I don't think I'm really ready to talk about Theo so publicly. One; we're just casual, nothing's set in stone, so I don't know if there's even any point in introducing him to people and two – well, I don't really want to go into detail about how we met and what he does to other people, you know?'

I watched Sade's face fall slightly as she processed what I'd said. I'd thought, of all people, she might understand where I was coming from.

Coming from an African background, the idea of paying for sex – or dating a sex worker as a woman – wasn't just taboo, it was scandalous. I could already hear the whispers, feel the judgement. And honestly, I just wanted to save myself the shame before it ever had a chance to start.

Sade replied, 'Oh, I mean I suppose I get where you're coming from. But Kofi wouldn't judge you; we're just happy that you're happy, to be honest. In any case, do you see anything happening between you guys?'

'Nah, not really. I'm big on keeping it light and casual at the moment. I'm just there for the sex; no strings, no feelings. God, this must be what men feel like all the time, huh?' I said, taking a sip of my rum and Coke.

'I guess,' replied Sade, pensively. 'I mean, as long as he feels the same way – are you both on the same page?'

'I reckon so; he hasn't mentioned anything to me about wanting to take things further, so I'm assuming he's into the whole "friends with benefits" thing,' I replied. That said, he had featured, and even tagged me a few times in his recent Instagram stories when we were out on dates. I mean, you don't really do that unless you're starting to take someone seriously . . . right?

Sade sighed, looking somewhat disappointed, to my confusion.

'Look, I know it was my idea in the first place to push you into this . . .' Sade started, taking my hand gently, 'like . . . *yay* for sexual reclamation and all that, but I'm not gonna lie, I can tell you like this guy – a LOT. And I just feel like . . . if there's an opportunity there for you to take things further with him, you should do it. You're so much happier, and I've noticed a confidence in you I've never seen before. I love all of this for you and if he's the one that's bringing this all out of you, I for one would like to shake the man's hand!'

I stared at Sade, at her gorgeous, symmetrical face. Her thick, voluminous Afro that had been swept into a clean top-knot bun only highlighted her razor-sharp cheekbones and perfectly plump lips. My best friend was stunning.

'Thank you, babes,' I replied, taking a sip from my glass. 'I'm just gonna see where it goes for now; there's nothing wrong in being a little guarded in the beginning, you know?'

'Yeah I hear you, I just wouldn't want you to ruin a prospectively good thing is all,' replied Sade, leaning back. Shit, me either.

Besides, I'm sure that Theo was still seeing his other clients on a weekly basis. I was sure that he was as content with this arrangement as I was. I carried the conversation with Sade home with me that evening, thinking about the fact that Theo had, in fact, broken his boundaries with me. I needed to be clear on where we stood before we could progress any further, just to avoid any mixed signals. I also thought about potentially introducing Sade to him; I needed to sort out my feelings around that before acting on anything. What me and Theo had at the moment felt so perfect that I was hesitant to introduce anything – or anyone – that could distract from that.

Theo was on his way to mine that evening anyway, so I decided that we would chat then.

A couple of hours later, Theo showed up, looking as effortlessly delicious as ever.

Usually, after we slept together, we'd linger in bed for a while, snuggling, talking, half watching whatever was on TV while he absentmindedly traced his fingers along my back. It was unexpectedly tender, almost romantic. And the more it happened, the more I realised just how much I'd been missing that kind of softness. As we lay in bed, our bodies hot and pulsating after a particularly vigorous session, I turned to face him; his face was a picture of calm and serenity. He had beads of sweat dripping down his forehead, forming a pool on my satin pillow.

'Hello, beautiful,' he said softly, and smiled as he kissed me lightly on the lips. I shivered subtly as his lips met mine. Don't get me wrong – sex with him was incredible. He knew how to navigate every inch of my body, holding me with a confidence and care that no one else ever had. With him, I felt free; able to speak my desires openly, to guide him, to take the lead in ways I never had before. And that in itself was empowering.

But it was the moments afterwards, the quiet, tender ones, that truly stayed with me. The way he held me, touched me like I was something to be cherished. That's when I felt most beautiful. Most wanted. But, in order for things to continue, clarity was needed.

'Hey you,' I responded, lightly booping him on the nose. 'So, this thing that we're doing right? What are your thoughts on it?'

At this, Theo raised his head slightly before resting it on his crooked arm to get a better look at me. 'What do you mean? As in, like, us hanging out?'

'Yup. Like, this is purely a sex thing right? Like a "friends with benefits" type thing? I just think it would be good to know where we're both at. For clarity.'

Theo's face was unreadable. He paused for a while, staring deeply into my eyes, his face neutral the whole time. After what seemed like two minutes of silence, he finally spoke.

'I mean. I suppose, if that's what you want it to be, Cassie.' His face again showing no traces of emotion.

'Isn't that what this is, though? Don't get me wrong, I enjoy you, I really do. I think this little thing we have going on is really fun and I love spending time with you but I just wanted to be clear that that's all it is – fun. Right?'

'Right,' he said, laying his head back on the pillow as he softly played with my hair. I might have been wrong, but he almost looked a little disappointed. My assumptions proved to be correct a moment later.

'I'd be lying if I said I didn't like you a little, to be honest, Cassie,' he said at last, sitting up in bed. I sat up too, slowly, my stomach doing that annoying little flip it does when things are about to get real.

So this was happening. The Talk™. I'd only known him for two months.

To be fair, a part of me had clocked it ages ago; probably right around the time he stopped charging me and we started hanging out like two people who actually *liked* each other. But did I acknowledge it? Absolutely not. I shoved that realisation into a mental drawer labelled 'Deal With Later' and slammed it shut. I guess it was better to have the conversation now and just get it over and done with. He continued on.

'I know we haven't known each other that long,' he began, his voice steady but careful, 'but over the past few weeks, I've found myself drawn to you, more than I expected. And not just in a sexual way. It's . . . something about your energy. Being around you just feels good. Easy. There's this pull I can't really explain. You kinda broke through all my boundaries and I wasn't mad at it.'

He paused for a moment, eyes searching mine.

'That said, if you'd prefer to keep things strictly transactional, I'll have to respect that. Whatever you decide, I'm good with it.'

There was a flicker of sadness in his eyes that tugged at something deep in me. I hadn't realised this was how he truly felt. And if I'm honest, a part of me was frustrated – frustrated that I couldn't meet him there, not yet.

I mean, here I was: completely naked in bed with a fine-as-fuck, successful younger guy who'd just opened up and admitted he was slowly falling for me. And what was I thinking about? My family. What they'd say if they ever found out what he actually did for a living.

The truth is, I did have feelings for him – maybe not fully formed, but they were there, lingering at the edges. Still, in the name of self-preservation – and avoiding any potential scandal – I knew I had to keep things light and easy.

And at that moment, I hated myself a little for it.

I caressed his cheek slowly, wanting him to feel heard and seen – the last thing I ever wanted to do was dismiss his feelings at this moment.

'Thank you for telling me and I appreciate you respecting my current stance on things. Would this mean I'd need to go back to booking you formally for things, moving forward?'

'Yeah, it would,' he stated, now getting out of bed and putting on his clothes. 'I'm not leaving because of this conversation, by the way – like I said, I respect what you have going on. I just have another home appointment with a client soon.'

For some reason, that admission landed hard – like a slap I didn't see coming. It was the first time he'd mentioned seeing another client in front of me since I'd asked about it a few weeks ago. The way he said it felt intentional, almost like he *wanted* a reaction – as if he was trying to make me jealous. But instead of stirring up any kind of desire, it just turned me off completely.

If anything, it gave me the ick.

'OK . . . ? Well, I hope your next appointment goes

smoothly, I guess,' I said in response, covering my body with my duvet. 'I suppose I'll see you another time?'

Theo finished getting dressed, walked over to the bed, and pressed a light kiss to my forehead. As he walked towards the door, I could see that he was clenching his jaw. Was he really upset? Was he . . . expecting things to develop into something more serious? No. I couldn't allow myself to assume that. Not when he was still seeing other clients.

'Sure. You know what to do. Have a great rest of the day.'

And just like that, he turned on his heel and left.

I sat there in silence, more agitated than anything. I could understand that he probably felt a little bruised by the rejection – he didn't exactly strike me as someone who was used to hearing 'no'. But the way he had left, so abruptly and coldly, left a bitter taste in my mouth.

Still, I didn't want to throw away the connection we'd built. The chemistry was undeniable, and he was, objectively, a phenomenal lover. So yeah, I figured I'd probably book him again when the mood struck – hopefully by then, his ego would've made a full recovery.

'You're actually a witch, you know?' Sade blasted at me on the phone after I let her know everything that had gone down between Theo and me earlier. 'WHY ON EARTH would you say that to him? You literally were on the cusp of potentially dating this fine-ass younger man who's been dicking you down several times a week, only to fuck it all up, for what reason? Have I taught you nothing, child?'

I had been expecting this reaction; and if I had had the guts to look at this situation externally, I'd probably be mad at myself too.

'Oh, Sade please, I kinda feel bad enough as it is. Imagine I take him to my parents and they start probing him with questions? I wouldn't want him to lie about what he did. Also, what if someone recognised him from the website? And another thing, he's still sleeping with his clients alongside me, so it's like . . . it was never really set up to last on a deeper level, was it?'

'Oh my God, you're acting as if you guys were about to get married. Why would you be introducing him to your parents already? It wouldn't have needed to even go that far! But I didn't know he was still sleeping with the other women – you sure he's been using protection, yeah?'

I paused at that last question – I genuinely didn't know. I guess I'd just assumed he was a responsible adult and took the same precautions with his other clients as he did with me. It hadn't even crossed my mind to question it.

'One. Yes, I think he is using protection with the others, and two, I was more so thinking about my mum's wedding in a couple of months. The thought quickly crossed my mind about inviting him as my plus one. You know what my parents are like; all the questions and stuff. And besides, as long as he's still active on *OuiMeet* doing what he's currently doing, there couldn't be any prospect of a relationship anyway. I'm a monogamous babe.'

Sade groaned. I changed the call to 'loudspeaker mode' as I flipped through the notifications on Instagram. I'd seen that he'd left a trail of 'likes' on some of my most recent photos. I sighed. Bless his heart.

As Sade continued her lecture about how I'd apparently sabotaged a good thing with Theo, I distracted myself by scrolling through my socials – LinkedIn being the final stop. Much as I enjoyed my job, I liked to keep one eye on the horizon. A little career window-shopping never hurt anyone, and let's be real: I wasn't about to stay stuck on an NHS Band 7 salary forever.

Checking through my LinkedIn profile friend requests, my eyes were drawn to one profile; it was Jeff. The *nerve*.

I eventually got off the phone with Sade, and allowed my curiosity to get the better of me as I clicked 'accept' on Jeff's friend request, just to have a nosy look at his profile; I'd planned to unfriend him as soon as I was done snooping. A quick glance at his profile told me he'd studied medicine at Cambridge, then gone on to complete his specialist training at St George's. Impressive – very 'future consultant who drinks oat matcha lattes' energy. I checked his friends list to see if he'd already connected with any of our colleagues. I saw that he had also connected to four of our other colleagues – as well as Kofi – over the last four days. All of a sudden a message popped up on my screen. It was from Jeff.

Oh, for goodness sake.

Hi Cassandra. I hope you've been well. Just to let you know that I'll be swinging by the office for a couple of hours tomorrow before going to the other surgery. I also wanted to again apologise for my terrible oversight and overstepping a few weeks ago. I'm sorry if this has put you in an uncomfortable position, and I'm hoping we can continue to maintain a civil, professional relationship moving forward.

I rolled my eyes. Sure, he *sounded* sorry, but the choice of platform said otherwise. Sending this through LinkedIn instead of our work email felt somewhat calculated – as if he was already cushioning himself in case I decided to go to HR. I typed back:

Hi Jeff. It's all good, thank you for checking in. I'll see you tomorrow.

I hit 'send', and instead, muted his account. The truth was, when Jeff first arrived, I was physically attracted to him, but I didn't believe I displayed my attraction towards him in any way.

However, what if subconsciously I had? What if he had been picking up on vibes that I was unintentionally giving out? I couldn't necessarily blame him 100 per cent (99 per cent was enough due to him being a colleague), and while what he did had been inappropriate, I also had to sit with the question: had it not been for Theo, would I have leaned in for that kiss too? I guess I'll never know, and I never wanted to find out. I logged out of LinkedIn and sighed.

Men. The initial plan was spending the day with Theo at mine, but since his abrupt exit a few hours ago, it had left me with nothing to do. To pass the time, I whipped out the £250 dark-green peplum dress I'd ordered from Karen Millen that I would be wearing at my mum's shotgun wedding. Somehow, she'd managed to tick off a surprising number of things in record time, from locking down a small venue to sorting the catering (thank God for aunties who could throw down in the kitchen), and even sending out the e-invites. Mum and Femi had both made it clear that since it was their second time down the aisle, the wedding would be intimate and fuss-free – which, honestly, suited me just fine.

The theme was green and ivory; Mum and Femi's favourite colours. I tried on the dress again, standing in the mirror to look at how the dress hugged every curve of my body.

The dress was a bit snug, but by periodically trying it on a couple of times a week, I was hoping that the fabric would be able to stretch just a tiny bit. The dress hugged and cinched me in all the right areas, something that the larger dress size wouldn't have been able to do. It had a low neckline that showed a respectable amount of cleavage, and a corseted bust, complete with a peplum waist that draped into an A-line skirt, complete with tulle gathering. It was absolutely stunning.

I still hadn't been able to find a date; something my mum kept reminding me of every time we spoke:

'Cassandra, have you got a plus one yet? I thought you were dating someone? What's the holdup?'

'I'm not dating anyone at the moment, Mum, and yeah, I'm still working on it, but would it be the worst thing in the world if I came alone?'

'Of course it would, don't be ridiculous! I wouldn't hear the end of it from your aunties and my cousins. I don't want there to be rumours started about you, you know? I don't want people to think you weren't raised right – that you aren't wife material.'

'And if I'm single, why is it that I am positioned as being the problem? Do you know the absolute lizards running around the dregs of London claiming to be real men? If it's not them listening to red pill, Andrew Tate-style nonsense, then it's them starting podcasts and I just can't be arsed, Mum.'

'Be that as it may, even if it's a friend, invite someone please. Don't come and embarrass me on my big day. Thank you very much.'

Africans. Sometimes you have no choice but to laugh. The alternative is screaming into the abyss at how our worth is still tied to how close we can orbit men, like desperate moons circling dusty little planets. In the matriarchal dystopia of my dreams, men would be born in solitary confinement, handed a syllabus on feminism, and only granted societal access after passing a rigorous series of trials: empathy exams! Basic hygiene evaluations! And a multi-stage consent obstacle course. And even then, parole would be conditional.

Chapter 16

I'll be honest (and a little dramatic): I'd gotten so used to Theo's daily check-ins and flirtatious calls and messages that a few days of radio silence felt like a bit of a tragic loss – the kind you don't cry over, but still mope about like someone stole your last piece of chocolate. Pathetic, really. But here we were. I hadn't heard from him since our little chat recently, and I'd found myself mindlessly going through random photos and videos we'd made together while on my work lunch break.

'D'you have a date for your mum's wedding yet, Cass?' Kofi asked me one day over lunch.

'Ugh. Don't remind me; my mum keeps calling me every day, asking about it. I don't really see the big deal in going alone but alas, the woman wants her wedding to be perfect. No one in mind yet, though,' I replied, tucking into my ham and cheese sandwich. It was at that point that I saw a flicker of mischief shift within Kofi 's eyes, followed by a swift smirk.

'Mm. I see,' he said, peering over his glasses at me with an amused look. 'Well, it's not long to go now and I figured, since you and Jeff seem to be getting along much better these days, why don't you ask him?'

I stopped mid-chew and stared at Kofi, willing my face not to betray me. I'd rather eat a jean jacket than ever ask him. I hadn't told Kofi about my run-in with Jeff, and tried as hard as possible to keep my face passive. In a different universe, it would probably have been ideal taking someone like Jeff to the wedding. He was older than me; an accomplished surgeon, attractive. Well dressed. With a fancy flat in Vauxhall and a pension plan. I could see my mum and the aunties practically fawning over him. But alas. *But then again . . .*

'Kofi! I don't think that would be appropriate, you know,' I said, trying to feign laughter. I really needed to chill out. 'I hardly know the guy! Plus, I wouldn't want him to get the wrong idea or anything. The last thing I'd ever want is an office romance – yuck.'

'OK, but I love that with everything you just said, not once did you deny finding him attractive – or that he might have a bit of a thing for you,' Kofi said, hands raised in mock innocence. 'I'm just saying! If the talent pool's looking a little dry, he could be an option. Let me play matchmaker for once, man!'

I rolled my eyes. I would have much preferred to have gone to the wedding with Theo. I suppose there could still be an opportunity to do that if I paid him to be my date, though. I couldn't deny that I did miss him a little bit. If only he could stick to the day job – I just couldn't risk the shame of bumping into someone who could potentially recognise him though.

Ugh; a dilemma.

I'd been working extra hours after my shift, trying to muffle the loneliness that crept in whenever I was home alone. It was surprising how quickly I'd grown used to spending time with Theo, talking, laughing, just being around each other every day. Now that our conversations had slowed, a quiet emptiness had started to settle in, one that even Sade and my other friends couldn't completely fill. Being with Theo these past few weeks had reminded me what it felt like to be seen – truly seen – and desired, openly and without hesitation. And I missed that. I missed *him*.

That evening after work, I found myself lingering on his *OuiMeet* profile, looming over the new pictures he had uploaded. One of the photos – a profile shot of him in the park wearing a beige co-ord set, diffused winter sun making his face glow handsomely – was one I'd taken of him while on one of our dates. I found myself briefly thinking back to that date; I'd organised a cute picnic in Larkhall park – a stone's throw away from my flat. He'd shown up at midday and we ended up spending approximately forty-five minutes on the grass frolicking before deciding it was too cold and clambered back to the flat, where we spent the rest of the day making love and drinking wine. It was wonderful.

I let out a sigh as I scrolled through the rest of his photos, debating whether I should take the leap and book him again. He'd been pretty clear that *OuiMeet* should be our main line of communication moving forward, and out of respect for his boundaries, I didn't want to risk making him uncomfortable by reaching out through calls or texts out of the blue.

I hovered over his booking menu. Maybe it wasn't just the sex. Maybe I did like him more than I let on. Without thinking, I clicked on 'overnight stay' and saw that he had availability for Saturday night. I booked it, closed the app and held my breath. Fuck it.

As expected, about twenty minutes later I received a message from him:

> Oh. I see. Just couldn't stay away, huh? I'll see you on Saturday, I guess. Thanks for the booking.

No kisses. No sign off. I couldn't quite make heads or tails of his response, but ultimately I was glad that I would be seeing him again, if only as one of his clients. I replied back, matching his aloof energy:

What can I say? I miss your company. And you're very welcome.

That was that, then. It was an uneventful week, but Friday had finally arrived, and I was dismayed upon finding out that I'd RSVP'd to another after-work drinks event that evening and had completely forgotten. Kofi and Sade had a date night, so I couldn't even use them as an excuse to dip. It wasn't until one of the nurses reminded me at 4 p.m. that I remembered. I checked the calendar invite and saw that Jeff was due to attend too. Fantastic . .

When the workday finally wrapped up, I logged off, fixed my make-up and decided to pop in for one quick drink – just to show my face. Part of me also wanted to signal to Jeff that things didn't have to be awkward; we needed to get used to being around each other again.

As we all entered the pub, I made a beeline for the corner booth again and tried to make a conscious effort to seem sociable. As the others placed their orders at the bar, Jeff approached me and asked for my order.

'I'll have a gin and tonic, I think, thanks,' I said, trying to appear normal.

'Coming right up,' he said, and wandered over to the bar to make the order. Minutes later, he was back, and took the seat opposite me. This couldn't have been any more awkward if it tried. 'So, how has your week been? It's been a pretty busy one at my end, so apologies for all the extra work I lumbered you with – I feel awful. I didn't anticipate the influx of new patients this week.'

OK, a bit of light chat; fair enough. We could just pretend as if it never happened.

'Ah, don't worry about it. It's literally what I'm here for. You're all good.' I smiled politely and sipped my drink, wishing I could be at home.

'I appreciate it a lot. Anyway, erm, it's been nice having these little work outings and getting to know the wider team – it's like a little family.'

'Haha – yeah, almost,' I replied; little did he know I barely knew anything about my other colleagues outside of their full names and roles. Our offices were situated away from the outpatients' department, meaning that outside of the consultant meeting rooms, Kofi and I were quite isolated.

We made polite conversation for the next twenty minutes, with Jeff starting on his second beer. After a swig, he suddenly became solemn. This was what I had been dreading.

'Cassandra . . . about that moment in the car, I just wanted to apo—'

I waved my hand lazily, cutting him off. 'It's fine, Mr Paulson; it's fine. You've already apologised, and I accept your apology. I don't think we need to go back to that, do you? I'd love to just move past it, if that's OK?'

Jeff nodded his head slightly, his mouth forming into a thin line. His face was unreadable. 'You're right . . . you're right. I just feel awful about it – I won't bring it up again. Deal?'

'Deal,' I replied, breathing a sigh of relief. I was hoping that things could now finally get back to normal.

We played a couple of rounds of friendly pool before heading back to the booth where I picked up my jacket. I'd done enough socialising for the night.

'So, any plans for the weekend?' he asked.

'Not much, to be honest. Just spending the evening with a friend, and maybe browsing a few flower shops for wedding bouquets during the day. My mum's getting married at the end of May, and at this point, floral arrangements are the only thing she trusts me with,' I replied, suddenly remembering that extra chore I'd been tasked with.

At this, he raised his glass. 'Congratulations to your mum!

That's super exciting. I'm going to a wedding at the end of May too; must be the season for it!'

'Yeah, I'm looking forward to it – it should be a decent day!' I said, stifling a yawn. I really wasn't good at small talk, but at least we were back to being semi-normal again.

On the taxi ride home, I sent Kofi a message to update him on how the evening went. I immediately received a message back:

> **Oh good, I'm glad it went well! Also, I forgot to give you the gist. I found out that he has a whole family by the way, lol, so ignore everything I said the other day about inviting him to the wedding as your +1.**

I read the last part of the message again.

Wife? A family?

Upon first meeting him, I made sure to note that he didn't have a wedding ring on. Not to mention that he's never brought up any mention of having a family in all the conversations we'd had. Not that he had to, of course, but still. Interesting. I typed back:

> **Wait wtf. How do you know he's married? Never seen him wear a ring??**

I arrived home and made a beeline straight to the bedroom to try and sleep off the alcohol. Propped up in bed, I read Kofi's eventual reply:

> **Didn't notice the ring thing but I randomly looked him up on Facebook after he friended me on LinkedIn. His profile is open and he's got photos of his wife and wedding pics and his two little kids on there and everything. Looks like he's been married for at least 10 years. xx**

Thank God for good friends like Kofi. I rushed onto Facebook – an app I hadn't actively used in at least four years – and searched 'Jeff Paulson' and, sure enough, his profile popped up immediately. Scrolling through it, I saw hundreds of photos – updated as recently as last week – of him and his wife, whose name was Veronica. She seemed to also be a doctor, and was stunning to boot, with the most gorgeous blonde dreadlocks. As Kofi said, they had two children; one was five years old and the other was two, and they looked like the perfect family; like something out of a Norman Rockwell painting, in fact. Just perfect.

Wow. A whole family. That just made what he did with me in the car even worse. A would-be cheater!! A scoundrel. Ragamuffin, some would even say! For the sake of my peace of mind at work, I decided that I wasn't going to crash out over it. I thought of his poor wife. How many times had he done this without her knowledge? A phone notification broke me out of my concentration. It was a *OuiMeet* message from Theo:

Hi. I'll see you tomorrow at 8 p.m.

The sharpness of the message stung; he still seemed a bit hurt by our last conversation, but I was hoping I could make it up to him tomorrow. I'd be lying if I said I wasn't looking forward to spending time with him again. I snuggled up to Toby and thought of Theo as I fell asleep, waiting to see what tomorrow would bring.

It was just past 3 p.m. the next day, and I was at Sade's flat, working my way through a bucket of KFC while we swapped stories about recent escapades. Things between her and Kofi were clearly still going strong – evidenced by the load of laundry she was halfway through when I showed up, which included more than a few pairs of men's boxers. I made sure she watched as I stared at the boxers on top of the laundry basket – Calvin Kleins – Kofi at least had good taste.

'So,' I started, biting a strip of chicken from the bone, 'it begins. So when's he moving in then?' Sade responded by playfully jabbing me in the ribs before coming to sit down and join in the feast.

'Oh, whatever – quit being so dramatic!' she exclaimed, tucking into a drumstick. 'Honestly, I really like having him around; it just feels . . . real, you know? I know we're moving fast, but I'm genuinely happy. He's like this big, excitable ball of light, and right now, that's exactly what I need. And seriously, thank you. You really came through for me – you're a real one!'

She then stared off into the distance for a moment, her eyes glazed over in what looked like a trance, and that's when it hit me: this bitch had fallen in love.

'You look like a bitch in love by the way,' I said, breaking the silence. 'Either way, you two are incredibly cute together – Kofi can't stop talking about you at work and I've never seen him this way with anyone else in all the years I've worked with him so you must be doing something right, girl. Anyway, I love you both and when you guys get engaged, just know that I will be claiming that maid of honour position.'

Sade didn't reply, but instead smiled warmly. It was truly great to see her so happy. If I could just get a crumb of that at some point, then life would be great.

'What's going on with you and Theo these days anyway?' Sade asked. 'Are you guys still seeing each other?' I updated her on the recent events taking place with Theo and me, making sure to ham up the reasoning as to why I couldn't allow for anything deeper with him at this point.

After I was done, Sade just stared at me and shook her head. Uh oh.

'Girl. You clearly like this guy. And if you're beginning to develop feelings for him, why do you care what your family will think?'

'Sade, have you forgotten that we are both African women who come from annoying-ass families? I don't want to be given the third degree by my parents if they ever found out how we met – it's so embarrassing.' I finished up the last of my food, feeling Sade's eyes burn into me, full of judgement. She was such a lover girl, this one.

'Cassie, babe, let's be real for a second. Your brother just had a baby with his girlfriend – no ring, no vows, just vibes. Your mum's gearing up for round two at the altar. And your dad? He's out there roaming around London like he's the star of a nineties R&B music video, trying to win her back instead of acting like a grown adult. Traditional? Babes, please. Your family left "traditional" in the dust years ago. Just admit that you like that male escort and have your happily ever after.'

My best friend had such a way with words, and that's why I loved her and her brutal honesty.

'When you put it like that, I see what you're saying . . . but . . . I don't know. We'll see. I'm seeing Theo tonight – he's staying over – so we'll probably chat then, I guess.'

At that, Sade cocked her perfectly groomed eyebrow at me. 'Uh huh. Well, you guys have your chat in between getting dicked down – I'm sure you'll change your mind eventually, and I can't wait until you do, so I can finally meet the guy and fully give him the third degree.'

'About that—' I started, knowing where this was about to go but being powerless to stop it '—Sade, I'll be honest, I've been a bit hesitant to introduce you both, not only because I'm trying to keep it on the downlow, but you know what my dating history's been like, right? I've never really had something that's been . . . all mine. I guess I was a bit nervous that he'd take one look at how gorgeous you are and somehow . . . forget all about me.'

I chewed on my thumb nervously as I braced myself for her response. I don't know what urged me to bring this up, but I knew I had to be honest about that niggling fear in the back of my head.

Out of nowhere, I felt a chip land on my nose at full force, with the chip dust breezing into my nostrils. I looked up at Sade, who looked livid. Here we go.

'Are you taking the piss, Cass? You're my best friend. Do you honestly think I would ever do that to you?' Her hands were crossed around her body defensively. Oh yikes.

I issued my retort: 'NO I absolutely don't! I know you would never cross that line . . . I think I'm just scared that he'd probably take a liking to you and—'

'Lemme stop you right there—' intervened Sade, picking up another chip and threatening to throw it at me again. 'Don't use me as a reason to sabotage what you have with him. From the way you've made it sound, he practically worships the ground you walk on. Has he ever given you a reason to doubt his attraction to you?'

'No, but—'

'Exactly,' she cut in. 'Has he ever flirted with, or even looked at another woman while you guys have been together?'

'Well, no—'

'Right,' Sade cut in again. 'So is this really about him or is this about you seeing a good thing for once and self-sabotaging because you're not used to being around good men?'

She had me there, my irritating-yet-always-right-best friend.

'I . . . maybe it's about me, I don't know. I panicked, OK?' I stared down at my hands, feeling sorry for myself.

'Oh, I know you did,' Sade replied, shoving the chip into her mouth and munching loudly. 'I'm a bit hurt that you think I'm some kind of a threat to you and him, if I'm being honest. I've always wanted nothing but the best for you, and I would never want you to think I would ever cross the line in that way. You're my sister, man.'

We stared at each other in silence, and in that moment I was grateful that I'd brought it up before it had the opportunity to turn into resentment.

'I'm sorry sis,' I replied, going in for a hug. 'I'm definitely overthinking. I shouldn't have brought you into this. Maybe I do need to do a bit more self-reflection.'

'I know you fucking do. Apology accepted. Now hurry up and get ready so you can get your man back, for fuck's sake.'

I threw a chip at her. I hated how she always ended up being right.

At 7.30 p.m., I began lighting the scented candles in my bedroom and living room. Toby had annoyingly shat up a storm during my absence, and despite me changing his cat litter, I could still faintly smell the shitty odour, forcing me to have to light my never-before-used Diptyque 34 Candle – a scent I'd only ever wanted to use for special occasions. I'd also decided to actually cook this time around, settling on steak, mashed potatoes and vegetables, which I knew was one of his favourite dishes.

With fifteen minutes to spare, I slipped into a simple but cute white dress. It was form-fitting, understated – almost virginal, if we're being dramatic. I kept my hair and make-up minimal, too. After all the time we'd spent together, I didn't feel the need to go all out. He'd always made me feel cute, even in an oversized T-shirt with zero make-up on.

At 8 p.m. on the dot, my buzzer rang and something in me shifted. I hadn't been this nervous to see him since our very first phone call, and wasn't sure why I suddenly had a case of the butterflies. He'd been pretty quiet on his socials since our last conversation, so I hadn't really been able to gauge his mood up until now. I guessed I was about to find out.

'Hey you,' he muttered, a slow grin spilling across his face lazily as I opened the door to greet him. Since we'd last seen each other, he'd grown out a bit of facial fur, which really suited him actually. He was dressed rather formally; wearing a pair of grey suit trousers paired with a crisp white shirt and matching grey blazer.

'Your office has you working on a Saturday?' I said, as he walked through the hallway, caught sight of Toby and gently picked him up to pet him. By now, Toby had become used to Theo coming to the flat, and had become quite taken with him, much to my relief.

'Nope,' he replied, putting Toby down and making his way to the sofa. 'Just thought I'd be professional, you know. You are, after all, a client of mine. I thought it would be good to be formal.'

He must have been taking the piss. Surely.

'Um . . . OK? Would you like a drink? I've got wine, Sprite, tea . . . coffee . . .' I responded, confused. I'm pretty sure he was doing this to spite me. Touché.

'I'll have a glass of wine, thanks.'

We made ourselves comfortable on the sofa after I served him his drink. The air was thick with tension; not necessarily bad, just awkward. I decided that it would be best to just confront the elephant in the room.

'Theo . . . I missed you,' I started, turning to face him. He was already facing me at this point, his eyes turned downwards as he listened quietly. 'This whole "formal client" thing you're doing? I get it; you're trying to make a point. And look, I understand that I was the one who brought up the whole thing about you breaking your boundaries in the first place, but things changed, I guess. And you were so adamant about keeping your work and personal life separate, that I just wanted to respect that too, you know?'

'I missed you too,' he began. As he turned to face me, he held my hands in his – *très* romantic.

'Look, I know. I was really clear about my boundaries at the beginning, especially when it came to clients. But something changed that night in the Uber. I don't even know exactly when it happened . . . I just know you're different. You're not like anyone I've met in a really long time, and it caught me off-guard. It's not just the sex – though that's honestly incredible – it's the way I can't seem to stop thinking about you when we're apart. I love how quick you are, how you never let anything rattle you. You're beautiful, but it's more than that. It's the way you carry yourself, how sure you are. Most women either put me on a pedestal or keep me at a distance, and it gets . . . lonely, sometimes. But you? You meet me eye to eye. You challenge me. You make me feel seen. I guess . . . I just wanted to hold onto that a little longer.'

I stared at him, open-mouthed, completely blindsided. No one had ever seen me like that before, let alone said it out loud. For a second, something inside me – something I thought had long since gone numb – began to thaw. All I wanted in that moment was to fall into him, to kiss him, to lose myself and not think about anything else. But I couldn't shake it; the sharp, unwelcome voice in the back of my mind, hissing, *'What would your friends say? What would your family think?'* It clashed painfully with the part of me that just wanted to be selfish, to reach for something that felt real. And for the first time in a long time, I didn't know which side of me was going to win.

It was as if Theo could read my mind. Without a word, he set his wine glass down on the table, his eyes never leaving mine. In the next breath, he closed the distance between us and swept me into his arms, his mouth finding mine in a kiss that was all heat.

I melted against him instantly, my hands gripping the fabric of his shirt as if grounding myself, almost as if to make sure he was really there. His kiss deepened, desperate; tasting of wine and something sweeter I couldn't put my finger on.

He pulled back just enough to look at me, his forehead pressed to mine, his breath ragged. For a long moment, we just stayed there, suspended between sense and surrender. His hands slid up my back, slowly, as if memorising the shape of me.

When he kissed me again, it was slower and more deliberate. His fingers threaded through my braids, tipping my head back so he could trail kisses along my jaw, down my neck, leaving a blazing path in their wake.

I could hear Toby meowing in the background, probably pissed off that I wasn't giving him any attention just then. Cuddles would just have to wait, my friend.

All of a sudden, Theo picked me up and backed me towards the wall, pinning me there with the weight of his body, and I let him, heart hammering against my ribs. His hands slid down to my hips, gripping hard enough to almost bruise, and I arched into him, craving more, craving *everything*. 'God, you drive me crazy,' he muttered against my skin, voice rough, before again trailing a line of frantic kisses down my neck, my collarbone, anywhere he could reach.

His hands were everywhere; my waist, my thighs, my back, touching like he was afraid I might slip away if he stopped for even a second.

When he finally lifted me, I wrapped my legs around his waist without thinking, clinging to him as he carried me towards the bedroom, his mouth never leaving mine for long. Every kiss, every touch, every ragged breath between us screamed of something bigger than lust – something urgent, desperate and real.

And for once, I didn't think. I didn't question.

I just let myself fall.

Chapter 17

I never imagined I'd find myself making a full English breakfast for a man on a Sunday morning. Me – a lifelong believer in a matriarchal society where men would have to prove their worth before even being welcomed into it – standing there in my bathrobe, blasting Sam Cooke on Spotify, and flipping bacon and eggs (with my good spatula!) for Theo like it was the most natural thing in the world.

Last night felt like something out of a movie. The way Theo and I made love was so natural; it was as if we'd known each other our whole lives. He allowed me yet again to take the reins – something he knew now turned me on – allowing me to fully bask in my femininity and confidence, making me feel invincible. We lost ourselves in each other again and again, three, maybe four times last night, until I was trembling, glowing, completely undone in the best way.

And now I was here making him breakfast; go figure.

I was mid-toast, butter knife still in hand, when his arms snuck under mine and spun me around, stealing a kiss so passionate it felt like something straight out of a romcom. I couldn't help but laugh – I thought moments like this only happened on screen?

'Hey you,' he murmured, cheekily grabbing a slice of toast.

'Morning, love,' I replied, returning to plate the fry-up. I could get used to this. After dishing the plates, we sat down on the sofa together, taking in the last few hours. I'd decided that I wanted to see him more regularly again, and wanted to know his thoughts on it.

'So, when do you want to see each other again?' I said, clearing the plates. Theo looked at his phone in response, his gaze focused intensely for a few moments before responding.

'Hmm. I've got a couple of clients I'm seeing tomorrow and Tuesday after work, so I'd be free from Wednesday onwards?'

And in that moment the strangest thing happened. It felt like my heart had frozen solid and dropped straight into the pit of my stomach. Of course I knew he was still seeing other women 'professionally', but I just didn't expect him to mention it so casually, especially after what he'd shared last night – especially after how we spent the last night.

'Clients as in *OuiMeet* clients?' I mumbled, turning my head slightly so he couldn't see the disappointment in my face. I could only hide this sudden jealousy for so long.

'Oh . . . yeah. Why?' he said with a subtle puzzled look on his face, which only made me feel more resentful. I decided to just spill; better out than in.

'I mean, after everything you were saying last night, you almost made it sound as if you wanted us to – I don't know – go steady or something. Why would you still be sleeping with other women if that were the case? Or maybe I misunderstood last night.'

The solemn expression Theo had worn all this time suddenly gave way to confusion; something I had anticipated. Just last night – in between us having sex and lying in each other's company, we'd had a few chats trying to come up with a suitable conclusion.

I'd reminded him that I wanted to keep things strictly transactional between us for now – that it was purely a sexual thing at the moment, which although he wasn't the most pleased about hearing, he seemed to accept for now. So at this moment, I could understand why he might be confused. The truth was, I didn't know where this sudden wave of jealousy had come from either.

'Cassandra – I'm confused. Last night you said you wanted to keep things transactional for now, so why do you care about who I'm sleeping with? It's a job. I don't have any emotional attachment to those ladies, if that's what you're really trying to find out.'

It felt like I was drifting outside my own body – watching, powerless, as the jealous, aching part of me took over. The logical side tried to reason with it, reminding me this was just part of his job, nothing personal. But reason felt distant, drowned out by something I couldn't quite name. Whatever I was supposed to feel for Theo was meant to be physical – just physical – but at that moment, I wasn't so sure any more.

Had I fallen for him? Obviously I had. Duh.

All I knew right there and then was that – as selfish as it was – I didn't like the idea of him seeing other women while we were together.

'It's not even about emotional attachment,' I started, trying to control my face. The last thing I wanted was for him to assume I was really upset. 'It's just weird, don't you think? To be seeing and sleeping with someone you like, as well as sleeping with other women. It just . . . it just makes me uncomfortable, I guess.'

Theo stood up and gave an exasperated sigh, holding his head in his hands. Considering my viewpoint on his arrangement, I knew I was asking for a lot.

'Cassie, you really need to figure out what you want. Am I someone you just want to keep hiring to fulfil your needs? Or do you actually like me? Because I like you. And at this point, I'm down for whatever it is you want; but you can't treat me like a disposable asset and also expect exclusivity – it doesn't work like that. You were the one who brought up the prospect of dating in the first place and now that I'm offering that to you, you don't want that either. What is it you want?'

I felt something the size of a grape fall pitifully into the depths of my stomach. It was the fact that I couldn't even fully refute what he was saying; he was absolutely right. I wanted exclusivity with him on my terms when it came to our physical relationship, but I was also in no position to commit to him in the way I perhaps wanted him to.

'Theo, I'm sorry. You're right – and I hate that I've put you in this position. The thing is, I really do think you're amazing. In another life, under different circumstances, I would've jumped at the chance to see where this could go, dating-wise. You're smart, kind, respectful, generous. You make me feel like a fucking queen every time we're together. You've helped me see myself in a way no one else ever has. But I'm scared to mess with whatever this is. Can't we just keep going the way we have been? Or . . . maybe just limit it to one other client instead of the three or four? I know it's not fair to ask, but I'm just being honest.'

I knew I was asking for a lot. I just needed to try my luck. I could see the wheels turning in Theo's head; I was stressing this boy out, but I didn't want to let go of a good thing. Theo paced from one end of the living room back to the other, trying to gather his thoughts, until he finally spoke again.

'Here's the thing; I'm not so sure that me still sleeping with other clients has anything to do with you not wanting to date me properly. If I told you right here and now that I'm leaving those clients in the dust and was prepared to go all-in for you, I have a feeling that you still wouldn't go for it. If you're saying you like me as much as you say, why don't you want to at least try with me?'

He was almost begging now. I felt awful. I couldn't say it.

'Theo – let's not do this now.'

'Nah, let's do it now. Let's get it over and done with because as much as I'm used to being used by people in the industry I'm in, I'm not the biggest fan of being used by people I've grown to like. So what is it?'

'I don't get why you need to know why? Some people just prefer casual options! I'm sure you've been in situations where you've preferred for things to be casual,' I retorted. I didn't like this line of questioning, because I knew what was coming.

'If you want it casual, then we can keep it casual. I'm not going to stop my job for someone who can't be bothered to take me seriously.'

'I DO take you seriously, it's just . . . I . . . I can't date someone who does what you do.'

There. The cards were fully on the table. Theo looked at me, dumbstruck. That wasn't the way I'd meant for it to come out, but we were here now.

'What's that supposed to mean?' Theo replied quietly.

'I think you're a great guy obviously, and if it were a thing where you just had your day job, it would be cool, but . . . I'd never hear the end of it from my friends and family if they ever found out about what you do on *OuiMeet*.'

The air in the living room was thick with tension; as soon as I spat it out, I wanted to take it back. I looked over at Theo; the look of hurt was written all over his face as he scoffed loudly.

'All right. So I'm good enough to fuck you but not good enough to be seen in public with you? I guess this is what it feels like to be slut-shamed. Cool. Well, seeing as I've fulfilled my purpose, I'll be going, Cass. It's been fun.'

Shit.

'Theo, please,' I started, making an attempt to grab his arm before he shrugged me off. 'I'm sorry, I didn't mean for it to come out like that. It's just my parents are really traditional and—'

'Cassandra, it's fine. I get it. African parents and all that. I just thought you were—' he stopped, shook his head and made for the door.

'I was what?' I replied.

Theo opened the door, sighed, and turned around to face me. He was wearing a sad smile, which made me feel even worse.

'You don't really seem the type to need validation from people, but I guess your loved ones are different. Take care of yourself, Cass.'

And with that, he turned and left, leaving me feeling like the worst person in the world. I had literally just slut-shamed him. Who would have thought?

I decided to give Theo some space. It felt like the right thing to do – especially since I needed room to sort through my own feelings, not just about him, but about what he'd said before leaving: 'You don't really seem like the type who needs validation from others.' He wasn't wrong – I didn't. But at the same time, the idea of being with someone who felt the need to keep themselves sexually available to others? That wasn't something I could easily accept.

I looked down at my phone, which had the screensaver of my baby nephew Aaron, and thought about my role being an aunt and what that meant. Not trying to live up to my parents' expectations. Setting new traditions in my family based not on judgement and expectations, but on unconditional love, grace and acceptance.

I lay down on my sofa and before I knew what was coming, the tears had begun. What had I done?

Sade wasted no time in letting me have it over the next few weeks.

'Girl. I've never seen someone fumble this hard in a long time,' she chastised over drinks one day. 'I still can't believe you? You had this prime steak of a man; premium quality-grade beef! Tall! Sexy! Charming! Witty! Sexy! Confident! Self-made! Well dressed! A good lay! Did I mention sexy?? And you let it slip through your fingers because you somehow turned into a slut-shaming hypocrite. I'm still screaming!'

'Ahh, Sade, don't, man. We've gone through this,' I replied, exasperated as I pressed the cool, chilled wine glass to my forehead, numbing the headache I could feel coming. We'd gone through this at least six times now.

'I know, I know. Sorry, babe. But if you ask me, I do think you've kind of fucked this up a little. That was a GOOD man, Savannah,' she said, mocking the famous quote from one of our favourite movies *Waiting to Exhale*. 'I know you had your reasons, but you said he mentioned that if you two started dating exclusively, he might be willing to drop his other clients. And honestly, you wouldn't even have to tell your family about *OuiMeet* – there's no way they'd have ever found out.'

'I miss him,' I sobbed, burying my face in my arms as Sade pulled me into a tight embrace. I knew I'd messed up – let go of a genuinely good man for no real reason. But now, all I could do was sit with regret, because there was nothing left to fix – at least I didn't think so anyway.

'I know this is really bad timing,' Sade continued, 'but have you found a date to your mum's wedding yet? It's in a month or something, isn't it?'

I've been trying to forget.

I'd spent the last month helping out with the guest invite list; replying to RSVPs and sorting out the seating arrangements. Luckily, it was set to be a super small wedding, with only fifty guests in total; twenty-five from each side. In a bid to try and have an excuse to ditch my plus one, I'd tried to invite a couple of distant relatives, but hadn't heard back as of yet, annoyingly. My mum – probably distracted by the wedding – had yet to ask again about my lack of date, which is how I needed it to stay.

The arrival of my nephew Aaron seemed to have mellowed Dad out a bit. He'd started leaning into the role of doting grandfather; spending more time with Steven and his family, and less time hovering around Mum or unloading his emotional baggage on me. It made the following few weeks easier to get through. Still, with the wedding fast approaching, I'd started to toy with the idea of logging back onto *OuiMeet* to hire someone else, just to get it over with. But I couldn't stop imagining what it would've been like to walk in with Theo. My aunties – and a few distant cousins I barely spoke to – would've been seething with jealousy. And honestly, that alone would've been worth it.

I spent my lunchtimes at work scrolling through Theo's Instagram, thinking about what he was probably getting up to. He'd uploaded new photos of him on nights out, alongside a couple of videos of him playing football. How he found the time to do a nine to five, do his *OuiMeet* stuff and still have an active social life was beyond me. He looked happy enough in the photos – happy without me. It's strange how someone could leave such a deep mark on your life in such a short amount of time, but here we were. I often thought of reaching out to him, but the fear of being rejected had taken hold of me. This was all my fault, and I had to deal with the consequences.

My thoughts eventually went back to Jeff. I'd been avoiding him again at work since finding out about his secret family – although could it be considered a 'secret' if I never really asked about it in the first place?

For someone who had a whole family at home, it definitely

felt like he was trying his luck. Not on me, but on some of the other female staff members. All sans a wedding ring too, although that could be argued that because he was a surgeon, wearing a ring all the time at work could be seen as impractical. But still. The next time I bumped into him was in the staffroom; I was in the corner scrolling through my phone, polishing off my packed lunch when he rolled into the room, grabbing his mug of coffee as always. He caught my eye and I smiled awkwardly, returning to my phone, but it was too late.

He sauntered over and plonked himself down, that smug grin of his instantly giving me the ick. Honestly, it made me wonder if charming female colleagues was just part of his onboarding process at every job. Nothing said 'faithful husband' like borderline sleaze in the staffroom.

'Heyyyy, Cassie, how are you doing? What have you got there?' He nodded at my sandwich.

I decided to turn up the sass and replied, 'Hey Jeff; I'm good, thanks. Well, in most societies, this is known as a sandwich,' and I took a huge bite. Jeff just grinned, which for some reason annoyed me more. Could a girl not enjoy her lunch break in peace? I should have stayed in the office with Kofi instead.

'Ha ha, very funny. I mean what's in it?' he replied, taking a sip of his coffee, his glasses perched delicately on the bridge of his nose, making him look pensive. 'Cheese and ham,' I said simply, trying to engage as little as possible.

'Nice, nice. Oh! Also, are you all set for your mum's wedding? It's quite soon, isn't it? Got your outfit ready and everything?'

I needed to nip this in the bud; this was excruciating. I went for it:

'Yeah, I'm all set! I didn't know weddings could be *that* stressful, with all the different options for outfits and making sure they kinda match with the rest of the wedding party. It's been such a ball ache. Did you have to go through all of this at your wedding?' And I smiled the biggest, most innocent smile I could muster, fluttering my eyelashes at him. Jeff stared at me – stumped. He then looked down at the place where his wedding ring should have been, and began to rub his ring finger frantically. Gotcha, bitch!

'Oh, um . . . yeah, haha, it was erm—' he started, and I could see his eyes darting back and forth from me to his ring finger, no doubt probably trying to come up with an excuse. I had to admit that it was delicious seeing him scramble in such a way.

'Haha, yeah, it was quite the day. Weddings can be quite frantic, I suppose—' he caught me looking at his left hand, no doubt noticing the phantom ring, and continued to spill.

'I don't usually wear my ring at work if you're wondering – I've always either got my hands in water or in someone's body and it's too easy to get lost, you know . . . haha'

I smiled. He was positively panicking now. I took another bite of my sandwich, finishing up my lunch. My work was done here.

'Oh, don't worry! It's easily understandable – I do that with some of my jewellery too. Anyway, I'm gonna get back to the office now; there's a few forms I need to draft up for you to fill out today, so I'll send the PDF forms to you a bit later this afternoon, if that's OK?'

And with the biggest smile I could muster, I got up and left, leaving Jeff squirming in his seat.

Chapter 18

It had been a few weeks since Theo and I last spoke, and the silence weighed heavier on me than I cared to admit. I missed him – more than I should've. But with Sade's reprimand still echoing in my head, guilt kept me from reaching out. Getting in contact felt selfish, and yet doing nothing felt just as wrong. I tried to concentrate all my energy into work, doing overtime and other tasks to keep my mind busy (with a now very meek and professional Jeff at bay), and spent my spare time with my little nephew, going over last-minute wedding details with Mum and Femi, and even dipping a toe back into the dating scene.

The rebound phase didn't last long. After a week of back-to-back dates with guys from every app under the sun, I tapped out. None of them came close to what I'd had with Theo – and the truth was, my heart still ached for him. It was now three weeks until the wedding and I was at Mum's house, helping her put together twelve bouquets of fake flowers she'd bought on Amazon for the reception tables after refusing to invest in purchasing real flowers for the day.

'That floral shop in town quoted me two grand for flower arrangements, as if we're not in a cost of living crisis?' she moaned, passing me the coloured bow to tie up the bouquets, kissing her teeth loudly. I chuckled as I tied up the plastic peony bouquet and placed it on the counter.

'I think flowers are such a scam, personally. Why are we paying for things that die as soon as you cut the stems? Also, if you're only using the flowers for a day, there should be an opportunity to just rent them instead of buying them. Makes more sense really.'

We spent the rest of the day knee-deep in floral decorations, as well as ticking off other wedding tasks that needed doing. It didn't take long to realise this wedding was less 'elegant soirée' and more 'Pinterest board' come to life – minus the budget and a team. I took a break after designing the fiftieth guest seating card on Canva and sat on her bed, watching her hem the Phase Eight wedding dress that she'd bought for £75 on eBay. Mum was determined to cut costs by any means necessary. She had bought a beautiful ivory halter neck-style maxi dress that featured hand-stitched ruffles with pearlescent beads that caught the light as she walked. It was a little long, hence the hemming, but she looked absolutely sensational in it.

'So, Cassie,' she started, as I helped her pin the lining of the dress, 'I know you said I shouldn't ask but, do you have an update about who you're bringing?' I let out an exasperated sigh. She refused to let this go.

'Mum, no offence, but why does this matter so much? It's your day; it's not about me. You don't need to worry about me, I'm fine.'

Mum dropped her pins and looked at me, her eyes sad. Were you truly an African parent if you didn't constantly worry about the marital status of your first-born daughter?

'I know you're fine, honey. You've always been fine. But I worry, you know? It's more than just you bringing a date to the wedding, I suppose. I always thought my first grandchild would be produced by my first-born – not that Aaron isn't a blessing served by God, of course—' she quickly added in, noticing my cocked eyebrow '—but I worry about you sometimes. I've heard from some of the younger girls at work about how hard dating is, and I just don't want that for you. You're an incredible spirit – so beautiful – with so much to offer. I just want to see you happy and settled is all. It took me a while to get over the fact that you didn't want to be a lawyer and now I can see that you're happy where you are at career-wise which is nice, but I also want more for you. I can't be blamed for that.'

'But why must my happiness be framed around settling down, though?' I asked. We'd had this discussion several times before; about the African urge to centre men in everything and how problematic and patriarchal it was. Despite the many conversations, it always seemed as if she never fully 'got' it. 'Why can't I just be happy and single? I promise you, Mum, I'm OK! I'm thriving. I'm a strong, independent woman who don't need no man.'

She looked at me quizzically. I knew she was sick of me at that point. 'If you say so, my child. I just want you to be happy,' she eventually answered, going back to hemming her dress.

'But let's say I had someone in mind to bring along,' I continued, a thought suddenly occurring to me. 'Would you and Dad judge him if he looked a particular way, or didn't go to university . . . or had a job that was a bit . . . unorthodox?'

It was quick, but I saw the subtle smile that emerged from her lips.

'First of all, your dad's not invited to the wedding. Let's start there.' We laughed in unison.

'Secondly, I wouldn't care what he does – as long as it's legal, he earns enough to take care of you, and most importantly, he makes you happy. That's what really matters!'

I side-eyed this slightly. It sounded good in practice, but in reality . . .

'So! Does this mean you do have someone in mind then?' Her eyes widened, full of excitement.

'Mm. Maybe; we'll see,' I muttered quietly. My mum's response had made me feel a tiny bit more confident about what I had been planning to do, but I still felt awkward.

After what I had put him through, what if he rejected me?

'Well, that's wonderful!' my mum practically yelled, throwing her dress down and clapping her hands. 'I won't ask you to elaborate; I just hope he has a corporate job and is tall. Is he from a good family? Are they Ghanaians too? Hopefully he'll be ready to settle down too!'

This woman.

I got home that evening, fuelled by determination and just the right amount of desperation. Reaching out to Theo directly was out of the question; the thought of being ignored twisted my stomach. But he wouldn't ignore a potential job opportunity, would he? With Toby snoring obliviously at my feet, I opened the *OuiMeet* app and pulled up his profile. My fingers hovered for a moment before I took the plunge. This was it – my last shot. If he rejected me here, then it was over. Done. But if he didn't . . . maybe, just maybe, the door between us wasn't fully closed.

I scrolled through to his menu and clicked on the '*One-off special event (weddings, school reunions etc) – £500 + expenses*' option. I clicked it, opened his calendar for the 30th of May and quickly transferred the £500 from my savings account into my current account before confirming the booking. Now all I had to do was wait.

Three days later, and no response from Theo. Normally, he was good at responding as soon as I made a booking, so I wasn't sure whether to note 'no response' as a good thing. The booking still appeared in my calendar as 'confirmed' on the app, so that was something, I supposed. The wedding was in ten days, so there was still a bit of time for him to respond.

I tried not to think about him as I went about my normal routine at work, making sure to lock in especially at work; I started working through lunch again, and stayed behind to start on new referrals for the following day. I needed distraction, and the spring influx of new patients – alongside Kofi's one week annual leave – provided me with enough to do to stop from catastrophising. I also tried to be as proactive as possible, even going so far as to look up other profiles on *OuiMeet* in the event that Theo cancelled at the last minute. I'd narrowed down my results to three other potential guys:

- Prophet, 33 from Dulwich
- Chad Thrustworthy, 35 from Chiswick **(What can I say? I like a pun)**
- Pretty Ricky, 32 from Stoke Newington

All corny. But they were all also incredibly handsome and well dressed from what I could see on their profiles. They would all do, for that night, anyway; I'd bookmarked them just in case.

It was now exactly a week until the wedding, and still no word from Theo, understandably. I had been checking his Instagram all week, and had seen various Instagram stories of him at dinner, and playing football with his friends after work, confirming that he was just ignoring me all along. Dismayed, I logged into *OuiMeet* and clicked onto Chad Thrustworthy's profile. He would have to do for the wedding.

I was just about to tap on his profile when my phone buzzed, blaring the *OuiMeet* notification like it was trying to startle me into cardiac arrest. I practically launched it onto the bed. Great – exactly the kind of calm, composed energy I wanted to bring into this emotionally reckless decision.

I slowly picked up the phone, navigating to my *OuiMeet* inbox, and saw that there was a message from Theo; however, it looked like an automated message. Great. It was probably a message to say he had declined the booking request – or worse, that he had blocked my account.

I squinted through one eye, as I clicked on the auto-reply, preparing for the humiliation of being rejected yet again:

> Jericho has applied a 50% discount code to your booking, Therefore you will only be charged £250 for this service.

I rubbed my eyes and looked at the message again. Had he forgiven me? I supposed it meant that he had in fact accepted the booking? I couldn't allow myself to feel a full sense of relief; I wasn't out of the woods yet. I had to confirm. Sitting upright, I quickly typed him a message, praying that he was still online.

> Hey Theo, thanks for the discount. Um . . . does this mean you'll be my plus one for the wedding? I'd really love for you to come with me, and meet my family. I hope you've been well. Cassie x

I held back, careful not to say too much too soon – I didn't want to scare him off. But deep down, I hoped we'd get the chance to talk properly. There were things I needed to say, and they'd been sitting heavy on my chest for far too long. Luckily, minutes later he had sent a response:

> Hi Cassandra. I've been well, thanks. I hope you have too. May I please have the time of the wedding, as well as the location? I can drive to your place about an hour beforehand so we can go through any last-minute details, and then I will drive us there.

I don't know what I had been anticipating, but it wasn't that. His response was cold and formal, yet he had agreed to come along, so I couldn't really gauge where his head was at. Was he pissed off at me or not? I quickly responded, matching his energy:

Thanks, Theo. Details below:

Ceremony (11 a.m.) – Emmanuel Gateway Church, 376 Lee High Street, SE12 8RS

Reception (1 p.m. – late) – The Dixon Hotel, Tower Bridge, SE1 2JX

I'm looking forward to seeing you; it would be good to talk. Cassie x

I didn't get an acknowledgement of my response until I was at work the next morning. He had sent a simple reply, **'thanks'**.

To be honest, I deserved the cool response. I was the one in the wrong, and I intended to make it right, if he would give me the chance.

I found myself counting down the days until the wedding, even catching myself browsing for a new dress – something more form-fitting, something that might turn Theo's head. But deep down, I knew the dress I had was perfectly fine. It wasn't really about the dress at all; it was just me, trying to control something small when everything else felt so uncertain between me and him.

'That's my girl! I think you're doing the right thing, personally,' said Sade over the phone, two days before the big day. I'd called her for a last-minute pep-talk beforehand, on the way home from work; I needed all of the positivity I could muster at this point.

'The fact that he's even coming is a big deal. It shows that he still cares about you! I think it'll probably mean a lot to him that you've extended the olive branch too; try not to be too nervous. You're going to absolutely smash it, OK?'

'I hear you, sis,' I whined, chewing the corner of my freshly manicured thumbnail. 'It's wild; I've never cared this much about any man before; and it low-key annoys me that I've been thinking about him as much as I have.'

'Mmhm,' Sade replied somewhat sarcastically. 'Because he's the first person to make you feel seen; truly seen and cherished. Don't think I haven't noticed how much more confident you've been over the last couple of months, babe. You owe it to yourself to at least try?'

Sade was right; she was always right, and I loved her for it. Outside of the crippling pain of rejection, what else was there to lose? I decided to send him a text, hoping he would respond.

Hey Theo, I'm really looking forward to seeing you on Saturday. I hope you've had a great week!

A few minutes later, he responded:

Hey Cassandra, my week has been great thanks, I hope yours has too, and I'm looking forward to Saturday too. I'll get to your place around 9.30 a.m. :)

A smiley face! We had made small progress, at last. I smiled to myself as I got off the bus and took the short walk home. Once home, I took out my dress again, admiring how pretty it was and how amazing I would look on the day. My excitement had been bumped up to a ten and I couldn't wait.

My alarm went off at 6.30 a.m. It was the day of the wedding, and after a brief phone call with my mum for moral support, I started my beauty regime. Bianca had volunteered months before to help my mum get ready in the morning for the wedding, as she was a qualified make-up artist and hair stylist, which my mum dutifully and enthusiastically accepted without hesitation. This left me free to wax, tint and beat my face and body into submission. After taking an 'everything' shower, I moved onto using my Palmer's Cocoa Butter body oil, to give my skin a gorgeous, subtle glow. I then sprayed a thin layer of my Diptyque perfume and allowed my body to dry before putting on my underwear: a pair of black lacy thongs with a matching black push-up strapless bra I'd gotten on sale from Curvy Kate.

After the underwear was on, it was time to quickly do my hair, which was easy. I bent my head down to gather all the strands of my freshly retwisted Senegalese twists into my large hair tie and swooped it into a tight high-bun, securing it with a few pins. It was formal, yet demure, and accentuated my cheekbones beautifully. After that was done, I started on my make-up. I decided to forego my usual signature red lipstick and instead opt for a soft-matte, neutral look, finishing off with a golden pearlescent highlighter on the tops of my cheeks, a deep plum blush from NARS and a translucent mauve lipstick from Fenty Beauty. To add a bit of pizazz, I had also carefully drawn on some fake freckles around my nose, to make the look more cherub-like.

The whole look had taken about an hour to do, but I had to admit, I looked sensational if I said so myself.

As I sat on the bed, I received a direct text from Theo, as opposed to a *OuiMeet* message – once again, progress!

> **Morning, Cassie, I'm on my way. I should be at yours by about 9.30 a.m.**

It was 8 a.m., which gave me a bit of time to chill out and calm myself down. I carefully refilled Toby's wet food for his breakfast and went to lie on my bed, making sure to stay completely still so as not to disrupt my make-up. There was something undeniably poetic about today – the quiet thread of second chances woven through it all. My mum, stepping into a new chapter of love and happiness. And me, holding onto the hope that I might still have a chance to make things right with Theo. It felt like a reminder that maybe, just maybe, it's never too late to start again.

At 9.20 a.m., I stepped into my dress, breathing in a little as the corseted bust went past my torso snugly. The fit was a little tighter than when I'd tried it on previously, and I realised I was having a bit of trouble doing the zip up. Shit. I hopped around in the mirror a few times, trying to force the zip up my back, but my arms were simply too short. Moments later came the sound of my intercom.

I shuffled towards the corridor to answer it; it was Theo, standing there looking as beautiful as ever. I let him in and opened my door while I went back to the mirror, slightly panicking over the dress. Moments later, he appeared, taking up the entire height and width of the doorframe, as usual. He looked *sharp.*

He was clean shaven, and smelled like oud and sandalwood; a rich and intense scent. He was wearing a grey three-piece suit, with the blazer having a slightly tailored silhouette, nipping in his waist and making his shoulders look massive. He didn't come to play around, he looked expensive, and gorgeous.

'Hey, Cassie,' he said, closing the door behind him as I continued to stare at him, open-mouthed. Looking like a male model, I could already tell that he would be the talk of the wedding today. *And he'll be all mine, if just for the day.*

'Need a hand with that?' he asked, stepping behind me. His fingers brushed the small of my back as he slowly pulled up the zip of my dress. The moment his touch met my skin, a shiver ran through me, electric and familiar. In an instant, I was transported back to all the moments we'd shared – the way he used to touch me, how effortlessly he could undo me. Right then, I wanted him. Completely. I hadn't realised just how much I'd missed him until that very second.

'Thanks; thank you so much,' I whispered, turning to face

him. I wanted to hug him, but I had to tread carefully and let him lead. We still needed to talk things out, after all. 'You look amazing by the way, is this a designer suit?' I playfully tapped his shoulder, smiling meekly at him. He returned my smile as he gave himself a quick peek in the mirror.

'I do scrub up well, don't I?' he teased, meeting my gaze. 'And thanks! It's an Issey Miyake suit. I rented it from one of those designer rental sites; thought I would treat myself seeing as it's a special occasion and all.' He spun around, giving me a full 360; he was really feeling himself and I loved that for him. He then turned round and gazed at me, his wide grin breaking into a smile. 'As for you,' he said quietly, 'you look breathtaking. You're so incredibly beautiful, Cassie, damn.'

If I were capable of blushing, I would've done so right then and there. We locked eyes for a brief moment, the air heavy with tension, both of us searching for some unspoken signal. He took a step towards me, then quickly pulled back. At that moment, all I wanted was to throw my arms around him, but I forced myself to hold back. We couldn't let everything unravel just yet. The wedding had to come first.

'Thank you so much,' I managed to muster in my raspiest, sexiest voice. The re-seduction was going to start now. 'We should get going; it'll probably take us about forty minutes to get to the church.'

In the car, we drove in near silence, stealing occasional glances at each other, followed by brief, shy, nervous smiles. It felt like we were two teenagers on our first date – awkward, a little clumsy, and wrapped in a thousand things left unsaid. I decided to break the tension by talking logistics.

'OK, so, when we get there and anyone asks you about us, you can just say we're dating and that we met through friends or something.'

'Gotcha,' Theo said.

'And if someone asks what you do, erm . . .' I trailed off awkwardly. I hadn't thought about how to finish the sentence. The air grew tense again.

'Don't worry. I'll talk about my day job,' Theo eventually said, scoffing loudly. 'I'll try not to embarrass you.'

It was like my heart sank into my stomach and just stayed there, heavy and unmoving. I didn't say a word for the rest of the drive to the church. Once we arrived, I quickly took Theo to the side.

'So um, just some last-minute things. We definitely need to talk after this; there are some things I really need to say to you, so if you aren't busy tomorrow, it would be great if you could come back to mine for a few minutes so we can chat? Also, my Aunt Gladys is nosy and a little handsy – I'll point her out to you, but if she comes up to you and compliments your cheeks – cover your bum.'

At this, Theo roared with laughter. 'Hey, I'm used to that kind of behaviour from older women, but I hear you! And for sure, we can talk after this. That'll be nice.'

'OK, amazing. I'm not sure how much you're used to being around African families, but mine can be loud, so fair warning.'

'Cassie, I'll be fine, don't worry. My only job today is making you look good and making sure you're comfortable, OK?' Theo rubbed the small of my back and I vibrated. If only he were mine, for real.

I took a deep breath, took Theo's hand and opened the double doors of the church. It was about time to get this show on the road.

As I walked into the church, with Theo in tow, I felt every eye in the venue on us. And it felt spectacular. As we walked up to find our place on the bride's side of the pew, I could see the faces of nearly every woman in my peripheral vision crane their necks to take a gawk at the hottie whose hand was in mine. This must have been what it felt like to be the popular kid at school. I caught a glance at Sade and Kofi in the corner – they looked so stunning as a couple – and dragged Theo to formally introduce him.

'Kofi, Sade . . . meet Theo!' I said shakily, looking from both Theo to Sade and Kofi, trying to decipher their body language. Sade let out a huge grin and went in to give Theo a bear hug, much to my relief.

'Sade, I've heard so many amazing things about you – it's lovely to finally meet you!' exclaimed Theo, before going on to give Kofi a handshake and a half-hug. 'What's going on bro? Good to meet you!'

Sade took both of us in, her face beaming. 'I've been wanting to meet you for ages; it's so good to bloody meet you at last—' in the corner of my eye, I could see a couple of aunties in the pew giving us the side-eye, which Sade caught onto as well '—but we'll catch up at the reception, yeah?'

I was delighted. One obstacle down, the rest of the day to go!

I indicated to Theo where we would be sitting – my plan was to quickly go into the back room of the church to hype my mother up before gathering my bouquet. She had tried to insist on having no bridesmaids, but me and Bianca managed to eventually change her mind. Femi was standing near the altar, looking dapper as anything, chatting with the minister. As the guests were still pouring in, I quickly walked up and gave Femi a hug. As I turned back towards the pew, I noticed a couple of the female family members on Femi's side staring at Theo pointedly. Further down the pews, I noticed one guest – a woman sitting near the aisle seat with her bag on the seat next to her, as if saving the seat for someone. She had blonde dreadlocks and looked vaguely familiar. She was staring at me and Theo pointedly, her face cold and unapproachable. Where did I recognise her from? I offered a friendly smile, but was met with a side-eye in response. Strange. I looked over at Theo, who had already begun engaging in conversation with Steven, who was cradling my nephew in his arms while trying to pontificate over last night's football results. Knowing he was in safe hands with Steven, I ran into the back room and saw my mum and Bianca, who both looked like visions. My mother has always been beautiful, but today she looked exquisite; Bianca had done an incredible job on her hair and make-up.

'Oh Mum! I'm not gonna cry but, you look sensational. I'm so, so happy for you!' I beamed, giving her an air hug to avoid transferring any make-up onto her dress. 'Thank you so much for this, Bianca – you look incredible too!'

'Awww shucks, thanks, sis!' Bianca said, gushing. 'I'm gonna grab my flowers and I'll meet you by the main doors in about five minutes yeah? It's five to eleven.'

'No problem, my love, will see you in five,' I said, still staring at my mum, who was preening in the mirror.

'Oh Cassie, I'm so happy. So so happy!' Mum gushed, struggling not to cry. 'As much as I'm ready to marry Femi, I'm also hungry, so I'm ready for this part to be over if I'm being honest. Your auntie Gladys made jollof rice. *That's* what I'm excited for.'

'I actually can't stand you, woman,' I laughed, picking up my plastic floral bouquet. 'You're going to absolutely smash it out there, I'll you in a sec outside the main doors!'

I walked back outside to the main church, greeting the guests and making sure the logistics were in place before we got this show on the road. I noticed that the blonde-haired woman was still staring at me. Wanting to nip it all in the bud, I made my way towards her – a megawatt smile in tow – in the hopes to greet and introduce myself to her. Despite her frown, she was very beautiful, and I still couldn't place where I'd seen her before.

'Hi there! Thank you so much for coming today,' I said, grinning brightly as I held out my hand. 'My name's Cassie, I'm the daughter of the bride – how do you know the groom?'

The woman peered up at me, her eyes almost turning into slits. After an uncomfortable few seconds, she replied, 'I know who you are; I recognise you from your photo, but thanks for confirming. Me and Femi work together.'

Photo? What the hell was she on about? And how did she know me?

I raised my eyebrows in response and made my way to sit down briefly on the empty seat next to her, but she suddenly tapped her hand onto her handbag, blocking my path.

'My husband's just parking the car, he'll be here in a second,' she said, her voice low and guarded.

'Um, OK,' I replied, confused. 'May I ask where you saw a photo of me? Funnily enough, you look familiar to me too, but I can't remember where we've met – maybe one of Femi's house gatherings?'

The woman squinted again, sizing me up and down. What was her problem? Finally, she spoke:

'No, we don't know each other, but you know my husband, I believe. And I recognised you from your LinkedIn picture, actually.'

I stared at her blankly, still utterly confused. Were we friends on LinkedIn?

'My LinkedIn—' I began, but the church doors swung open and whatever words were about to follow died immediately in my throat. I snapped upright and stared at the man making his way down the aisle. The man saw me, and froze. His mouth opened in disbelief, before he flicked his gaze to the woman who I assumed was his wife – the blonde dreadlocked woman.

'Jeff?' I breathed, barely audible, my feet cemented to the floor.

Jeff's face was a mess of panic and recognition. His eyes ricocheted between me and the woman I now realised was *Veronica* – his wife. The same Veronica I'd found on Facebook.

'Cassandra . . . hi. What are you doing here?' His voice cracked as he tugged a handkerchief from his pocket, blotting his forehead with trembling hands. He sank down beside Veronica, who watched us both with a taut, unreadable expression, her lips pressed into a razor-thin line.

I prayed desperately that she wouldn't make a scene. Not here. Not today.

'This is my mum's wedding,' I said shortly, wanting more than anything to go back and sit next to Theo. I glanced behind me and saw Kofi staring at us, his mouth forming a perfect 'O' before mouthing to me 'what the fuck??' I rolled my eyes quickly and returned to the awkward scene in front of me. Veronica had recognised me from my LinkedIn photo, meaning that she'd probably seen the messages exchanged between Jeff and I, hence her current demeanour towards me. *Shit.*

Jeff started to crack his knuckles, looking perplexed. 'Oh wow, I wasn't aware! It's a . . . a small world, isn't it?' He laughed nervously. Veronica stared at him grimly, before cutting her teeth at him loudly and turning to me again. 'I'm sure we can talk at the reception,' she murmured, her gaze sliding over my shoulder to Theo with a pensive sort of curiosity. The entire encounter was bizarre, but I forced myself to shelve it until after the ceremony. Weddings always save their juiciest plot twists for the reception anyway . . . right?

'Right,' I replied shakily. 'Well, bye.' And I strolled over briefly towards Kofi and Sade, with Kofi beckoning me to sit down so he could get the tea.

'What the hell is Jeff doing here? Please don't tell me you actually invited him? Why is his wife staring at you like that?' Kofi whispered excitedly. I looked behind me briefly and saw Jeff and Veronica quietly exchanging heated words.

'What? No! Apparently his wife works with Femi; that's how she was invited. Also, I can't get into it now, and I didn't wanna tell you guys at the time, but there was a time when Jeff tried to make a move on me and I rebuffed him – but we'll talk about all that after the wedding yeah?'

Kofi and Sade's mouths opened and closed in quick succession like goldfish. I peeked up ahead at Theo, who was still happily chatting to some of my family members, oblivious to the drama that was happening behind him.

'SIS, you are TRIFLING. Why didn't you tell me?!' Sade said, struggling to maintain her composure. Kofi's face was a picture. He looked over at Jeff, shaking his head.

'It wasn't a big deal, honestly. He didn't hurt me or anything, it was just a miscommunication, but look – the wedding's about to start – I promise you I'll explain everything afterwards yeah?'

Moments later, Bianca and I took our places outside the inner entrance, with Mum behind us, waiting patiently for the wedding march music to begin. The doors opened, and Bianca and I slowly made our way down the aisle in unison. As I walked down, I noticed Jeff trying his hardest not to look at me, while Veronica glared straight ahead, refusing any eye contact whatsoever. This would be hilarious if it wasn't so awkward. I continued looking straight ahead, and eventually caught Theo's eye. Theo was gazing at me as if he wanted to devour me there and then. I slipped him a cheeky wink and added an extra sway to my hips as I glided down the aisle.

Bianca and I reached the end of the aisle and stepped to the side. I kept my eye on Veronica, who had now focused on Theo as my mum floated down the aisle, her mouth beaming as everyone took their phones out to film her. Mum reached the altar, and I went to sit back next to Theo in an attempt to enjoy the rest of the ceremony. I couldn't shake the uneasy feeling that had developed in the pit of my stomach. During the vows, I whispered softly to Theo:

'Hey, so, there's a woman with blonde dreads behind you on the groom's side who keeps looking at you; do you know her?'

Theo subtly looked over to the right quickly before responding. 'Nope. Never seen her before. Maybe she's just taken by my beauty. Don't worry, it happens sometimes.'

I forced down a chuckle as I watched on, my mum and Femi looking beautiful as they stared into each other's eyes. It was all so romantic and perfect. I had hoped that my run-in with Jeff and Veronica would be the only awkward thing that would happen today.

Guess who was wrong, again?

As the ceremony continued, I could faintly hear the main doors opening and closing, alongside muted – yet intense – conversation.

God, please.

I tried to ignore it, but the conversation only became louder, with other members of the congregation turning around to see who was making the noise. I recognised the voice immediately.

Not this. I really hoped it wasn't this.

The voices at the back of the church were getting louder.

'If anyone here objects to the marriage,' continued the pastor, speaking drearily, oblivious to the growing ruckus outside the chapel doors, 'speak now, or forever hold your—'

Fuck!

'REGINA! Leave me alone! Get off me! REGINA PLEASE. Don't do this. Ow! Get off me!'

And of course – like the final act of a badly written romcom – there he was. My dad, bursting through the church doors like a man possessed, gasping for breath as two frantic ushers clung to him like toddlers on a runaway shopping trolley. He looked completely unhinged: unshaven, dark circles the size of dinner plates, hair doing its own thing entirely.

'REGINA, PLEASE!' he bellowed, arms flailing like a soap opera extra. 'I STILL LOVE YOU, WOMAN! DON'T DO THIS!'

It was pure chaos. Honestly, all he needed was a boombox and a trench coat to complete the cliché.

I looked at my mum and Femi, who were both looking at my dad in horror. The congregation turned from them to my dad, still being restrained by the two ushers. Theo glanced at my dad, with a slight smile on his face, as if impressed by his audacity. A real lover boy, this one. I, however, wanted the ground to swallow me up.

'WHAT IS THE MEANING OF THIS, DANIEL?' screamed Femi in a voice I had never heard before. I'd never seen him truly angry before; it was terrifying. I stood up instinctively, wanting to protect Mum, who at this point was standing with her mouth open in shock, looking royally pissed off.

'Regina, please – just hear me out. Please, I still love you!' Dad roared, still trying to make his way down the aisle while being pulled back by the two men. By this point, all eyes and phone cameras were on Dad, and at this point, I couldn't have been more embarrassed if I tried. I clocked Jeff and Veronica staring up at the altar in shock. At one point, Jeff glanced over at me, and quickly turned his head away. I was mortified; never mind what happened between Jeff and me personally, on a professional level, this was humiliating. Steven was busy with baby Aaron, so it was up to me.

'Dad – NOT HERE!' I shouted as I ran up the aisle towards him. I grabbed him by the hem of his shirt and walked him back towards the corridor, leaving the two ushers to close the doors behind us. If the whole ordeal wasn't so mortifying, I would have found this hilarious.

'Cassie – I'm . . . I'm sorry, I just . . .' Dad started, trying to catch his breath as I walked him outside the church. He stank of tequila: clearly a motivating factor for this outburst. 'I just love her. I couldn't stand by and let her marry him, I just couldn't!'

'So you decide to burst into the chapel like Grandpa Simpson in an attempt to crash the wedding in the hopes that, what? She'd just randomly comply?' I chastised, also trying to catch my breath. 'Do you know you've just ruined what was supposed to be the happiest day of her life? If you loved her, you wouldn't have done that!'

'Grandpa who? I don't get the reference, I . . . I'm sorry.' Dad breathed, now looking forlorn.

'Ugh, don't worry about it, it's a cartoon thing. Anyway, what on earth did you think would happen from you making a scene like that? You've just embarrassed her in front of the family – do you think she's ever going to want to talk to you or forgive you now? You have to let go, once and for all. You HAVE to move on.'

Dad was now sitting on the steps of the church, silent tears spilling down his face. For once, I actually felt a little sorry for the guy. For all his fuck-ups as a dad and a husband, he seemed to truly love my mum and was genuinely struggling to move on.

'I can't move on, my dear.' He sighed heavily, confirming my theory. 'Your mum was my first love. The only woman I've loved. You don't just let that go.'

I sat beside him, seething that I was missing the ceremony – but, if I was being honest, a little grateful too. At least the chaos meant all eyes were on the dramatic mess at the altar, not on me and Theo.

'Dad,' I said, trying to keep my voice calm, 'I get that this is hard. I can't imagine what you're feeling right now – but if you really love her, then you have to let her go. You should want her to be happy . . . even if that happiness involves someone who isn't, well, *you*.'

I gave him a look.

'Let's be real – you weren't exactly Husband of the Year. Or Father of the Year, for that matter. And at some point, you've got to own that. What matters now is who you decide to be from here on out.' I gestured towards the chaos he'd just created. 'And crashing a wedding? Not exactly the redemption arc you want to start with. You're going to find someone again – I'm sure of it. But first, maybe let's focus on healing . . . and staying out of church buildings unless invited, yeah?'

While I was busy tearing into him, my mind flicked back to all the other times I'd been forced to step in – for him, and for Mum. I'd always had to play the peacekeeper, the moderator, the one who held everything together. Being the emotional breadwinner had been exhausting, and I was tired of being in the middle of everything.

'Dad . . . please don't take this the wrong way, and I know I briefly brought this up when Aaron was born, but I can't keep doing this with you and Mum any more. It's not fair on me. Because of this, I'm missing the wedding – and that breaks my heart more than you probably realise. My whole life I've been the one caught in the middle, the one you both turn to when you want to let it all out about each other. Do you know how lonely that feels? How heavy it's been to carry all of that? And then when it comes to my own life, the choices I've made, it still feels like nothing I do is ever quite enough for either of you. I've tried so hard, Dad . . . but I'm so tired of this; I just want a dad who cares about me too.'

Dad looked up to stare at me; his eyes glazed with tears. I waited for him to interject, but when nothing came, I continued.

'I know that being the oldest comes with responsibilities, I absolutely do, but I'm your child. Not your caretaker, or your therapist, or a trophy you get to show off whenever you want to score points against other members of the family. I'm your daughter, and I just wished that growing up, you could have treated me like one. I needed looking after too. The same way I've been trying to look after you, despite it not being reciprocated. I needed your love and approval also.'

Dad looked at me, his eyes red with tears. I stared at him back, time standing still as, for the first time in what seemed like a long time, a true bonding moment was had between us.

'You're right. This has . . . been hard to hear. When did you get so wise? I'm sorry. I truly am. For all of it. I've made a fool of myself; this is so unlike me. Please tell your mother I'm sorry also.'

'No, Dad,' I said sternly, asserting my temporary dominance in this moment – who knew if I'd ever get the opportunity again? 'When you've cleaned yourself up and had some time to think, *you* need to tell her you're sorry. It can't come from me any more.'

Dad continued to stare at me, his eyes forming into a squint. He wasn't used to hearing me stand up for myself in this manner. Well, there was more where that came from!

I continued: 'I'm assuming it's the tequila on your breath that made you do this, and I can understand that today was always going to be a hard one for you. I'm going to call you an Uber and have it drop you at Uncle Tony's house, OK? Spend some time with your brother and the cousins today. I'll call you this evening and check on you.'

I turned to see Theo standing a few yards away, watching me with a soft, sad smile. I looked back at Dad, who was quietly fumbling with his shirt buttons, and my heart ached at the sight of him – dishevelled, defeated, and entirely human. I called the Uber, and when it pulled up, I gently guided him to the car.

'I love you, Dad,' I said, giving his hand a squeeze. 'Remember what I said, OK? I'll call you later, and we can have a proper chat then.'

I wrapped him in a firm hug, held on for a beat longer than usual, then watched as the car pulled away, taking him – and the drama – with it.

I turned back towards Theo, whose arms were outreached towards me.

'Jesus, I'm so sorry, Cass,' he said as he swept me into his embrace, his hug warm and comforting. 'That must have been tough, but you handled it so well.'

'*Fuuuuuuuuck me*,' I cried out, exhaling and half-laughing. 'That was fucking wild. But hey, welcome to my chaotic, weird-ass family!'

At the reception, Theo and I had been placed on the head table, just a few seats away from the newlyweds, who were currently on their second bottle of champagne, understandably. I was on my second glass of red wine, trying to erase the details of earlier in the chapel. To my utter surprise, although Femi was furious, my mum had apparently seen the funny side – which I shouldn't have been surprised about in retrospect – Mum always had a habit of using humour to tackle difficult or awkward situations.

'Cassie? If that man thinks he's ever going to see me again, he's got another think coming,' Mum slurred, champagne glass in one hand, slice of wedding cake in the other. 'An absolute disgrace. I'm going to call his mother and disgrace him. What a farce.'

'Mum, just try and enjoy the rest of the night, yeah?' I shouted over the loud music. 'This is still your day. What's a wedding without drama anyway? One day we're gonna look back and laugh, to be honest.'

'Maybe, but the family will talk about this for years. It's humiliating,' Mum said, slumping over slightly. 'This was the sort of embarrassment I wanted to avoid.'

'Yeah, well, at least the onus will be on Dad, not you,' I started, taking the champagne glass out of her hands. 'You're gonna come off as the gorgeous ex who moved on with her life and was so unforgettable that she had her ex trying to stop her wedding. You're the real hero here if you think about it.'

Mum sat up, her eyes suddenly bright. 'You're right, you know. Hehe, you always know how to make me feel better. Thank you, dear. Also, I didn't get a chance to say earlier, your date is very handsome – Theo, is it? Keep that one close, you hear?'

Theo was deep in conversation with a flock of my aunties, who had descended on him like a pack of gossip-hungry vultures. They were firing off questions about his job, his parents, and – of course – his salary. From what I could overhear while shamelessly eavesdropping, he was holding his own surprisingly well. I had to admit, it was kind of impressive.

'GIRL!' shouted Sade at me across the dancefloor, a plate of jollof rice in one hand and a bottle of Supermalt in the other. 'I'm glad you and Theo are here together – do you know how sexy you both look as a couple?? I've been seeing how some of the other women are looking at you both – I can smell the envy from here!'

I laughed as I stole a piece of plantain from Sade's plate, earning a mock glare in return. The truth was, I owed so much to her – more than I could ever properly put into words. Sade wasn't just my wise, loyal friend; she was my anchor, the one person who reminded me who I was when I forgot. Without her, I don't think I'd ever have found the courage to finally stand up to my dad, let alone the confidence to risk opening my heart to Theo again. She was my bestie for life, my ride-or-die, the sister the universe gifted me.

'I love you, d'you know that?' I said, giving her a hug. 'Thank you so much for just being you, and for scolding me, and for motivating me when I needed it, and for supporting me today. You mean everything to me and I'm so glad that things are going well with you and Kofi! Your wedding next, yeah??'

'Girl, please. The engagement ring I want is saved on my Pinterest. He's gonna need to save up for at least two years to afford it. Give us some time!'

As Mum joined Femi on the dancefloor for the Electric Slide, I scanned the rest of the room. Steven and Bianca had left the reception earlier; the casualties of being newly exhausted parents. Sade and Kofi were twerking against each other, much to the disdain of the aunties sitting on the sidelines.

Considering the chaos that had unfolded just hours ago, the guests were in surprisingly high spirits – laughing, dancing, and definitely a few drinks past sober.

But then there was *her*. Veronica. It seemed that Jeff had decided to pass on attending the reception – which I couldn't blame him for. Veronica sat in the corner of the reception hall, eyes darting between her phone and Theo with unnerving focus – scrolling, pausing, staring, then back to scrolling again.

Something about her just didn't sit right with me. I could understand why she might not be my biggest fan – finding out your husband tried to prey on a colleague who shut him down would ruffle anyone's feathers. But what I couldn't shake was the way she kept looking at Theo.

I wanted to go over to her to at least try and smooth things over, but then I felt a tug on my arm.

'Cass, why don't you show me your best moves on the dancefloor?' Theo exclaimed over the music, his eyes full of pure panic. He winked at me a few times before I got the hint.

'Oh, uh, yeah, of course! Love a good Electric Slide – let's go!' I replied as I allowed him to drag me onto the dancefloor and started to dance. I'd speak with Veronica later.

'Thanks so much for inviting me again, by the way – you were right – your Aunt Gladys is very erm . . . touchy feely,' he said, moving effortlessly as we line danced to the beat.

'I told you! She's a freak, that one,' I replied, laughing. We danced for a few minutes, watching the dancefloor fill with fellow millennials as Juvenile's 'Back That Azz Up' came on. I proceeded to offer a light twerk in respect of the elders in the room, with Theo behind me, slowly grinding into me, as respectfully as he could pull off in a room full of elders.

Out of the corner of my eye, I again spotted Veronica deep in conversation with a cluster of my aunts. They were all huddled around her, eyes glued to something on her phone. She glanced up at me and Theo, then casually returned to whatever she was showing them.

I kept watching, heart creeping into my throat, as Aunt Gladys looked up – eyes wide, mouth agape – then leaned in to whisper urgently to the others. One by one, they began murmuring to nearby guests, heads turning towards us like a slow-moving wave of suspicion.

I froze mid-step and stopped dancing. Something was very, very wrong.

What was happening?

I turned to Theo, who was in the middle of doing the Harlem Shake.

'Theo, are you sure you don't know that blonde woman?' I said, fear gripping my voice.

Theo stopped and stared at her, squinting his eyes. He then turned to me, staring blankly.

'Nope, I swear, never seen her before. What's going on? Is she still looking at me?'

'Yeah, something weird is going on, I think I'm gonna—'

I trailed off mid-sentence as my eyes landed on Aunt Gladys, leaning across the table to whisper something into Mum's ear. Whatever she said wiped the smile clean off Mum's face. By now, nearly every guest in the reception hall had their eyes locked on Theo and me – and not with the usual curiosity or admiration. This was something else entirely.

We slipped off the dancefloor and sat at a nearby table, hoping to disappear into the background, but the stares followed us like spotlights. Then I saw Mum – expression unreadable, jaw tight – silently motioning for me to come over to where she and Aunt Gladys were seated.

My stomach dropped.

'Wait here,' I said to Theo. 'Lemme find out what's going on.'

I walked over to Mum, trying to appear relaxed but conscious of the watchful eyes on me. Whatever Veronica had shown the gaggle of aunties, it had now spread.

'Cassie . . . your aunt has shared some troubling information,' she started, her face filled with concern. Aunt Gladys on the other hand, looked furious and proceeded to shout at the top of her lungs for everyone to hear.

'A PROSTITUTE, Cassandra?? Is that how low you have sunk? Why would you embarrass the family like this? Why would you bring a whore to a family gathering? Are you not embarrassed?'

It was as if you could hear a pin drop. I stopped breathing as I felt the heads of people in our vicinity turn towards me. I looked around to see people whispering to each other, looking at their phones in disgust.

'Cassie, Femi's work colleague recognised Theo from some online gossip forum,' Mum started, her hushed tones now filled with concern. Ah. 'There was an article in there about some famous American actress called Catherine Thompson he used to date, before he was outed for being a prostitute she hired a few years ago while cheating on her NFL player husband. Apparently it caused a huge fuss in Hollywood.' Mum handed me her phone, showing the article posted on the gossip website. It was dated back to 2021 and showed articles featuring paparazzi photos of Theo and said actress outside several nightclubs, as well as his *OuiMeet* profile, and a few of his nude-adjacent photos. My jaw dropped. Everything I feared had come true. Catherine Thompson; I recognised the name. She was that 40-something-year-old actress who had been in a few superhero franchise movies over the last few years and was known for her heavy party lifestyle more than anything. Theo's bracelet in his bathroom; 'C.T'. It belonged to her. The gaggle of girls who recognised him on our first date – it was because of Catherine. Mystery solved.

Aunt Gladys wouldn't let up though. 'You have really disgraced this family, I hope you know that. Your cousin Rachel would never do something like this; I'm glad I raised my kids well.'

I turned around to spot the guests whispering and looking down at their phones. From a short distance I could see a few of the guests googling 'Catherine Thompson' into their phones, and bringing up her photo. This was horrifying. It felt as if the room was spinning. I saw Theo, looking like a wounded dog, his eyes wide and pathetic.

'Cassie, I'm sorry – I'm *so* sorry,' he said, his voice thick with regret. He looked at me, pitiful and sad. But I couldn't hear him any more. I turned, zeroing in on Veronica like a missile locking onto a target. My pulse roared in my ears as I stormed up to her. If this was some sort of payback on me for her husband's indiscretions, I guess we were all going to lay it out on the dancefloor today.

'Why would you do this, Veronica? It's not my fault that your husband tried to cheat on you and I rejected him. You should be angry at *him*, not me! I didn't do anything with him,' I hissed, my voice trembling with fury. 'Why the hell are you on a gossip site anyway? You're a grown ass *woman*!'

The words came out sharp and cold, each syllable crackling with rage. My chest was tight, my breathing shallow, and I could feel the heat of a hundred stares pressing into my skin. Shame and anger were battling for control – and both were winning.

Theo looked ashen upon hearing this nugget of information. Sade and Kofi looked at each other – aghast – then both glared at Veronica, venomous.

Veronica glared at me, a look of hatred burned across her face. 'I'm sure you must have led him on. Girls like you always lead men like him on. What was it you liked about him? Was it his money? Did he compliment you?' Her face cracked into a grin.

At that moment, my mum strode across the dancefloor, another flute of champagne in her shaking hands. 'I don't care if you work with Femi or not and, frankly, I don't care or know what happened between your husband and my daughter; you're not going to talk about my daughter like that – especially not on a day like this! You need to get out. Now.'

I wanted to hug my mum there and then. I knew what it probably cost her to have my back like this, especially so publicly, when I knew she was probably feeling just as humiliated too.

Veronica looked from me to my mum, her face contorted with rage. She held up her phone with the article featuring Theo to my face and continued to shout.

'Me? I'm the problem? Clearly your daughter is the one who seems to go around fraternising with men she shouldn't be fraternising with. It's shameful, and hopefully this will teach you—' she looked over at me as she spat '—not to go after people's husbands!'

I continued to stand there, glued to the spot – my stomach in absolute knots. I could no longer speak. Silent tears began to trickle down my face. At that, Sade had sprung into action as only a best friend could, by verbally dragging Veronica within an inch of her life:

'First of all, yeah, you and your ashy, dry-ass locks can get the hell out of here. My bestie hasn't told me the full story yet but I don't need to know the full story at this point. Because who the hell do you think you are rolling up here and trying to ruin our day? Looking like you let a blindfolded kid do your make-up, and whatever that *outfit* is – sis those colours are fighting each other harder than you're fighting for your marriage—'

I needed to leave. Now.

Chapter 19

'Cassie! CASSIE wait!' I heard Theo's booming voice behind me as I jaywalked into traffic trying to find solace in the park opposite the hotel. I needed air, and to feel the earth beneath my feet. As I approached the park, I took off my heels and sat in a slump on the grass, slowly counting to ten to soothe my breathing.

Everything I had feared when it came to Theo had come true. Someone had recognised him, and now I was the shame of my family. Now they all knew that I was too pathetic to find a man organically, and that I'd had to lower myself to paying for company. I would forever be known as my mother's failure.

I was too shell-shocked to even cry. All I could do was gaze into the distance, regretting all my life choices thus far. Out of the corner of my eye I could see Theo crossing the road towards me, panic and concern in his eyes. As he came over and joined me on the grass, I stared at him, motionless.

'Cassie? Cassie, are you OK? Say something,' he said, his voice filled with worry. His eyes were frantic, searching mine for some form of recognition or acknowledgement on my end.

'Cassie, I'm so sorry,' he said softly, his eyes locked on mine. 'I don't even know where to begin. I never thought that story would see the light of day again – I didn't even *know* I had a fucking gossip page and that that situation would have been news in the UK, but apparently I guess some people know. It happened years ago, when I was living in the States for a while. It was a mess, and I was a mess. But I swear to you, I never meant to keep it from you.'

He took a shaky breath, his voice thick with emotion.

'You have every right to be angry. I just . . . I didn't want anything from my past to ruin this. I know I should've said something. I know I've probably blown it. But please believe me when I say I never wanted to hurt you or your family. You mean more to me than I know how to put into words.'

He looked down, then back at me with pleading eyes. I just stared at him wordlessly. He continued.

'I've made so many mistakes in my life. But you? You're the one thing I wanted to get right. That's why I messaged you back when you booked me again. I know you said you wanted to have a talk earlier, but I also wanted to talk to you too. I haven't been able to get you out of my head. And I'm terrified I just lost you. Cassie, please say something.'

I stared at his eyes, his beautiful, red-tinged eyes that had become so big and sad, and uttered the only thing that came to mind at that moment.

'Prostitute. A damn prostitute.'

And before I knew it, I burst into fits of laughter.

Theo looked at me, incredulous. 'Cassie, what—?'

'She could've at least been a little more politically correct and called you a *sex worker*,' I said, half laughing. I wasn't even sure why I was laughing – maybe because it was the only thing I had the energy left to do.

The truth was, I wasn't angry or even hurt by Theo's revelation. He had always shown up as his full, unapologetic self – and he'd been nothing but honest about what he did for a living. He didn't owe me every detail of his past; we hadn't known each other long enough for that kind of deep disclosure.

So really, how could I be mad at him?

Nah – what I felt was anger at myself. For judging him. For letting my own biases, my internalised shame, and whatever I thought people would say cloud my vision. I was angry at the fact that I had been a hypocrite; that I was preaching empowerment on one hand whilst casting judgement on the other hand. I was furious that I'd let something so irrelevant stop me from seeing what was right in front of me – a guy who saw me. *Really* saw me. And maybe, just maybe, desired and wanted me in a way I'd always said I wanted but never truly believed I deserved.

I looked up at Theo, my eyes filling with tears. Out of the corner of my eye, I could see some of my family members spilling onto the pavement on the opposite side of the road, my mum included, I guess checking to see if I was OK. But it wasn't about them now.

I looked back at Theo and smiled.

'You have nothing to apologise for, Theo – none of this is your fault,' I said, nodding towards the wedding guests gathered outside. '*They're* the ones with the problem. Honestly, I was too. I let my own hang-ups and assumptions get in the way.'

I took a breath, steadying my voice.

'I like you. I *really* like you. And it's not just about the sex – though, yeah, that's been incredible – but it's more than that. I like who I am when I'm with you. I think I've been pushing you away because I couldn't reconcile how we met with how I felt . . . but the truth is, I can't ignore what you've made me feel these past few months. You've changed the way I see my body, my sexuality, and most importantly, the way I see myself.'

As I finished speaking, I reached out and gently cupped his face, my thumb brushing across his cheek in a tender gesture. His eyes softened as I rocked slightly, my breath catching in my chest.

'I don't want to run any more,' I whispered, the words barely leaving my lips before I closed the distance between us, kissing him softly, tentatively at first, like the world around us had quieted for just that moment. It felt freeing, more so that we had an audience watching our every move.

'Cassie, I only want to be with you.' Theo grinned between kisses, his words a little breathless. 'I want to actually try this. Since we last saw each other, I haven't had any other bookings except yours. Honestly, with what I've saved up so far, I'm pretty good on that front now. I could use a girlfriend . . . preferably one as amazing as you?'

I grinned back and kissed him as we embraced in the middle of the park, fully aware that everyone could see us. The feeling of his arms around me, the warmth of his lips on mine – it was like the world had shrunk down to just the two of us. I pulled back for a second, our foreheads touching, and laughed softly. 'Well, if they're going to gossip, they might as well have something good to talk about, right?'

Theo chuckled, his hands resting on my waist. 'You're dangerous, you know that?'

I shrugged, a playful glint in my eyes. 'Maybe, but I'm only dangerous when I'm with you, it seems.'

He raised an eyebrow, smirking. 'Good thing I'm all in, then.'

We stayed like that for a few moments longer, just soaking in the quiet joy of being in each other's arms, the world around us blurring into the background.

In the distance, I heard Aunt Gladys's voice rise, 'This is disgraceful!'

Without missing a beat, my mum shot back, her tone sharp, 'Oh, shut up and mind your own business, Gladys! Don't you have an embezzlement case to worry about? Leave my daughter alone!'

Theo and I looked at the chaos across the street, and burst

into fits of laughter. He eventually leaned into me and whispered, 'I could give you a refund for today, you know.'

I kissed him on the cheek, and stared into his eyes, allowing myself to fall even further.

'I apparently specialise in humiliating myself in public and falling for men I can't afford, so keep it. Consider it hazard pay.'

Epilogue

8 Months Later

'Can you help me grab this one, babe? It's a little heavy.'

I could feel the heavy, medium-sized box sliding out of my hands like a greased watermelon before Theo swooped in and saved it, setting it down with ease. We'd spent the past two days shuttling back and forth between his shoebox East London flat and mine, stuffing furniture into storage and tripping over boxes labelled things like '*miscellaneous wires that will never be used*.'

'Sit down, babe, I've got the rest,' Theo said, pressing a kiss against my forehead like the gallant man he was.

After bringing in the last of the boxes, we both sat on my sofa, sweaty and tired, yet content. Theo took out his phone and, after a few minutes, played the latest episode of *The Jungle Diaries* on loudspeaker, while I cuddled up to him and placed my legs on his lap.

'Is this the episode?' I asked, excitedly.

'Yep, Simi's producer emailed me a couple of days ago,' Theo responded, grinning proudly.

'Yo, yo, yo! Welcome back to The Jungle Diaries, *with your girl, the one and only, Simi P! And listen, you lot have been wilding in the listener letters this week. I mean, the inbox has been on fire – questions*

about spicing up your sex life, shaking things up in the bedroom, and let's be honest, who doesn't need a little upgrade now and then?

'But here's the real tea: I've got a special treat for you. We've only gone and bagged ourselves a brand-new contributor – our very own resident sex and relationship expert. That's right, baby: Jericho is in the building! He's gonna be diving headfirst into some of your juiciest, most unfiltered questions, and trust me, you do not want to miss this. Stay locked in – he's coming up in the next half-hour, and it's about to get real spicy!'

Confused, dear reader? Allow me to catch you up.

Yes, Theo and I are officially a *thing*. A proper thing. Capital T. No more transactions, no more *OuiMeet*, no more wondering if his car ride to Aldi was included in the hourly rate. Two weeks after my mum's wedding showdown, he asked me to be his girlfriend. Naturally, I said yes – but only on the condition that he retire from his escorting gig. I wanted him to be mine, and mine alone. He admitted he needed a month to get his finances in order, and like the progressive, supportive feminist I am, I waited . . . (OK fine, I sulked for the first week, but growth, people, growth).

And now here we are: Theo's temporarily moved in with me while house-hunting in Stockwell; a mere six-minute walk from my flat. He's eyed up a gorgeous three-bedroom semi-detached house opposite Larkhall Park that's a bit of a fixer upper, but it meant it only cost a mere £800k. I didn't even want to begin to think about how many *OuiMeet* dates he'd had to go on over the last three years in order to save up the deposit on that.

He's even dropped the casual 'you could move in with me, you know' bomb, which I pretended not to hear because I was too busy silently screaming into the abyss. Our relationship? Going from strength to strength. We've both said the L-word now – mmhmm, *that* L-word – and shockingly, neither of us combusted afterwards.

Funnily enough, my mum eventually came around to the whole Theo situation – though not before Aunt Gladys got herself excommunicated from all future family events. (Honestly? Served her right. She can take her passive-aggressive potato salad elsewhere.)

As for my mum and Femi, they insisted on having a Very Serious Chat™ with Theo about his *OuiMeet* escapades. I refused to attend on the grounds of 'absolutely not', but Theo came back looking alive and intact, so I assumed it went . . . well enough. Apparently, once they realised I was happy *and* that Theo had a well-paying full-time job (because God forbid we don't quantify love in annual salary), they relaxed. In fact, Mum even whispered that he was 'quite handsome', which, frankly, I didn't need to hear.

Things between my dad and me seem to be going OK. I can see that he's making the effort to repair our relationship with his daily telephone call check-ins and fortnightly dinner dates. He now ends every call telling me he loves me, which has meant the world, and we've slowly been able to establish boundaries where he can still share and be vulnerable with me without the trauma dumping. He still isn't 100 per cent over Mum, but I did spot the Hinge app on his phone a couple of months ago, so . . . progress, I guess? He still doesn't know about Theo's 'other' job, because he left the church before the exposure, and that's how it'll stay.

Sade and Kofi also moved in together, I'm happy to report! About two months ago, Sade also stopped ordering alcohol with her meals whenever we'd go out. Mm. Wonder what that means . . .

Around the same time, Kofi also got a new job; a higher position at a private hospital in Chelsea, leaving me to man the admin on my own, which was great for me as it meant an increased pay packet and my own office, at last.

Oh! And Jeff? Gone. Fired. Turned out he'd been having an affair with Tanya, the 22-year-old junior member of our orthopaedic team until she finally grassed him up after he broke it off – classic Jeff move, the slippery bastard. Honestly, good riddance; he always gave me the kind of weird ick you can't wash off, like when your Uber driver insists on telling you about crypto. Apparently, according to Femi, Jeff and Veronica have initiated divorce proceedings. Tough titty, I guess. Back to Theo – so, in a stroke of sheer genius (or chaos, depending how you look at it), I convinced him to write into Simi P's podcast. She'd put a call out for dating, sex and relationship experts, and at first I'd only suggested it as a joke. But Theo, being Theo, went full PhD dissertation mode and sent in this long, heartfelt email detailing his years in the escorting industry and all the wisdom he'd gathered along the way. And guess what? They actually messaged him back!

What started as a few trial runs answering listener questions about sex, body image and the occasional 'why won't he text me back?' spiralled quickly. Simi P and her producers loved him – like, *really* loved him. Next thing I know, my boyfriend has a six-week stint as their resident sex and relationships expert. And yes, he's doing it under his old 'Jericho' moniker, which makes it sound way more mysterious and sultry than 'Theo, from South London'.

I'm looking forward to doing life with this very handsome, very caring, safe man and, even though it's been less than a year, I can honestly say I'm the happiest I've ever been. Who would have thought?

But here's the real kicker: somewhere between him making me laugh until I cried and him always kissing me on the forehead like I'm his most precious thing on earth, I started to feel . . . secure. In myself. With him, yes, but also just with me. That confidence has bled into everything: I've been advocating for myself at work, setting boundaries with my parents, and walking around like I'm the CEO of my own damn life.

So, yeah. Turns out I *do* believe in love now. And apparently, all it took was an ex-escort, a bit of family drama, and a meltdown or five to get me there.

Acknowledgements

First of all, I dedicate this book to Sareeta Domingo, my former commissioning editor at Trapeze Books. Sareeta was, in every sense of the phrase, a rare and radiant force – a nurturing, brilliant woman who championed under-represented voices throughout her career. Thank you, Sareeta, for seeing me, for believing in me, and constantly pouring positivity and confidence into me, giving me the determination to constantly write. I love and miss you.

I'd also love to thank my literary agent Hattie who has been on this journey with me – constantly championing and supporting me for many years now. Thank you so much for all your hard work, and for believing in my stories. You are simply the best agent EVER.

Thank you so much to Sanah at Trapeze for helping me shape this story with your brilliant, witty and sharp ideas when it came to editing; I'm such a fan of the final turnout and I appreciate you and the team at Trapeze for all your unwavering support.

To my family, who allowed me to doss out in their living rooms and bedrooms to write this book due to not wanting to pay for a workspace membership, I thank you all!

I hope this book speaks to anyone who feels pressured to

settle in dating. Modern dating can feel brutal and disorienting (it's a CESSPIT out there, I fear!), but it doesn't mean we have to surrender our agency. We're allowed to take control of our sexuality, redefine what intimacy means to us and pursue connections on our own terms – even when that means choosing paths that fall outside conventional expectations.

Finally, in the spirit of Niecy Nash-Betts during her Golden Globes win for Best Supporting Actress in 2024, I want to thank ME. I never really tend to give myself credit for things, but I'm very proud of this book, and I'm proud of my hard work and tenacity, so yeah, well done Steph!

Credits

Trapeze would like to thank everyone at Orion who worked on the publication of *Doing it for the Plot*.

Agent
Hattie Grunewald

Editor
Sanah Ahmed

Copy-editor
Donna Hillyer

Proofreader
Kim Bishop

Editorial Management
Ciara Mongey
Jane Hughes
Charlie Panayiotou
Lucy Bilton
Patrice Nelson

Audio
Paul Stark
Louise Richardson
Georgina Cutler-Ross

Contracts
Rachel Monte
Ellie Bowker
Phoebe Miller

Design
Charlotte Abrams-Simpson
Nick Shah
Deborah Francois
Helen Ewing

Photo Shoots & Image Research
Natalie Dawkins

Finance
Nick Gibson
Jasdip Nandra
Sue Baker
Tom Costello

Inventory
Jo Jacobs
Erika Andrejuskinaite

Production
Ruth Sharvell
Katie Horrocks

Marketing
Kirsty Moore

Publicity
Kate Moreton

Sales
Dave Murphy
Victoria Laws
Sammy Luton
Group Sales teams across Digital, Field, International and Non-Trade

Operations
Group Sales Operations team

Rights
Rebecca Folland
Tara Hiatt
Ben Fowler
Maddie Stephenson
Ruth Blakemore
Marie Matuschka

RAISING READERS

Books Build Bright Futures

Dear Reader,

We'd love your attention for one more page to tell you about the crisis in children's reading, and what we can all do.

Studies have shown that reading for fun is the **single biggest predictor of a child's future life chances** – more than family circumstance, parents' educational background or income. It improves academic results, mental health, wealth, communication skills, ambition and happiness.[1]

The number of children reading for fun is in rapid decline. Young people have a lot of competition for their time. In 2024, 1 in 10 children and young people in the UK aged 5 to 18 did not own a single book at home.[2]

Hachette works extensively with schools, libraries and literacy charities, but here are some ways we can all raise more readers:

- Reading to children for just 10 minutes a day makes a difference
- Don't give up if children aren't regular readers – there will be books for them!
- Visit bookshops and libraries to get recommendations
- Encourage them to listen to audiobooks
- Support school libraries
- Give books as gifts

There's a lot more information about how to encourage children to read on our website: **www.RaisingReaders.co.uk**

Thank you for reading.

hachette UK

[1] OECD, '21st-Century Readers: Developing Literacy Skills in a Digital World', 2021, https://www.oecd.org/en/publications/21st-century-readers_a83d84cb-en.html

[2] National Literacy Trust, 'Book Ownership in 2024', November 2024, https://literacytrust.org.uk/research-services/research-reports/book-ownership-in-2024